S0-BDQ-973

TIME SLOWS DOWN

She lifted her gaze to his and their eyes locked. Kurt tried not to feel anything, but the air between them suddenly felt prickly—charged with electricity, as if the thunderstorm had turned around and come back.

Her eyes darkened, and something in her experssion made Kurt suck in a breath. He could feel every cell in his body, every thread in his shirt. Time seemed to slow, and for an instant he understood that time really could alter to let someone move through it.

No other woman had ever made him feel like this with just a glance. No other woman had ever looked straight into his soul without even trying. He had the uncomfortable notion that he wouldn't be able to hide anything from this woman, and he wasn't at all sure he liked that.

Olivia might still think he was dangerous, but it seemed to Kurt that *he* was the one who needed to worry . . .

Titles by Sherry Lewis

A TIME TO DREAM
WHISPERS THROUGH TIME

WHISPERS THROUGH TIME

Sherry Lewis

JOVE BOOKS, NEW YORK

If you purchased this book without a cover, you should be aware that this book is stolen property. It was reported as "unsold and destroyed" to the publisher, and neither the author nor the publisher has received any payment for this "stripped book."

This is a work of fiction. Names, characters, places, and incidents are either the product of the author's imagination or are used fictitiously, and any resemblance to actual persons, living or dead, business establishments, events, or locales is entirely coincidental.

TIME PASSAGES is a registered trademark of Penguin Putnam Inc.

WHISPERS THROUGH TIME

A Jove Book / published by arrangement with
the author

PRINTING HISTORY
Jove edition / November 2000

All rights reserved.
Copyright © 2000 by Sherry Lewis.
This book, or parts thereof, may not be
reproduced in any form without permission.
For information address: The Berkley Publishing Group,
a division of Penguin Putnam Inc.,
375 Hudson Street, New York, New York 10014.

The Penguin Putnam Inc. World Wide Web site address is
http://www.penguinputnam.com

ISBN: 0-515-12952-6

A JOVE BOOK®
Jove Books are published by The Berkley Publishing Group,
a division of Penguin Putnam Inc.,
375 Hudson Street, New York, New York 10014.
JOVE and the "J" design
are trademarks belonging to Penguin Putnam Inc.

PRINTED IN THE UNITED STATES OF AMERICA

10 9 8 7 6 5 4 3 2 1

For Leon
and
for Ruby

Your light still shines in our lives.

Acknowledgments

I would like to gratefully acknowledge the help of Victoria Atkins, archaeologist with the Bureau of Land Management at the Anasazi Heritage Center, for taking the time to answer questions and set me on the right path, and for providing such incredible research materials. I'd also like to acknowledge the help of my daughter, Valerie, who took time away from her own studies to further my research through the University Library. Many thanks to you both.

Chapter 1

CLOTHES SPILLED FROM the closet to the bedroom floor, bureau drawers stood open. Shoes lay in the middle of the room and the bookshelf on the far wall was nearly empty. If it hadn't been for the two suitcases near the door, a third half-packed on the bed, and Charlotte standing in front of the bureau, her arms filled with underclothes, Kurt Richards would have called the police to report a robbery.

He recognized the signs immediately, of course. This wasn't the first time someone had walked out on him. But some part of his brain refused to acknowledge it could be happening again. He stopped unbuttoning his shirt and stood there for a moment to let the realization sink in.

"What are you doing?" An unnecessary question, but the only thing he could think of to say.

Charlotte sent him the look of raw disgust that had

become all too familiar over the past few months. "I'm leaving."

Well, there it was. He couldn't even try to deny it now.

It shouldn't have come as such a big surprise. Their relationship had been slipping into the hauntingly familiar pattern for a long time. When welcoming smiles disappeared and sex cooled into something resembling duty or habit, when bitterness began to fill a woman's voice and accusations loomed beneath every word, the end couldn't be far behind.

The past came rushing back to haunt him—not just losing Holly, but every unhappy experience since his father had walked out the door twenty years earlier. When his mother died two years later, leaving him in her aunt Dorothy's care, Kurt had quickly learned to hide his emotions in a crisis. This one was no exception.

Kurt kept the bitter spear of pain inside and worked up an insolent expression instead. "I can see that you're leaving. Do you mind if I ask why?"

Charlotte propped her hands on her narrow hips, her tanned skin a stark contrast to the white of her shorts and tank top. She shook her dark hair, slightly damp from the August heat, out of her eyes. "Do you have to ask?"

He hated when she started a discussion that way. He wasn't a mind reader, for hell's sake. He thought back over the last few fruitless arguments they'd had and tried to come up with one that might have pushed her to this. "Is this about last night?"

She laughed bitterly. "It's about the past six months, Kurt. But, yes. Last night was the final straw."

The room grew hotter and it felt as if someone had sucked the oxygen from the air, as it always did when the subject came up. "I didn't say I *wouldn't* marry you." He dashed a trickle of sweat from his temple. "Just that this isn't the best time. This latest rash of vandalism at Black

Mesa is going to keep me working longer hours than ever."

"Longer than twenty-four hours a day?" Charlotte tossed the clothes she held into the suitcase and turned back to the dresser for more. "Why don't you tell the truth? You don't *want* to get married. I was just too gullible to realize it before now."

"You know how I feel about marriage. I've never lied about that."

"Yes, and I know why you feel that way." Charlotte jerked something from the dresser and wheeled around to face him. "But I'm not Holly, and I'm tired of paying for what she did. *I* didn't cheat on you, Kurt. I've done everything I could to make you happy and help you forget. But it hasn't done any good, has it? You're determined to be miserable, and I can't live this way anymore."

The accusation made his temper flare, more at himself for being foolish enough to share the details of Holly's betrayal than at Charlotte for using it against him. Women had a way of turning whispered confidences into weapons when the chips were down. He knew that, but he'd trusted her anyway. "I'm not determined to be miserable—"

"No?" Anger flashed in Charlotte's eyes and distorted her mouth. She pushed a damp lock of hair from her forehead. "You've been divorced for three years and you're *still* moping about it."

Resentment twisted through him, but he refused to let it show. "Are you trying to make me believe that you've forgotten *your* past?"

"No. Of course not." She took a steadying breath and shook her head sadly. "Nobody forgets, but most people don't let the past consume them. They don't let it color everything that happens afterward."

"Obviously," he drawled carelessly, "*most people* never walked in on their wives and their best friends in bed together. I know you didn't."

Tiny white lines of frustration formed around Charlotte's mouth. "No, I didn't. But I've had other things happen, and you know it. I've tried not to make you pay for things other people have done. All I ever asked for was the same courtesy."

Much as Kurt hated to admit it, she had a point, but stubborn pride wouldn't let him acknowledge it. Later, maybe. If they could work through this. If he ever felt secure again. But not now, when his heart and emotions lay on the floor, vulnerable, exposed, raw.

Charlotte studied him for a moment, as if she expected some response. When he didn't say anything, she shook her head and started in again. "It's not just that, anyway."

"So we're going to air the entire list, are we?" Kurt let a bitter smile contort his mouth. "Well, please . . . don't stop now. Tell me what else I've done to deserve this."

She sighed heavily and glanced away. "I'm tired of coming in a distant second to your career, Kurt."

He let out a harsh laugh. Too harsh, perhaps. It gave away how much he cared. "I've never put you behind my work."

"Haven't you?" Charlotte stepped into the connecting bathroom and emerged with a collection of makeup and facial cleansers. "What time is it? Do you have any idea?"

He refrained from glancing at his watch. "I know I'm late getting home tonight, but I've told you about the trouble at Black Mesa."

Charlotte waved his explanation away with a jerk of her arm. "It's after nine o'clock. You've been gone since before the sun came up. And don't blame it on the trouble at Black Mesa. Even when you're not having problems at the site, you're never here." She scooped up the shoes from the floor, tossed them into the suitcase, and closed it with an ominous click. "I'm beginning to feel as if the only time you want to be around me is when you want sex."

"That's not true." His voice rose in protest at the unfair accusation. He softened it quickly. The walls of the tract houses in this neighborhood were as thin as cardboard and he didn't want the neighbors—people he had to work with every day—to overhear. "You know it's not true."

"Do I?" Charlotte propped her hands on her hips again. "We haven't gone out together in months—not that there's anywhere *to* go in this godforsaken place. But you could at least take me to the Burger Barn or Chuck's Lounge once in a while, couldn't you? It feels like you're embarrassed to be seen with me."

Nothing could have been further from the truth. Charlotte was an incredibly beautiful woman. That was part of the trouble. Kurt didn't like the looks she got from other members of the crew, and he hated the nagging insecurity that inevitably came along with them.

He wanted to argue with her, to explain his reasons, but she'd only use that as proof that he was moping over Holly. Aunt Dorothy's stern admonitions to be strong echoed in his head, and memories of the stinging slaps she'd administered whenever he'd weakened kept him silent.

"Maybe you're right," he said after a long moment. "Not about me being embarrassed to be seen with you, but about the rest. God knows I'm no good at relationships. Just look at my track record."

"I'm not *interested* in your track record," Charlotte shouted. "That's what I'm talking about. You can't even have an argument with me without bringing Holly into it."

He bit his tongue to keep from pointing out that she was the one who'd mentioned Holly first. Nothing could turn a woman vicious faster than telling her she was wrong.

"You're so consumed with your divorce, you don't even notice me." She hoisted the suitcase from the bed and lowered it to the floor beside the others. "You're so busy with your thousand-year-old pottery shards and broken tools, you can't see what's going on in front of your eyes. Well, I won't *be* in front of your eyes anymore. I hope you're happy."

Kurt ran a hand across his face, moved it to the back of his neck, and tried like hell to think. Part of him wanted to ask her to stay. The other part told him to cut his losses and let her go. Once a relationship began to falter, there was no salvaging it. He'd learned that lesson the hard way.

He studied Charlotte's face, wondering at the emotions he saw written there. Was it hope or resolve flickering in her eyes? Wistfulness or bitterness curving her lips? Regret or disgust tightening the muscles of her jaw?

When he didn't speak, she sighed again and broke the silence. "You don't care, do you? The minute the going gets tough, you run away."

He resented the accusation bitterly. He'd never run from a fight in his life. "I care."

"You have a strange way of showing it." She picked up two of the suitcases and started toward the door. "There's not an ounce of expression on your face."

Kurt turned away, wanting to make sure none of the searing pain inside spilled over into his eyes. He resisted the impulse to carry the other bags for her. Maybe he couldn't stop her from walking out on him, but he sure as hell wasn't going to help her.

Charlotte stopped just inside the door, brushing the hair from her forehead once more as she turned to face him. This time, there was no mistaking the look in her eyes, the curl of her lips, the set of her jaw. "Do yourself a favor, Kurt. If you ever think about getting involved again, don't. You'll be much happier living alone . . . and so will the women you meet."

He kept his mouth shut, knowing that this was the dangerous moment, the time when he was most likely to weaken. Let Charlotte think him a heartless beast. It didn't matter. Let her think he didn't care. It would be better in the long run.

Only when she disappeared into the living room did he allow his feelings to show, and then only for the briefest of moments. He pulled himself under control quickly, shoving the emotions away, tamping them deep below the surface where he kept the others.

He could almost hear Aunt Dorothy's crisp voice warning him that big boys don't cry. He could almost see her deep-set black eyes boring into his, waiting for him to show some sign of weakness so she could box his ears or, as she'd so often put it, give him something to cry about.

It had been a long time since Kurt had felt the urge to cry—not since he was eleven years old and Jeff Conover had bloodied his nose on the playground over a kiss on the cheek from Victoria Grant. Somehow, he'd managed not to cry when his marriage fell apart, and he sure as hell wouldn't cry now.

Instead, he stepped into the bathroom and closed the door behind him. He could feel tears dangerously close to the surface, stinging, scratching, clawing their way out. He studied his face in the mirror, almost daring himself to betray some sign of emotion. There, deep in his eyes, he could see the wounded ten-year-old who'd stood beside his mother's grave.

Disgusted with himself for weakening, he turned on the faucet and scrubbed away the dirt he'd picked up on Black Mesa during the day. He kept his mind on his job as he washed, thinking about vandals instead of Charlotte carrying out the last two suitcases, deliberately tuning out the final click of the front door, stubbornly refusing to let regret get the best of him as he heard her car leaving the driveway for the last time.

Charlotte was right about one thing. He was better off alone.

Sand swirled into Kurt's mouth and nose, dusted his eyes and filtered through his clothing. Sweat beaded his upper lip, and his mouth and throat felt as dry as if he'd swallowed a pair of old gym socks. The sharp scent of ozone and the quickly darkening sky carried the threat of a thunderstorm, so common in southern Colorado during the heat of the summer.

Maybe he should turn back and take shelter in the Jeep he'd left behind a bluff, using Sleeping Ute Mountain as his point of reference to find it again. The one-man tent in his pack wouldn't offer much protection against the forces of nature, but he decided to keep going. He could find shelter somewhere in the maze of canyons carved into the mesa.

Shifting his heavy backpack, he cast a glance over his shoulder to make sure the Jeep was hidden from view, uncapped his canteen, and rinsed his mouth with tepid water. The wind, unceasing here on the top of the mesa, seemed to carry the voices of the Anasazi, nearly silent whispers urging him forward. Far below, the lights of Cortez twinkled in the evening sky.

Like a man possessed, he'd spent the past two days and nights on the mesa guarding the cliff dwellings from looters, taking chances he'd have fired anyone else on his crew for taking. But he welcomed the discomfort and held on with both hands to the chance to keep himself busy.

A few more days, he reasoned, and the memory of Charlotte leaving would begin to fade. A few more nights and he'd be back to his old self. Meanwhile, with luck, he might catch the thieves who'd been raiding the cliff dwellings under cover of darkness.

Robbing a protected site was a federal offense, but even more it felt like sacrilege to Kurt. The Anasazi had made their homes on this land for nearly a thousand years. They'd created farms, carved dwellings from the sand, loved, laughed, hurt, and cried here. They'd made miracles out of nothing and wrought a civilization out of the desert. And then, without explanation, their civilization had disappeared around the year 1300.

Kurt had made it his life's work to learn more about them, but so many artifacts had already disappeared, carted off during the late 1800s when white men first discovered the ruins, it was difficult to piece information together.

Black Mesa seemed to be a frequent target for looters, not only because it was a remarkable site, but because of the old legend about a city of gold hidden in its mysterious labyrinth of canyons. Unbelievably, there were still people who believed and came looking.

Kurt refused to sit by while selfish, greedy people pillaged the few remaining scattered remnants of the ancient culture. With Charlotte gone, he told himself as he walked along the edge of the cliff, he could devote all his time and attention to his life's work. There was nothing left to distract him. He should be glad.

Running his arm across his forehead, he gazed into the narrow *arroyo* and tried to concentrate on finding shelter instead of dwelling on his failures. He tried to focus on the twisted trunks and green-black heads of the juniper and piñon dotting the red sand and the clusters of gray-green sage at their feet.

He loved this land. Something in it spoke to him and kept him here in spite of its remote location and sparse population. This evening, as the sun dipped past the western horizon and painted the sky every color from fiery orange to deep indigo, the voices on the wind seemed louder than usual.

He took another drink from his canteen and turned toward the spring at the head of the canyon, knowing he should replenish his supply of fresh water before darkness fell and the storm hit. As the sun sank, the wind grew cooler and traced an icy finger along his spine.

Before long, the night air would seem almost frigid after the intense heat of the day, but he wouldn't indulge himself with a fire. If the looters were out there, a fire would only give him away. He'd make do with his sleeping bag and blankets.

Shifting his pack again, he started his descent carefully, moving slowly and keeping his eyes trained on the path for rocks and roots breaking the ground. Even with the man-made paths leading to the ruins, the steep descent was treacherous.

Getting hurt wasn't on his agenda. A man could lie hidden in the network of canyons forever while search parties passed him by.

He'd only gone a few feet into the crevice when a noise caught his attention. Something that shouldn't have been there. Human. He froze in place, held his breath, and listened, but the silence around him seemed complete. Maybe he'd been imagining it.

And maybe not.

He cast about for cover and stepped off the path toward a stand of piñon pine a few feet away. The sun had disappeared now and the sky had faded to deep gray-black. A sprinkling of stars gave him some light but clouds covered the rising moon and made him wary of moving too quickly.

Again, the sound came. A voice. A whisper. A brush of boot-shod foot against soft rock. Definitely human. Definitely wrong.

Kurt touched the butt of his rifle, but he didn't pull it out of his pack yet. It was possible the intruders weren't treasure hunters. They might be perfectly harmless— members of the nearby Navajo nation, lovers seeking solitude, children searching for adventure.

He glanced at the sky, half wishing the clouds would dissipate so he could see, half praying they'd keep him hidden for a while. If the voices were innocent, the last thing he wanted to do was leap onto the path brandishing a weapon like the Lone Ranger. If they weren't, the element of surprise would work in his favor.

He listened, trying to identify which direction the voices were coming from. One minute it sounded as if they were in front of him; the next, behind or to one side. The wind gusted, drowning out the sounds one moment, magnifying them the next.

Go to her.

The whisper, coming from directly behind him, nearly cost Kurt his footing. He grasped a low-hanging branch to keep himself upright and held his breath while he searched the gathering darkness. An icy shiver raced up his spine along with another gust of wind. Dirt swirled in front of him and the clouds seemed to close in on him.

Go to her.

This time, he could have sworn he heard the soft sound of a woman's voice. No, not a voice. It sounded like crying.

Charlotte? Kurt shook off that idea with a silent laugh. He couldn't imagine Charlotte crying, and he knew for damned sure she wouldn't be out here. She'd never even bothered to visit the ruins with him after that first time, and he'd had to *beg* her to come then.

Not Charlotte. But who? One of the thieves? Unlike some of his crewmates, he knew women were as capable of carting off priceless artifacts as men. But if someone was hurt—especially a woman—he had to do something.

Moving slowly from the cover of the trees, he spoke for the first time. "Is someone out there?"

The soft crying stopped immediately and silence engulfed him. He stepped further away from the trees, moving closer to the cliff's edge and pulling his rifle from his pack in case it was a trick. "Ma'am? Are you hurt?"

Only the rustling of the branches and the distant rumble of thunder answered. Swallowing convulsively, he inched further away from cover and scoured the ravine and the rim of the mesa.

Nothing moved except dust and trees in the wind. No one spoke.

He strained to hear the whisper, the muffled sobbing, the sound of wildlife scurrying for cover, but total silence greeted him. "Ma'am?"

In the distance, lightning split the sky. The deep crackle of thunder followed, and Kurt cursed himself for coming out here alone. Maybe he should go back to the Jeep and call for help. But his supervisor would have his hide for taking a chance like this and he'd probably reward Kurt with a suspension from duty. The last thing Kurt needed right now was empty time with nothing to do but think.

Go to her.

The whisper, so close, so insistent, made him spin around, half-convinced he'd find someone breathing down his neck. But that move was his biggest mistake of all.

His foot slipped in the soft sandstone and the earth seemed to crumble beneath his feet. Frantically trying to save himself, he caught at a nearby juniper but he was too far away to reach it. He let out a shout and windmilled his arms, trying to catch his balance. But it didn't help.

Like a rag doll, he slipped off the side of the mountain into the inky blackness below.

Pain.

In his leg. In his shoulder. In his head. His pulse pounded through him with every heartbeat. A rock jabbed into his back. Another into his hip. His knee throbbed, sweat trickled down his face and pooled beneath his arms, and dust filled his nostrils. He felt like hell and he hadn't even opened his eyes yet.

At least he was alive. That was something to be grateful for.

With the return of consciousness came a wave of nausea. Kurt kept his eyes shut, hoping a few more minutes would get rid of the worst of it. This just might qualify as the worst damned week of his life.

A bug buzzed near his ear. A raven squawked in a nearby tree. Something else set up a steady stream of chatter.

Slowly, reluctantly, he squinted open his eyes and took in his surroundings. The sun had already begun to rise over the eastern slope of the canyon and the sky had gone from jet black to pale lavender, blue, and peach. He'd been lying there all night.

Inching onto his elbow, he checked his position. He hadn't fallen far, thank God, before a smooth, flat boulder had broken his fall. But in this shape, the climb back up would be torture.

He checked himself gingerly for broken bones, let out a sigh when he didn't find any, and rubbed his ankle. In the cold light of day, his decision to come out here alone seemed far less heroic than it had last night. Far more foolish. He was damned lucky the vandals hadn't finished him off while he lay here.

He tried getting to his feet, but his right knee buckled as soon as he put his weight on it. He clutched an exposed root to keep from landing on his ass again, felt about for his canteen, and uncapped it eagerly. He filled his mouth with stale-tasting water, swallowed slowly, and took another sip.

He'd have given almost anything for a hot shower, and he'd have sold his right arm for a steaming cup of coffee and a soft place to sit. But if he couldn't make it back to the Jeep, coffee, cushions, and showers wouldn't be an issue.

Funny, but just thinking about coffee sent his imagination into high gear. He could have sworn he could smell some on the still morning air. The wind had died down, and with it the voices he'd heard in the night. The spirits of the ancients seemed weaker, as well. In fact, the morning seemed peaceful, serene, and harmless.

Maybe he'd imagined the voices last night. Now that he thought about it, the haunting whisper *could* have been the wind. Or the product of some deep-seated regret at letting Charlotte walk out without trying to stop her. Either way, he felt like a fool for letting it send him ass over teakettle down the cliff.

It seemed to take forever to drag himself up the side of the canyon and he had to stop several times to rest. The fall had left him weaker than he'd first thought. But the imagined scent of coffee, and even the aroma of breakfast cooking, spurred him on.

Dirt crusted beneath his fingernails and covered every inch of his jeans and shirt. Rocks and roots had scraped his knuckles and blood oozed from beneath the skin. Never again, he told himself firmly. He'd never set off into the wilderness alone again.

At long last, he reached the surface. Taking a deep breath, he planted his hands on the top of the canyon wall, found a solid foothold, and heaved with all his might. Twice, he nearly tumbled back into the canyon, but he managed to hold himself upright and keep his footing. On the third try, his chest and shoulders landed on the mesa, leaving his legs dangling over the yawning ravine.

While he sought something solid to hang onto with his hands, he curved his good knee and tried to bring the lower half of his body out of the canyon. He ignored the rustle of lizards through the sagebrush and gave one last heave-ho. Finally out of danger, he lay there for a minute, eyes closed against the rising sun, and tried to catch his breath.

But the aroma of fresh coffee, stronger now, and the

nicker of a horse teased his eyes open again. Maybe there *were* people out here. Hikers. Backpackers. Back-country cyclists who'd wandered from the approved trails. And maybe they had coffee. And aspirin. At this moment, he'd kill for either.

If he could make it to the Jeep, he'd spend a few minutes looking before he drove back to Cortez. He just hoped his leg wasn't hurt so badly he couldn't work the clutch or his shoulder too banged up to shift gears.

Feeling stronger, he lifted his gaze and looked out over the mesa top to orient himself. Sunlight bathed Sleeping Ute Mountain, gilded the tops of the distant pines, and beckoned him closer. He crossed the mesa top slowly until he should have been able to see Cortez in the valley below. But instead of the small city with its cluster of houses and businesses, he saw only a few low buildings in the distance and a small house set into a small clearing almost directly below him.

He must have gotten turned around somehow.

He circled slowly, trying to align himself, then looked again. But Cortez still wasn't where it should have been.

He rubbed his eyes, studied the landscape all around him, and tried to figure out what he'd done wrong. Something wasn't right. Had someone moved him? No, Sleeping Ute Mountain was right where it was supposed to be, it was just the town that looked different.

Limping, he hurried as quickly as he could across the mesa top, checking landmarks, reassuring himself that he wasn't on the wrong track. When the bluff where he'd hidden the Jeep appeared from behind a thick stand of juniper—thicker by far than he remembered—he let out a sigh of relief.

He dug his keys from his pocket and rounded the bluff, but he saw nothing but sage, piñon pine, and juniper, dirt and rocks and sky.

The Jeep—and everything in it—was gone.

Chapter 2

OUTSIDE CORTEZ, COLORADO
1889

"ALL RIGHT, YOU stubborn creature, it's you or me." Olivia Hamilton held onto the reins with both hands and stared straight into the horse's eyes. One or the other would have to back down soon, but it wouldn't be Olivia. Not this time. Not if her life depended on it.

Much as she hated to let Harvey's horse go, she couldn't afford to keep him any longer. Sentiment wouldn't pay the upcoming mortgage payment on the Lazy H Ranch or buy the tools she needed, and it sure wouldn't put food on the table.

From behind her on the fence rail, she heard a deep, rumbling laugh. She mopped her forehead with the sleeve of her heavy cotton dress and resisted the urge to look back at her closest neighbor, Sam Evans. If she took her eyes off Nightmare, even for a second, she'd lose the battle.

The horse's eyes rounded at the sound of Sam's laugh.

He tossed his magnificent head and tried to jerk the reins from her hand.

"Oh, no you don't." Olivia tightened her grip, clenched her teeth, and held on for dear life. "Stop it, Sam," she called over her shoulder. "You're only encouraging him."

"Sorry. It's just that the two of you make quite a sight."

"I'm sure we do," she muttered, grimacing when a trickle of perspiration started on her forehead and worked its way past her eye to her cheek. "But it's not funny. I'm determined to show this beast who's the boss."

Sam jumped to the ground and crossed the corral to stand behind her. "Why don't you let me do this for you, Livvy?"

"Because it's my responsibility." Olivia strained against another determined toss of Nightmare's huge head and neck. "I own the Lazy H now. If I can't even make one stupid horse pay attention to me, what chance do I have of running this place on my own?"

"You don't have to run it on your own. I'm here." Sam stepped into her line of vision, scowling so deeply the tips of his thick, drooping moustache nearly touched beneath his chin. He towered over her by a good eight inches. Tall and dark, pleasant to look at. The perpetual twinkle in his deep gray eyes kept him from looking ominous. "Besides, Harvey'd never forgive me if I let you struggle alone."

Olivia sent her late husband's friend a thin smile. "I appreciate your concern, Sam, but I can do this."

Sam ran a hand along his chin and shook his head slowly. "You are without a doubt the stubbornest woman I've ever met."

She laughed softly. "Thank you."

"It's not a compliment."

"It is to me. I've never wanted to be one of those simpering, pampered women who sits in her parlor all day drinking tea and entertaining friends." She'd come a long way from those days and she had no desire to go back.

If her mother could see her now, brown as a native and so thin the curves so highly prized in the genteel society of Virginia long gone, she'd give in to an attack of the vapors.

Soft skin and smooth curves had no value in this new, untamed land called Colorado. Silken hands couldn't gentle a critter as mulish as the horse that stared into her eyes, challenging her to give up. They couldn't eke a living out of the soil at her feet.

Sam gave her a slow once over. "I don't think there's much danger of you turning into one of those ladies. You're not like most women I've known."

"I'll take that as a compliment, too." Olivia laughed again and let her gaze leave Nightmare's just long enough to break the spell. Sighing with frustration, she gave up the battle and turned to face Sam fully.

Sometimes the ease she felt around him surprised her. Harvey had taken to him the instant they met so, of course, it hadn't taken Olivia long to count Sam as a friend as well. With Harvey gone, they'd slipped into an easy companionship that had Sam riding the miles separating their properties to check on her at least twice every week.

"It's a very kind offer, Sam, and you know how much I appreciate you looking in on me. If it weren't for you, I wouldn't even see another human being for weeks on end. But I'll be fine."

The twinkle faded from Sam's eyes and his expression sobered. "Selling Nightmare might give you enough cash to hold off this latest crisis, but what about the next one? You don't have a whole lot to sell—except the land."

Irritated with Sam for reminding her how precarious her position was, Olivia tugged on Nightmare's reins and started toward the barn. Harvey had been gone nearly ten months already, and though she'd been fine until now, she didn't have any idea how she'd get through the rapidly approaching winter. "Harvey died for this land," she told Sam with more bravado than she felt. "I won't sell it."

Sam fell into step beside her, his hands clasped behind his back. "Harvey killed himself on this land, Livvy. I don't want the same thing to happen to you."

"It won't."

"Face it, Liv. This is no place for a woman alone. Maybe you ought to take your parents' advice."

"Sell the Lazy H and go back to Virginia?" Olivia laughed harshly. "I can't even imagine going back there." Or maybe the truth was, she could imagine too well. Leaving the strict confines of her mother's house had been the best thing that ever happened to her. "I'm not about to go back, especially not as a widow. My mother would wrap me in black, tuck me away in a stuffy room, and leave me there to mold."

Sam stopped walking, but he didn't speak again until she turned to face him. "There's another option."

"What?"

"I've thought about it from time to time, but I didn't want to suggest it so soon after Harvey's death."

"If it'll let me stay in Colorado, you'd better suggest it," she warned. "I'm *not* going back to Virginia."

Sam shifted his weight, pushed his hat onto the back of his head, then inched it forward again and let his gaze drift away toward the nearby bluffs of Black Mesa. "You might think I've lost my mind."

"Oh, for heaven's sake, Sam. Spit it out. I'm not likely to be offended by whatever you have to say."

"I hope not." His cheeks turned the most unusual shade of red. His gaze flickered from her face to the corral fence and back again. He pulled off his hat and clutched it in front of him with both hands. "I've been thinking that maybe you and me ought to get married."

Married? To Sam? Olivia gaped at him, then forced

her mouth shut. He couldn't have said anything more surprising if he'd suggested she take up residence in Cortez's
fancy house. Sam was a dear and trusted friend, but she'd
never once thought of him as anything more than that.

Now that he'd opened the floodgate, words spilled out
of his mouth as he tried to justify his suggestion. "I've
always admired you, Livvy. You know that. And with
Harvey gone . . ." He broke off, mopped his face with his
hand, and shifted his weight again. "I know you don't
love me, not like you did Harv, and I'm not suggesting
that I take his place. But if we put the two ranches together, I reckon we could make a go of it. Or you could
sell the Lazy H and come to live on the Cinnabar with
Jesse and me. He'll be getting married soon—"

Heat rushed into Olivia's face and stunned disbelief
kept her silent. Everything inside insisted that she refuse
the offer. Everything, that is, except one niggling whisper
that said his suggestion made an odd sort of sense.

She took a deep breath and let it out again slowly, turning the idea over in her mind. She wouldn't even consider
selling the Lazy H, but combining the two ranches didn't
feel right, either. "I'm fond of you," she began, "but—"

The color in Sam's cheeks deepened and made him
look as if he'd spent three days in the sun. He cut her off
before she could finish. "That's all I'd ask, Liv, I swear."
He lifted his gaze to hers, then looked away at the dirt
beneath his feet.

"And it's very sweet of you to offer—"

"I'm not being sweet." His voice sounded funny—thick
and deep the way it had when Harvey died. "I admire
you, Liv. Always have."

"And I admire you. You know that. I know people
marry for those reasons all the time—especially way out
here. But I don't think I can, Sam. It just feels wrong."

Sam nodded slowly, accepting her refusal like a gen-

tleman. Thank God for that. The last thing Olivia wanted
was to lose the one friend she had.

"You know," he said, working his hat back into place
again, "I've always wished I'd met you before Harv did.
Somehow, I got myself to believin' that it might have
made a difference."

Surely he didn't mean that the way it sounded. Olivia
ran a hand along Nightmare's muzzle, needing the touch
to keep her grounded. She forced a thin laugh and tried
to joke. "Now you're talking nonsense, flattering me because I'm out here all alone and you think I need to hear
a man say nice things about me."

Sam's eyes grew nearly black with concern. "Ah, shoot,
Liv. I've made you uncomfortable, haven't I?"

"Of course not," she lied, certain they could salvage
their friendship if Sam would only stop talking that way.
Olivia didn't expect to *ever* fall in love again. And the
thought of marrying her husband's friend, of sharing a
house—a *bed*—with him. Well, it was unthinkable. "It's
just that I'm not used to hearing pretty words these days.
But you know that if I ever fell in love with anyone else,
it would be you."

The pain in his eyes stunned her, but he managed a
deep chuckle. "Well, that's something, I guess. When a
dog goes begging he ought to be satisfied with what he
gets. I won't pressure you, Livvy, but if you ever change
your mind, the offer stands."

"Thank you." Dear, sweet Sam. Other than Harvey and
her family, no one had ever held such a huge place in her
heart. And if she did marry him, her mother wouldn't be
able to force her back to Virginia. Olivia forced that
thought away immediately. What was wrong with her?
She might be desperate to stay in Colorado, but she
wouldn't let herself stoop that low. Sam deserved better
than that.

She tugged Nightmare toward the barn again and nodded toward the house. "Coffee's on if you'd like some. I'll be there in a minute."

Sam stood his ground for a second or two, then shook his head. "Naw. Thanks. I think I'd best be on my way. I've overstayed my welcome as it is."

She wanted to argue with him, and until five minutes ago, she would have. Sam always had coffee with her when he came over from the Cinnabar—and usually stayed for supper as well. She looked forward to those shared meals, the laughter, the conversation. Now, she watched him ride away and wondered when she'd see him again and how they'd face each other when she did.

His proposal had changed everything. It had robbed her of the easy camaraderie they'd shared, stolen her only companion, and made the days alone on the Lazy H stretch endlessly in front of her.

Still second-guessing herself, Olivia carried her third cup of coffee to the rough pine table in the center of the room. She had a dozen things she should be doing, but she couldn't seem to concentrate on any of them. All she could think of was Sam's proposal.

Blast!

Why couldn't he have left well enough alone? What was wrong with men, anyway? Why did they always have to try to fix things? Especially things that didn't *need* fixing.

A soft breeze stirred the curtains she'd sewn for the two small windows and carried the scent of the country she loved so much indoors. The thought of leaving here and going back east made her almost sick, but without some quick cash, she just might have to leave.

Maybe she should have accepted Sam's offer. It wasn't too late. She could saddle one of the horses, ride to Sam's ranch, and tell him she'd changed her mind. But the thought of marrying for money still left a sour taste in her mouth. If she was going to do that, she might as well have stayed in Virginia and married the man her mother had picked out for her.

She scowled into her coffee, so deep in thought the sound of footsteps on the wooden porch caught her completely by surprise. She jerked her head up and started to her feet, amazed that she hadn't heard a horse approaching and suddenly filled with hope that Sam had come back after all.

She was halfway to the door when the knock sounded, and it took only another two steps to reach it. "You changed your mind," she said as she pulled open the heavy wooden door.

Her welcoming smile turned to stone when she saw the man standing in front of her. Not Sam, but a stranger. Tall, dark-haired, with clear blue eyes and blood caked on his cheeks and forehead.

"You're hurt."

"Not badly." He propped one hand against the wall and sagged against the door frame. "I'll be all right. Just tell me you have a phone."

"A phone?" She shook her head slowly. "I'm afraid not." The truth was, she didn't even know what one was, but she didn't admit that. "Are you sure you're all right? It looks like you've been bleeding."

He checked his hands and shook his head. "It's nothing, really. I made it this far."

"Not there. Your face has been bleeding. And your arm." She looked him over quickly. "And your leg."

He touched his cheek as if he'd never felt it before, then shrugged. "I wouldn't be surprised. I took quite a fall. I was hoping to call a friend to come out and pick me up. Someone stole my Jeep during the night." He looked past her into the single room that served as parlor and kitchen. "If you don't have a phone, do you have a two-way radio?"

"No. Sorry." Phone. Jeep. Two-way radio. He must be a foreigner. Olivia didn't understand half of what he said. "I have a horse if you're interested in buying one."

"Maybe." He paused, sniffed the air, and smiled. "You do have coffee, though. I knew I could smell it."

"Yes. Would you like a cup?"

"I'd just about kill for one."

Olivia hoped he didn't mean that. She studied his eyes for a moment and decided he looked quite nice. Other than his strange speech, he didn't seem dangerous. "Set your bedroll down and come inside," she said. "I'll get you some."

He slipped the odd-looking bedroll from his shoulders and lowered it to the porch, then glanced out at the barn. "I don't remember ever seeing this place before. How long have you been here?"

"Five years." Olivia stepped aside to let him enter and stole another glance at him as he ducked his head beneath the door frame. "Are you passing through?"

"No. I live in Cortez." He stopped inside the darkened room and looked around as if the sparse furnishings fascinated him. "You're really into authenticity, aren't you?"

Olivia moved past him to the heavy stove Harvey had bought for her the year before he died—her favorite luxury—and poured two cups of coffee. "I'm afraid I don't understand."

"This." The man waved one hand around the room. "Everything in here must be at least a hundred years old."

Olivia frowned, handed him a cup, and sat across from him. "Is that how they teach you to repay someone's hospitality where you come from? With insults?"

The man's smile faded and a look of sheepish embarrassment took its place. "I didn't mean it to sound rude. It's just that you don't see people living this way very often these days. At least *I* don't. Most of the people I know can't exist without modern conveniences. You don't even have a microwave." He took a sip of coffee and sighed as if he'd never tasted anything better. "I have friends who'd think you were seriously deprived."

Thoroughly confused now, Olivia admitted, "I don't understand most of what you're saying. Where did you come from?"

His brows knit as if *she'd* confused *him*. "California originally. Los Angeles."

"That's odd. You don't look Spanish. You don't sound Spanish, either. And the words you've been saying don't sound like any of the Spanish I know."

The confusion on his face deepened. "Which ones?"

"Microwave. Phone." Cradling her cup between her hands, she tried in vain to remember the others. "I don't remember them all."

"You've never heard of a microwave or a telephone?"

"No, but I doubt many people around here have. We're not exactly on the beaten track." She pushed her cup away and let her gaze linger on the scrapes on his face. "Maybe you should let me take a look at those cuts. Some of them look pretty rough."

"Thanks, but I'll just stop by the hospital on my way home."

"Hospital?" Olivia laughed, feeling superior for the first time since he knocked on the door. "There's not a hospital within a hundred miles—maybe more. What happened to you, anyway?"

"I was on my way to guard the Black Mesa site when I heard voices. I was trying to stay out of sight and I guess I stepped too close to the edge of the cliff. The next thing I knew, it was morning and my Jeep was gone."

A tickle of nervousness fluttered in Olivia's stomach, but she tried not to let it show. Nothing he said made much sense. Visitors had recently started coming to the Montezuma Valley to look at the ruins on the Wetherills's property, but nobody came to Black Mesa. Other than a

few broken pots scattered around the ranch site, there'd
been no sign of any ruins on this side of the valley. So
why was this stranger snooping around her land?

Maybe he'd heard the legend. Maybe he believed it.
Funny. She wouldn't have placed him as a treasure hunter
to look at him. And why was he hiding last night?

She stole a glance at Harvey's rifle above the mantle.
There were only a few reasons she knew of for a man to
hide, none of them good. She just hoped she hadn't made
a mistake offering this one her hospitality. "What were
you hiding from?"

"I wasn't sure if the voices I heard belonged to vandals
or someone else. Maybe I just heard you and your husband talking."

Olivia didn't bother setting him straight. If he thought
she had a husband somewhere nearby, he might be more
careful.

"I wasn't aware there was anyone living out here," he
went on. "Last time I came by this spot, this was just an
abandoned cabin. You've done a lot of work with it."

"You must be confused." The flicker of nervousness
grew stronger. "No one lived here before Harvey and I
homesteaded this land."

As if he could tell he was making her edgy, the man
leaned back in his seat and widened his smile. Dimples
dipped into his cheeks, making him look deceptively
harmless. "Maybe I am confused. I wouldn't be a bit surprised." He finished his coffee and set the empty cup
aside. "That helped. Thank you. Can I ask you another
favor?"

"What?"

"Can you give me a lift into town? It's a bit far to walk
on a gimped-up leg."

Olivia hesitated before answering. She didn't relish the
idea of losing an entire day by taking the buckboard into
town, but she didn't want the stranger hanging around too

long, either. No matter who he was or why he'd been hiding, she didn't feel right about letting him set off on foot. In the summer heat, the land was unforgiving. She didn't want a man's death on her conscience—even if he was a bank robber or a gunslinger.

When she didn't respond immediately, the stranger tossed out an incentive. "I'll pay you for gas."

"For gas?"

"I wouldn't expect you to make the trip for nothing."

She shook her head and stood. "You don't need to pay me for anything. I'll be glad to take you to town." And gladder still to be rid of him.

He stood to face her, held out one swollen hand, and tried to smile, but this time a grimace of pain crossed his face and his knees buckled.

"You *are* hurt," she cried, hurrying around the table to help him as he sagged back into the chair.

"I've had better days," he admitted. "I've had better weeks. When my boss finds out about this, he'll kill me."

Kill? Lord above, she was right. He *was* an outlaw, and it sounded as if he had more than the law on his trail.

Through the haze of pain, Kurt watched the conflicting emotions playing across the woman's face. He saw a dozen different things flitting through her dark eyes, but the predominant one—fear—made him suspicious.

"You're hurt too badly to travel that far," she said firmly. "We'll see how you feel tomorrow."

Tomorrow? What was she trying to pull? Kurt could think of only one reason for her to be afraid of him. She had to be hiding something. Only one reason for her to want to keep him here. She was trying to keep him from telling anyone about her.

He knew she hadn't bought property so close to Black Mesa. The federally protected land wasn't for sale to the general public. But why hadn't he heard that someone was squatting out here? How had they built a cabin, a barn, a corral, and dug a garden without someone noticing? It made absolutely no sense.

Maybe she was one of the vandals he'd been looking for. But how stupid would she have to be to squat here *and* steal? Maybe she and her husband were just crazy. Kurt loved nature more than most people, but even he couldn't imagine living like this.

There wasn't one concession to modern times in the roughly constructed house. Not a clock, a sink, or a television set. Not a satellite dish, a computer, or a lamp anywhere.

Maybe she was Amish. The simple clothes she wore certainly made her look the part. With a little makeup, she'd be lovely. Hell, all that dark hair and those deep brown eyes made her beautiful even without it. But her clothes . . . That dress she had on must be uncomfortably warm, especially in this stuffy cabin with only two small windows and no air-conditioning.

He stood to face her, keeping his smile carefully in place. "I'd rather go to town today."

"Absolutely not. I won't have you dying on me."

"I'm not going to die. I'm not hurt *that* badly."

"*I'm* not going to take the chance."

Kurt let out a frustrated sigh. "Look, lady—"

"Don't argue with me." Anger lit a fire in her eyes and tinted her cheeks.

"All I want is a ride into town."

"And you'll get it. Tomorrow."

The set of her jaw and the tilt of her head told Kurt she meant business. He obviously couldn't walk into town, and he didn't appear to be in any immediate danger. And maybe he could make her change her mind. Meanwhile, he'd use the time to do a little sleuthing. "You haven't noticed anyone hanging out up on Black Mesa, have you?"

The woman's face shut down as if he'd asked something odd or dangerous. "Why would anyone want to hang out up there?"

"Someone's been looting the Anasazi ruins at Black Mesa." Kurt's head, shoulder, and leg throbbed in rhythm. The pain began to curdle his stomach. "I figure anyone leaving there would likely come by your place."

"There aren't any ruins on Black Mesa." She took a step backward and put the chair between them. "Who are you, anyway?"

He tried not to retch. "Kurt Richards. And you?"

"Olivia Hamilton. *Mrs.* Hamilton. What are you doing here?"

"I live in Cortez. I work on Black Mesa."

Her eyes flashed. "You don't live in Cortez. If you did, I'd have seen you before. And you don't work on Black Mesa. There's nothing up there. Why are you lying to me?"

Why was *he* . . . ? Oh, that was rich. Kurt kept his gaze riveted on hers, noting her fear and her wide-eyed vulnerability. "I'm not lying. And I'm not going to hurt you. If you're nervous, maybe you should call your husband." This was looking more suspicious by the minute. Kurt would love a chance to question the guy.

She ignored the suggestion and asked again, "What are you doing out here?"

"I work for the Department of the Interior. It's my job to keep people from looting the ruins."

"You're a government man?"

"I am."

"The *United States* government?"

"Yes."

"You're a lawman?"

"In a manner of speaking, yes." He bit back a smile at the outdated term.

"Then show me your badge."

His *badge*? Kurt thought quickly, remembered the government identification card in his wallet, and decided that would have to do. He pulled it out and handed it to her.

She reached for it, eyes narrowed, mouth drawn. "What is this?"

"My badge."

She turned it over in her hand and scanned the back. "I've never seen a badge like this before. How did your likeness get on it? How'd you get the color in it?"

"Into my picture?" Kurt shrugged and another pain zinged through his shoulder. "I don't know," he said through clenched teeth. "Modern technology, I guess."

She glanced at him, then back at the card. "Things sure have changed since I left Virginia . . . but this can't be right." Her eyes shot to his again. "It says here you were born in 'seventy-two. But that'd make you only seventeen years old. You don't look seventeen."

"Not quite." Kurt let out a pain-edged laugh. "More like twenty-eight."

"No." Olivia shook her head grimly. "I know how to do numbers, Mr. Richards."

"I'm sure you do."

She turned his ID card over again. "If you're really a lawman, why are you sneaking around? And why does someone want to kill you?"

"Nobody wants to kill me. What gave you that idea?"

"You just said so."

He had? Kurt shook his head to clear it. This was without a doubt the strangest morning of his life. "I never said someone was trying to kill me."

She put a few more steps between them. "Yes, you did. Look, mister, I don't mind helping you, but I won't if you keep lying to me."

Too late, he realized she was making her way toward the fireplace where an old-fashioned rifle hung over the mantle. Kurt tried to stop her, but she reached it before he could get around the chair and table.

When she yanked it down and aimed it at him, he ground to an abrupt halt and held up both hands in a gesture of surrender. "Don't shoot."

"Give me a reason not to."

"Like what?"

"The truth, mister." She moved a step closer, her eyes wide with fear and determination. "Tell me the unvarnished truth or I'll drop you where you stand."

Chapter 3

SWEATING LIKE A banshee, Kurt kept both arms up and tried desperately to look peaceful and harmless— especially harmless. Without moving, he glanced toward the door and tried to calculate the possibilities of escape or at least of reaching his backpack and rifle.

They weren't good.

If this crazy woman's husband was anywhere nearby, all she had to do was raise a shout and Kurt would be outnumbered. The last thing he needed was two crazy people trying to hurt him.

He let his gaze slip back to hers and took in the grim expression in her eyes. She might be beautiful, but beautiful didn't necessarily mean nice. Kurt wasn't about to underestimate her.

Nervous sweat trickled down his back. Obviously, she thought she could shoot him and get away with it. And maybe she could. They were out here in the middle of nowhere with miles and miles of remote gullies, ditches, and canyons in which to hide his body. If a search party came looking for him, it might be years before they found him—if they ever did.

"I want the truth," Olivia said, keeping the rifle pointed at his head. "Who are you?"

Kurt had never been on the opposite end of a rifle before, and it gave him a new respect for the people he'd looked at from the safe end. "I told you, my name is Kurt Richards, I live in Cortez, and I work for the Bureau of Land Management. If you had a telephone, I'd suggest you call someone to verify that."

She nudged the rifle closer, scowling darkly. "Quit using words I don't understand. I don't have a whatchamacallit. I don't even know what one is."

"A telephone?" Kurt inadvertently let his hands drop a fraction of an inch. When her eyes narrowed dangerously, he jerked them back up again. "Are you serious? You don't know what a telephone is?"

"No, and I don't want to know. You still haven't explained why your badge says you were born in 'seventy-two."

"That's simple," he said with a light shrug. "I *was* born in 'seventy-two." His hands began to tingle and he took a calculated risk by lowering them an inch or two. When she didn't pull the trigger, he took another chance. "Maybe you could explain why that upsets you so much?"

"If that's not obvious," she snapped, "I don't know what is."

"It's not obvious or I wouldn't have asked." He lowered his hands a bit further and tried to gauge the distance between them. "Tell me."

Olivia's face flamed and her eyes widened again. She cocked the rifle and zeroed in on the bridge of his nose. "Don't even *think* about trying to jump me. I'm as good a shot as my husband ever was."

Cursing silently, Kurt inched his hands back into the air. "Don't worry, I won't." The air in the tiny cabin grew even hotter and the pain in his leg intensified. "Look, Mrs. Hamilton—"

"Don't talk. You're only trying to confuse me."

"You have no idea how hard I'm trying *not* to confuse you," Kurt assured her. "The last thing I want to do is upset you. Standing here with the blood draining out of my arms and a loaded rifle in my face isn't exactly my idea of a good time."

Her gaze left his for a heartbeat, darted to his leg, then back to his face again. But now he could see a flicker of uncertainty in her eyes. "Let me take a look at that leg."

Not in a million years. He wasn't stupid enough to get caught with his pants down. "If you could just take me into town," he began.

She shook her head brusquely. "Not if you're hurt bad. You won't make it that far."

"I'm not hurt that badly," he assured her. "It's only half an hour drive."

"See what I mean? You don't even know where town is from here. It takes half a *day* to get there in the buckboard. Less on horseback. But you're in no condition to ride."

Kurt felt as if he'd been trapped in a nightmare. "You've got to be kidding. You don't have a car?" Even as he asked, he wondered why that should surprise him.

"No."

He rubbed his forehead gingerly. "Can I ask you one question? Why in the hell are you living way out here alone?"

She lifted her chin and let her gaze settle on his. "This is my home, and I'm not leaving it."

"That's fair enough, I suppose." He gave the cramped cabin another once-over, but the pain in his leg was beginning to affect him in other ways. The room swam in front of his eyes and his head felt as if it had begun to spin. "But what's with the Wild West reenactment? If you're determined to stay here, why not at least make yourself comfortable?"

"I am comfortable. I have everything I need."

Kurt ran a hand across his stomach and fought another surge of nausea. He must be hurt worse than he first imagined. If he didn't know better, he'd swear he'd been swept up during the night and carried through a timewarp. "Look," he said, rapidly running low on patience, "why don't we hitch the wagon and head into town? You can be rid of me, I can get to a hospital, and we'll both be happy. If you're worried about me telling someone you're out here—"

Olivia inched the gun into his face again. "Why would I be worried about that? Seems to me, *you* have more reason to be worried than I do."

"You might be right." The room pitched beneath his feet. Kurt longed to sit again before he fell over or lost consciousness. "All I know is, I hurt like hell all over and I'd really like to see a doctor."

Concern took the place of distrust on her face—but only for a moment. "Is this some sort of trick?"

"Lady, I don't have the energy to play tricks. I'm running out of steam fast. Do you have any aspirin? Maybe that would help."

She lowered the gun an inch or two and studied him carefully. "What's that?"

"Aspirin?" He let out a sharp laugh and kneaded his temples. This had to be the most bizarre situation he'd ever been in—and Olivia Hamilton was certainly the most bizarre woman he'd ever met. "If you have to ask," he said as he grabbed the table to hold himself upright, "you don't have any."

Amazingly, she lowered the rifle and took a hesitant step closer. "You're feeling poorly?"

"Poorly isn't the word for it."

"Maybe you should sit down for a minute."

That was the best idea he'd heard yet. He dropped into the chair, rested his head in his hands, and took several deep breaths hoping to get his balance back. His shoulder throbbed and another sharp pain shot up his leg. His head pounded as if someone had hit it with a boulder.

Wincing, he lifted his gaze to hers again. "Do you have *anything* for pain?"

She rested the rifle on the floor beside the front door and studied him for a long moment as if she still suspected him of trying to trick her. But the look in his eyes must have convinced her. "I have something in the bedroom."

"Do you mind if I take some of it?"

"I suppose not." She picked up the rifle and carried it with her toward a closed door. She disappeared for a minute and came back carrying an amber-colored bottle half filled with liquid. *He'd* been thinking along the lines of ibuprofen.

She found a spoon that looked big enough to choke a horse, filled it with the medicine, and urged it toward him. "I still think you should let me take a look at that leg."

When he hesitated, trying to decide whether to risk taking the unidentifiable concoction or not, she nudged it closer and half-smiled at him. "Go on. Take it. If it puts you to sleep, I promise I won't shoot you."

"That," he said honestly, "is the best news I've had all day. What is it?"

"Just a pain tincture. I may be living in the back of beyond, but that doesn't mean I don't have up-to-date medicine." She pressed the spoon against his lips and he reluctantly opened his mouth. As the vile-tasting stuff trickled onto his tongue, she added, "This *is* eighteen eighty-nine, after all."

He swallowed half the medicine convulsively but the other half sputtered out onto the table. "Eighteen eighty-nine?" He tried to stand but another sharp pain tore through his leg and up into his side. He dropped back into the chair and stared at her, no doubt looking like a complete idiot. "What kind of joke is this?"

Olivia lowered the spoon to the table and worked the cork back into the bottle. "Don't tell me you don't even know what year it is."

"I may be in pain, lady, but I haven't lost my head completely. It sure as hell isn't eighteen eighty-nine."

She sent a lingering glance at the rifle. "You're awfully rude for someone in your condition. My rifle is in here. Yours is outside. You're hurt. I'm not. And *I* didn't just take a dose of laudanum."

Laudanum? Impossible. Unless . . .

Unless this really *was* 1889.

Olivia rinsed the spoon beneath an old-fashioned pump, then propped both hands on her hips. "Now take off your shirt and trousers. I want to see how badly you're hurt."

He shook his head softly, but not softly enough to stop the pain from ricocheting everywhere. "I don't want to sound rude, but I think I'll wait to see the doctor."

"Doc Winters doesn't get out this way very often," she said, reaching for his buttons as if she intended to strip the shirt away herself. "I'm afraid you'll have to put up with me." Kurt could think of a hundred things he'd rather do than strip down in front of this woman. She cut him off before he could say so. "Don't tell me you're bashful about letting a strange woman see you in your skivvies."

He laughed, then immediately wished he hadn't. Another searing pain shot down his neck, traced the muscles on his shoulder, and ping-ponged into his leg. "I've never been accused of being shy before."

"Then take off your clothes." Olivia started toward the door. "I'll turn my back if it makes you feel better. When you're finished, lay down in the bedroom and give a shout so I can look you over."

He studied her face, searching for some sign of trickery, malice, or even dementia. But she looked absolutely genuine and perfectly normal. Maybe she knew what she was doing. Maybe not. But at the moment, Kurt didn't seem to have many other options. He could dig in his heels and hold out until he saw the doctor, or he could let this woman do her best with home remedies. If nothing else, she could clean the wounds.

He pushed slowly to his feet, turned toward the rough-hewn wooden door, and tried to lighten the moment with a small joke. "This is by far the oddest excuse any woman's ever given to get me into bed."

An ominous-sounding click brought him back around to find Olivia, red-faced with anger, aiming the rifle at him again. "That," she said with false bravado, "is the last thing in the world I want from you."

An embarrassed smile twisted his lips, but he didn't have the strength to raise his arms again. Instead, he gripped the back of the chair and held on. "It was a joke."

"Some joke."

"I didn't mean it."

"You'd better not have meant it. If you lay one finger on me, you'll *wish* you'd died last night."

"I'm beginning to wish that already." His head whirled, his stomach pitched, and the floor rose up to meet him. He sagged against the table, but it wouldn't hold him. He heard a resounding crash, the splintering of wood, and a second later, everything went black.

Olivia stood back, panting from exertion, and stared at the man's inert body. She hadn't been able to move him to the bed—he was far too heavy and densely muscled for that—but she'd tried to make him as comfortable as she could by rolling him onto a blanket on the floor.

She tried not to look at the chair he'd shattered when he fell. It was one of the chairs Harvey had made for her, and it broke her heart to lose it. But crying wouldn't bring it back. And just now, she had to keep her wits about her.

Kurt turned his head slightly and muttered something

under his breath. A lock of dark hair fell over his fore-head.

She studied the clean-shaven planes of his cheeks, the slightly open mouth, the eyelids covering the startling blue eyes. He was a strikingly handsome man, she couldn't deny that, but she'd never trusted good-looking men.

Not that Harvey hadn't been handsome in his own way, she thought quickly. And Sam was certainly nice-looking. But Kurt Richards was that dangerous kind of handsome, and a traveling man to boot—the same treacherous combination as Nathaniel Park, the man who'd wooed her sister Melody using pretty words and soft-spoken promises, and then left her alone and pregnant, and still unmarried.

In Olivia's experience, men like Kurt Richards were the kind a smart woman should avoid. She'd always considered herself to be reasonably intelligent, so what was she doing with him passed out on her floor? And what was she going to do with him now?

She could ride to Sam's place and ask him for help, but she felt uncomfortable asking after turning down his marriage proposal. Her other closest neighbors were the Wetherills, but it would take hours to reach their place, and she didn't like the idea of leaving a stranger alone in her house.

Everything she owned was here. Every memory of Harvey along with the few things she still had from her childhood in Virginia. He'd already broken one of her chairs. She didn't want to risk something happening to the rest of her belongings if he woke while she was gone.

Besides, she reasoned as she settled herself in the rocker near the window, if she went running for help now, she might as well admit that staying here alone was too much for her. She'd be fine. She had a rifle, and she knew how to use it.

She rocked for a minute or two longer, then crossed to the pump and filled a bowl with cool water. After finding some clean rags, she knelt beside Kurt's inert body and began to wash the blood away from his forehead. She found a small cut beneath his hair, another over his ear, but sighed with relief when she realized they weren't deep.

Sitting back on her heels, she took a deep breath for courage and moved lower. She unfastened his shirt, peeling away the fabric from his chest and shoulders. It had been a long time since she'd seen a man's bare torso, and the sight of his chest, broad, tanned, and well-muscled, stirred an unwelcome reaction in her.

Biting her bottom lip in determination, she washed away the dirt and dried blood and smoothed salve over the cuts and scrapes. Now for the rest of him.

She rinsed the rags in the water and stared at the waist of his trousers for what felt like forever. When she realized the idea of undressing him further made her uncomfortable, she chided herself silently, unbuckled his belt, and tried to pull off his trousers.

The strange shoes on his feet stopped her, so she removed them and set them aside, then gently tugged off his dust-covered pants. He wore the strangest underclothes she'd ever seen. Skimpy was the only word that came to mind. And colorful. And made of silk.

She laughed softly, trying to imagine Harvey's reaction if she'd ever suggested he wear a fancy pair of underclothes like that. He'd have thought she'd lost her mind.

Remembering Harvey helped keep her from reacting to the sight of the man's bare legs. One thing for certain, it was hard for *any* man to look tough and threatening in his underwear.

She felt his legs gingerly, checking for broken bones, then cleaned him as far up as she dared, applied the salve to the cuts and scrapes on his thigh, and called it a job well done. There might be bruises beneath those fancy underclothes but since he wasn't bleeding, she wasn't about to look.

She found another blanket and covered him so she wouldn't have to look at his bare legs and chest now that she'd finished her doctoring. Scooping up his dusty clothing, she carried it outside and hung it over the porch rail. But curiosity got the best of her and she took a minute to search his pockets first. If he had another weapon hidden somewhere, she wanted to know about it.

She found only a few coins and a leather contraption that held some paper money and some strange-looking things all embossed with his name. Since that was the only name she came across, she figured he'd probably told her the truth about that.

She started to slip the coins back into his pocket, then decided to take a closer look. Maybe she could find out where he was really from. It looked like United States money, all right. It said so on every single coin, even though they didn't look like any coins she'd ever seen. But what caught her attention was the date stamped on the first one she studied.

1995? Impossible. She checked another, then another, her hands trembling as she did so. But by the time she finished, a cold ball had settled in her stomach.

Every coin in her hand was dated at least a hundred years in the future.

Kurt awoke slowly, trying to figure out why he hurt so much. Every inch of his body ached or pulsed with pain, a hard surface pressed into his back, and he knew without even trying to move that his muscles were stiff and tight. Not only that, but something hot and scratchy covered him.

He tossed back the cover, finding only mild relief from the August heat. His air conditioner must be on the fritz—

again. But why was he asleep on the floor?

Forcing his eyes open, he took in his surroundings. Rough cabin walls surrounded him. An uneven wooden floor stretched away from him. The old-fashioned stove, thick leaded windows with hand-sewn curtains, and a pile of wood where a chair had once been brought everything back in a rush . . . or as much of a rush as possible with his mind still fogged from the laudanum.

He tried to sit, but stiff, sore muscles dropped him back to the floor like a wet rag. A groan escaped his lips. Another hovered just behind it. "Mrs. Hamilton?" His voice cracked on the two simple words and the effort sucked his breath away.

He filled his lungs and tried again. "Mrs. Hamilton? Are you there?"

No answer.

Gritting his teeth, he forced himself upright. His brain cleared enough to realize that the woman had taken his clothes, leaving him nothing but the silk hot-pepper boxers one of his friends had given him as a gag gift. He had to give her credit. He wouldn't be much of a threat to her in these.

A strong medicinal scent stung his nostrils and drew his gaze toward the wound on his leg. Mrs. Hamilton might have stripped him nearly naked, but at least she'd cleaned and treated his wounds. He gave his leg a cursory inspection, wincing when his fingers brushed the skin around the cut, the bruises, and even places that didn't look hurt.

He'd taken a beating when he fell off the cliff. He felt every second of his twenty-eight years—and another twenty-eight on top of those. But the salve and bandages gave him heart. It wouldn't make much sense for Mrs. Hamilton to doctor him if she planned to kill him later.

He rubbed his eyes and wondered how long he'd slept. Squinting to clear his vision, he checked his watch. But his bad luck was holding. The damned thing had stopped working.

Hoping to guess the time from the angle of the sun, he scooted toward the open front door. Leggy evening shadows stretched from the house onto the baked earth. He must have slept the better part of the day. Long enough for Mrs. Hamilton's husband to come back.

She might be harmless, but Kurt didn't think any man would be thrilled to find a drugged-up, half-naked stranger lying on his floor. He needed clothes and he needed them now. And while he was at it, he'd find his rifle and ammunition, just in case.

He inched toward the table and used the legs, then the top to pull himself to his feet. But the effort left him weak and panting. No matter what was happening here, he wouldn't be going anywhere on foot. He'd die before he made it to town. Holding his head, he bent to retrieve the blanket.

"You're up." The sound of her voice caught him by surprise. He dropped the blanket to the floor and stood there in all his chili-peppered glory. She held a rusted hoe in one hand and a faded bonnet covered her hair. "Are you feeling better?"

"Not much." He glanced down at the blanket pooled on the floor, though he didn't know why he worried. She'd already seen him this way. "Thanks for . . ." He gestured vaguely, not quite sure where to begin.

"You're welcome." She set the hoe aside and came through the door, removing her bonnet as she walked and letting loose a tumble of thick, dark hair that bounced from her shoulders and ended in a lazy curl just above the place where her breasts swelled against faded green cotton. "You must be hungry."

Hungry? The word sounded almost foreign to him, but his stomach reacted automatically with a deep, demanding growl. "Starving."

"Sit down and I'll fix you a plate." Letting her gaze flick across his boxers, she moved toward the stove and lifted a lid from a pot. The rich, warm scent of simmering beef and broth floated across the room to him.

Kurt picked up the blanket and wrapped it around his waist. "Thanks. Out of curiosity, where are my clothes?"

"Outside." Olivia ladled stew into a heavy bowl and motioned him toward the table. "What's left of them, anyway. I was planning to wash them for you, but I'm not sure if they're worth the effort."

"They're all I have." Kurt's stomach rumbled again as she carried the bowl across the room and set it in front of him. Beef and vegetables swam together in a thick broth, and the aroma nearly knocked him off the chair.

Olivia smiled, amused, as if she'd heard the echo of his hunger, and handed him a spoon. "We can see if any of my husband's things will fit you."

Kurt spooned up some of the stew. "I'm not going far. My things will be fine." He doubted Mr. Hamilton had clothes to spare, but he didn't want to insult her again. "I don't want to put either of you to any trouble."

Olivia filled a bowl for herself and sat across the table from him.

Surprised that she'd start supper without her husband, Kurt stopped with the spoon halfway to his mouth. "Maybe I should introduce myself to him. Where is he?"

Olivia handed him a round loaf of crusty bread. "I'm afraid you can't do that. He passed away last October."

Kurt lowered the bread to the table and shifted uneasily inside the scratchy blanket. "I'm sorry."

Her lips curved ever so slightly. "Thank you."

"So you're living here alone?"

"Yes." Wariness flickered in her dark eyes. "But don't get any ideas. My friend Sam lives on the neighboring property and he stops by often to make sure I'm doing all right."

"You're perfectly safe with me." Kurt couldn't resist the aroma of dinner any longer. He filled his mouth and nearly moaned aloud at the taste. He'd eaten at some of the best restaurants in the west, but not even the most expensive meals had ever tasted this good.

Olivia smiled, once again leaving him with the impression that she could read his mind. "Is the stew all right?"

"*All right*? It's probably the best thing I've ever tasted."

"You *must* be hungry," she said with a laugh. She ate in silence for a few minutes, then set her spoon aside with her bowl still half full and held out a handful of coins. "Since you're feeling better, Mr. Richards, maybe you can explain these."

Kurt dragged his attention away from his bowl and gave the coins a quick once-over. Nothing special there. A few quarters. Nickels. Dimes. Too many pennies. "What about them?"

"I found them in your pockets."

He lowered his spoon to the table with a clank that hurt his head. "You searched my pockets?"

"I certainly did. I wanted to know if you had any other weapons hidden."

"And did I?"

"No. But you had these."

Kurt pushed his bowl away and held out his hand for the coins. She closed her fist around them as if they were secret government weapons. "If you expect me to explain them," he said, "you'll have to let me see them."

She hesitated, dragging her bottom lip between her teeth as if she were facing a momentous decision.

Kurt held his hand out a little further. "I'm not dangerous . . . unless you're the one who's been looting the ruins."

Her eyes flicked across his face, her lips curved into a scowl, but she loosened her grip on the coins. "I haven't looted anything," she said as she dropped the money into his hand. "I'd never steal something that didn't belong to me." She nodded toward the coins in his hand and demanded, "Are they counterfeit? Is that why you're hiding?"

"What in the hell makes you think they're counterfeit? For that matter, what makes you think I'm in hiding?"

"They don't look like any money *I've* ever seen." Olivia stood and gathered the bowls. "If they are, whoever made them isn't very bright. The dates are all wrong."

His head began to buzz again, the throbbing in his leg returned. He studied several of the coins, but he'd be damned if he could see anything wrong.

Olivia set the bowls aside and turned back to face him. "How do you think you're going to fool anyone with that money?"

"I wasn't *planning* to fool anyone."

"Then, somebody took you for a ride. Either that, or you did this to somebody else and that's who's gunning for you."

Kurt made to slip the coins into his pocket, remembered he didn't have one, and dumped them onto the table instead. "*Nobody's* gunning for me," he said, standing to face her. "And I'm not in hiding." He jerked his hand toward the table. "If there's something wrong with the coins, I wish you'd show me what it is."

She crossed the room quickly, snagged several of them from the table, and held them under his nose. "Any fool can see they're not silver. And how can they have been minted in nineteen-something when it's not even the turn of the century yet? Tell me *that*."

Kurt could only stare at her for a long moment while he tried to process the question and the implications behind it. "What you said before," he finally managed. "About the year being 1889 . . . It's true?"

"Of course it's true. What other year could it be?"

Confused and uncertain, he shook his head slowly. "If

I told you, you'd probably think I was crazy."

"I'm beginning to wonder about that already."

"I'm sure you are." He dropped into his seat again, barely noticing that the blanket loosened and fell away. He'd always considered time travel the product of peoples' overactive imaginations. But here he was, eating dinner in a ranch house that hadn't been occupied for over a hundred years, arguing with a woman who certainly looked as if she'd come from the nineteenth century, and wearing nothing but a pair of hot pepper boxer shorts. He was either in the middle of a very realistic nightmare or he'd done the utterly impossible and traveled through time.

Chapter 4

KURT TOOK A deep breath and let it out again slowly while he tried to decide what to do next. If he *had* traveled through time, he'd be smart not to antagonize his hostess. She had the food, the water, and the shelter he'd need to survive. But what possible explanation could he give for having coins minted over a hundred years in the future?

The truth? She already thought he was crazy. He could just imagine how she'd react to hearing that he'd come from the twenty-first century.

Admit to counterfeiting? If she didn't shoot him, she might see that he wound up in jail. Not exactly top on his list of things to do while in the past.

"I don't—" His voice cracked. He cleared his throat and tried again. "I don't have an explanation," he admitted. "I must have been given the coins in change."

She pulled back slightly, studying his eyes as if she could see the difference between truth and lie in them. And why not? Aunt Dorothy always could. So could Charlotte. And Holly might have been able to if she'd ever bothered to look. His eyes were one of the reasons Kurt had never been a poker player.

"Who are you hiding from?" she demanded.

"No one, and that's the God's honest truth. I fell. I told you that. And I became disoriented in the night. But I'm not hiding, I'm not dangerous, and nobody's looking for me."

She folded her arms and tilted her head from side to side as she raked him with her eyes. "You'd better be telling the truth."

"I wouldn't dare lie," he said honestly. When she relaxed slightly, he nodded toward the door. "Do you think I could get my clothes back?"

Her gaze drifted toward the chili peppers below his waist, then snapped back to his face. A light blush flamed in her cheeks, but she averted her head so quickly Kurt almost missed it. To his surprise, the sign of vulnerability pleased him. Maybe she was made of something other than iron and cactus needles after all.

"You can't wear your things," she said without looking at him. "I'll find you some of Harvey's."

"Thanks." At this point he'd take anything . . . gladly.

She darted a quick look at him. "You can stay in the barn tonight. You'll be comfortable enough there."

Kurt could only imagine. But common sense told him to accept the offer and be glad of it. He stayed put while she disappeared into the back room and emerged a few minutes later clutching a small stack of clothing and bedding.

She held out the clothes to him, but that quick glance at his boxer shorts had changed something between them. When their fingers brushed, a current shot through him and he could tell by the way she jerked her hand away that she'd felt it too.

"Clothes and blankets," she said stiffly. "If you want to follow me, I'll show you where you can bed down."

He set the clothes aside while he knotted the blanket around his waist once more, then limped behind her onto the porch of the cabin. But one look at the dusty yard brought him to an abrupt halt. "Can I at least have my shoes?"

She glanced at his stockinged feet and almost smiled. "Of course." She disappeared around a corner and came back with his shoes in hand. The laces drooped from the eyelets and the tongue protruded at an odd angle, as if she'd given the shoes a thorough search, as well.

She didn't admit to it, but handed him the shoes and waited while he sat on the splintered porch to slip his feet into them. The sun had settled even further onto the western horizon and only a few reddish-gold rays still lit the sky. But out of the grand expanse of landscape, they found Olivia's hair and lit the dusky locks on fire.

He forced his attention back to his shoes and took his time tying them. She was beautiful, there was no denying that, but Kurt wasn't entirely sure that at least part of his reaction hadn't been sparked by losing Charlotte. Even in his own time, he wouldn't risk using another woman to soothe his battered ego. He sure as hell wasn't stupid enough to mess around with the past.

He might have been brought here by some freak accident of nature, but he'd have to be very careful not to alter history while he was here. He'd read books. He'd seen movies. Sooner or later, he'd go back to his own time, and when he did, he didn't want to find out he was his own great-grandson. A thing like that could give a guy nightmares for the rest of his life.

Sam scowled into the dancing flames inside the fireplace, the ledger on the desk in front of him all but forgotten. Outside, wind rustled the piñon and junipers. Inside, the fire cast flickering light across the floor to dance on his feet.

His kid brother, Jesse, sat across the room near an oil

lamp, a book in his lap, his reading glasses perched on the end of his nose. Jesse liked all the paperwork that went with running a spread the size of the Cinnabar. It made Sam nervous. Columns of figures had never appealed to him, and too much time in a chair made his legs twitch.

He'd inherited the Cinnabar when his father died, but only the responsibility of keeping a roof over Jesse's head kept him here. And Olivia. Of course, Olivia.

He let out an unwitting sigh and returned his gaze to the ledger, pretending the sound hadn't come from him.

Jesse looked up from his book and pushed his glasses up on his nose. "What was that?"

"What was what?"

"Sounds like something's bothering you."

Sam shook his head and kept his gaze firmly focused on the account books. "No."

Jesse marked his place in the book with one finger and shook back a lock of russet hair from his eyes. "Did something happen on the range today?"

"No."

Jesse set his book aside slowly. "Were you on the range today, or did you go to the Lazy H?"

And here we go, Sam thought. *The inquisition begins.* Jesse had always been hardheaded. Once he got his teeth into something, he didn't let go easily. That tenacity was one of his best qualities—and one of his worst. Nobody ever pulled the wool over Jesse's eyes, not even Sam.

Avoiding the subject wouldn't accomplish anything. Jesse'd keep hounding until he either got an answer or made one up. Sam flicked a glance at him. "I went to the Lazy H."

"Did you see Olivia?"

"I did." Sam made another note on the ledger and tried to look bored with their conversation.

"How *is* Olivia?"

"She seemed fine." Sam pulled the oil lamp closer and found a fresh sheet of paper in the desk. "You up to riding to Devil's Canyon with me tomorrow? We ought to check on the cattle up there."

"Sure." Jesse rested an ankle on his knee and hooked one arm over the back of his chair. "I can go alone if you want me to. If there's something here that needs your attention . . ."

"No. Nothing." Sam looked at his brother from under his eyebrows, saw the phony innocence on his face, and bit back a murmur of irritation.

". . . or if you need to ride over to the Lazy H again."

Sam turned several pages of the ledger without responding. Ever since Jesse had fallen in love with Elizabeth Langley from town, he'd been trying to convince Sam to bite the bullet and get married himself. Come to think of it, the pressure Sam got at home probably had a lot to do with the humiliation he'd suffered that morning.

Not that Sam resented Jesse's happiness. He couldn't think of anyone he'd rather see smiling like a dimwit all the time. It just didn't help Sam's mood to see it, that's all. And though he knew that Jesse worried about him, he wasn't about to let him find out what a fool he'd made of himself with Olivia.

"I don't need to go to the Lazy H again for a few days," he said. "I'll go again on Monday, like I usually do." Maybe in a few days he'd be able to actually look at Olivia again.

Jesse picked up his book again but he didn't go back to it right away. "You could go if you want. I don't mind. I can go to Devil's Canyon alone and there's not a whole lot else that needs doing around here."

"Obviously not enough to keep your mind on what's important," Sam snarled.

Jesse laughed, not even slightly intimidated by Sam's

most irritated scowl. "Is she still thinking about selling that horse of Harvey's?"

Now, there was a subject Sam didn't mind talking about. He abandoned the ledger and leaned back in his chair. "She's going to have to if she wants to keep the ranch. It's either sell the stock or sell the land."

"And she's still not willing to sell the land?"

"She's not even considering it." Sam drummed his fingers on the desk, frustrated all over again by her stubborn determination. "She's convinced Harvey would want her to stay."

Jesse pulled off his glasses and set them on top of his book. "Harvey wouldn't have wanted her to stay here alone. She's just using that as an excuse to do what she wants."

"What's wrong with that? Everyone ought to do what they really want."

"Even you?"

The question sounded innocent enough, but the look on Jesse's narrow face sure wasn't. "What's that supposed to mean?"

Jesse shrugged. "Whatever you want it to."

Sam drilled Jesse with another glare, this one stern and unyielding. "Uh-huh."

Jesse wagged the hand that dangled over the back of his chair. "Oh, come on, Sam. You know this isn't what you want to do with your life. *I* sure as hell know it."

"Oh?" Sam arched an eyebrow at him. "All right, Mr. Know-It-All, what do I want to do?"

"Not sit around adding up figures all night, that's for sure." Jesse disentangled himself from the chair and came to stand in front of their father's huge mahogany desk. "Do you want me to finish that?"

The offer was tempting, but Sam shook his head. He'd set himself to the task, he'd damned well finish it—even if it took all night. "I'm doing all right. You go on back to your book."

Jesse cleared a corner of the desk and perched there. "I need to talk to you about something first."

That brought Sam's head up again. "What?"

"Elizabeth and I have been talking. When we get married, we'd like to travel some. Maybe settle down near Denver. She . . ." Jesse rubbed his neck and laughed uncomfortably. "She doesn't want to stay here."

"She what?" Sam closed the ledger book with a bang. What was it with women, anyway? He had one on his hands who wouldn't budge if the walls came crashing down around her, another who turned her nose up at one of the best ranches in the Montezuma Valley. "And what's wrong with the Cinnabar?"

"Nothing. It's just that she'd like us to have our own place."

"The Cinnabar *is* your own place."

"No. The Cinnabar is yours. Pa made sure of that."

"Only because you were so young when he died."

"Doesn't matter." Jesse set his jaw and pushed to his feet. "I'll never be anything but second fiddle around here. You'll get married one of these days and fill the house with a family."

"Yeah?" Sam stood to face him. "You know that for a fact, do you?"

"When you do," Jesse went on, "I'll be about as necessary as a fifth wheel."

Sam crossed to the fireplace and rested his arm on the mantle. He stared into the fire for a second or two, trying to get his temper under control. He didn't want to take out his frustrations with Olivia on Jesse. "Even if I did get married," Sam said carefully, "it wouldn't be for years. If I had children, I might have daughters. If I have sons, they're not going to be born ready to ranch."

"True enough. But I could use those years to set up my own place."

Sam wheeled around to face him. "So you're going to up and leave just because the old man was too short-sighted to officially leave half of the Cinnabar to you. Damn it, I'll give you your half. Will that make you happy?"

"He wasn't short-sighted," Jesse snapped. His voice had a rough edge, but his eyes were calm—as if he'd been thinking about this for more than just a day. "The Cinnabar is what it is *because* of the way the old man set it up. He knew this place would crumble if he broke it in half."

Sam opened his mouth to argue, then snapped it shut again. Jesse was right. They both knew it. But Sam couldn't just stand by and twiddle his thumbs while Jesse made a decision like this. Jesse loved the Cinnabar as much as Sam did—maybe even more.

"Does Elizabeth want to leave the valley? Or is it just because of the ranch?"

"She loves it here," Jesse admitted. "She's a little afraid to leave her family. But she wants to see me happy."

At least Sam had that. "There has to be a better solution," he said. "Just give me some time to think about it."

"Elizabeth and I have already thought of everything."

"Another head working on the problem can't hurt," Sam insisted.

"I suppose not." Jesse looked hesitant, and sounded downright reluctant.

"A few weeks, Jesse. That's all I ask."

"All right," Jesse said slowly. "I won't do anything yet. But Elizabeth and I are talking about getting married in December, so I can't wait forever."

Sam had a reprieve, but not much of one. It wasn't enough for one bad thing to happen in a day. Everything had to hit at once. A huge weight settled on his shoulders.

One side held Olivia's security; Jesse and Elizabeth perched solidly on the other.

If he hadn't destroyed everything with Olivia, he could have talked to her about Jesse and Elizabeth. She had a level head on her shoulders, and she knew a sight more about women than he did. But he'd had to open his big mouth.

He twitched his shoulders as if he could settle the weight more comfortably, but it didn't help. His father had entrusted the Cinnabar and Jesse's future to him. Harvey had left him with Olivia's happiness in his hands. And Sam had no idea what to do about either one.

The pounding in Kurt's head had subsided greatly by the next morning. The throbbing in his shoulder and the shooting pains in his leg had all but disappeared. Must say something about the healing properties of hay dust crawling up his nose, horses nickering him to sleep, and the pungent aroma of livestock sweeping around him like a dark cloud.

He stretched, watching dust motes dance on the morning sun as it streamed into the barn through chinks in the wood. His sleeping bag formed a barrier between him and the sharp, stabbing bits of hay. He'd used Olivia's blanket for comfort and the one from his backpack rolled up under his head as a pillow. Not bad.

"Are you awake?"

The unexpected voice so close made him jerk upright. Hay dust stirred into the air and tore a sneeze from him.

Olivia rested both arms on the stable wall and looked down at him. He must have made quite a sight with his bare chest and hair spiked from sleep. He scrambled to cover himself with the blanket, and her lips curved into a smile. "Did you sleep well?"

"Surprisingly, yes." Once his mind had stopped reeling from the idea of bedding down in the nineteenth century.

"I'm glad. Do you still want to go to town today?"

"Yes, if you're willing to take me." There was still a chance that he'd find Cortez just the way he remembered it and that he'd fall asleep in his own soft bed at the end of the day.

"Are you sure you're feeling up to it?"

"I'll take my chances. I'm sure people are beginning to wonder where I am."

"Which people?"

"Friends. People I work with."

"In Cortez?"

"Maybe." Kurt stood clumsily, trying to keep the blanket together and his chili peppers hidden as he got to his feet. "I hope so, anyway."

Wariness flickered in the depths of her eyes, making Kurt wonder if he'd inadvertently said the wrong thing again. "You can wash up in the trough if you want to," she said. "And come on up to the house when you're through. Breakfast's ready. But don't take too long. It's half a day into town, and half a day back after I've got you there." She started to turn away, then stopped and looked back at him. "Did the clothes fit all right?"

Actually, the worn cotton work shirt she'd handed him carried about five extra inches through the shoulders and was equally too short in the tail, but he wasn't about to insult her again. "They're fine, thank you."

She nodded as if the answer pleased her and stepped off whatever she'd been standing on. "Don't be long. The day's wasting."

Kurt dug soap, deodorant, and a disposable razor from his backpack, then limped outside and across the uneven yard to the trough. He scooped off the film of dust and layer of bugs covering the water and spent a few minutes remembering how to prime the pump before he had fresh water.

He scrubbed furiously, washing away the dust, sweat,

and grime. The water felt cool against his skin and far
more refreshing than it looked. He plunged his head into
the water and shook out the cool droplets in the rising
sun.

He wondered if Olivia was watching from inside the
house. If their situations had been reversed, he most certainly would have been watching her. But she was a recent
widow and probably not at all interested in a half-naked
stranger washing in a horse trough. Still, there had been
that moment last night when he'd glimpsed the woman
beneath that backbone of steel.

It didn't matter, he told himself firmly. She'd be taking
him into Cortez this morning and that would be the end
of it. He'd discover that this whole thing was a delusion
brought on by whatever pain medication she'd really
given him, and he'd never see her again.

He shook his head once more to clear his thoughts,
dressed quickly and hurried across the yard to the porch.
All business. Mind firmly under control. Women forgotten. It hadn't even been a week since Charlotte walked
out on him. Far too soon to be thinking about women
anyway.

Olivia appeared in the doorway almost the second his
foot hit the bottom step, which meant she'd either been
watching or listening. But again he told himself it didn't
matter. Meant nothing.

She stepped aside to let him enter, shoulders back, chin
held high. As full of purpose as he was. Determined not
to let another moment pass between them like the one
they'd shared last night.

He had to turn to sidle past her and their eyes met. And
held.

That was his first big mistake. His second was not looking away. Her eyes held his—deep, wide, night-dark eyes
both glimmering with awareness and shadowed with
worry. He swallowed convulsively and his hands grew

clammy. He rubbed them against the legs of her late husband's Levi's and tried to break the moment with some inane bit of conversation.

"I appreciate your hospitality, Mrs. Hamilton. I don't know what I would have done if I hadn't come upon your place."

It worked. Her eyes shuttered immediately. "There's no reason to thank me. I'm just doing what anyone would do."

He swiped water from the back of his neck and managed to step past her to the safety of her cabin. As if being anywhere alone with her was truly safe. "I'll repay you somehow."

"No need." She stepped inside behind him, making sure to keep a distance between them. "I'll get you into town, but after that you're on your own." The softness he'd seen a moment ago had vanished completely. She was back to business, bustling between stove and table with plates of eggs, biscuits, and sizzling beefsteak, a crock of butter, a pitcher of milk, and a pot of coffee. "I hope this is enough."

"*Enough?*" Kurt's laugh came out sharp-edged and he realized with a start that he was angry—with her for being so damned attractive, with himself for noticing, with fate for dropping him here. "I can't remember the last time someone cooked me a real breakfast." If he was lucky—or if he'd been damned near miraculous in bed the night before—Charlotte had made toast to go with his coffee. Otherwise, he made do with a trip through the drive-through.

"You're not married, then?" The question sounded casual, but Kurt caught the slight tensing of her shoulders and the merest flick of her eyes in his direction.

"No. Not anymore."

"You were once?"

"Once. I'm divorced."

"Divorced?" The idea seemed to throw her. "Oh. I see. I—I've never actually known anyone who was divorced before."

Definitely not a twenty-first-century kind of thing to say.

She pulled up a chair and sat across from him. "Was it awful?"

"The divorce?" Kurt laughed softly. Curiosity had broken right through the tension. "Actually, yes it was."

"Is that why you came here? To start over?"

"You might say that."

"And what about her?" Olivia caught herself and blushed. "I'm sorry. I shouldn't have asked. It's really none of my business and I *was* brought up with better manners."

"I don't mind talking about it," Kurt assured her. "It's better than looking into the business end of your rifle."

The color in her cheeks deepened and her eyes disappeared behind a long sweep of lashes. But before she could say anything, the sound of an approaching horse whipped her around toward the door. She stood quickly and hurried to the window. "Oh, dear." She darted a glance over her shoulder. "It's Sam. What is he doing here?"

The warm fuzzies disappeared at once. "Sam?"

"My neighbor." She straightened and gave the curtain a twitch to make sure the window was covered. "The one I told you about last night. I didn't expect him this morning. He usually doesn't show up on Fridays."

Kurt vaguely remembered her mentioning a neighbor, but he hadn't given it much thought at the time. Considering how agitated she seemed, maybe he should have. Too late now. Sam was nearing the house and Kurt's leg started to throb again as if it were sending out trouble warnings.

Olivia threw open the door and hurried outside. Kurt

abandoned breakfast and limped behind her.

The rider was alone, but that was the only piece of luck fate tossed Kurt's way. He was a giant of a man, every bit as old-fashioned as Olivia, from his faded hat to the guns on his hips and on down to the tips of his dust-covered boots.

Even from a distance Kurt could see the deep-set eyes boring out from beneath his hat, the thick handlebar moustache drooping over his mouth, the face deeply tanned by long days in the sun. He wore a duster that lived up to its name and it looked to Kurt as if he'd stand about eight feet tall out of the saddle.

He could have been an actor straight off the set of the movie *Tombstone*—only this guy was the real thing, bulked up with muscles that could only come from honest labor and fully capable of shooting a man just for looking at him the wrong way.

Kurt waited for his life to flash before his eyes. Any second now . . . He searched his memory of the local histories he'd read. Sam. Sam. Oh, good Lord. He had to be Samuel J. Evans, owner of the Cinnabar Ranch. According to the journals Kurt had read, Evans was considered mean as a snake and twice as deadly.

No doubt about it, Kurt was a dead man.

Chapter 5

KURT FORCED AIR into his lungs and back out again while Sam did a slow once-over of the ranch yard. He could almost hear Clint Eastwood–movie music in the background. He knew the instant Sam caught sight of him standing on the porch behind Olivia because the ends of the moustache drew together and his eyes narrowed into snake slits.

Apparently, he'd been smiling before. He sure as hell wasn't smiling now.

Olivia didn't seem to notice. She stepped from the porch and hurried toward him. A light breeze flicked the hem of her dress as she walked and should have cooled the morning a bit, but it seemed to Kurt as if the temperature rose by a good twenty degrees.

Kurt was no coward. Far from it. He'd never backed down from a fight in his life, but he wasn't in shape this morning to go into battle. On the other hand, Sam was wearing a holster and gun, so the chances of an actual fight were pretty slim. Sam would probably just shoot him.

At least it would be quick.

"This is a surprise," Olivia sang out as she crossed the yard. "I wasn't expecting you today—but I'm so glad you're here."

Sam slid from the saddle without taking his eyes from Kurt. "Had a feeling I ought to check and make sure everything was all right." His voice matched the rest of him—deep, bass, and edged with a slight drawl. He sent a distinctly unfriendly nod in Kurt's direction. "Guess I can see why."

Olivia glanced over her shoulder as if she were seeing Kurt for the first time. "That's Mr. Richards. He showed up yesterday after you left. He's been hurt."

"He's been here all night?"

Olivia stood so much shorter she didn't even come close to looking Sam in the eye, but she sure gave it hell. "He's *hurt*, Sam. I couldn't turn him away."

To Kurt's surprise, the challenge in Olivia's voice had an effect. Sam didn't back down, but he did look slightly less murderous. "What's wrong with him?"

Kurt left the porch and gimped across the yard toward them. If he waited any longer, Sam would think he was a coward.

Sam took in his limp and the scratches on his face without the slightest sign of concern—probably because he figured he'd be putting Kurt out of his misery any minute.

In spite of Sam's sneer, Kurt made the offer of a handshake. It couldn't hurt, and it might even help. Sam might think twice about shooting a man he'd just shaken hands with. "Mrs. Hamilton very kindly let me sleep in her barn last night."

Sam tugged off one glove and took Kurt's offered hand, just about crushing Kurt's bones before he let go. "Passing through?"

Kurt resisted the urge to massage his hand when he got

it back. "I don't know how long I'll be here," he said honestly. "Mrs. Hamilton has offered to take me into Cortez. I'll make up my mind once I get there."

Sam's thick eyebrows formed a solid line above his deep-set eyes. "Cortez?" He turned his head slowly toward Olivia. "You got time to take him all the way into town, Livvy?"

"I can make time. I need to talk with Sloan Durrant about the mortgage, anyway."

Sam stuffed his gloves into a pocket of his duster and turned his deep, dark stare back to Kurt. "What business do you have in Cortez?"

The look in his eyes was more chilling than that of even the worst movie bad guy Kurt had seen as a kid. And to think he'd spent countless childhood hours dreaming of a chance to live this life. He squared his shoulders and tried to look a few inches taller. "I guess that will depend on whether I can reach anyone I know when I get there."

"You have folks around here?"

"Not exactly. I've been working nearby."

"Working?" The moustache gave a twitch. "Where?"

Kurt waved a hand in the general direction of the ruins. "In the canyons."

The snake squint returned. "Doin' what?"

"He's a government man." Olivia stepped between them and slipped a hand beneath Sam's arm. The action put her so close to the man's bulk, Kurt had to battle a twinge of envy. "Now, stop bristling like a porcupine and come inside. Coffee's on and breakfast's ready. We were just getting started when you rode up."

"Bit late, isn't it?" Sam asked, as if he suspected Kurt of trying to starve Olivia.

"A little. I wanted to feed the horses first."

Sam gave that a moment's thought. "Wasn't planning to eat. I just came to see if you wanted help with the stallion this morning."

Olivia shook her head up at him and a look passed between them. "I won't be able to work with him again until tomorrow. And I'm certainly not going to ask you to work with Nightmare if I'm gallivanting off to town. So come inside and have breakfast . . . please?"

That look passed between them again and Kurt had the uneasy feeling that he'd walked smack into the middle of a moment he wasn't meant to share. Another twinge of envy shot through him.

He let it slide right on past. Hadn't he just been irritated with himself for being attracted to her? Wasn't he in just about the worst position possible at the moment? So why did he envy Sam that look in Olivia's eyes?

"Guess I will join you," Sam conceded at last. He hitched his horse to the railing and let Olivia lead him toward the house, effectively shutting Kurt out. "Sloan Durrant shouldn't have a problem giving you an extension. Nightmare'll fetch a pretty penny when you sell him."

"Then you're—" Olivia darted a glance over her shoulder and lowered her voice. "You're not angry with me about yesterday?"

"I was never angry, Livvy."

She smiled as she had a few minutes earlier, but this time the smile was for Sam alone. "I'm so glad. I could hardly sleep last night for worrying about it."

Obviously, Olivia and Sam had a history together. Kurt told himself to be glad he'd found out so soon. Not that he had any ideas about Olivia, but after Holly's betrayal, he'd sworn never to come between another man and a woman. He'd hate to be responsible for putting anyone else through that kind of blistering pain—even inadvertently.

Olivia paused with one foot on the step and looked back at Kurt. The breeze gusted again, molding her skirt against her thighs for an instant and teasing the hem of her dress away from her ankles. Kurt's body reacted immediately and abruptly.

He froze, thoroughly dumbfounded by his reaction. He'd come from a time when a man could see hundreds of bare thighs—and a helluva lot more than that—during the course of a single day, yet he was panting after a glimpse of forbidden ankle.

"Are you going to join us, Mr. Richards?"

Her voice jerked his gaze away from the tiny ribbon of flesh. He nodded and started after them, but the look on Sam's face left him cold. Sam hadn't missed the way Kurt had been watching Olivia. Kurt would have to watch his step if he wanted to make it into Cortez alive.

Olivia could feel Sam tense as Kurt crossed the yard and joined them on the porch. She hadn't expected him to be happy at finding Kurt here, but she hadn't expected such blatant jealousy, either. It poured from his body in tight coils and kept his expression tight and his eyes stormy gray.

She tried not to resent his reaction, but she had enough to think about this morning without having to worry about Sam. She hadn't expected a chance to talk with Sloan Durrant so soon, and her mind kept bogging down when she tried to figure out how to approach him.

Inside, Sam took off his hat, helped himself to coffee, and leaned the back of his chair against the wall. He watched Kurt over the rim of his cup, every movement slow, languid, and deliberately menacing. "Government man, huh?"

Kurt stared back with the same cautious expression. "That's right."

"You got proof?"

"Yes. I showed it to Mrs. Hamilton."

Sam's gaze shot to hers for confirmation.

She nodded and poured a cup of coffee for herself. "He has a badge, Sam."

"Does he, now?" Sam bit a hunk from a biscuit and slid his gaze back to Kurt. "Folks around here don't hold much with the government. They're partial to keeping what belongs to them."

"I'm not here to take away anyone's property."

"That right?" Sam polished off his first biscuit and tore open another, slanting a quick glance at Olivia. "When are you planning to leave for Cortez?"

"As soon as I clean up from breakfast."

"Wagon hitched?"

"Not yet."

"I'll do it after we eat." Sam shot a look at Kurt, almost daring him to argue.

Olivia spoke before Kurt could get a word in. "Thank you, Sam. It would save time."

"Anything else need doing?"

"Not today." Both men sat with shoulders squared and jaws set. Kurt watching Sam. Sam watching Kurt. The air between them felt like a summer night in Virginia. Thick. Heavy. Uncomfortable. *Unbelievable.* Sam had been around often when Harvey was alive, but she couldn't remember feeling this kind of tension even once.

When the conversation fell into a natural lull, she ignored her upbringing and made no effort to start it again. Thank goodness it wouldn't last long. She and Kurt would leave for town and Sam would head back to the Cinnabar, and it would be over.

But as she stood to begin gathering dishes, Kurt shot to his feet and picked up his plate and cup. Sam's face tightened into a deep frown, and the tension rose again.

Olivia waved Kurt back to his seat. "Stay where you are, Mr. Richards. Would you like more coffee?"

"In a minute." Kurt ignored her and carried his plate

and utensils to the dry sink anyway. "Let me clear while you start washing."

Watching Kurt carry dirty dishes from the table—as if clearing away the meal was the most natural thing in the world to him—struck her as odd . . . but nice. She couldn't remember Harvey ever helping her with the dishes in their five years together.

Sam didn't seem nearly so impressed. He stood quickly, scraping his chair on her floor on his way up. "Can I talk to you for a minute, Olivia?"

Olivia. Sam never called her that unless he was upset. She forced a smile and made room on the dry sink for a stack of plates. "Of course. What is it?"

He jerked his head toward the door. "Outside?"

"It's getting late—"

"I know that. It'll just take a minute."

She couldn't think of a graceful way to refuse, but she wished she could. Sam's expression left no doubt what he wanted to discuss. She wiped her hands on her skirt. "Will you excuse us, Mr. Richards?"

Kurt picked up another load of dirty dishes. "Take all the time you need. I'll start washing up."

Sam muttered something under his breath while Olivia followed him into the yard.

Olivia didn't even try to figure out what he'd said. When he showed no sign of slowing, she called after him. "What is it, Sam?"

He looked back at the house, motioned for her to be quiet, and moved even further away. "There's something wrong with that guy. What do you know about him?"

"Not much. Only what I already told you. But what does it matter? I took care of his wounds and gave him something to eat and a place to sleep. This morning, I'm taking him into Cortez and leaving him there."

Sam's brows furrowed. "I don't like it."

"I can tell. But you don't need to worry. If he was

going to hurt me, he'd have done it already."

Sam took two long, jerky steps away, then wheeled back to face her. "It's not right, Livvy. I don't like knowing that some stranger can come riding in here and find you alone."

And Olivia didn't like the direction this conversation was going. "He wasn't riding," she threw in just to be obstinate.

Sam took her by the shoulders and stared into her eyes. "I don't like knowing that some strange man can come *walking* in here and find you alone. I spent all night convincing myself to forget about yesterday, but now—"

He looked so agonized Olivia regretted teasing him. "Please don't worry, Sam. I'm fine. Mr. Richards is perfectly harmless."

"Harmless?" Sam curled his lip and glanced at the house again. "There's something wrong with him. A man doing dishes? It's not right."

"*That's* your big objection? Does that mean you think a woman running a ranch isn't right, either?"

Sam ran a hand along the back of his neck. "That's not what I meant."

Olivia stepped away and folded her arms. "Mr. Richards won't be a problem once I take him to town."

The tips of Sam's moustache drew together. "For the sake of argument, let's say I agree with you. What about the next time some stranger wanders in?"

Olivia held back a sigh of impatience. "You know how much I care for you, but I'm not going to marry you just to feel safe. I need you to understand that and accept it."

"I'm trying. But I need you to understand, too. You're not safe here alone. I can't help but worry about you."

"I've been perfectly safe for the past ten months," Olivia reminded him.

"There weren't strangers wandering all over the hills

then," Sam said dourly. "And you weren't looking your mortgage in the eye."

He wasn't going to back down an inch, but neither was Olivia. "You're right," she said. "I am looking my mortgage payment in the eye, and if I don't get busy I'll be driving back from town after dark . . . or Mr. Richards will have to stay another night."

A quick scowl tugged on Sam's face and near panic filled his eyes. "Let me ride into town with you. That way you won't have to drive back alone."

Before yesterday, she'd have been pleased to have Sam's company. Today, she dreaded it. She hated realizing how much strain the last two days had put on their friendship. But if she said no, she might drive a wedge between them they'd never be able to remove.

She forced a smile. "All right. If you promise to be nice to Mr. Richards."

Sam glowered at her. "Aw, come on, Liv—"

"At least be civil. And not another word about me living out here alone."

Sam hesitated before giving a brisk nod. He turned toward the barn, and she could swear she heard him complaining all the way there. But since he didn't say it loud enough for her to hear the actual words, she ignored it.

She didn't have time for male egos. She needed to concentrate on what she was going to say to Sloan Durrant when she got to the bank.

Several hours later, Olivia's old wagon rattled to a stop in the middle of town and the last of Kurt's illusions faded like mist under the hot August sun. If this was Cortez, he was a long way from home.

A dusty main street stretched only a few blocks before civilization disappeared again. A tumbleweed rolled down the center of town and bumped up against a hitching post, and the few people on the street looked like actors on an Old West movie set.

Sam shifted on the wagon seat to see him better. "Well . . . here you are."

Terrific. With no money to his name, Kurt had no idea what his next move should be. "This is Cortez?"

"Yep. Anyplace special you want to go?"

Kurt took another long glance around. There weren't many options to choose from. "Is there a hotel?"

Sam nodded toward a two-story building on the other side of the street. "Right there." His eyes narrowed and he watched from the shadow of his hat brim as Kurt tossed his backpack to the street and jumped down after it. "You got a problem?"

Kurt dusted off his pantlegs. "No problem." As if to make him a liar, one of the horses chose that minute to relieve itself near his shoe. He sidestepped quickly and caught Sam's pleased smile as he jumped down from the seat. He glanced at Olivia for her reaction and saw a deep frown creasing her brow.

Not for the world would he let Sam think he bothered him. He moved closer to Olivia and sent her his best smile. "Thank you again for your hospitality, Mrs. Hamilton. If there's ever anything I can do to repay you, all you have to do is ask."

Sam's smile vanished so quickly, Kurt felt as if he'd scored his first point all day.

But the look on Olivia's face dashed cold water on his mood. She looked sad and nervous, and he remembered suddenly that she hadn't come to town just for him. He wondered how dire her financial picture was. A widow, alone on a ranch in the 1800s. . . . Her outlook must be fairly dismal. And just from the little Kurt knew of her, he'd bet she had too much pride to ask for help unless she couldn't see any other option.

But why didn't she have options? For all Sam's bluster,

he must not be doing a whole lot to help her. She needed more than bluster, guns, and muscles.

"Out of curiosity," she said, pulling Kurt back to the moment, "how do you plan to pay for your room?"

Sam's voice sounded almost in Kurt's ear. "Don't tell me you're broke."

Technically, Kurt supposed he was. He might have cash in his pocket and credit cards in his wallet, but none of them would do him a bit of good in 1889. He ignored Sam and answered Olivia. "Don't worry about me. I'll figure something out. I'm sure I can find a job somewhere."

"Thought you already had one," Sam muttered. "Or was all that talk about being a government man just a lot of hot air?"

"It was all true," Kurt assured him. "But while I'm waiting for my pay from the government," which would be a long time coming, "I might as well see about picking up a little extra cash."

Sam snorted in derision and sent a meaningful look at Olivia over Kurt's shoulder.

After everything she'd done for him, Kurt didn't want Olivia to suffer because of him. The sooner he disappeared from her life, the better. Surely he could find some kind of work. Some good, honest, physical labor might help him make sense out of the situation.

Why had he been brought back through time? Was it some freaky quirk of nature, or was he here for a purpose?

Slowly, memories of things Olivia said came floating back through yesterday's haze of pain, shock, and laudanum. If this was 1889, the Black Mesa site wouldn't even be discovered for another two years.

He'd read every account he could find about the initial explorations of the ruins, and the articles listed in those journal entries boggled his mind. By the time politicians in Washington DC could be persuaded to care, the most valuable finds had disappeared into private collections and many of the fragile walls of the cliff dwellings had been destroyed by people clambering over them.

But if he was here . . . *Now* . . . He had a chance to save the ruins for future generations. He had no idea how he'd do it, but this was a dream come true for him. He wouldn't let a few little things like lack of money, unemployment, and no place to sleep stand in his way.

He glanced around quickly to see if Sam or Olivia had noticed his sudden excitement. Sam had helped Olivia out of the wagon and was doing his level best to monopolize her attention. It seemed for the moment that he was succeeding.

She scowled and said something too low for Kurt to hear. Sam answered, reaching for her arm, but she jerked away from his touch. Poor dumb cowboy. Trying so hard to hang on, he was actually pushing her away.

Kurt attributed most of his satisfaction to the realization he'd just had about the Black Mesa ruins, though he wouldn't deny that after the way Sam had acted all morning, he got a little pleasure from watching him dig himself into a hole.

At that moment, Olivia moved away from Sam with a heavy sigh and a deep-set frown. "I mean it, Sam. I'm not going to talk about it anymore." She turned to Kurt and pasted on a smile. "Good luck, Mr. Richards."

"Thank you. I have a feeling I'll need it." Kurt picked up his pack and slung it over his shoulder. "Any suggestions about where I should look for work?"

"You could try the Montezuma Irrigation Company." Olivia nodded toward a squat wooden building on the other side of the street.

Yes, of course. James Hanna and his irrigation company had started working on a system to bring water from the Dolores River a few years ago, with the first trickles actually hitting the Montezuma Valley in 1888. No doubt, they would still be working on the system.

He smiled wearily. "I suppose there are worse things than digging ditches for a living."

"If you don't like that idea," Sam grumbled as he hitched the horses, "try the livery stable."

Kurt refused to let the man goad him into showing any irritation. He flashed Sam a smile. "Good idea. Thanks."

Olivia motioned him a few steps away from Sam. "You won't try to use the funny money, will you?"

Was she worried about him? Kurt couldn't deny a quick flush of pleasure at the thought. "Don't worry. I'll keep it well hidden."

"You'd better, or you might land in jail."

Kurt pretended to give that serious consideration. "Free room and board? Not a bad idea." The look on Olivia's face made him regret teasing her. He put a reassuring hand on her shoulder, completely unprepared for what happened next. A warm tingle began in his hand and surged up his arm. Before he could take a breath, the heat flashed into his chest.

Her eyes shot to his, just as they had earlier, and Kurt felt as if the air had been sucked out of his lungs. He could see only Olivia—the deep brown of her eyes, the soft curl of her hair, the satiny curve of her cheek. Time seemed to stand still and the town and everything in it seemed to fade into the background.

Stay with her.

The unexpected whisper jerked him out of his daze.

Stay? With Olivia? Sure. And let Sam shoot him before the end of the day. Great idea.

Stay with her.

Kurt shook the voice away and pulled his hand from Olivia's shoulder. His libido might want to stay with Olivia, but his conscience didn't. He wasn't a big enough jerk to take advantage of a lonely widow in financial trouble just to make himself feel like a man again.

He gripped his pack tightly and put another foot or two between them. "Good luck at the bank," he muttered. "And thanks again. I'd better—" The words seemed to stick in his throat, but he forced himself to keep speaking. "I'd better let you get to it."

"Yes." She looked almost sorry to say good-bye. Another good reason why Kurt should put as much distance between her and himself as possible. He had the feeling those wide, doe eyes could easily make him do something stupid and count himself lucky for the chance.

The woman was dangerous. Pure, damned dangerous.

He hurried away, resisting the urge to look back, but the strangest feeling of emptiness washed over him as he reached the other side of the street.

Nonsense. He'd been able to put Charlotte out of his mind and they'd been together six long months. He ought to be able to forget Olivia Hamilton after just one day.

Chapter 6

WITH SAM KEEPING a suspicious eye on him from the doorway, Kurt crossed the hotel lobby toward the front desk. The polished wooden counter and stair railings, gleaming glass lamps on the walls, and faded oriental carpet gave the hotel a quaint charm. It might not be the Ritz, but Kurt figured he could be comfortable here. Certainly more comfortable than on a bed of hay or the hard ground.

He shifted his backpack and tried to ignore Sam's glowering presence. He'd rather get far away from Sam and his gun, but Sam showed no signs of leaving him alone. He was probably on a fool's errand, asking for a room without money, but Kurt had to try. A little friendly charm, an honest smile, and some smooth talk *might* get him a bed for a night or two.

He pasted on a smile as he approached the desk, but when the hotel clerk came out from a back room his smile slipped. The round, grizzled man only stood about as high as Kurt's shoulders. But his craggy face with one continuous thick eyebrow didn't look particularly friendly or susceptible to charm of any kind.

The clerk gave Kurt a long, slow, appraising glance, shifted his gaze to Sam, and finally settled it back on Kurt. He looked even less friendly than he had a moment before. "Afternoon."

"Good afternoon."

Kurt heard Sam shift position behind him an instant before his deep drawl filled the room. "This fella's looking for a place to stay."

"Well, he's come to the right place."

"Maybe." Sam's footsteps echoed on the rough wood floor as he moved closer. "Except he doesn't have any money."

Thanks for the help, buddy. Remind me I owe you one.

The clerk laughed in disbelief. "Is that right?"

"I'm temporarily without funds," Kurt admitted, "but I'm hoping to get work."

"Are you, now?" The clerk leaned an elbow on the counter and looked him over again. "And you expect me to give you a room on credit?"

"Just for a day or two."

Sam took another step closer. "What do you think, Isaac? You want to give him a room? He claims to be working for the United States government."

Isaac's gaze narrowed. "Is that so."

If Sam hadn't been wearing a gun, Kurt might have given in to the urge to stuff a sock in his mouth. "That's so."

"Well, now." Isaac scratched at the few days' growth on his chin lazily. "And what would the United States government be wanting out here?"

"A bed."

The clerk shot him a foul look. "No call to get smart, mister."

Kurt held up both hands in surrender. "I'm not getting smart. I just want a bed."

"And you can have one," Isaac said, "for two dollars a day. Cash. In advance."

It might as well have been two hundred. "Look, I'm not trying to pull anything. I'll pay you—"

"Damn right you will. In advance. No cash, no bed."

"But I don't *have* cash at the moment."

"Then I don't have a bed."

Kurt kneaded his forehead with one hand. "If I found work, would you give me a room?"

"Sure thing. Soon as you get paid." Isaac sent a knowing smirk in Sam's direction. "But you ain't gonna *get* work."

Aching with futility, Kurt snapped, "How in the hell can you know that?"

The clerk's eyes narrowed and his smile thinned. "Cuz Sam here's a respected man in these parts, and if he don't trust you, nobody will. 'Sides, we've had enough trouble with your kind already. Nobody's going to be willing to bring on more."

"My kind? What *kind* am I?"

"U-nited States government. Prissy pants."

Kurt barely resisted the urge to grab the man's scruffy collar and yank him over the counter with it. And he only managed that because Sam's low chuckle reminded him he'd be smart to watch his step. "What kind of trouble?"

"You name it," the clerk said cryptically. "We don't cotton to folks who've never been west of the Mississippi coming out here telling us what to do. Don't like 'em taking land that doesn't belong to 'em neither." He pulled the hotel register closer, as if he wanted to protect it from Kurt's foul hands. "And lastly, folks around here was getting along just fine with the Injuns 'til you folks come along."

Kurt stole a glance at Sam, who stood near a pillar, arms crossed on his chest, a satisfied smile peeking out from beneath his moustache.

"What if I said I *wasn't* with the government? What if I'm just a drifter?"

Isaac shrugged. "Then you might get work. Might not. No way to tell."

"And I can't have a room until I do."

"That's right."

Sam unfolded his arms slowly and took two steps closer. "Changing your story now?"

The hair on the back of Kurt's neck stood on end, but frustration was quickly overpowering caution. "I might not have to if you weren't so determined to sabotage me before I can even get started."

Sam's moustache twitched. "Well, now, here's the thing. I care about my friends and neighbors. Don't want to see anyone take advantage of them."

Kurt turned to face him squarely. "I don't plan to take advantage of them. All I want is a room."

"All you need is some money."

Kurt balled his hands into fists but he kept them at his side. He hadn't lost *all* common sense. "Well, then, what do you suggest I do?"

"Me?" Sam looked taken aback by the question, but he recovered quickly. "I suggest you go back to where you came from."

"You have no idea how much I'd love to do exactly that."

"There's the door," Sam said with a jerk of his head toward it.

"It's not that simple." Kurt turned back to the clerk, who'd been watching the exchange with unconcealed interest. There'd be talk in town tonight. Kurt would bet on it. And once it got out that Sam didn't approve of him being here, he probably wouldn't stand a snowball's chance in hell of getting work anywhere.

"Is there anyone in town who might be willing to sell me some food?"

"Sure." The clerk grinned as if he was having great fun. "T. J. Mortensen down at the mercantile will sell you anything you need—if you've got cash. He don't give credit neither."

"Is there anyone in town who *does* give credit?"

"To a drifter?" Isaac pretended to ponder that. "No, can't say there is."

Kurt's fingers itched to wipe the smile off Isaac's face. They ached to show Sam exactly what he thought of his interference. Instead, he gave his pack a hitch higher onto his shoulder, gathered what little dignity he still had left, and turned toward the door.

He wasn't a bit surprised to hear Sam's footsteps echoing behind him on the hardwood floor. Luckily, he still had his pack with him, his tent, blankets, and rifle. He even had a little ammunition. God willing, he might actually be able to shoot something and find a safe place to set up camp. But that would only work for a day or two. If he was still here after that, he'd be up a creek.

And Sam would still be holding the paddle.

The closer Olivia got to the bank, the more nervous she became. She had no experience with begging someone for time to pay what she owed. Her father had never worried about money. He'd never had to. *She'd* never had to worry either until she married Harvey.

No, she amended silently, their problems hadn't started immediately. They'd been fine until Harvey heard about the legend. That's when he'd changed. That's when everything changed. If not for the legend, she wouldn't be in this position.

She knew instinctively that even a friend like Sloan Durrant wouldn't grant her an extension if she seemed desperate. Harvey had said a million times that banks only gave money to those who didn't need it. She had to convince Sloan that money was coming and the extension nothing more than a convenience.

She kept her chin up and smiled at people she recognized as she passed, alternately wishing she lived closer to town when she saw a smiling woman in a beautiful morning frock twirling a parasol that must have been the latest fashion from Paris, then counting her blessings when she passed a man whose rank odor could have wilted any living thing within a hundred paces.

Outside the bank, she paused and took a deep breath for courage. She smoothed the folds of her best dress, noticing for the first time how shabby her clothes had become. She certainly *looked* destitute and desperate. She'd have to be mighty convincing to make Sloan believe she wasn't.

She waited while a tall, thin man paused just outside the door to light a cigar, then forced herself to step over the threshold into the bank. It had been more than a year since she'd been inside. The plank floors that had been new the last time she saw them were now stained by hundreds of muddy footprints, but the lamps on the walls gleamed as if they'd recently been polished and the place radiated the scent of money and beeswax.

Sloan noticed her the minute she walked through the doors. He sprang to his feet inside his tiny glassed-in office and came out to greet her. His trousers and cutaway jacket fit like kid gloves, showing off his legs and shoulders to perfection. One of these days one of the belles of Cortez society would snap him up and make a happily married man of him. For now, he kept the single women happy by dancing attendance on all of them.

"Olivia. What a delightful surprise." His voice still carried his native Boston accent even though he'd come West several years before.

She smiled as if she hadn't a care in the world. "I had some other business in town, but since I'm here I wondered if I might speak with you for a moment."

"Of course. Of course." His gaze swept around the lobby, then settled back on her face. "Of course." He led her into his office and shut the glass door behind them. "Is something wrong?"

"Wrong? No, everything's fine." She settled into a plush leather chair and made a pretense of adjusting her skirts while she tried to remember the speech she'd planned. "You're probably aware that the mortgage on the Lazy H is due on the first of next month."

"Is it?" Sloan slid into his own chair and laced his fingers together on his stomach. "I'll take your word for it. Does this visit mean you've had second thoughts about what you're going to do?"

Olivia tried to look equally comfortable but she could tell she failed miserably. "No, not at all. I still plan to stay."

Sloan unlaced his fingers and straightened in his seat. "Is that wise, Olivia? A woman alone—"

"Oh, please, Sloan. Not you, too." Olivia let out a tight laugh. "I don't think I can bear to hear another person try to talk me out of staying. My only problem—if you could call it that—is that I'm a little short of cash at the moment. I came to ask you for a brief extension on the mortgage."

"I see." Sloan rubbed his chin thoughtfully. "An extension." He said the word as if no one in Cortez had ever asked for one.

Olivia tried not to panic. Surely he dealt with such requests all the time. "It would just be until I can turn some of my assets into cash."

"Yes. I see." He rubbed harder, faster, then dropped his hand and leaned back in his chair again. "I'd like to speak as your friend for a moment, rather than your banker . . . if you'll allow me to?" At her nod, he went on. "I'll be honest, Olivia. I'm worried. I have been for some time, even before Harvey's . . . unfortunate accident."

Worried? Olivia twisted her hands together, praying he wouldn't say no.

"The truth is," he went on, "I'm not certain the Lazy H can be made to pay for itself. Even when Harvey was alive, the place was always in the red. The ranch has yet to pay for itself."

"But it will." She caught the desperation in her voice and forced a thin smile. "I'm sure it will. It's only a matter of time."

"Perhaps." Sloan spent another few agonizing moments thinking. "Let me propose something before we discuss extensions . . . as a friend." He leaned up again, locked his hands on the desk, and met her gaze. "I know how much you'd like to make the Lazy H a viable proposition, but I don't know how you'll do it. Harvey certainly didn't choose to settle in a prime location. Most of the land isn't workable and there's not enough vegetation to run cattle."

Olivia thought she might be sick. She took several shallow breaths and tried to still the shaking of her hands. Apparently, she was the only person who had faith in her husband, or in her ranch.

Sloan looked almost as miserable as she was. "I know you must be in a precarious position, Olivia. I know how little cash Harvey had when he died. I know how quickly he spent it. I tried to warn him, but he refused to listen. And now I'm watching a beautiful woman working her fingers to the bone for nothing."

"The land *is* good," she said evenly. "The potential is there."

"Perhaps." Sloan dipped his head as if the concession cost him dearly. "But not in the way Harvey wanted to use it." He stood slowly and came out from behind his desk, hands locked behind his back. "It's not smart business on my part, but I'm offering to take the Lazy H off your hands. I'll pay off the mortgage myself and give you enough cash on top of that to see you safely back to Virginia."

Everything inside tightened and burned. "I'm *not* going back to Virginia. This is my home."

"I understand why you feel that way, Olivia. I truly do. But Cortez is no place for a woman alone. Especially not a woman of your breeding and background. And I know Harvey wouldn't have wanted you to struggle like this."

If he only knew how miserable she'd been with her breeding and background, he wouldn't have said that.

"Let me pay off the mortgage, help you get settled somewhere else, then." Sloan waved a hand. "Denver, perhaps. Kansas City. St. Louis. Wherever you choose. I can guarantee you won't get another offer like it."

"Maybe not," Olivia hedged. *Definitely not.* Who would pay that much for a worthless tract of land? Sloan's generosity made her eyes sting with tears of gratitude and doubts race through her mind.

Was she being foolish to insist on staying? She felt so strongly about the Lazy H, but could she really make it pay for itself? Or was its name ironically prophetic?

Sloan watched her carefully. "You don't have to answer right away," he said gently. "Think about it for a few days. As you reminded me, the mortgage isn't due until the first."

"That's only a month," she said. "I can't possibly make a decision in such a short time. If you'd just consider my request for an extension—"

Sloan leaned back in his chair and linked his fingers across his stomach again. "If you hold out too long, I might have to withdraw my offer. If you don't decide before the mortgage is due, my hands will be tied. I'd hate to see that happen."

"But a month—" Olivia's head whirled. The swimming nausea returned, followed closely by an oddly peaceful feeling that her original decision was the right one. She clung to it desperately. "Your offer is more than generous, Sloan, but I can't accept." She stood quickly, aware that his smile had evaporated. "Once I sell Harvey's horse, I'll have the money for you."

Sloan's eyebrows quirked with interest. "The black?" He flicked an imaginary speck of dust from his trouser leg. "I might be willing to take him off your hands as well. Shall we say . . . a hundred dollars?"

"A hundred?" This was getting worse by the second. "He's worth three times that."

Sloan smiled as if she were a small child he found amusing. "He's a competent horse, I'll grant you that. But I'm afraid Harvey may have misled you about more than just the ranch."

"Harvey was an excellent judge of horses."

Sloan shrugged. "Harvey was a friend of mine, but he did sometimes like to inflate things."

"Harvey did *not* mislead me," Olivia insisted. "I know how much that horse is worth."

"And *I* know how difficult this must be for you. Believe me, it's not easy for me, either." He stood and smoothed his long fingers over his pantlegs. "I hope you do get enough to bring your debts current. Foreclosing on a friend is always uncomfortable."

Olivia's mother would have slapped her silly if she'd heard the things that were running through her head. She had to get out of there quickly, before she said a few of them. "You won't have to foreclose, Sloan. I can promise you that." And without giving him a chance to argue, she swept from his office, trying desperately to look dignified instead of frightened.

But she had no idea how she'd keep that vow. In spite of her bravado, Sloan Durrant had put the fear of God into her.

•   •   •

Olivia put some distance between herself and the bank, then stopped to catch her breath. Frightened as she was, she couldn't waste time feeling sorry for herself. She'd never save the Lazy H that way. She was in town, surrounded by people. Surely, she could find someone willing to pay what Nightmare was worth.

Gathering her skirts, she lifted her chin and headed toward Mortensen's Mercantile. She might as well pick up a few supplies while she was here. She still had credit with T. J. Mortensen—at least, she thought she did. And what better way to get the word out about Nightmare than to ask T. J. and Isabella Mortensen to do it for her?

She forced a smile and nodded in greeting at the people she passed. Harvey had been content to stay on the ranch or on the mesa most of the time, so she'd never spent much time in town. Today, as she scanned faces for someone familiar, she realized how little she knew her neighbors. She could put a few names with faces, but most of them were unfamiliar.

A flicker of regret darted through her. She'd spent five long years telling herself she had no need of neighbors. That she had everything she needed on the Lazy H. Even Harvey's death hadn't changed that because Sam visited so frequently. But having someone to talk with over supper last night and again at breakfast *had* been awfully nice.

Two women walking and laughing together on the street ahead caught her eye and the flicker grew to a huge spear of regret. She hadn't had a woman friend since she left Virginia. She hadn't had someone to share secrets with since Melody ran off with Nathaniel Park.

When they were younger, they'd laughed and whispered together well into the night. They'd giggled about beaux and whispered about weddings, and even speculated about the private side of marriage as they grew older.

But after Nathaniel Park's heartless desertion, Melody had stayed locked in her room, emerging only for meals . . . and not even always for those. She'd been a different woman—quiet, hurt, shamed by her circumstances, and bitter about the way their mother treated her. Things had never been the same between the sisters after that.

As always, thinking about Melody saddened Olivia and the longing for a female companion intensified. She told herself sternly that today wasn't the day for thinking about that. Nothing would matter if she couldn't sell Nightmare and pay the mortgage on the Lazy H.

She walked quickly toward the mercantile and tried to pull her mind back to important matters. But it darted here and there, wondering whether Kurt had found a place to stay, whether he'd tried to pay for something with his counterfeit money, or whether he'd be moving on.

A laugh broke into her thoughts and pulled her back to the present. She stopped abruptly and narrowly missed plowing into the back of a young woman in front of her. Laughing sheepishly, she mumbled an apology and started around the woman and her companion.

"Olivia?"

The voice, so like Sam's, brought her back around quickly. A tall young man with auburn hair and glasses stood beside the woman she'd nearly run into. "Jesse? Goodness, it's been so long since I've seen you, I didn't even recognize you."

Jesse's warm laugh burned off some of the chill left by her visit with Sloan Durrant. "I like *that*. It hasn't even been a year since I saw you at the service—" He broke off, suddenly uncomfortable.

Olivia had had enough of sour faces and maudlin thinking for one day. She wouldn't let the mere mention of Harvey's funeral ruin the rest of it. "Yes, I suppose I did see you then, but ten months has made an awfully big difference in you. You really should ride over with Sam now and then."

Jesse grinned impishly. "I had the feeling Sam didn't want company when he rode over to your place."

"Sam might not," she said with a quick frown, "but I'd love to see you."

"Well, then, I'll do it." He drew the small blond woman at his side forward. "You've met Elizabeth Langley, haven't you?"

"If I have," Olivia said honestly, "I don't remember."

Elizabeth, a pretty young woman with a friendly smile, nodded shyly and tugged a lacy shawl around her shoulders. "I don't believe I've had the pleasure. But, then, I've only been here a short while."

Maybe it was all the thinking she'd been doing about Melody, but Elizabeth's soft Southern voice sounded like home. "You're from the South."

"Savannah. My mother and I came West last autumn after my father died, to live with my brother and his wife."

So, she'd experienced loss, as well. Olivia's heart went out to her. She offered her condolences, but Elizabeth only turned a smile on Jesse.

"Thank you, but they do say that good things can come out of the worst of circumstances. I do believe that's been true in this case. If I hadn't come out here, I never would have met Jesse." Such love filled her eyes, Olivia felt a twinge of envy.

It had been a long time since she'd been so dewy-eyed and optimistic, forever since she'd believed any man could carry the world on his shoulders or solve all of its problems. In fact, she wondered if she'd ever believed it.

Her parents' marriage had hardly been what she'd call romantic, and Melody's experience had left its mark on both sisters. As for her own marriage, she'd loved Harvey but she couldn't remember ever gazing up at him quite so adoringly. By the time he came along, Olivia had been quite able to see men, romance, and love in a clear light. She'd always considered that a blessing . . . until now.

As she watched Elizabeth blush under Jesse's smile, a faint wistfulness curled through her. "Welcome to Cortez, Miss Langley. It's always nice to have new neighbors."

"Thank you, but I'm afraid we may not be neighbors for long."

"Oh? Are you leaving?" Olivia battled a pang of disappointment and glanced at Jesse to see how he reacted to the news.

His secretive smile surprised her. "Nothing's decided yet," he warned Elizabeth gently. "I promised Sam I'd wait to make a decision."

Olivia stared from one to the other. "You're *both* thinking of leaving?"

Jesse took one of Elizabeth's hands in his and brought it to his lips. He beamed at Olivia over the delicate fingers. "Elizabeth has consented to marry me in December. We'd like to strike out on our own, come spring."

"And Sam doesn't want you to?" She understood only too well how Jesse and Olivia felt. She and Harvey had done the same thing over the objections of her parents. But she also knew how deep Sam's feelings for his younger brother ran, and her heart ached for him. No wonder he'd been acting so strangely the past few days.

The light in Jesse's eyes faded. "No, he doesn't. He made me promise to wait to make a final decision until he could think of some way to keep us here."

He looked so young and vulnerable, Olivia couldn't resist the urge to put a hand on his arm. "I thought you loved the Cinnabar."

"I do." Jesse shot a guilty glance at his fiancée. "We both love it here."

"Then why leave?"

"The Cinnabar belongs to Sam. It'll never belong to me. Not that I want to take it away from him," Jesse added quickly. "But . . . well . . . everyone thinks of me as Sam's little brother. As long as I stay on the Cinnabar, that's all I'll ever be."

The look on his face made Olivia's heart sink even further. Poor Sam. Poor Jesse. She drew her hand away slowly. "I'm sure between you, you'll come up with a solution."

She could think of one right off the top of her head that would solve all their problems. If she married Sam, she could sell the Lazy H to Jesse and Elizabeth. She'd be out of debt, Jesse and Elizabeth would be happy, and Sam wouldn't have to suffer the torment of losing his little brother the way she'd lost Melody.

It was a perfect solution, except for one tiny detail—she wouldn't marry a man she didn't love. Yes, she might learn to love him the way a wife should love her husband . . . in time. But time was just one more luxury she couldn't afford.

Chapter 7

"WELL? WHAT NOW?" Sam leaned against a hitching post and tried not to gloat. He'd followed Kurt everywhere in town as he looked for a place to stay and a way to earn a living. Not surprisingly, he'd come up empty on every count. Even Jim Hanna had turned him down. Sam couldn't help being a little proud of himself.

"Now?" Kurt ran a hand across his face. He didn't look amused. In fact, he looked worried. "I haven't got the foggiest idea."

"Pretty sad when a man can't even get a job digging ditches."

"Pathetic might be a better word. Maybe I *should* let them throw me in jail just for the free board and food."

Sam might've felt sorry for the guy under other circumstances. He hadn't actually tried anything funny, but that might just have been because Sam had dogged his footsteps all day. "Guess you'll be moving on, then."

Kurt adjusted the pack he carried on his back. Strange way of carrying things in Sam's view, although for a man on foot it might be handier than a bedroll.

"I don't think so," Kurt said. His gaze traveled up the street, then back down again. "I need to stay here. Something'll turn up."

Sam crossed one booted foot over the other and let his gaze follow Kurt's. "I thought you said you'd been working in these parts." He slanted his glance back at Kurt. "*And* that you knew folks in town."

"It's a long story."

"Well, now," Sam said slowly. "By the strangest coincidence, I have time to hear one."

Kurt stole a glance at the Colt resting on Sam's hip.

Sam wouldn't have shot him. He'd never killed a man yet, and he wouldn't unless his life or someone else's was in danger. But he didn't figure Kurt needed to know that.

Just when Sam thought he had Kurt dead to rights, frightened enough to spill his guts, relief stole across Kurt's face and he nodded up the street. "Maybe you don't have as much time as you think. Looks like Olivia's through at the bank."

Even from a distance Sam could tell her meeting with Sloan Durrant hadn't gone well. His urge to protect her rose sure and strong and pushed aside his need to intimidate Kurt—for the moment. He started toward her, muttering under his breath when he realized Kurt was following him.

He picked up his pace a little, just to make sure he reached Olivia first. "How'd it go?"

She forced a smile. "Not very well. Sloan refuses to give me an extension on the mortgage."

"Why in the hell—" Sam caught himself and started again. "Why not?"

"He says his hands are tied." She sent him a wan smile that included Kurt. "He thinks the land is worthless and doesn't believe I'll be able to make it pay for itself. But he *did* offer to buy the ranch from me. I suppose I should be grateful for that."

"Grateful?" Sam snorted in derision. "If the land's so worthless, why's he willing to buy it?"

"He made the offer as a friend," Olivia said. "Not as a banker."

Kurt crowded his way into the conversation. "Don't sell it to him."

"I don't want to," Olivia said. "I told him no."

Sam had had just about enough of Kurt. He glared at him to make sure he knew what Sam—and his Colt—thought of his opinion. "I suppose you're an expert on ranching now, in addition to being a government man who can't find a job."

"No, I just have a feeling her land will be valuable someday." He looked deep into Olivia's eyes and added, "*Extremely* valuable."

"You have a *feeling*?" Sam snorted a laugh and looked at Olivia to make sure she realized how ridiculous that sounded.

But she was smiling at Kurt in that way she had and skipped right over the foolishness as if he hadn't said anything. "You couldn't find work? I guess your day isn't going well, either."

Kurt shook his head. "You could say that."

Sam glowered. She was acting as if Kurt was a long-time friend, not a drifter whose story didn't add up. What did she think she was doing? "Seems our friend here is short on cash. Can't get a room at the hotel, either." At the flash of concern in Olivia's eyes, he added, "But don't you worry about it. He got here somehow. He can go on the same way." And Sam was here to make sure he did.

Kurt let out an odd-sounding laugh. "Believe me, I can't go *anywhere* the way I got here."

"Don't matter to me how you move on," Sam snarled, "long as you do."

Olivia frowned at him. "Be civil, Sam. You promised."

"I *am* being civil."

But Olivia had already stopped listening. She tilted her head to one side the way she always did when she got an idea, and a slow smile curved her lips. "So, you're staying around?"

"He's got no place *to* stay," Sam reminded her.

"Oh, but he does." Olivia clapped her hands together in front of her. "I've just had the most wonderful idea. It just might be the answer we're all looking for."

Sam had serious doubts about that.

"What if Kurt stayed with me on the Lazy H?"

"With you? Be serious, Livvy."

"But I *am* serious." She turned to Kurt, more excited than Sam had seen her in a long time. "You could work for me in exchange for room and board."

"Are you crazy?" Sam said, louder this time. "You can't do that."

He knew from the way Olivia's lips thinned and her eyes narrowed into dangerous slits that he'd said the wrong thing, but it was too late to take it back now. "I most certainly can." She swept back a lock of wind-mussed hair with one small hand. A hand much too small to take on everything she thought she had to. "You're a dear friend, Sam, but I don't need your permission to make decisions about my ranch."

He took her arm, intending to lead her a few steps away from Kurt. She refused to budge. Fine. If she wanted to have this conversation in front of Kurt, Sam wouldn't argue. "You can't let some drifter hang around the ranch, Livvy. It's not safe. You don't know a thing about him except what he's told you, and God only knows how much of that is true."

"Oh, for heaven's sake, Sam—"

"If he's working for the government, why does he need a job? Why can't he afford a place to stay? His story just doesn't make sense. Besides, you have me. You know I'll do whatever needs doing at the Lazy H."

"You're already doing as much as you can." Her eyes softened a little, but not enough to make Sam feel a whole lot better. "In fact, you're doing too much. It's not fair for me to let you ignore the Cinnabar the way I have."

"Jesse's there," Sam argued. "I could easily give you an extra day or two every week—"

"Jesse won't be there forever. He just told me he's planning to leave after he marries Elizabeth. You need to take care of the Cinnabar, Sam. I can't let myself take any more of your time."

Sam clenched his fists and turned away for a second, but he didn't want Olivia to think he was through. If Jesse had been there, Sam might have relieved his tension by popping him one just for opening his big mouth to Olivia. As it was, he had to think fast. "I wouldn't have to help for long," he bargained. "Once we sell Nightmare, we can hire someone to help out. Someone we both know. Meanwhile—"

"Not *we*, Sam. This is my decision, and I've made it." She put her hand on his arm as if that might take away the sting of the verbal slap she'd just administered. "You know how much I appreciate everything you've done, but I have to do what I think best. If Kurt's willing, I think this is the perfect solution."

"It's about the farthest thing from a perfect solution I can think of," Sam snarled. "I already offered you a solution that would work a helluva lot better than this."

"And I already told you why that won't work." Olivia turned away from him, resisting his one last effort to get her to stay. The breeze lifted the hem of her skirt, revealing the worn leather of her boots. How long had it been since she'd had a new dress? How long since she'd had a decent pair of boots?

If she'd just stop being so damned fool stubborn, Sam could give her pretty things. If she'd stop thinking she had to battle the world alone, Sam could make up for the years of Harvey's neglect while he chased his treasure.

"What about it, Mr. Richards," she said, dragging Sam back to the moment. "Are you interested?"

Kurt sent Sam a shuttered look. "It sounds fine to me . . . except that I don't know a whole lot about working a ranch."

"I'll teach you."

Sam kicked a rock out of his way, wishing he could plant his boot on Kurt's backside instead. "Aw, for hell's sake, Livvy—"

Olivia didn't even spare Sam a glance. "And Sam will help."

Help? She had to be joking. He sputtered an objection.

But she wasn't listening. "As far as I can see, Mr. Richards, your options are as limited as mine."

"I believe you're right." Kurt smiled in relief. "I don't know how long I'll be around, but I'd be grateful for a place to stay and more than glad to give you a hand in exchange for it."

And that was that. All decided and done up pretty with a big red bow. Olivia smiled as if life couldn't get any better. Kurt looked pleased with himself. But Sam could have sworn he felt a piece of his world fall away.

Soft lamplight cast shadows across the table as Olivia threw together an evening meal of cold leftover beef on thick slabs of bread and two slices of the pie she'd made the day before. She worked quickly, uncomfortable now that she and Kurt were alone together.

Not because she didn't trust him, but because she was so aware of his every movement. Of his eyes as he glanced up to watch her work. Of his scent, his dimples, the rhythm of his breathing. The awareness made her feel clumsy, as if her hands, arms, and fingers were each moving independently of the others.

The strong scent of sage, fresh from the quick, violent

rainstorm that had just passed, drifted in through the open windows. She stole a glance at Kurt, who sat at the table behind her working on something out of his strange bed-roll. A lock of hair fell over his forehead and his face scrunched in concentration.

He seemed stronger tonight, his limp less pronounced, his eyes a clearer, deeper blue. Lamplight flickered across his sun-bronzed skin and a memory of evenings spent like this with Harvey skittered across her consciousness.

Harvey had often sat in that same spot and watched her fixing supper. In the beginning, he'd chatted about his day's work, about his hopes, his dreams for the future, and his plans. By the end, he'd only been interested in one subject—the treasure of Black Mesa.

She shook the thoughts away. She had no business comparing the two men. "I hope this will be enough," she said, turning toward Kurt. "It's too late to make a big supper."

Kurt glanced up and nodded, his eyes the color of a cloudless summer sky. "Anything's fine. I'm grateful for whatever you're willing to give me."

She wiped her hands on her apron and carried the tray to the table. "I'll be grateful for any work you do around here, so I guess that makes us even."

A slow smile curved his lips and the flickering of the oil lamp threw his face into stark relief. "Not quite even, but if I can help you save the ranch maybe we will be."

He looked so strong, so sure, so determined, she let her doubts swim to the surface again. "Do you think we can save it?"

"I hope so. I'll do my best, but I don't know how much help I'll be." He cleared away his things and linked his hands on the table. "If you don't mind my asking, what's your relationship with Babe the Blue Ox?"

"With who?"

He smiled wryly. "Sam."

"Why do you ask?"

He lifted one shoulder and leaned back against his seat. "I got the impression that there's something between you."

"What gave you that impression?"

"He did."

"He did?" She dropped into the seat across from Kurt, trying not to be angry with Sam but losing the battle. "What did he say?"

"It wasn't what he said, exactly. It was the way he acted. Protective. Watchful. Like he wished I'd do something stupid so he could shoot me."

That description was so accurate, it tore a laugh from her throat. "I'll admit he's not thrilled that you're here, but I don't think he wants to shoot you . . . unless you hurt me in some way."

Kurt shook his head and stuffed whatever he'd been looking at into his bedroll. "Oh, he wants to, all right. But I guess maybe he won't as long as you ask him not to. It's pretty clear he'll do whatever you ask of him."

"Except let me make my own decisions about running the Lazy H." As soon as the complaint left her lips, she wished she could take it back. She might be angry with Sam, but he was too good a friend to criticize him in front of someone else. "If Sam's overprotective of me, it's only because he feels a responsibility to look after me now that my husband's gone."

Kurt shrugged. "If you say so."

"I do."

"Okay." He reached for a slice of bread, as if he'd accepted her explanation. But she could tell by the look on his face that he still didn't believe her.

"Maybe things are different where you come from," she said. "But out here, there's nothing unusual about neighbors helping one another."

Kurt slanted a glance at her and twitched a doubtful smile. "Okay."

His attitude unnerved her. She stood and went in search of something—anything—she could add to their supper. But his silence grated on her. She watched him pile beef onto the bread in his hand and grew more irritated with every languid movement. "What makes you such an expert, anyway?"

"On men?" He looked away from his food and laughed. The sound echoed in the tiny house, reminding her how long it had been since the house had known joy. "Maybe it's escaped your notice," he said with a grin, "but I am one."

It had definitely *not* escaped her notice, but she wasn't about to admit it. "I'm a woman, but that doesn't mean I know what other women are thinking."

"No, but you'd probably be able to read their body language and understand what's going on inside them better than a man would."

"Maybe." She snatched up a crock of butter and carried it back to the table. Her feelings about Sam were too confusing and her loyalty to their friendship too powerful to want to keep discussing him. She decided to turn the tables and put Kurt on the spot for a change.

"Now that I've offered you a roof over your head," she said, "maybe you'll finally tell me the truth. Where *are* you from, and what are you really doing here?"

"I've told you the truth."

She shook her head quickly. "You've told me *something*, but I'm pretty sure it isn't the truth. People don't come to country like this unless they're either running from the past or chasing after the future."

"Which was it for you?"

"A little of both, I guess. But we're talking about you. If you're going to stay here, you can't keep dodging my questions. If you do, maybe I *will* let Sam shoot you."

Kurt half-smiled. "What makes you think I'm not telling the truth?"

How could she explain? There was nothing solid she could base her beliefs on, but she knew, nonetheless. "You're not a very good liar," she said after a lengthy pause. "Your face gives you away."

"Really? I've always been told I lie rather well."

"Well, you don't. So? What is the truth?"

His smile evaporated and he looked her over slowly.

He might have been trying to decide what to say, but his scrutiny increased her discomfort and heightened her irritation. "If you're worried about me putting you out, don't. I can't afford to change my mind. Maybe it's escaped *your* notice, but I need you here."

He considered for another moment, then nodded slowly. "I suppose you're right. You deserve the truth. Besides, you've probably pieced most of it together anyway."

Then she was right! There was more than he'd told her. She didn't tell him how wrong he was. She hadn't figured *anything* out, but it couldn't hurt to let him think she had.

He pushed away from the table and paced to the window, wiping his face with one hand and shaking his head as if he couldn't quite get a handle on what he was about to say. Wind gusted outside and showered the windows and walls with tiny bits of dust and pebbles. The silence between them grew heavy as he considered his words.

After what felt like hours, he met her gaze again. "Remember those coins you found in my pocket?"

"The counterfeit ones?"

"They're not counterfeit. They're real. Legal tender. Minted by the United States government."

"Nonsense. Why would the government make money and date it a hundred years or more in the future?"

"They didn't." He leaned against the windowsill and looked deep into her eyes. "They made it a hundred years or more in the future, and I brought it with me."

She started to respond, then stopped cold. Surely he hadn't meant that the way it sounded.

As if he could read her mind, he sketched an X across his heart and took a step toward her. "Are you sure you want to hear the rest? I'll warn you up front, it sounds pretty far-fetched."

"I asked," she said with a forced laugh.

"Yes, you did. And you've been honest with me since I came here. You might not believe what I have to say, but I swear to you, every word is true."

"Go on." Her mouth was so dry she could hardly get the words out.

"The truth is, I was living in the year 2000 when I fell down the side of that cliff. When I woke up, I was here. More than a hundred years earlier."

"Don't tease me," she warned. "I'm not as naive as you might think."

"It's the truth."

"It's impossible."

"You think *I* don't know that?"

The agony on Kurt's face looked so real, Olivia's head began to buzz and the feeling in her limbs slowly drained away. "Two *thousand*?"

"Two thousand."

She gripped the edge of the table to keep herself from fainting to the floor or bolting out the door. Either she'd let a crazy man into her life and her home, or *she'd* gone mad. The trouble was, she didn't know which.

Kurt knew the instant he told Olivia that he should have kept the truth to himself. She took a quick, sharp breath, turned bright red, and began to choke. Her eyes brimmed with tears, but when he started toward her, she nearly fell off her chair trying to get away.

He tried to remember what little he knew about the Heimlich maneuver, but he wasn't sure the maneuver would work if someone was choking on air. "Are you okay? Let me help. I didn't mean to upset you—"

She pulled away sharply and managed to choke out a few words. "You really must think I'm naive . . . or stupid."

"Neither."

"I'm so sick to death of men thinking they're so much smarter than me." She began pacing up one side of the tiny room and down the other. "Sam treats me like a child. Sloan Durrant thinks I'm too stupid to recognize good horseflesh or run the Lazy H. My father—even Harvey thought he was smarter than I am simply because he was a man. I don't need this from *you*!"

"I'm not making this up, Olivia. I'm not trying to fool you. I am from the future."

She shot a dagger sharp look at him.

"Think about it," he insisted. "Think about the photograph on my identification, about the money, about all the things you didn't understand when I showed up here yesterday."

She shook his arguments away. "You're hiding from someone, aren't you?"

"No. I work for the United States Government Department of the Interior. It's my job to preserve ancient native ruins. There's a site not far from here that I think I've been sent here to discover and save."

She acted as if she hadn't even heard him. "You've robbed someone."

"No."

"Shot someone?"

"Wrong again. You want to hear about the future? I can tell you. We have machines that fly. Machines that talk. Machines that cool houses and buildings even in the hottest weather and heat them in the winter without fire or stove. We can cook food in an instant and keep it frozen in the summer until you're ready to use it."

"Someone's gunning for you."

"The only person who's angry with me is my ex-girlfriend. And Sam, of course. The only one of those two who might be gunning for me is Sam."

"Sam." Olivia's eyes flew open wide. "I don't even want to think about what he'll say about this."

"I don't either," Kurt assured her. "I shared this with you in confidence. I'd rather Sam didn't hear about it."

Her eyes shot to his face again. "I can't lie to Sam. I have no patience with liars."

"I'm not asking you to lie," Kurt hedged. "Withholding information isn't the same as lying. But if you think you have to tell him every little thing, I guess it's no wonder he thinks he's supposed to make decisions for you."

Okay, that was a cheap shot, but Kurt was desperate. If Sam got wind of this, Kurt might as well kiss the past—*and* the future—good-bye.

Olivia scowled up at him, but he could tell that he'd gotten through to her. "If this is the God's honest truth—and I'm not saying I believe you—why are you worried about telling him?"

"I'd think that should be obvious. He'll think I'm crazy. And dangerous. And he's already looking for any excuse to get rid of me."

"But you're not crazy." A broad ribbon of skepticism wound around the words.

"Not at all."

"Or dangerous?"

"Absolutely not. Harmless as a lamb."

Olivia rolled her eyes and folded her arms. "As a *lamb*? I doubt that."

The almost teasing tone gave Kurt hope. He reached to touch her shoulder, but she moved just as his hand reached its mark and he touched her hand instead. The contact of flesh on flesh stopped them both in their tracks.

Olivia's breath came out on a trembling sigh. And

Kurt—Hell. He'd probably touched a thousand female hands in his lifetime—maybe more—but the feel of Olivia's slim fingers beneath his made his skin tingle all the way to his shoulder.

It was over in an instant. Olivia snatched her hand away and hid it behind her back. She put a chair between them and lifted her chin defiantly, but Kurt could see that the touch had shaken her every bit as much as it had him.

"I don't like the idea of lying to Sam," she said, obviously trying to get them back on an even keel.

"And I don't like the idea of giving him one more reason to get rid of me."

She started to protest, cut herself off, and rubbed her forehead with one shaking hand. "That just might do it."

"It just might." He caught her eye again and smiled. "I know it sounds crazy, Olivia. If I were in your place I'd think the same thing. But I swear on my life it's the truth."

Skepticism flashed across her face again.

"Why would I say something that I *know* sounds crazy if it weren't true?" Kurt argued. "You could shoot me. You could tell Sam to do it. You could tell people in town and let them cart me off or lock me up. When you think about it, I've put my life on the line by telling you."

Some of the fear in her eyes faded and a dab of uncertainty replaced it. "That's true, but—"

He dug the coins from his pocket and held them out to her. "Look at these again. They're not newly minted. There are a dozen different dates on them. And how do you explain the credit cards and other things in my wallet? At least admit there's a possibility that I'm not crazy."

She took the coins reluctantly and looked them over. "They don't look like new coins," she admitted after what felt like eternity.

Yes! He pulled out his wallet next and flipped it open. "Look through this. Have you ever seen color photographs before?" He found one and held it out to her. "This one is of me when I was ten—taken in 1982 just before my mother died." It wasn't his favorite. His ears stuck out and his teeth were about three times too big for his body, but he'd live through the embarrassment if it would help convince her.

A brief smile curved her lips and her eyes lifted to his face, searching for similarities.

"Had you ever seen a color photograph before I showed up?"

She shook her head and flipped to the next picture in his wallet. "Is this you, too?"

He craned to see it. "My graduation picture from high school."

"And this?" She held up his wallet this time to reveal a picture of him with Charlotte in better days.

"Me with my ex-girlfriend, Charlotte. That's my Jeep in the background, and we're standing in front of my house in Cortez."

"In your underwear?"

"Not underwear," Kurt assured her. "We're both wearing shorts, and she's in what's called a tank top. Everyone dresses like that."

Olivia scowled uncertainly. "To go out in public?"

"Absolutely."

She looked thoroughly scandalized but she stole another glance at the picture. "Oh my. My." She tapped a finger on the picture. "And this is your house?"

"It doesn't exist yet, of course. It won't be built until the nineteen-eighties." He thought about showing her the photos of the ruins he had buried deep in his backpack, then thought better of it. He didn't want to get her hopes up before he had something to show for it, nor did he want to risk word of them getting out before he was ready.

Shaking her head slightly, Olivia handed back his wallet. "It's not possible, you know."

"I know."

She paced for a few agonizing moments.

Kurt could feel his life and the future of Black Mesa hanging in the balance. She held everything in those slim hands of hers. At last, she stopped and turned to face him. "As long as you don't do anything crazy, I won't say anything to Sam," she conceded. "And I won't say anything to anyone from town, either. Some folks might be kind, but there are a few—" She broke off and looked away. "Well, I don't like thinking what they'd do."

Kurt's breath came out in a gust of relief. "Does that mean you believe me?"

"I'm not sure *that's* what it means. But I won't tell anyone else that I might have a crazy man living here on the ranch with me—unless, of course, I find out you're lying."

He'd take what he could get. "Thank you."

She lifted her gaze to his and their eyes locked. Kurt tried not to feel anything, but the air between them suddenly felt prickly—charged with electricity, as if the thunderstorm had turned around and come back.

Her eyes darkened, and something in her expression made Kurt suck in a breath. He could feel every cell in his body, every thread in his shirt. Time seemed to slow, and for an instant he understood that time really could alter to let someone move through it.

No other woman had ever made him feel like this with just a glance. No other woman had ever looked straight into his soul without even trying. He had the uncomfortable notion that he wouldn't be able to hide anything from this woman, and he wasn't at all sure he liked that.

Olivia might still think he was dangerous, but it seemed to Kurt that *he* was the one who needed to worry.

Chapter 8

SAM DRAGGED HIMSELF down the stairs the next morning, squinting to see through the early morning shadows and raking his fingers through his hair. Exhaustion scratched his eyes and set up an unsteady rhythm inside his head.

He'd spent the whole night tossing and turning, thinking about Olivia alone on the Lazy H with a drifter and, much as Sam hated to admit it, one who just might have a thing or two that would appeal to a woman.

Sam didn't see it himself. Far as he was concerned, Kurt was an ugly cuss. What grown man walked around with dimples in his cheeks? The man didn't have a moustache or a beard, and Sam seriously doubted he could even grow one.

And he was strange. Damned strange, if you asked Sam, from his shoes all the way up to his hair. He couldn't understand why Olivia was so dead set on trusting him. The odd way he'd acted as if he knew Cortez one minute and like he'd never seen it the next. The way his story just didn't add up.

Sam shook his head slowly. There was something wrong, all right. Most definitely something wrong. He just wished he could put his finger on it.

He threw open the front door and took a deep breath of clear morning air. The sun was just beginning to lighten the sky from deep night black to slate gray and to paint the underbellies of the clouds gold and pink.

Sam needed to get the day underway. Long as he had something to do, he could put uncomfortable thoughts out of his mind. But he couldn't seem to get moving.

He shouldn't have this problem. He'd had lots of practice putting things out of his mind over the years. He'd learned to put aside the urge to strike out on his own and the irritation he'd felt so often with his father's expectations. Surely he could stop thinking about Olivia and Kurt for a few hours.

A noise behind him brought him around to find Jesse on the landing stuffing his shirttail into his waistband. "How do you expect us to get anything done today without sleep?"

"You didn't sleep?"

Jesse started down the stairs toward him. "How could I with you pacing in the next room all night?"

Sam turned back to the door. "Sorry. I didn't think I was making that much noise."

"Well, you were." Jesse came to a stop beside him. "So, what's bothering you?"

"It's not important."

"You'd better not have kept me awake all night over something trivial." Jesse leaned against the wall and yawned noisily. "Spit it out, brother. I'm not in the mood to pry it out of you." When Sam didn't immediately answer, he pried anyway. "What is it? The ranch or Olivia?"

Sam turned away so Jesse couldn't see his face. "What makes you think it's either one?"

"You don't care enough about anything else to stay

awake worrying." Jesse shuffled toward the kitchen. "Come on. You can decide what you want to tell me while I get coffee on."

Sam wouldn't say no to a cup. It might help clear his mind. He followed Jesse into the kitchen and gathered wood for the stove. It had been far too long since this house had felt the benefit of a woman's touch. Apparently, Sam wouldn't be bringing one home anytime soon. No doubt about it, this would be a lonely old place if Jesse and Elizabeth left.

Jesse gave him a few blessed moments of silence while he got everything ready, and Sam found himself hoping he'd forgotten—or at least given up.

But the minute he had the coffee brewing, he sat down at the table and fixed Sam with a steady stare. "Now."

"Now, what?"

"Now tell me what's had you tied in knots all night." Jesse kicked his feet onto an empty chair. "Don't leave anything out."

Sam knew better than to think Jesse would let the matter drop. He'd follow him around all day, nagging him for an answer. Sam would have to give him something. "I guess I am a little worried," he admitted. "Olivia has a new ranch hand."

"That's good news, isn't it?"

"It would be if she'd hired someone reliable. But this guy drifted onto her place a couple of days ago."

"So? We hire drifters all the time. We couldn't run this ranch without help. Olivia's got to be in the same boat— only without money."

"Yeah, well, this guy had some cockamamie story about being from Washington. But when we took him into town yesterday, he didn't even have money for a room. Even tried to find a job with Jim Hanna on the irrigation system."

"No luck?"

"None." Sam saw no reason to explain his part in Kurt's failure.

"So, Olivia took him back to the Lazy H."

Sam nodded miserably. "She's giving him room and board in exchange for a hand around the ranch." And he felt responsible. If he'd known, he might have helped Kurt get a room in town. He stretched his legs out in front of him and tried to blink away some of the exhaustion. "She could get herself killed with no one to watch out for her."

Jesse gave him a long look. "Maybe. And maybe the guy's all right. Olivia seemed fine when Elizabeth and I saw her yesterday."

"Where did *you* see her?"

"In town." Jesse twirled a spoon around on the table for an irritatingly long time. "You don't always have to be the one watching out for her, you know."

"You aren't suggesting that I just ignore the fact that she's alone over there?"

"Of course not." Jesse stopped the spoon, switched direction, and started spinning again. "But you know what the trouble with you is?"

"No, but I'll bet you're going to tell me."

"Your trouble is, you think you're responsible for everyone."

"Pa didn't raise me to turn my back on my neighbors," Sam snarled. He snagged Jesse's hand and took the spoon away. "Folks have to look out for each other."

"True. But you aren't her only neighbor. *I* could ride over once in a while. So could a lot of other people. But you won't hear of it. You know what I think? I think you're sweet on her."

"Is that right?"

"That's right." Jesse pulled off his glasses and began polishing them with his shirttail. "*And* I think you're upset about this new ranch hand of hers because you're jealous."

"Jealous?"

"Don't tell me I'm wrong," Jesse warned. "It's as plain as the nose on your face." He put his glasses back on and blinked to adjust his eyes. "The question is, what are you going to do about it?"

"Nothing I can do about it."

"Why not? She's not married anymore."

Sam stood abruptly and checked the coffee. He had to talk to someone, and if he couldn't trust his brother, who could he trust? "Maybe not," he said, "but she doesn't want to marry me."

"How do you know?"

Sam filled two cups and carried them back to the table. "I know," he said with a thin smile, "because I asked her."

Jesse nearly let the cup slip through his fingers. "You *what*?"

"I asked her." Sam took his seat again and sipped carefully. "She said no."

Jesse fell back against his chair and shook his head in disbelief. "When did this happen?"

Sam waved a hand as if it didn't matter. "Couple of days ago. Same day the drifter showed up."

"Why didn't you tell me?"

"Didn't see any reason to."

Jesse pulled off his glasses and rubbed his eyes. "Well, I do. If nothing else, talking about it might have helped you sleep."

"It might have." Sam sipped again and set his cup aside. "There's no sense fretting about it, I guess. She's given me her answer. Nothing I can do about it now."

"Isn't there?" Jesse's eyes glinted. "Exactly what did she say when you asked her?"

"I told you, she said 'no'."

"I mean *exactly*. Did she say 'no,' just like that? Or did she give you a reason? Did she say she didn't want to look at your ugly face every morning? Or maybe that it was too soon after Harvey's death to think about marrying again? Did she give you *any* encouragement?"

"Does it matter? No is no."

Jesse rolled his eyes in exasperation. "Not always. Sometimes no means not until you change something about yourself, or not until you have more money, or not until she has a chance to finish grieving for her husband. With Elizabeth, it meant not until I gave her some hope that we'd eventually have a life on our own."

Sam jumped at the chance to change the subject. "So, you'll give up the Cinnabar for a woman."

"Wouldn't you?"

"Never." Sam could say that with confidence. "Pa trusted me with it. I owe it to him—"

Red-faced with irritation, Jesse cut him off. "Pa's dead. You don't owe him anything, except to make yourself happy. But you won't even consider it, will you? You'll spend the rest of your life here, tied to Olivia because you think you owe *her* something and to the Cinnabar because you think you owe *me* something."

Bristling with anger, Sam stood slowly. "There's more to being a man than thinking about myself all the time."

"There's more to life than always doing what someone else expects you to." Jesse's voice rose a little higher with every word. "That's exactly what Ma did, and she was just about the most miserable person I've ever known, right up until the day she died."

"Well, *I'm* not Ma," Sam roared back. "And I'm not miserable." Shaking with fury, he shoved his chair under the table. It hit too hard and sent coffee over the edges of both cups. "I'm just about as *happy* as a person can get."

"I can see that."

"You," Sam bellowed, "need to learn how to mind your own damned business." And with that, he slammed out into the morning. It wasn't until hours later, when he'd worked off most of his anger, that he started wondering whether there was some truth in what Jesse had said.

Olivia peered anxiously out the window until she saw Kurt leaving the yard. Breathing a sigh of relief, she slipped from the house and tiptoed to the end of the porch.

She watched him walk away, ignoring the way his stride chewed up the distance, paying no attention whatsoever to the swing of his shoulders or the taper of his waist. And she *most definitely* didn't let herself remember the way he'd looked in those skimpy underdrawers.

It had taken three long days to think of a chore that would keep him away from the barn for a while. It wouldn't take him long to figure out that the creek in back of the garden wasn't ready to flood its banks, but if she worked quickly she should have plenty of time.

When he disappeared over a low hill, she raced toward the barn and let herself inside. Maybe she shouldn't be doing this, but curiosity was getting the best of her. Besides, it *was* her ranch. She had the right to know what was going on. And Kurt's story about traveling through time was just too . . . too *strange* to believe.

But she felt so devious. She'd done more snooping since Kurt showed up three days ago than she'd ever done in her life. Then again, she'd never had a reason to before. Harvey had always been up-front with her. Even when he'd started to ignore the ranch for the treasure, he'd never lied about it. And she doubted Sam could lie if his life depended on it. He certainly couldn't make up a story like the one Kurt had told her.

Either Kurt was an accomplished liar, or he was crazy. Or maybe he was just confused. Maybe that blow to his head had done more damage than she'd thought.

Before closing the door, she glanced over her shoulder to make sure Kurt hadn't doubled back for some reason. It took a moment for her eyes to adjust to the dim interior after the bright summer sunlight but the barn was so familiar she didn't have to wait long.

With her heart high in her throat, she crept across the hay-strewn floor toward the stall where Kurt had been sleeping. If her mother could see her now, she'd never recover.

Nightmare looked over his stall door and nickered softly.

"Yes, I know," Olivia whispered. "It's sneaky and underhanded. But you know why I'm doing it. There must be something in his things that will answer my questions."

The horse actually looked skeptical.

Olivia paused at the entrance to Kurt's area and frowned at the horse. "Don't tell me you believe him."

Nightmare tossed his head and backed up a step or two.

"Good. Now, keep watch. Let me know if you hear him coming back."

Her hands tingled with apprehension and her pulse quickened as she crept inside and tried to memorize where Kurt had left everything. She had to be sure she could put it all back the same way. She might be willing to snoop, but she wasn't all that excited about getting caught.

The blanket she'd given him lay spread on top of his strange-looking bedroll. Another rolled-up blanket marked where he lay his head at night. His pack sat on one side, tightly closed.

Why couldn't he have been disorderly? If everything had been strewn around the stall, she wouldn't have had to worry so much. As it was, she'd have to be very careful not to give herself away.

Her pulse picked up more speed as she took stock and the hammering of her heart nearly deafened her. Even so, her imagination found sounds from the barn and yard and magnified them. Creaks turned into footsteps. Settling wood turned into the huge barn door opening.

What would he do if he caught her? What excuse could she possibly give?

She forced away the apprehension and decided to tackle the bed first. Taking a deep breath, she plunged her hands into the hay beneath his bedroll and felt around to see if he'd hidden anything there. When she didn't find anything, she shifted to the other side and tried again.

Nothing.

If he had anything to hide, it must be inside his pack. The thought of actually searching it made her ears buzz, but she'd gone this far; she might as well keep going.

She took a moment to smooth his bed and stepped back to admire her handiwork. Perfect. He'd never know she'd been here.

After another deep breath, she picked up Kurt's pack. It seemed innocent enough for all that it looked odd. But it was heavy. He could have anything hidden inside.

She carried it to a corner of the stall and sat on an overturned bucket to work. It wasn't comfortable by any means, but she didn't plan to be there long.

She studied the pack for several seconds, turning it over in her lap while she tried to figure out how to open it. It shouldn't be too hard. It had a flap like a saddlebag, even if the fasteners were different.

She looked for a buckle or anything else familiar, but the metal closures weren't like anything she'd ever seen before. She lifted one corner of the flap and gave it an experimental tug. The metal fastenings held fast. She lifted both corners at once, but they still wouldn't give way.

Where *did* he come from?

Losing patience and acutely aware of passing time, she gave the pack's flap a sharp tug. It still refused to open. *Damn and blast!* This should have been easy.

A lock of hair fell into her eyes. She blew it back onto her forehead and tried again.

"Can I help?"

With a tiny scream, she dropped the pack, lost her balance on the bucket, and landed on her backside on the stable floor. She looked up to find Kurt watching her from the stall door wearing a bemused smile. Her face burned with embarrassment and she wished she could melt into the hay at her feet and disappear.

"I was . . . I just . . ."

"Let me guess. You wanted to look through my things while I was out of the way?"

"No! I . . . That is, I . . ."

"Wanted to find proof that I'm lying?"

She scrambled to her feet and shoved the pack at him. "Not lying. Just confused. Or . . . or . . ."

"Crazy?"

He didn't seem at all concerned. In fact, he seemed amused. And that made her angry. She hated to be laughed at.

"Well, can you blame me?"

He lifted one shoulder in a casual shrug and stepped into the stall with her. "Not really. But I'm not, you know."

"Not what?"

"Not lying. Not confused. Not crazy."

He was too close. The stall too small. His eyes *far* too blue. She straightened her shoulders and tried not to look like the fool she'd been.

He held the pack out in invitation. "Do you want to see what's inside?"

More than anything. But pride—what little she had left—wouldn't let her admit it. "Not at all. I was just checking to see if you needed another blanket."

Kurt's smile widened and the twinkle in his eye danced. "I see."

"And I was—I was making sure your pack hadn't gotten dirty or torn when you fell."

His lips twitched. "Oh. Well. Thank you. That's very kind. Please, accept my apology for misjudging you."

"I don't appreciate your sarcasm."

He dipped his head and tossed the pack onto his bed. "Next time, just ask."

"There won't *be* a next time," she assured him. And she managed somehow, in spite of her mortification, to lift her chin and step past him.

She could feel him watching her as she walked toward the barn door, but she resisted the urge to run. But as she passed Nightmare's stall, she flicked an annoyed glance at the horse and whispered, "Some help *you* are."

It was ridiculous, she knew, but Nightmare's whinny sounded for all the world like a laugh.

Kurt stood on the lip of the mesa and stared into the narrow canyon below him. The sun had already begun its westward slide to the horizon, and the piñon and cedar trees dotting the mesa's crest cast long shadows at his feet.

Darkness already engulfed much of the wooded valley far below. The scents of sage and pine filled the air and only the occasional call of a raven circling overhead broke the stillness. But Kurt wasn't enjoying the solitude or the landscape the way he usually did. In fact, he couldn't believe his eyes.

He'd waited three long days for a chance to slip away from Olivia's to search for the ruins. He'd been certain he knew his way back. After working this maze of canyons for three years, he'd learned how to read the landscape, how to tell one blunt, dead-end *arroyo* from another.

So where were the ruins?

Miles of canyon surrounded him. Hundreds of miles, in fact. One unmarked finger canyon after another, stretching away from the main gouge in the mesa. Though many of the landmarks he'd relied on in his own time were man-made and didn't exist yet, he knew he hadn't taken a wrong turn. He'd been so careful to backtrack the route he'd taken to Olivia's that first day.

He searched in the gathering darkness for his own footprints, but they'd either been blown away by the wind or washed away by the afternoon thunderstorms. He refused to believe they might be on some other part of the mesa entirely.

Swearing under his breath, he dashed away a trickle of sweat and propped both hands on his hips. His supervisor at the Bureau of Land Management had made such a point of telling everyone that the canyon area had been left more or less natural. Apparently, "less" was the key word.

He'd never find the ruins tonight. The cliff dwellers had built them into caves in the sheer rock walls, impossible to see from above. But Kurt had been certain he knew the right vantage points to see them without climbing down the cliff face. Apparently, he'd been wrong.

The only other choice was to go down into the canyons, but without the footpaths and stairs that had been built to supplement the Anasazi paths, that could be treacherous work. He'd have to go down on the end of a rope, and only a fool would try a trick like that alone, especially this late in the evening.

Kurt might be desperate, but he was no fool. He perched on the edge of a rock and mopped his face with his sleeve. Uncapping his canteen, he took a long drink, then let out a sigh heavy with frustration.

If the ruins had been easy to find, he reminded himself, they'd have been discovered long before now. In that case, there'd be no reason for him to be here. But all the logic in the world couldn't completely wipe out his disappointment.

He'd entertained the grand notion that he'd find the ruins and set Olivia's mind at ease about her mortgage.

Now, he'd have to ask for her help. And maybe Sam's as well.

In spite of the stunt she'd pulled that afternoon, he trusted Olivia. Sam was another matter entirely. But Kurt wouldn't dare lower himself into the canyon without someone on the other end of the rope to control his rate of descent and make sure he got back out again.

Once he found the ruins, he'd decide what his next step should be. The first time around, the federal government had been supremely uninterested in protecting the ruins of the Southwest until after the turn of the century—long after most of the damage had already been done.

Kurt didn't plan to waste time with the feds. He'd try instead to interest the local government. He'd read about some local people who'd been instrumental in protecting the ruins the first time around. But he had to have something to show them first.

He sat for a while, pondering his options as the sun slid further toward the horizon. Streaks of orange and indigo stretched across the sky and the shadows at his feet lengthened and deepened by the minute. The inevitable evening thunder boomed in the distance and a gust of wind danced past him.

He stood quickly, knowing he should head back toward the Lazy H before the storm hit. But the sudden strong sensation of being watched pricked the back of his neck and inched up his spine. Without breaking stride, he glanced along the canyon rim, but the setting sun made it hard to tell whether the shapes looming there were trees or people.

Who would be watching him? He'd been careful not to let Olivia see him leave, so he doubted very much she was out there. Besides, he really didn't think she'd do much more skulking around after today.

Could it be Sam? That seemed more likely, except that Sam hadn't even been near the Lazy H for two days.

There were Navajo, Ute, and Pueblo still living in the area during the late 1800s and relations between them and settlers hadn't always been peaceful. He just hoped he didn't inadvertently stir up trouble. That would really win friends for him in town.

Still uncomfortably aware that someone was watching him, Kurt kept moving toward his horse, making every effort to look as if he were out for a casual stroll. Right. Sight-seeing at sundown in the middle of nowhere.

Help her.

As always, the whisper came out of nowhere. Kurt ground to a halt and glanced around instinctively, though he already knew what he'd find. Nothing. No one. Just like always.

But tonight, the presence felt different somehow. This time, he could almost feel someone creating a target of concentric circles on his back. He forced himself to start walking again.

Help her.

"I'm *trying*," he muttered. "It would help if you'd give more detailed instructions."

The only answer was a sudden gust of wind that swirled on the ground directly in front of him before lifting into the sky. Creepy. Kurt watched it for a moment and repressed a shudder.

"I wish you'd just tell me what the hell's going on here," he shouted to the dust devil as it disappeared. "How did I get here? *Why* am I here? Nothing's the way it should be."

The wind ruffled his hair, but it didn't give him any answers.

Kurt very nearly demanded one when the prickly sensation on the back of his neck became stronger. He clamped his mouth shut and put his feet in gear. There was someone else out there, someone more substantial than the wind, and he was standing here shouting at nothing.

Ducking his head into the wind, he stole one last glance at the canyon rim. The feeling faded slowly, and he knew with a certainty he couldn't explain that he was alone again.

But the sensation of having been watched left him a little uneasy as he rode back to the Lazy H. Someone had their eye on him. He'd have to be very careful in the future.

Chapter 9

SWEAT POURED DOWN Kurt's back and trickled into his eyes. Dust from the dirt and hay tickled his nose. The air inside the barn was stifling, the air outside scalding. He couldn't decide which was worse.

So far, he'd been able to figure out how to do everything Olivia had given him to do—and she'd given him enough work to keep two men busy. By the end of every day he collapsed in the hay and slept hard until morning.

He'd fallen asleep two nights in a row trying to read the paperback novel he'd found in the bottom of his backpack, and awoken both mornings to find it lying open on his face. Since then he'd given up trying to do much of anything but eat, sleep, and work.

Another hard day's work had kept him from thinking much about his experience on the mesa the night before. Tomorrow, she wanted him to go somewhere with Sam and learn how to mend fences.

An entire day alone with Sam. Kurt couldn't wait.

He ran an arm across his forehead and caught a whiff of sweat from the shirt he'd borrowed. It had been clean yesterday. By tomorrow, he'd be so rank the animals would probably run from him.

As if he'd spoken aloud, Nightmare nickered softly from the stall behind him.

Grateful for the excuse to take a breather, Kurt answered. "What's the matter, boy? Am I grossing you out?"

When the horse nickered again, Kurt left the pitchfork in a stack of hay and turned around to carry on the conversation face-to-muzzle. "You're no petunia yourself, you know."

Nightmare tossed his head, then lowered his muzzle over the stall door, inviting Kurt to draw closer.

Kurt ran a hand along the horse's soft snout. "You might not smell so great," Kurt said softly, "but you're a beautiful thing and the best roommate I've ever had. How can she bear to part with you?"

Nightmare snorted softly.

"I know. I know. The woman's gotta do what she's gotta do. But you're too fine a horse to sell just because she needs money." Olivia's decisions weren't any of his business, of course. He might not even wake up here tomorrow.

He fished a carrot he'd saved from lunch from his pocket and offered it. Nightmare nibbled experimentally, then took the whole thing and moved away from the door.

Kurt turned back to the pitchfork. He still had a barn full of chores to finish and the day was quickly spinning to a close. He worked in rhythm, reciting song lyrics as he worked to keep his mind off his aching muscles and all the questions running through his mind. Lift. Grunt. Toss. Groan.

He hated being dependent on anyone, but beggars couldn't afford to be choosers. He was completely dependent on Olivia for as long as he stayed. And that meant he ought to at least try to call a truce with Sam. His instinct for self-preservation didn't want to take a chance on Sam convincing Olivia to send him packing. Besides, it would make her happy if they got along and Kurt would like to see her smile once in a while.

Lift. Grunt. Toss. Groan.

Now, why had he thought that? He wasn't supposed to care about her one way or the other. But she made it pretty hard *not* to care. Besides, the Lazy H was the best possible location for him to "discover" the ruins, the best place to keep an eye on them, and the only chance he had of protecting them. So it made perfect sense to up his chances of staying.

When a shadow fell across the floor of the barn, he looked up with a grateful smile. But when he realized it was Sam blocking the door instead of Olivia, his smile froze. Guess there was no time like the present for making a new friend.

He nodded a greeting. "Evening."

"Evening." Sam strolled into the barn like an ox with an attitude. "Saw you in the canyons yesterday."

Kurt didn't know whether to be concerned or relieved. "So that was you?"

Sam dipped his head in a semblance of a nod. "What were you doing?"

"Looking around."

"Looking around." Sam's eyes narrowed and his moustache twitched in disbelief. He took two slow steps closer. "At what?"

The man's attitude was beginning to get real old, real fast. "Was I on Cinnabar property?"

The merest flicker of surprise showed in Sam's eyes. "Close."

Kurt held back the sarcastic retort about "close" and "horseshoes" that perched on the tip of his tongue. Antagonizing Sam wasn't in his game plan. "Well, then, I'll be more careful."

Sam crossed his arms and leaned against one rough plank wall beneath a collection of ropes and bridles. Great pose. It would make a terrific postcard. "Just what is it you want from Olivia?"

"A place to sleep and three meals a day."

"Is that right?"

Kurt had been in his share of bar fights when he was young. He knew how to square off against someone. How to look intimidating. He knew all the body language from *Don't mess with me* to *Run while you still can*. If he was reading Sam right, the messages hadn't changed much over the years.

He affected boredom. "That's right." He lifted a bale of hay and moved it onto the stack, fighting the grimace of pain that went along with it.

"I don't think so." Sam crossed one foot over the other. "I think you're lookin' for more."

"Such as?"

"I think you're planning to take advantage of her."

The look on his face made it impossible to mistake his meaning. He wasn't worried about a few meals or a hay mattress in the barn. He was worried about Olivia's virtue. Funny. Kurt would have bet the balance on his VISA card that Sam wouldn't hesitate to claim her virtue if she gave him the chance.

Kurt had never considered himself a small man, but Sam dwarfed him. When he got back to his own time— *if* he got back—he'd make working out at the gym a priority. He tugged off his gloves and stepped around Sam. "You couldn't be more wrong."

"That so?" Sam pushed the brim of his hat back with one finger.

"That's so."

"Olivia's a mighty fine-looking woman."

"That's true, but you're still way off base."

"Could be." Sam circled Kurt slowly. "And it *could* be

that you're thinking she'd be a fine catch. Poor widow woman all alone on a ranch out here in the middle of nowhere."

"She's not alone," Kurt said. "She's got you."

Sam's step slowed, his brow wrinkled. "Wasn't sure if you realized that or not."

Kurt leaned on the pitchfork handle and sent Sam a thin smile. "You're kind of hard to miss, Sam. No offense meant."

Sam stopped completely, gave his hat brim a twitch. "None taken." He looked Kurt over carefully. "So, you're not looking to court Olivia?"

"Nothing could be further from my mind." Not *entirely* true, but close enough. Kurt sat on a bale of hay and tried to ignore the stalks jabbing into his legs through the soft, worn denim. "The truth is, I just got out of a relationship back where I come from. I'm not ready for another."

Sam nudged his hat back another inch and leaned an arm on the stall door. He looked almost human. "You have a wife?"

"Not a wife." Kurt scratched his ankle and decided to set the poor man's mind at ease. "I wasn't interested in settling down, so she left me."

"So, you're saying you don't want to settle down with Olivia, either?"

"That's exactly what I'm saying."

"You planning to run out on her?"

"I'm not planning anything," Kurt said honestly. "I'm taking life one day at a time."

Sam's voice grew heavy with disapproval. "Olivia doesn't need temporary. She needs someone she can count on."

"But *you'd* like it if I rode out tomorrow."

"I'd rather you rode out than hurt her."

Kurt leaned forward and rested his arms on his knees. "Look, Sam, I know you don't like me being here. I wouldn't either in your shoes. But saving the ranch is important to Olivia and she's been kind to me, so I'm going to do what I can to help her. I don't plan to hurt her. I'm not here to cheat her. And I'm not going to take advantage of her."

"So why *are* you here? It'd make it easier to believe you if you'd give me a straight answer."

A little of the hostility had faded from Sam's steely eyes, but Kurt was reasonably certain that the truth—the whole truth—could still get him killed. "I wish I could give you the answer you want," he said carefully. "But I can't. Not now. All I can do is give you my word that you have nothing to worry about."

Sam considered that for a long time. "I still don't like it," he said at last, "but out here, a man's word is his bond." He pointed one long finger at Kurt's face. "But I warn you, if I find out you're lying, if you hurt Olivia in any way, you won't be able to run far enough to get away from me."

Kurt didn't move until Sam had left the barn. The warning was duly noted and filed away for safekeeping. From his stall, Nightmare nickered softly.

"Well," Kurt said, pushing to his feet again and rolling his eyes at the horse, "I think that went well, don't you? I think he's starting to like me."

Nightmare snorted and turned his back.

"Well, I do. I'm growing on him. I can tell."

He'd just about started breathing normally again when he heard Olivia call him in to supper. He washed quickly in the trough and climbed the porch, trying to figure out the best way to approach her about searching for the ruins—and how to convince her not to tell Sam about them.

Neither of them had mentioned her escapade the previous afternoon, and Kurt didn't intend to bring it up tonight. He wanted her on his side. He couldn't get her there by embarrassing her.

He knocked softly and, when she called out to him, stepped inside. Dinner sat on the table already. A man's meal of roasted beef, potatoes, steaming biscuits, greens of some sort, pinto beans and onion, slabs of butter, and pots of homemade preserves. And milk. Raw milk. Straight from the cow.

Kurt hid his grimace of distaste. He'd gulped his first mouthful his first day here, expecting the kind of milk that came out of a carton. Homogenized. Pasteurized. Drinkable. Milk wasn't his beverage of choice under the best of circumstances, but he'd rather drink from the water trough in the yard than this vile stuff still heavy with the gamey taste of cow.

But the sight of Olivia more than made up for it. Hair cascading to her shoulders and beyond—featherlight wisps of night-dark silk that danced across her back. A nip of waist cinched in by the faded pink cotton of her dress. The gentle swell of hips below that. Soft. Rounded. Full enough to set her skirt in gentle motion as she walked from the stove to the table.

Remembering his vow to Sam, Kurt looked away quickly and concentrated on the spread on the table. She caught his rapt attention and smiled. "It's nothing special."

It could have been shoe leather, he wouldn't have cared. "It looks perfect."

She motioned for him to sit, then took the chair across from his and linked her hands on the table. "I'd like to apologize for what happened yesterday. I don't know what got into me."

Blunt. Straightforward. She knocked Kurt off balance. There was no way to avoid the subject now, but he didn't have to dwell on it. "Don't worry about it. Like I said, just ask if there's anything you want to know."

Olivia made a face. "I *do* worry about it. What I did was unforgivable."

"I'm sure you have questions. I sure would."

"Thank you for that." She unclasped her hands and passed the platter of beef. "I've been thinking that maybe it would help if we talked about what happened right before you fell."

"You mean it might help me realize that I'm crazy?"

Color crept into her cheeks, but she didn't look away. "I don't think you're crazy. Just . . . confused. Tell me, what's the last thing you remember before you fell?"

She looked so eager to help him, Kurt hated to disappoint her. And anything was better than another conversation with Nightmare. "The last thing I remember is hearing voices near the ruins."

Olivia spooned potatoes onto her plate. "You keep talking about these ruins, but surely you know there aren't any on Black Mesa."

"But there are," Kurt assured her. "They just haven't been discovered yet. In the future, they're protected by the federal government and it's my job to keep an eye on them. I'm supposed to make sure they're not disturbed or looted."

Olivia gave her head a determined shake. "If there were ancient artifacts on Black Mesa, Harvey would have found them."

Kurt's pulse jumped. This was the first clue of any kind that might help. "Harvey spent time on Black Mesa?"

"Yes." A deep sadness filled her eyes as she remembered her late husband. "A great deal of time."

"Did you ever go with him?"

"Once or twice."

"But you didn't see any cliff dwellings?"

"No." Olivia reached for her fork and her fingers trembled. She snatched her hand back and hid it in her lap. "Harvey wasn't interested in ancient native ruins."

"What was he interested in?"

Olivia looked as if she might answer, then caught herself and laughed softly. "Oh, no you don't. We're talking about *you*, remember? You heard voices. What do you remember before that?"

If he wanted answers, he'd better be prepared to give a few. He thought back, trying to stir the memories. "A storm. Was there a storm here the night before I showed up?"

"Yes, of course there was. A horrible thunderstorm. What else?"

"Leaving my Jeep behind a bluff so I could find it again." Kurt carefully moved his glass out of the way and hoped she wouldn't be offended. "And two days before that, I remember breaking up with my girlfriend."

Olivia's eyes shot to his face. "This girlfriend . . . Is she from around here? Maybe if we could find her, it would help you remember."

"I don't think that will be possible. By now, she's probably back in Los Angeles . . . in the year two thousand."

"Is that where you met her?"

Kurt nodded and spooned greens onto his plate. "We met when I went home for my aunt's funeral." That alone should have warned him how things would eventually turn out.

Olivia's cheeks glowed. Her eyes sparkled. Even her lips seemed suddenly more colorful and inviting. It was becoming painfully easy to understand what Sam saw in her. "Why?"

"Why what?"

"Why did you end your relationship with Charlotte? If you could remember that—"

"Oh, I can remember." How could he forget? "It was her decision."

"Why?" Olivia blushed and added, "There might be a clue that will help."

"There isn't." He popped a bite into his mouth and hoped she'd drop the subject.

"Well, *something* made you go up on the mesa that night." She accepted the bowl of greens from him, but they didn't hold her attention for long. "You've told me a story that's a little hard to swallow, you know. And when you dodge questions like this, it's even harder to believe you."

Kurt chewed, swallowed, and forced himself to answer. "She thought I spent too much time working and not enough time with her."

"And did you?"

Kurt laughed harshly. This was getting *way* too personal. He really didn't want to talk about his failures any longer. "Maybe. Probably. What about you and Sam? How long have the two of you been an item?"

This time *she* looked uncomfortable. "What makes you think Sam and I are courting?"

"Aren't you?"

"No."

Kurt's heart gave a leap. *Traitor*. He tried to keep his expression indifferent—or at least to not grin like an idiot. "Somebody ought to tell Sam that."

"Somebody has. He asked me to marry him. I turned him down."

So *Sam* was courting, Olivia wasn't. "Well, that might help explain why he's so worried about me being here." Kurt crossed his feet at the ankles. "Why did you turn him down?"

"I had my reasons."

"I'm sure you did. But turnabout is fair play, isn't it? I answered your question about Charlotte."

Olivia's lips curved ever so slightly. "Yes, you did. But Charlotte isn't here, and Sam is. I may have turned him down, but he's still a dear friend and I'm quite sure he wouldn't appreciate me telling you something so personal."

The soft look in her eye when she spoke of Sam wiped away the exhilaration Kurt had been feeling. If she wasn't in love with Sam, Kurt would eat oats with Nightmare for supper tomorrow.

In spite of his disappointment, he admired her for being able to keep a secret. He'd never understood why some women needed to tell friends every last detail about their relationships. He wouldn't have minded a *few* shared confidences, especially if they'd been something good—like confessing that he was the best lover the woman had ever had—but he didn't like it when his numerous faults were the topic of conversation over Caesar salads.

Olivia sent him a stern look. "We've strayed from the subject again. We were trying to remember what happened to you."

"I've told you what happened to me," Kurt told her. "You're just going to have to believe me."

Olivia stood quickly, realized they'd barely started eating, and sat down again. "I *can't* believe you."

She looked so confused, worried, even frightened that Kurt scooted his chair closer and deliberately covered her hand with his. She stiffened but made no move to draw it away. "Try," he urged gently. "And I'll try to think of some way to prove it to you. In the meantime, I'm here to find the ruins on Black Mesa, and I'm going to need your help."

Her worried eyes shot to his face. "What kind of help?"

"I need you to come with me to look for the ruins. I need you to control the horse while I climb down the cliffs on a rope."

She jerked her hand away as if she'd discovered something creepy crawling over it. "No."

"It won't be hard. All I need is a second person along. If I get hurt—"

"*No*!" Her eyes blazed and she stood to get away from

him. "I know what you want up on Black Mesa. You're after the treasure, aren't you?"

"Treasure? You mean that old legend? No. Of course not. I'm searching for the Anasazi ruins—"

Olivia's eyes grew wild. "I *hate* that legend, and I *hate* that stupid treasure, and I will *not* help you look for it."

"Why?"

But she was gone before he could even get the word out, and the bedroom door slammed to make sure he knew she wouldn't be coming back. He stood there for a few minutes, more confused than ever, waiting in case she changed her mind and decided to apologize for the hysterics. But it didn't take long for him to realize that she wouldn't be coming back tonight.

He crossed the yard toward the barn, muttering to himself and trying to make sense of what just happened. *Women.* There was just no understanding them.

Without warning, the image of her face tilted to meet his, of his hands woven through the deep chestnut strands of hair, of his lips covering hers, filled his mind and almost staggered him.

"Oh, no," he said firmly to the moon and the stars. "No."

Go to her.

"No way."

Go to her.

"Forget it."

Go to her.

Kurt ground to a halt. "Are you crazy? Leave me alone."

The air stilled. Even the slight breeze quieted. The coyote calls faded to nothing, and that haunting whisper might never have been.

Slowly, reason returned. Kurt looked around at the deserted ranch yard and realized he'd been shouting at nothing, angry with the wind.

Maybe Olivia was right. Maybe he *was* crazy.

•   •   •

Kurt awoke to soft, fading moonlight spilling in through the chinks in the barn and hay turning to silver dust right in front of his eyes. He stretched, yawned, and tugged the blanket up to his shoulders. He tried to lose himself in sleep again, but apparently he'd had all the rest he was going to get.

Animal sounds—including Olivia's endlessly annoying rooster—filtered in through his consciousness and the hay pricked through the blanket beneath him. He sat quickly and let out a heavy sigh.

Another day in the past. Another chance to find the ruins. Another chance to change the course of history. Maybe he'd even find out what had turned Olivia from a rational woman to an hysterical one in the blink of an eye last night.

A good night's sleep had helped him feel a whole lot more sensible. A whole lot less likely to have an argument with Mother Nature in the middle of the night. A whole lot more capable of ignoring Olivia's charms.

In fact, he was glad last night had happened. He really was. He couldn't afford to be attracted to her.

He reached for the shirt Olivia had washed for him, slung it over his shoulder, and stepped into the yard. The air was still cool and comfortable. The sun had just begun to creep over the eastern horizon and the light cast a golden web over the mesa. The morning breeze ruffled his hair and made his shirt skip across his back, but thankfully it didn't talk to him.

He stretched, bent to touch his toes and warm up the muscles in his back. By nightfall, every muscle in his body would ache again, but the pain of honest labor felt better than any burn he'd ever gotten from a workout.

He scrubbed quickly, rinsing dust from his hair and savoring the mixture of breeze-cooled air and water on his body. He dried his face with a cloth Olivia had given him and shook the water from his hair. To his surprise, Olivia appeared in the doorway and watched him silently.

Determined not to act weird about last night, Kurt called out to her. "Good morning."

"Good morning." She turned her gaze toward the horizon. "Sam should be here soon."

Kurt draped the cloth around his neck and looked toward the road. "Anything you want me to do before we leave?"

"I don't think so. I'm sure Sam will have plenty lined up for you."

Kurt laughed softly. "I'm sure he will." He crossed the yard to stand at the bottom of the steps. "Anything I should know about him before we head out alone? Subjects I should avoid? Things that make him touchy?"

Olivia's lips twitched. "Don't tell me you're nervous."

"Only a little."

He climbed the porch to stand in front of her. He knew better but he couldn't resist the urge to be closer. Or maybe he just needed to see once more how deeply she felt about Sam so he could get a grip on the thoughts that kept bugging him. "So, why did you turn down Sam's proposal?"

"I told you last night, I don't want to talk about it."

"Yeah, but I wasn't about to head out into the wilderness with him last night. Call me chicken if you want to, but I don't want to inadvertently say the wrong thing while he and I are out there alone with his gun."

She smoothed back a stray lock of hair. "If I was worried about what Sam would do to you, I wouldn't have asked him to let you ride out with him."

"Well, that's something, I guess."

She lifted her chin and let the breeze tease her hair away from her face. "Sam isn't going to kill you."

Kurt went on as if she hadn't answered, determined to break through that wall of reserve. His determination wasn't entirely self-serving, he told himself. If she stayed here and married Sam, she'd be able to hang on to the Lazy H and reap all the benefits of the ruins when he found them. *And* she just might be interested in helping to preserve them.

"It's pretty obvious Sam's in love with you," Kurt said. "You know what they say—two things a man can't hide, when he's drunk and when he's in love."

Olivia's eyes flashed. "Sam is one of the dearest people on earth to me . . ."

"But?"

"But I don't believe he's in love with me."

"You think he proposed to be nice?" Kurt had news for her. Men like Sam didn't do things like that.

"I think he feels responsible for me since Harvey's death and marrying me would make it easier to fulfill that responsibility."

"Does he know you feel that way?"

She started to answer, then sent him an annoyed look. "How on earth did we get on this subject?"

"I'm curious. I figure I ought to know what's what if I'm going to be around."

"Things may be different where you come from, but here people don't discuss things of such a delicate personal nature. I find your question to be the height of rudeness."

He almost fell for it. Almost muttered an apology and backed away. She had the look down pat—slightly haughty and starched with disapproval. She had the tone—Southern upper crust tinged with reproach. But her eyes gave her away.

"Is that some subtle way of asking me to drop the subject?"

She turned a serious expression on him. "Subtle. Yes."

"None of my business?"

"In a word."

"Four."

"*Four*?"

"Words." Kurt grinned, liking the feel of teasing her, liking the way she responded even more. " 'None of my business' is four words."

She stared at him for a second or two before she laughed. The sound swept across the yard like a morning bird's song and settled in his heart like some ancient warrior's spear. An unexpected yearning coiled tightly inside him. Strong. Almost overpowering.

Her eyes glittered with amusement, her cheeks flushed. Kurt had the strangest impulse to take her into his arms. He resisted, of course. Sam *was* in love with her. If Kurt had even the tiniest piece of moral fiber he'd put Olivia completely out of his mind. But the longing left him shaken.

He put some distance between them, trying to look cool, but knowing he probably looked more like a twelve-year-old boy who'd just realized that girls weren't geeks after all.

Olivia's smile faded suddenly and horror filled her eyes. "Breakfast!" She clutched her apron with both hands and turned toward the house. "I've forgotten all about it."

It was a lie, and they both knew it. The moment had made her equally uncomfortable. But Kurt pretended to believe her. "You'd better get back inside. You don't want it to burn." He grinned and added, "*I* don't want it to burn."

But she was already gone, nearly flying into the house in a swish of faded cotton, as if she couldn't get away from him fast enough.

Kurt expelled his breath in one long gust and turned away. He couldn't let things go on this way. He had to get himself under control. Holly's affair had devastated him and ultimately ruined his relationship with Charlotte.

Kurt wouldn't even consider hurting another human being that way. Not even Sam.

So what was he going to do about it? The smartest thing would be to leave. Absolutely. Just head toward town and get as far away from Olivia as he could get. But in the intense summer heat, he'd probably never make it. And if he did, what would he do once he got there?

Face it, buddy, as long as you're here in the past, you're stuck.

He'd just have to use every opportunity to search for the ruins. If there was any chance of getting out of this Wild West calamity and returning to his own time, he'd find it there. That was the sensible solution. Let Olivia and Sam make a life together here in the past. He'd head back to the future and get on with his own life. He'd bury himself in his work and forget about women.

It was the sensible solution. The *only* solution. So why did just thinking about it leave him feeling so hollow inside?

Chapter 10

OLIVIA LEANED HER head against the door and closed her eyes. What was she doing? She had no business responding to Kurt, but the smoldering look in his eyes had left her weak in the knees and gasping for breath. There'd even been a moment when she half expected him to scoop her up and carry her away.

What would she have done if he had?

She'd have fought him, of course. She might live here in the back of beyond, but she was still a lady. But just the thought of being cradled against his bare chest, of his male scent permeating everything . . .

She pushed away from the door and rubbed her arms. She had to stop thinking about him that way. She hadn't meant to catch him washing up this morning. She'd simply stepped outside to escape the heat of the stove and catch a breath of fresh air. She'd wanted only to enjoy the sunrise like she did so many mornings.

But all those other mornings she hadn't found a half-naked man dripping water in the middle of her yard. A half-naked man with a fine set of shoulders, well-muscled thighs, and a smooth, flat stomach.

She shook off the image and rubbed her arms a little harder. Maybe she was missing Harvey. Maybe she was just longing for the comfort of his embrace, the shared moments at the end of the day when he'd gathered her into his arms and cradled her against his chest. But if that was true, why didn't she respond to Sam the same way?

Of course, Sam didn't go around peeling off his clothes in front of her. She'd glimpsed him without a shirt once or twice, but always from a distance. Whenever she approached, he covered himself.

She tried to make Sam's image form in her mind, but Kurt's eclipsed him. Dark hair, clear blue eyes. His smile. His dimples. His shoulders, waist, and legs.

She blinked rapidly to force him away again, but she had the sinking feeling that even if she *had* seen Sam standing half undressed by the trough, she wouldn't have been overwhelmed by sensation. Even Harvey had never affected her in quite the same way.

She dropped into her rocking chair, but she couldn't sit still. Bolting to her feet again, she paced the tiny distance between the stove and the door.

She'd loved Harvey. Deeply. She'd married him, followed him into the wilderness, and spent five happy years with him. *Blissfully* happy years.

The lie tweaked her conscience and set her feet moving even faster. The years may not have been blissful, she admitted sadly, but she'd been happy. For the most part.

She certainly hadn't been *unhappy*.

And that wasn't the problem now, anyway. The problem was her inexplicable, overwhelming, totally inappropriate— not to mention unladylike—reaction to Kurt.

Ladies didn't behave that way. Hadn't her mother told her that a thousand times? Ladies didn't have longings like the ones Olivia had felt outside on the porch.

She lifted her hands to her burning cheeks and rolled her eyes to the ceiling. Lordamercy, what was wrong with her? The thoughts running through her head would have made a painted woman blush.

Rubbing her forehead hard enough to wipe out every thought in there, she stopped in front of the stove, but visions of Kurt still danced through her head. She filled his plate quickly, but the echo of his laugh and the memory of the way his eyes picked up the color of the sky teased her as she crossed the room again.

She couldn't let him into the house this morning. She'd have to feed him on the porch where she wouldn't feel as if they were quite so alone. But the sight of him sitting there, fully clothed again but so achingly handsome she wanted to touch him, nearly did her in.

He accepted the plate gratefully, taking care not to let his fingers brush hers or their eyes meet as they made the exchange. He ate in silence, breaking it only to compliment her cooking or ask a question about some chore she'd asked him to do.

Fences, hay, feeding, mending . . . She could hardly make herself think about any of them, but she nodded and answered as if she cared. Three times as he ate she told herself to go back inside and leave him alone, but she couldn't seem to make her feet move.

She willed Sam to ride into the yard and give her someone else to look at and talk to, but no matter how hard she watched the road from the Cinnabar, he didn't come.

She needed to stop indulging in fairy tales and start thinking about real life. First and foremost, Kurt was a stranger. A stranger with serious problems. Even if he hadn't been, she had to concentrate on saving the Lazy H. She couldn't afford to let daydreams distract her.

At last, Kurt handed back his empty plate and smiled at her. "Wonderful as usual. Thank you."

She pushed aside an almost unbearable sadness and forced an answering smile. "You're welcome."

"Is there anything you want done if Sam's not here after I feed the horses?"

Kiss me. The thought darted through her head before she could stop it. Blushing deeply, she turned away and started toward the door. "No. Just relax. I'm sure Sam'll keep you busy in the field."

"Olivia?"

She didn't want to look at him, but how could she ignore him? She turned back warily. "Yes?"

"Are you all right?"

"Yes. Fine. I'm a little tired this morning, that's all."

"You're not sick, are you?"

"No. Nothing like that."

His eyes darkened with concern. "If you're feeling bad, don't push yourself. Stay in bed. Read a book. Watch—" He broke off with a laugh and shook his head. "Read a book."

She smiled weakly. "That sounds lovely, but I don't have a book to read." It sounded more than lovely. It sounded like pure heaven. She hadn't allowed herself to miss luxuries like her father's library in years, but just the mention of a good book made her ache with longing. And it had been longer than she could remember since anyone had suggested that she take to her bed in the middle of the day.

A slow smile spread across Kurt's face. "I have a book in my backpack if you're interested. Let me get it." He started away, then turned back again. "I'll warn you, the language in the book might seem a little odd to you. And rough. It may be confusing, but it's a book." This time he actually started across the yard and called back over his shoulder, "It's been on the bestseller list for weeks."

"On the *what*?"

But he didn't hear her. He disappeared for a few minutes, then came out again, grinning from ear to ear and holding a book and several small pieces of paper as if they were the treasure from Black Mesa. He handed her the book first, bound in thick paper bearing the oddest picture she'd ever seen.

"John Grisham?"

"A very popular author in my day." Kurt shoved the photographs at her. "But these . . . look at these. *These* are the ruins we're looking for."

She took them hesitantly, a little thrown by the glimmer of excitement in his eyes. She studied the photographs with interest since she'd never seen even a sketch of the Wetherills's ruins. They were like nothing she'd ever seen before, magnificent structures built into caves beneath the cliffs. But there was nothing here to prove that these cliff dwellings were on her property. And even if they were, she still had no intention of going up onto the mesa.

Thankfully, Sam chose that moment to ride up, and spared her having to argue her point. Instinctively, she tucked the pictures into the book and hid the book inside the folds of her skirt.

She had no idea why, but the look of approval in Kurt's eyes warmed her clear through. If she'd thought toughening her heart against him would be easy, she couldn't have been more wrong.

The sound of an approaching horse brought Olivia out from Kurt's book with a start. Late morning sunlight streamed through the window and beamed across her lap. The air inside had already grown stuffy and almost unbearably hot. She must have been reading for hours. How utterly irresponsible when she had so much to do.

The feel of a book in her hands after so long had made her lose track of time. The utter joy of words on paper had made it impossible to stop, even though there were huge gaps in her understanding of the world in it.

Impossible as it was to believe, the book had finally convinced her that Kurt was telling the truth. Imagine living in a world such as the one the book described.

Setting it aside reluctantly, she hurried to the door. She expected to see Kurt and Sam riding back into the yard, but to her surprise, she didn't recognize the lone rider. She shielded her eyes with one hand and watched as he rode closer. She rarely had visitors, except for Sam. People in town seemed content to leave her on her own.

The rider finally drew close enough for her to recognize the long, lanky figure of Abner Grimley, who owned a small ranch on the west side of the valley. She knew him by sight, and Harvey had briefly mentioned meeting him in town a few times, but she couldn't imagine what brought him to the Lazy H today.

After making sure Kurt's book was hidden, she walked toward the gate to greet him. "Afternoon, Mr. Grimley. This is a surprise."

"Afternoon." His narrow eyes darted about the yard, skimming everything, landing nowhere. "Sam Evans around?"

So he hadn't come to see her after all. "He's out with my ranch hand mending fences. Do you want to leave some word for him when he rides in?"

"Naw." Abner shoved his hat back and skittered his eyes around the yard again. "Heard tell you was thinking of selling that black horse of Harv's."

Bless T. J. Mortensen. He'd obviously been spreading the word for her. "I'm thinking about it. But why come looking for Sam if you're asking about my horse?"

Abner shifted in his saddle. "It was my understanding that he's the one I should talk to."

Had Sam given him that impression? If he had, Olivia would have a few things to say to him. "You've been misinformed. The black is my horse. You'll have to do business with me."

"Makes no difference to me," Abner said with a shrug.

He dismounted, tethered his horse, and propped his hands on his hips. "Can I see it?"

Olivia led him to the barn, chafing with irritation as she realized he was looking closely at the farm and taking in every sign of disrepair. Inside the barn, his greedy eyes bounced from floor to ceiling, tool to tool. "You been getting along okay?"

"Just fine, thank you."

"This is a big spread for a woman to run alone."

"Oh, but I'm not running it alone," she said, smiling coolly. "I've hired a ranch hand."

"Hired?" Abner's step faltered and he shot a quick look at her. "I didn't realize—" He cut himself off and mumbled something under his breath.

But his meaning wasn't lost on Olivia. How had he heard that she was short of cash? As far as she knew, only two people knew the extent of her trouble—Sam and Sloan Durrant. Not even T. J. Mortensen knew how tight things were for her, and she owed him money. Sam would rather cut off his hand than break a confidence, but she couldn't imagine Sloan gossiping about her troubles either.

Abner drew to a stop in front of Nightmare's stall. She could see the gleam of appreciation in his eye, the slight licking of his lips in anticipation. He looked to her for permission, then let himself into the stall and checked Nightmare over carefully. Olivia tried not to let the sight of someone looking so closely at her horse bother her, but the reality of having to sell him made a lump burn in her throat.

"Fine horse," Abner said at last. He stood and patted Nightmare's haunch. "I'd be willing to take him off your hands, seeing as you're in need of cash and all."

How sweet. She forced away her irritation. She *had* to sell Nightmare, like it or not. "What kind of offer are you making?"

Abner ran a hand along his chin, thinking—which must have been difficult for him. "I could go as high as a hundred twenty."

Her stomach flopped to her feet and her heart landed somewhere nearby. That was higher than Sloan's offer, but not by much—and not enough to do her any good. She'd been so certain that Sloan's offer was ridiculously low, but now . . .

Had Harvey been wrong? Had he been such a bad judge of land and horses?

No. *No!* Sam believed she could get enough for Nightmare to pay the mortgage. *She* had to believe it as well. "That's ridiculous," she told Abner. "And you know it is."

"Mrs. Hamilton—" Pity flooded Abner's eyes and made her blood boil.

"I won't accept a hundred twenty dollars, Mr. Grimley."

"I understand your disappointment, Mrs. Hamilton. Truly, I do. But I can't see my way clear to giving you more than what the horse is worth just to be neighborly." He sent her a smile that made her want to slap it straight off his face. "Maybe there is something I could do, though—seeing as how you're a widow and all."

"Really? And what might that be?"

"I could . . ." Abner hesitated, shot a glance at her, and thought some more. "I could give you a hundred dollars for the horse and throw in a dollar an acre for that land of yours up on the mesa."

This was the second offer she'd had for her "worthless" land in a week. She was beginning to think maybe her land wasn't so worthless after all.

She pretended confusion. "But the land on the mesa isn't good for anything. Why on earth would you want it?"

Abner filched an apple from a barrel and rubbed it on his sleeve. "I'm a forward-looking man, Mrs. Hamilton.

No telling what that land may be worth some day. You and me may not live to see it come to pass, but I've got five young sons who might."

Olivia walked slowly toward the barn door, irritated by his offer, angered by the syrupy tone of his voice, and just plain tired of being treated like an idiot. "I'm sure your offer is a generous one, but I have no intention of breaking up my husband's holdings."

Abner followed her outside and squinted up at the mesa. "I understand that, too. But if I can be blunt, your husband isn't here any longer. If my wife suddenly found herself alone, I'd expect her to sell everything I own to keep herself." He turned a tight smile in her direction. "A man's dreams only last as long as he does."

Olivia banged the barn door shut and dropped the latch into place. "Maybe so, Mr. Grimley, but *my* dreams are very much alive."

"Your dreams?" Abner looked at the apple he'd stolen as if it might clear up his confusion. "Why would a woman want to run a place like this on her own? Seems to me, you'd want to live in town, at least, where you could take things a mite easier."

"Well, I don't."

"Then your answer is no?"

"It is."

"You won't reconsider?"

"Absolutely not."

Abner shook his head as if he'd never heard anything so foolish in his life, but the light in his eyes told a different story. She'd made him angry.

She didn't care. She refused to let him, or anyone else, intimidate her. She kept her head high and her back stiff as he mounted his horse and wheeled it around toward the gate. But as the dust settled behind him, she gave up all pretense and sagged against the porch rail.

Two offers for her land in such a short time could only mean one thing. Harvey had been talking about that stupid, *stupid* legend. He'd given people the idea that the treasure was on her land. And he'd been gone just long enough for the vultures to come circling.

Sam worked the shovel into the hard-packed ground and paused to mop his forehead with his sleeve. He'd been working beside Kurt for half a day already, trying to outwork, out-muscle, and outlast him. Now, he was ready to admit—grudgingly—that maybe Olivia hadn't done so badly for herself.

Sam had expected Kurt to call for a break several times, but he hadn't yet. He'd gritted his teeth, clenched his jaw, and put his back to the tasks he'd been given. He'd kept his mouth shut and worked without complaint until sweat soaked his shirt and even Sam was ready to call it quits.

He supposed any man who could hold his own like that deserved a little respect, but he wasn't ready to concede too much. He suspected that Olivia was growing fond of Kurt. And in spite of Kurt's assurances that he didn't intend to court Olivia, Sam couldn't imagine any man spending twenty-four hours a day around her and remaining unaffected. It just wasn't possible.

Women weren't a dime a dozen in the Montezuma Valley. Even the plainest, thinnest, and meanest could have found a husband without much trouble. And Olivia didn't fall into any of those categories.

Just thinking about it gave Sam a second wind. He dug another fence hole or two, making sure he worked harder and faster than Kurt. But the effort finally took its toll. Panting from exertion, he set aside his tools, pushed his hat back on his head, and uncapped his canteen. "You want a break, take one."

Kurt settled a stack of fence posts on the ground and

tugged off his gloves. "Thanks. I hope I'm not slowing you down too much."

"Not too much. I'm used to working alone."

To Sam's surprise, Kurt laughed. "And having me around isn't much better?"

A smile tugged at Sam's lips, but he fought it away. "Not much better, not much worse." He took a long drink, recorked the canteen, and set it beside him on the ground. "I still want to know how long you're going to stick with this before something new drags you off again."

Kurt filled a hand with water and rubbed his face. "Wish I had an answer for you." He let out a heavy groan and stretched out beneath a juniper. He shaded his face with one arm and groaned again. "Why didn't you tell me last night that you'd proposed to Olivia?"

"Didn't think it concerned you. How'd you find out?"

Kurt lifted his arm and grinned at Sam before covering his eyes again. "She told me, of course."

"She did?" Sam battled a pleased smile. Didn't want to get all calf-eyed in front of Kurt. "Well."

"Well."

"Did she happen to mention that she turned me down?"

Kurt nodded without looking at him. "Yep."

"That make you change your mind about her?"

"No." Kurt pulled his arm away and glanced at Sam. "I told you I'm not going to cut in on you, and I meant it."

Sam plucked a blade of dried grass and put it between his teeth. "Reckon that's all right."

Kurt dropped his head to the ground again. "You're a man of few words, aren't you?"

"Can't see any reason to overdo." Feeling better than he had in days, Sam stretched his legs out in front of him.

Kurt chuckled. "All I want is a place to stay. All Olivia wants is a friend. Someone to talk to. She's got you, but you can't be there all the time. And for some reason, she's not ready to say yes and marry you. But she will."

Sam raised an eyebrow. "Reckon that's all right, too."

Kurt's smile grew. "Reckon so. Now that you know I'm not here to steal the woman you love, can I ask you a question?"

Sam grew wary again. "What?"

"Black Mesa. How well do you know it?"

"I know it's a worthless stretch of land so covered with scrub oak and sand a man can't even run cattle on it. Why are you asking?"

Kurt brushed loose dirt from the toe of his shoe and pushed a couple of small rocks into a pile before he answered. "I heard an old native legend that mentioned it and thought I'd check it out while I was here."

"You after the treasure?" Olivia would *love* that.

"There is no treasure."

Sam's smile faded. "Then what *do* you want?"

Kurt pulled his hat brim down to shield his eyes. "Have you ever seen anything out of the ordinary up there?"

"Saw an owl once."

"Anything else?"

"Sorry. Can't help you. I never was as fond of that place as Harvey." He let the silence hang for a minute and tried to put the conversation out of his mind.

He tried closing his eyes, tried eating a hunk of the bread Olivia had packed with their lunch, even tried thinking about Jesse and Elizabeth and what he was going to do about them. But in the end, his curiosity got the best of him.

"You said Olivia would accept my proposal," he said, trying to sound nonchalant. "What makes you think so?"

One of Kurt's eyes popped open. "Because one of these days she'll figure out that you really do love her."

Sam pulled his knife from his pocket and set to work on a chunk of piñon wood, whittling nothing from nothing just to have something to do. "You saying she doesn't think I love her?"

"That's what she told me."

She'd only known Kurt a few days, and she'd already told him more than she'd ever confided in Sam. He didn't like the sound of that at all. "What else did she tell you?"

"Just that." Kurt struggled to sit up, groaning with every movement. "She's afraid you made the offer just to fulfill your responsibility to her husband."

Sam snorted a laugh. "Don't know what more I could do to convince her. I've done everything I know."

Kurt wrapped his arms around his bent knees. "Have you told her you love her?"

"Not in those *exact* words."

Kurt scowled thoughtfully. "Well, if I know women, you'd better *use* those exact words. I've never been with a woman who didn't like hearing them—and often."

"How many women have you been with?" Obviously more than one. Didn't seem quite fair when Sam couldn't even get one to pay attention to him.

Kurt shrugged. "A few. Enough to know that women don't think the same way we do, and if you want to hook up with one you have to make some adjustments."

"Like what?"

Kurt rolled his eyes skyward. "For one thing, they rarely say what they mean. They may *tell* you they want a new broom to sweep the floor, but heaven help you if you get it for them for Christmas or their birthday."

Sam shook his head quickly. "Olivia's not like that."

Kurt ignored him. "For another, they always want what they can't have."

"Olivia's not like that, either."

"No?" Kurt slanted a glance at Sam. "You know her better than I do."

Sam whittled a while longer, waiting for Kurt to elaborate, but he remained irritatingly silent. "Livvy wants me to be civil to you," Sam said at last to get things moving again. "I guess I might as well hear you out."

Kurt rolled slowly onto his side. If he thought anything about Sam's sudden change of heart, he was smart enough not to show it. "You're upset because Olivia turned you down, right?"

Fair assumption.

"But you're always there. Olivia *knows* you'll come running if she needs anything. Maybe you should quit being so available. Play hard to get. Be more mysterious."

Sam considered that for a moment. He didn't like the sound of it. Wasn't much for playing anything. But he had to admit there might be something to what Kurt said. He'd seen those looks Olivia gave Kurt before they left the yard that morning.

"I've known Livvy a long time. Not much I can do to become mysterious at this point."

"No, I suppose not," Kurt conceded as he watched Sam's knife. "Not about what's done, anyway. But there's always tomorrow. Maybe you ought to change your routine a little. Don't be so dependable."

"I won't leave her hurting," Sam warned.

"I'm not suggesting that you should. But you're as regular as a clock. She never has to wonder when she'll see you again. She knows. You don't give her anything to look forward to or figure out. Believe me, women *love* trying to figure men out. It's like a hobby."

Sam still wasn't completely sold. "Never thought being considerate would work against me," he muttered.

Kurt pushed to his feet, groaning all the way up. "Give it a try and see if I'm not right. Keep her guessing for a few days and I'll bet things will be a whole lot different between the two of you."

Sam tossed away the lump of wood he'd whittled into a shapeless knob, folded his knife into his pocket, and slapped his hat on his head. Might as well give it a try, he supposed. What did he have to lose?

Chapter 11

KURT WAS FEELING quite pleased with himself that evening. A soft breeze had dropped the temperature enough to make the air inside the barn almost comfortable. A day of hard work had left him exhausted, but he was even beginning to enjoy that. It was the fatigue of honest, hard work. Even better, Sam had taken his advice, riding off much earlier than usual and without explanation for the change.

Kurt had seen the flicker of curiosity in Olivia's eyes, the slight scowl of uncertainty as Sam rode through the gate in a cloud of dust. It wouldn't take long for Sam to win her over, and once she accepted Sam's proposal, Kurt would be able to get his attraction for her under control.

Once he *knew* she belonged with someone else, he'd stop seeing her as a beautiful, desirable woman. And he could stop searching—even unwittingly—for someone to fill the empty spot inside.

He could blame Charlotte for creating it, but in his heart he knew she hadn't. His father had blasted the first hole. Each subsequent desertion had only widened and deepened it so that Charlotte's leaving had left him poised on the edge of a moral chasm.

The big question facing him now was how much he wanted love and acceptance. Not enough to come between two people who obviously loved each other and belonged together. He'd never stoop that low.

He washed up quickly and tried to find something to occupy him while he waited for Olivia to call him for supper. If he stayed busy, he wouldn't have to look into her eyes or watch the light play in her hair. He wouldn't even notice the way her breasts swelled against her dress as she breathed.

The sound of footsteps broke into his thoughts and warned him she was on her way. Almost frantic for a distraction, he grabbed a shovel and hurried toward Nightmare's stall.

"Kurt?"

Her voice swept through him like a soft, warm breeze but he didn't let himself turn around. "Yeah?"

"Supper is nearly ready."

"Good. Thanks." *Stay focused on the dung,* he warned himself. *Don't look at her.*

"I've been reading your book."

"Do you like it?"

"Very much. I've also been looking at the photographs you left." She broke off and every cell in his body, every nerve, felt her coming closer. "I thought you should know that I believe you."

In spite of his resolve, the words brought him around to face her. He thought he'd steeled himself for the effect she had on him, but either she'd done something different to herself this evening or the attraction was growing stronger.

Her eyes caught his and he could hardly breathe. The slight flush on her cheeks almost buckled his knees. And when she pulled her bottom lip between her teeth and half smiled, the temperature inside the barn soared. "You believe me? About what?"

"About being from the future."

"You do?" The shovel slipped out of his hands and landed flat in Nightmare's business. "Why?"

She smiled and glanced back toward the house. "The book talks about things I can't even imagine, but it doesn't feel made up, either."

Kurt nudged the shovel out of the stall with his shoe, latched the stall behind him, and wiped his feet on the floor. "Thank you."

Olivia's eyes flashed with a strange light. "Don't thank me yet. I want you to tell me what you know about Black Mesa. Is there a treasure?"

Touchy subject. He didn't want to send her into hysterics again, but he still believed Black Mesa was the reason he'd been brought to the past. "Not the treasure of the legend, but those cliff dwellings are a treasure of a different kind."

"And that's what you came here for?"

"In a roundabout way. Maybe." He ran his fingers through his hair, not happy with himself for caring how he looked, but caring anyway. "I really don't know why I'm here, but that's my guess."

"And when you find it?"

"Then I suppose I'll have to go back. I don't know. It's not exactly up to me." Did she look disappointed? He couldn't tell.

"This treasure you're after . . . what is it?"

Usually, Kurt loved talking about the ruins. He knew fact and legend and everything in between. But he couldn't work up his usual enthusiasm tonight. Tonight, he felt as if he were letting her down.

With it came the familiar feeling that he'd been here before. First with Holly, then with Charlotte. Holly had been his wife. He'd been in a committed relationship with

Charlotte. Yet he'd never felt quite so low about disappointing either of them. The realization made him feel like a worm.

He inched a little further away, outside the range of whatever it was that seemed to affect him whenever Olivia got too close. "Have you seen the Anasazi ruins at Mesa Verde?"

"The Wetherills's ruins?" She shook her head. "They're charging five dollars a day just to see the closest ones. I don't have money like that."

"But you've heard of them."

"Of course. Everyone's heard of them. Are they like the ones in the photographs?"

"Basically, yes. But the ruins at Black Mesa—*your* ruins—are even more impressive. They've been better protected from the elements, so the artifacts are even more complete." His enthusiasm began to return. "Just imagine, Olivia. There are pots and jars, baskets, sandals, clothing, blankets, and tools up there that were used by people who lived here a thousand years ago. While people in Europe were building castles, the Anasazi were building here. Imagine what we could learn about their culture if we could preserve their belongings instead of letting people carry them off or thoughtlessly destroy them."

"All of this is on Black Mesa? Where?"

"I could show you."

The small spark of excitement he'd seen in her eyes died away. "I won't go up there. Ever."

"Why are you afraid of it?"

"Afraid?" She backed a step away. "I'm not afraid. I hate that place."

"But why?"

"Because Harvey died up there."

The pain on her face was so raw, Kurt felt as if he'd been gut-punched. "I'm sorry." He took a step toward her but managed to fight off the urge to take her into his arms. "I didn't know."

"He was always looking for the treasure," she said quietly. "Sam and I both told him a hundred times there wasn't anything up there, but he wouldn't listen. One day, he didn't come home." She rubbed her arms against the chill of memory. "I didn't worry at first. He often spent the night out there, certain that this time he'd find his precious gold. I didn't realize anything was wrong until I woke up the next morning and found that Nightmare had come back without him."

Kurt ached for her. "You don't need to talk about it if you don't want to."

She forced a weak smile. "Thank you, but I think it's time I did talk about it—if only to save you from the same thing. I went to look for him, of course. I found him lying at the bottom of one of those horrible canyons." She blinked away tears. Her hands trembled. The pulse point in her neck jumped.

And the ache in Kurt's chest turned into a needle-sharp pain.

"When I realized he was gone, I rode to the Cinnabar for Sam. He brought Harvey back up for me." She lifted her chin and looked deep into Kurt's eyes. "Harvey died because he wouldn't stop dreaming a fool's dream. I don't want to see you do the same thing."

"It's not the same. I know those canyons and I respect nature. I don't take foolish chances."

"It's *exactly* the same. One treasure is no different from another. Please, Kurt, stay away from Black Mesa."

"Stay away? You can't be serious."

"I've never been more serious in my life."

"Olivia, listen to reason. That's why I'm here. If I stay away—"

"You'll stay alive."

"And I'll be stuck in limbo for the rest of that life."

"But you'll *be* alive. And as long as you are, there's always hope."

"Hope? Of what?"

"Of something better. Of finding someone to love. Of having children and being happy. Of doing something important."

"*This* is important."

"More important than your life?"

"What kind of life can I have here?" he snapped. *Without you?*

Her eyes blazed. "Then go! Go find your precious ruins. Just don't expect me to help you."

She spun away and raced out of the barn. All of Kurt's instincts told him to let her leave. He'd never chased after a woman in his life. But Olivia wasn't just any woman.

It wasn't only the ruins that got his feet moving, it was something deeper. Something he'd never felt before. It started somewhere in his core and radiated outward to every extremity. "Olivia, wait!"

She ignored him and ran faster.

He put himself into high gear and caught up with her halfway to the house. Grabbing her by the shoulders, he pulled her around to face him and realized again how small and fragile she was. Small and fragile with a will of iron and a backbone of steel.

For the first time since he'd known her, she'd let down her guard, and he felt honored to be the one to share in the moment with her. He ran his thumbs in circles along her shoulders, knowing he should pull his hands away. But he no longer wanted to do what he should. Her gaze shot to his and he knew she must feel the same acute awareness he did.

"If it means that much to you," he whispered hoarsely. *What was he saying?* He told himself to shut up, but his mouth wouldn't listen. "If it means that much to you, I'll stay away from the mesa."

She drew a shuddering breath and tried to smile. "Do you mean that?"

The circles grew until his thumbs came dangerously near her breasts, but he couldn't seem to control them. "I mean it."

Tears pooled in her eyes and spilled onto her cheek.

Without taking time to think through the action, he wiped them away and barely stopped himself from following the trail with his lips. "It's all right," he whispered. "If anyone deserves to let down her defenses for a little while, you do."

Before he knew what was happening, she leaned against his chest and let out a soft sigh. Her breath went through the thin cloth of his shirt and teased his skin. Her breasts, soft and full, brushed against him as she moved and an urgent need he couldn't defend against tore through him.

Common sense warned him to step away and stop this before he did something he'd regret, but it was little more than a whisper against the desire screaming through him. Slowly, knowing he shouldn't, he slid his arms around her and cradled her against him. Easily—too easily—he tilted her chin and looked into her eyes.

Even then, he might still have been able to stop himself if she'd looked even slightly hesitant. But the need in her eyes matched his own and he knew he wouldn't be able to walk away. Not now. Maybe not ever.

Olivia lifted her lips to meet Kurt's, surprised at the urgency pulsing through her, stunned by the need that seemed to consume her. Half a dozen reasons why she should push him away flitted into her mind. Melody. Harvey. Sam. The ranch. The future. But they disappeared the instant Kurt's lips closed over hers.

Warmth. No . . . heat. Searing fire. Silk and granite. He was solid and strong, yet incredibly gentle. His lips brushed hers hesitantly at first, but his hesitation vanished with the next breath. His touch stole her will and her reason at the same time.

Somehow, she'd known it would be like this. Too intense to even think. Too powerful to resist. His hands moved along her back but they created sensation everywhere. He lifted his hands to cup her face. Callouses and blisters turned to velvet as he touched her.

His tongue brushed her lips, teasing her mouth open. Though she knew she shouldn't respond, she couldn't seem to help it. With incredible tenderness his tongue searched her mouth and the sensation exploded like a prairie fire in dry timber. Never in her life had she felt anything so strong and sweet.

Her hands behaved as if they belonged to someone else. Someone who hadn't spent hours convincing herself not to do exactly what she was doing. Someone who had nothing to lose. They trailed across his shoulders and chest, then curled into his hair, caressed the back of his neck, and slipped down to the small of his back as if they had done this before.

It was that thought that broke the spell. Of course she'd done this before. This and more. But even with Harvey, she'd never been so wanton. She pulled away sharply and covered her mouth with her hands.

Kurt's eyes roamed her face and she watched the passion fade slowly away. He must have seen the horror on her face, the realization of what she'd done, the guilt and anger with herself.

When she tried to explain, he pressed one finger to her lips. "I'm sorry, Olivia. I shouldn't have done that."

She swallowed thickly, unable to speak. Even worse, mixed in with all the other emotions was the strangest one of all—disappointment.

Kurt released her slowly, regretfully, a slow slide of his hands down her shoulders and arms as he pulled away. "I promise you, it won't happen again."

And before she could pull herself together enough to answer, he was gone.

Later that night, Kurt slipped away from the barn and made his way by moonlight to the mesa. He walked quickly, determined to get away from the ranch before Olivia saw him leaving.

Of all the mistakes he'd ever made, losing his head and kissing her had to be the stupidest. How could he have done it? Not that he hadn't enjoyed it—thoroughly. It had been like no other kiss he'd ever experienced. But that only made it worse.

She belonged with Sam. Sam loved her. She loved Sam, even if she hadn't admitted it yet. Though the look in her eyes had made Kurt wonder . . .

Stop it! The look in her eyes meant nothing. For the first time in his life, he understood how Holly's lover had been caught up in the web. Maybe Kurt had been wrong to blame the guy all this time. He'd certainly been no worse than Kurt . . . and no better.

How was any man expected to keep his head when a woman looked at him that way? He stumbled over an exposed root and common sense came rushing back. Who was he trying to kid? It wasn't Olivia's fault. Kurt had known how things were almost from the beginning, yet he'd continually placed himself in risky situations with her.

He could have avoided her. He could have kept his hands to himself. How could he blame Olivia, even for an instant? She hadn't known how he felt before tonight. She'd trusted him, felt safe with him. Once again, he'd taken a woman's trust and thrown it away. What the hell was wrong with him? Was he *determined* to screw up his life?

His thoughts drove him to the mesa, harder, faster, until his lungs labored for air and the only coherent thought in his head was the need to get the hell out of here. If he stayed, he'd ruin everything for Olivia and for Sam.

Kurt liked Sam, yet he'd tossed *his* trust to the wind along with Olivia's. And he didn't even want to get started on how thoroughly he'd messed up the future.

He couldn't stay here. It was too risky. He was going to do what he *should* have done in the first place. If he could recreate the night he'd been brought through time, maybe he could get back where he belonged. At least in his own time, the only life he'd destroy was his own.

A hot, dry wind stirred the dust beneath him and released the scent of dry earth and sun-baked piñon into the air. What if he couldn't get back home? Could he stay here and watch Sam and Olivia together?

He couldn't bear the thought. Right or wrong, smart or not, he was beginning to care far too much for her. But he still had a shred or two of human decency, and he knew what he had to do.

He slowed and took stock of his surroundings, trying to calculate how far he still had to go. Finding his way by moonlight wasn't easy. The mesa stretched away from him, a seemingly endless plateau of red rock and juniper. But he *knew* this area, damnit—even if it didn't look familiar to him tonight.

He took his bearings again, mentally calculating the distance to the mouth of the draw, counting the number of fingers that cut off from the main part of the canyon. Convinced he'd found the right place, he made himself comfortable and waited.

Though the sun had set long ago, the day's heat still radiated from the ground. The wind began to pick up, bending the junipers and piñons in its path and stirring the drying wild grasses. Overhead, cool air clashed with warm and a slash of bright white lightning cut through the sky. A moment later, a deep rumble shook the earth.

The rising storm matched Kurt's mood, drew him to

his feet again and soon had him pacing the lip of the mesa. Another lightning flash. Another roll of thunder. The sharp smell of ozone pierced the air and dirt swirled in front of his face.

He closed his eyes against the grit, and Olivia's image floated in front of him, smiling, laughing, scowling at him in suspicion, tilting back her head and waiting for his kiss. He forced away the swell of disappointment and told himself not to think about her.

She'd be fine without him. This was as it should be.

He waited, resigned, for the forces that had brought him here to do their job and take him back. But back to what? To an empty, lonely life? To an apartment that still bore the traces of his latest failure? To a job he'd devote endless hours to because he didn't have the courage to be honest with himself or let anyone into his life?

He didn't know how many times he paced from one end of the clearing to the other, how many times he sat on the smooth red rock, how many times he resisted the urge to take cover beneath the trees until the storm finally drove him to it.

The ragged fingers of the wind tore at his clothes. Stinging drops of rain slashed at him and splattered the ground, turning the top level of dust to mud almost immediately. When he couldn't stop thinking about Olivia, he tried to imagine her in Sam's arms, in Sam's bed, and at Sam's side for the rest of her life. A sharp bolt of jealousy shot through him and grew stronger with every minute. He gave *that* idea up at once.

At long last the storm began to wane. He lay there, listening to the hush of leaves and grass, trying to reconcile his feelings with his decision. He must have drifted off to sleep some time later because he awoke with a start to the sun rising over the mesa top. The sound of a bird cawing overhead and the rustle of grouse and game in the brush brought him fully awake.

Within seconds, everything came back. The kiss. The storm. The decision to leave. The bitter disappointment.

He struggled to his feet, knocking caked mud from his shirt and pants, and glanced around quickly. Had he been successful, or had he failed again? It wouldn't take long to find out. He had only to walk a little way and look into the valley. He'd either see Olivia's cabin nestled against the bluff or the modern city of Cortez.

Success or failure? The trouble was, he had no idea which was which.

In the early morning sunlight, Olivia picked her way across the muddy hillside toward the lonely grave where Harvey lay. Last night's kiss had left her sleepless and confused. She'd tossed and turned, listening to the storm lash at the house until the sky began to lighten and the birds began to sing. Finally admitting defeat, she'd crawled out of bed and dressed.

Maybe she should have been sorry about kissing Kurt, but even though she'd been unable to sleep, she hadn't been able to work up much regret. Worry, yes. Guilt, definitely. But regret just wouldn't come.

For the first time since Melody ran off with her traveling man, Olivia could begin to understand why she'd done it. But she was also smart enough to know that a few incredible, mind-numbing seconds weren't enough to base long-term decisions on. If she didn't know it instinctively, she had Melody's experience to help her remember.

Her situation wasn't any less worrisome than Melody's. It might even be more so. Was there any chance that Kurt would stay here? Fate had brought him here to find the ruins, and he would, no matter how difficult she made it for him. And then he'd leave again.

Shivering in the shadow of the mesa, she wrapped her shawl more tightly around her shoulders and cast a furtive glance behind her as she crested the small hill separating the ranch from the makeshift cemetery.

The few mourners who'd attended Harvey's burial had expected her to bury him closer to the house where she could see the hand-hewn cross Sam had made for him. But even in her deepest grief, she'd known that she wouldn't want to see the marker every time she looked out the window or stepped out the door. Having Harvey's grave close to the house and in plain view would have kept her rooted in the moment of his death instead of allowing her to move on.

After her uncle Jonathan's death many years ago, she'd watched her once vital aunt Ellen wallow in mourning and wither in grief. Since then, she'd recoiled against the practice of locking widows away from the world and swathing them in black for years. The death of a loved one was difficult enough to endure without that.

Here, miles from her nearest neighbors, free from the constraints of Southern society, she'd made her own rules. If anyone wanted to gossip about the way she mourned Harvey, at least she didn't have to hear it.

She tugged the shawl closer again and stopped completely. Just ahead, she could see the weathered cross, the straggly wildflowers that she'd planted in the spring. Grass had begun to grow on the softly mounded dirt again, but someone had cut it recently.

Sam, of course. Who else? The realization that he'd been here more recently than she had twisted in her heart. She should be the one who tended Harvey's grave, not Sam. But she hadn't been able to face it more than once or twice.

She looked at the lovingly tended grave and felt another tug at her heart. How could she have forgotten—even for a moment—what a dear, dear man Sam was? How could she have overlooked everything he'd done for her since Harvey's death?

Sam loved her. He wanted to marry her. She could definitely do worse. People like Abner Grimley wouldn't dare try to take advantage of Sam Evans's wife. But did *she* love Sam? She wasn't even sure she knew what love was anymore.

With Sam, she felt peaceful. Like floating on the pond on a calm summer day with one hand trailing in the water. Sam was the sound of crickets on a late summer's evening. The cloudless sky overhead, deep, and blue, and never changing. The smell of homemade bread, the soft drawl of her father's voice as he sipped bourbon on the veranda, the sun on her shoulders.

Kurt was none of those things. He was sneaking away from the nurse with Melody to roll down the hills. He was that breathless rush of emotion, the thrill of doing something forbidden. The sky and grass and trees all blurring together until she couldn't tell one from another. The dizziness that had her and Melody giggling and collapsing into one another's arms afterward.

Sam was trust and understanding and friendship. Kurt was tingling skin and breathlessness and uncertainty. The trouble was, Olivia didn't know which she wanted more.

She wanted both.

She stayed beside Harvey's grave while the sun rose, clearing away weeds, picking off the spent blooms from her pathetic flowers, and running questions through her mind. She discarded the thin shawl almost as soon as she began to work and pushed up her sleeves shortly afterward. The sun climbed higher in the sky and she had the vague impression that she should go back home before Kurt grew worried about her and Sam arrived. But confusion kept her working.

Tendrils of hair escaped the careless bun she'd pulled it into before she left the house. Smudges of dirt gathered on her skirts. Sweat trickled between her breasts and dampened the cloth beneath her arms.

Finally, with a wide swath of weeds cleared and the flowers looking a bit perkier, she wiped her forehead with the back of her arm and sat back on her heels. But satisfaction eluded her. The more she thought about the two men in her life, the more confused she became.

Chapter 12

KURT WALKED QUICKLY, scanning the horizon for some sign of modern Cortez or for smoke rising from Olivia's chimney. He couldn't see either.

He tried to make plans for the future—either future—but a deep sadness filled him and not even thinking about the ruins could shake it. Leaving Olivia had seemed like the only solution last night. Now, in the cold light of morning, it felt like a coward's choice.

There was nothing he could do about it now. If he'd gone home, he'd get on with his life. If he'd stayed in the past, he'd put Olivia out of his mind and focus on the reasons for being here.

He crested the last small hill and sucked in his breath when he saw the ranch lying quietly in the silvery dawn. His heart lurched, his pulse raised, and a buzz raced along his skin.

How could he not have known what he wanted? How could he have imagined he wanted to return to the future? Olivia might belong with Sam, but Kurt would rather stay here and share whatever piece of her he could than return to the future and lose her completely.

He just hoped Sam would win her over quickly and ease his torment a little. Once they were married and Olivia's future was secure, Kurt could begin the task of getting over her. Until then, every day would be torture.

He slowed, watching the ranch lying in stillness for several minutes before he realized how odd it was to see it that way. Olivia always beat the sun up. She had a fire going and breakfast underway long before now. But there were no signs of a fire, no smoke curling from the chimney, no aromas of cooking steak and eggs.

It was so unlike Olivia, he started toward the ranch— slowly at first, then more rapidly with every step. Dirt and pebbles skittered from beneath his feet as he ran. His heart beat against his chest. Had someone come during the night and hurt her? Was she ill or injured?

If so, it was his fault. He'd run away. The instant the going got tough, he'd been on his way. He'd left Olivia alone, and now anything might have happened to her.

He'd gone about halfway down the bluff when he caught sight of her below him, moving toward the ranch house. He was nearly at the bottom of the hill before he could bring himself to a stop. He made so much noise and stirred up so much dust, the horses moved restlessly inside the barn.

But Olivia didn't seem to notice. Wisps of hair drifted around her face. Deep rust blotches stained her skin and dress, and for a moment Kurt worried that they were blood stains. But when he realized that she wasn't limping, that she looked tired but otherwise okay, he breathed a sigh of relief.

He waited until she'd slipped into the house, then carried his things into the barn and left them there. He stayed there long enough for Olivia to start the fire in the stove, then knocked on the front door.

She answered almost immediately but the shadows in

her eyes caught him off-guard. "I'm sorry, Kurt. I haven't started breakfast yet."

"Sorry?" He cut her off quickly, hating the thought of her apologizing to him for anything. "I'm the one who needs to apologize. I went out early this morning and didn't get back until just now."

Did she know that he left last night? She didn't seem to know—or care.

The deep shadows beneath her eyes and streaks of dirt on her cheeks cut him to the quick. "You look as if you've been out yourself."

She nodded vaguely. "Yes, I—" She folded her arms as if she wanted to protect herself and took an almost imperceptible step backward. "I went to Harvey's grave."

The words came so softly he could scarcely hear them. If he'd had any doubts about how she reacted to his kiss, they were gone now. Kurt didn't have to be a rocket scientist to understand the look in her eyes.

"Don't worry about breakfast," he said stupidly. "I'll just grab something—" Where? At the local McDonald's? "I'll find something somewhere."

He turned to leave, but Olivia called him back. "About last night . . ."

That was the last thing he wanted to talk about. He could feel the walls closing in on him as they always did when his emotions were about to come under fire. "There's no need to talk about that," he said. "I'm still sorry. I overstepped my bounds."

"It wasn't entirely your fault. I seem to remember being part of it."

The memory of her fingers in his hair, her arms around him, her lips under his hit him all at once. All the work he'd done overnight shot in one short sentence. "Then you're not angry?"

"Angry? No." A brief smile curved her lips. "But I do agree that it was a mistake."

As it always did when he sensed someone pulling away, cynicism rose to the surface and eclipsed the pain. "Like I said, it won't happen again."

Her brows knit and a scowl replaced the smile. "It's not what you think, Kurt. It isn't you."

It isn't you, it's me. Had that awful brush-off line existed this far back?

Olivia smoothed a wayward lock of hair away from her eyes. "You didn't do anything wrong. I did. I told you I went to Harvey's grave this morning. Well, it had been months since the last time I went to visit it. *Sam* had been there more recently than I had."

She made it damned difficult to resent her. "Everyone grieves differently—" he began.

She shook her head and waved away his words. "That's not what's bothering me. I'm confused, Kurt. I don't know how I feel. Sam has been wonderful to me. He's done so much for me. I *should* love him."

"He's a good man."

"I owe him everything."

Why did those words skewer him? Hadn't he spent the entire night reminding himself that Olivia and Sam belonged together? Hadn't he tried to leap into the future and leave her here alone? "Not *everything*," Kurt said. "Gratitude and friendship ought to be enough." Sam *would* kill him for that.

She sent him a sad smile. "The point is that what happened between us last night has only confused me more. I don't know how I feel about you, or about Sam. I don't know that I should feel anything for either one of you. Harvey hasn't even been gone a year yet, and I'm acting as if I've forgotten he ever existed."

"That's not true—"

Despair filled her dark eyes. Sadness shadowed her face. "I *kissed* you. That's unforgivable."

"You didn't do anything wrong. I kissed you. And even

that—" He took a deep breath and tried to reorder his thoughts. "You may be a widow, but you're still a woman."

She ran a trembling hand across her forehead and lowered it to her neck. "That's no excuse." She drew her shoulders back and looked him square in the eye. "I think we should stop spending so much time together. Sharing meals is only making things harder on both of us. It's . . ." She broke off, obviously having a rough time getting the words out.

Kurt had no intention of helping her.

"It's making us feel as if we belong together when I'm not sure that we do," she said at last. "I think it would be best if I brought your meals to the barn from now on."

Angry and hurt, Kurt could only nod and turn away. He covered the distance to the barn quickly, asking himself over and over why her decision bothered him so much.

Hadn't he reached the same conclusion himself?

He'd never done well with rejection, and this was no exception. But it made him feel like a real jerk to realize that he'd have been perfectly comfortable putting the skids on their relationship, but he hated the fact that *she'd* gotten there first.

Sam stopped just inside the door of Mortensen's Mercantile and bit back a groan of dismay. Behind the crowded counter, Isabella Mortensen filled a bag with lemon drops from one of the glass containers behind her. Her husband, T. J., was nowhere in sight, which made Sam have second thoughts about going inside, considering the lone customer who stood at the counter chatting with Isabella.

With her long, hooked nose and broad forehead, Hesther Parsons couldn't be considered a comely woman by any stretch of the imagination. Her rail-thin body only made her more unattractive. Even so, she'd somehow managed to install herself in a position of social authority in town, and the other women tended to follow wherever she led.

For some reason, Hesther had taken a liking to him. Sam usually didn't mind knowing that she was a little sweet on him. He wasn't about to encourage her, but being on her good side didn't hurt and it cost little enough effort to smile and offer a friendly word.

But he wasn't in the mood to do either this morning. Jesse's frequent talk about leaving the Cinnabar combined with Olivia's odd behavior over the past few weeks had left him increasingly foul-tempered.

He couldn't understand either one of them. Jesse was being a damned stubborn fool. And Olivia . . . He didn't know what to make of her.

She'd started acting strangely a few days after Kurt showed up and still wasn't acting like herself. Sam had no idea why, and neither Olivia nor Kurt seemed interested in talking about it. The only thing that made him feel better was that she didn't seem any warmer to Kurt than she was to him.

On top of his worries about Olivia, he'd had another disagreement with Jesse on the ride into town. Every reasonable argument Sam offered Jesse for staying fell on deaf ears. He'd have had better luck arguing with his saddle than he had with his damned brother. Jesse might pretend to give Sam time, but he'd made up his mind to leave, and nothing Sam could say seemed to make a dent.

It had all left Sam feeling decidedly irritable, anxious, and edgy.

With a smile as thin as she was, Hesther accepted her lemon drops from Isabella and turned toward him. "Why, good morning, Sam."

"Morning, Hesther."

"We haven't seen you in town for a while." She turned

back to include Isabella in the conversation. "How are things out Cinnabar way?"

Sam handed his list to Isabella. "We're doing all right, thanks."

"You must be keeping yourself awfully busy," Isabella said in softly accented English. "Are you still helping Olivia Hamilton?"

Sam nodded, reluctant to discuss Olivia behind her back—especially with Hesther. "Now and then."

Genuine concern filled Isabella's eyes. "Tell me, is she doing all right? I had thought we'd see more of her after Harvey's death. I worry about her out there all alone."

Sam relaxed slightly. Olivia needed all the friends she could get, and he'd always liked Isabella. She was one of the few people in town Hesther Parsons didn't intimidate. "She's fine, far as I know."

Hesther's mouth pursed. "I guess she's still planning to keep the ranch."

"Far as I know."

"Well, I suppose she knows what she's doing. And I suppose now that she has someone else to help her, you'll be able to get back to your own business."

Sam's shoulders stiffened. How did she know about Kurt? So help him, if Jesse had opened his big mouth in front of Hesther Parsons, Sam would take him apart.

"Mind you," Hesther went on primly, "I *still* think she's being selfish."

"Selfish? Olivia?" Sam barely held back a laugh.

Isabella frowned in disapproval. "I think you're being a bit unfair—"

"Indeed?" Somehow, even though the top of Hesther's head only came to the bottom of Sam's chin, she still managed to look down her nose at both of them. "It's Olivia who's being unfair, if you ask me."

"Really?" In spite of his sour mood—or maybe because of it—Sam couldn't wait to hear why. He rested one hip against the counter and folded his arms. "How, exactly?"

"Doesn't she say she wants to stay out there on the Lazy H to remain . . . *independent*?" Hesther gave the lace on her sleeve a twitch and looked to Isabella for support. "It seems to me that she's anything *but* independent. She has Sam here dancing attendance on her and leaving his own ranch to help her. If she were truly independent, she wouldn't want or need Sam's help."

Isabella's gaze darted to Sam's and he could read a silent apology in their depths.

He smiled to show that he didn't blame her for Hesther's narrow mind. "I'm a fairly independent fella," he said, struggling to keep his voice level, "and even I can't run a ranch alone. But, then, I don't guess it's any of your concern what Olivia does, is it?"

Hesther's eyes narrowed and a pink flush crept up her neck onto her cheeks. She pulled a lace handkerchief from her sleeve and waved it languidly in front of her narrow horse-face. "I beg to differ with you. I believe we all have a right to be concerned about the moral standards of those around us."

Sam didn't know where this was going, but he had a bad feeling about it.

Isabella frowned and shook her head almost imperceptibly. "*Really*, Hesther—"

Hesther wasn't about to let Isabella stop her. "I'm most concerned about the impressionable young ladies in Cortez. What *must* they think when they hear that a seemingly respectable widow is suddenly living alone on her ranch with a perfect stranger?"

Sam had been so worried about what Kurt would mean to his chances with Olivia, he hadn't considered what this might do to her reputation. He knew she didn't much care what people in town said about her, but she couldn't ignore this.

From Isabella's reaction he knew this wasn't the first

time Hesther had speculated aloud. A thing like this could destroy Olivia.

He unfolded his arms slowly and fixed Hesther with a deep stare—one he knew could stop someone twice her size in their tracks. "I must have heard you wrong," he said. "You aren't suggesting that there's something inappropriate going on out at the Lazy H."

Hesther met his gaze steadily. "*I'm* not suggesting anything, Sam. I hardly know Olivia. None of us do, more's the pity. But Abner Grimley says—"

"Abner Grimley?" Sam looked to Isabella for an explanation. How did he know anything about the Lazy H?

Isabella looked almost embarrassed. "Abner came in a few days ago and told T. J. that he'd offered to buy that stretch of mesa land from her. Hesther happened to be here at the time."

Sam tried not to let the news bother him, but he hated knowing that Olivia hadn't wanted to discuss Abner's offer with him.

"She turned him down," Hesther said. "Imagine. What possible use could she have for that mesa land? Especially after what happened to her husband up there?"

"What possible use could *Abner* have for it?" Sam demanded. "That land's not good for farming. It's not even good for running cattle. And where did he get the money to buy anything?"

"Maybe he just wants to help her out," Isabella suggested.

Her habit of looking for the best in people annoyed the hell out of Sam right now. "*Abner*? Abner Grimley's never done a nice thing for anybody in his life."

Isabella frowned in confusion. "Well, then, why *would* he want it?"

Sam didn't know, but he had a very bad feeling. He nodded toward his list on the counter. "I'd appreciate it if you could get those things together for me." Meanwhile, he'd find Jesse and tell him to ride back to the Cinnabar alone. Sam wanted to pay a visit to Olivia and find out just what was really going on.

He thought he'd been in a sour mood before, but by comparison he'd been downright cheery.

Olivia watched Sam pace between the table and the door. His expression worried her. She couldn't remember ever seeing him look so grim. "There's talk in town, Livvy," he said at last. "Folks are speculating about what you're doing out here alone with Kurt."

Olivia half-expected Sam to laugh after making the announcement, but his expression remained somber. "But that's silly," she said. "He's my ranch hand. Besides, it's none of their concern."

"Whether it is or isn't, they're talking." He stopped pacing and sent an agonized glance at her. "Hesther Parsons—"

"That old busybody?" Olivia interrupted with a relieved laugh. "Be serious, Sam. Why would you be concerned about anything she says? Why would *anyone* listen to what she says?"

"People *do* listen, Liv. Whether they want to believe it or not, they listen. Can't help it. Once you hear something it's always there. They won't be able to forget it."

"I don't care what they think."

"If you want to do business with the folks in town, you'd better care. If you get a reputation as a loose woman, no woman in town will let her husband buy that horse from you. No woman will want her husband to do any kind of business with you. And the men who do—" He broke off suddenly. Angry as he was, he couldn't make himself say the rest.

"You mean they'd treat me like some fancy woman from the bawdy house?" Olivia laughed bitterly. "Let them. I don't care."

Color flooded Sam's cheeks. "You have to care. You can't stay out here alone with Kurt. People like Hesther Parsons can be dangerous."

"I'm not going to ask Kurt to leave just to make someone I don't even care about happy." Olivia knew only too well how sanctimonious people could be. She'd watched Melody's life be destroyed by that very thing, and she refused to cave in. "How *dare* anyone say anything? They have no idea what's going on out here."

Sam let his breath out in a huff. "Why do you have to be so blamed stubborn?"

"I'm not stubborn. I'm loyal. I'd never let anyone tell me to stop being friends with you, either."

Sam looked as if he'd like to hit something. He took a couple of jerky steps away, then blasted her again. "She's also saying that Abner Grimley made an offer on that mesa land of yours and that you turned it down."

This time, there was no mistaking the hurt in his eyes. He had every right to be hurt. She'd discussed everything with him since Harvey's death and she knew she'd feel the same way if their situations were reversed. "He did," she admitted quietly. "And yes, I refused his offer."

"I see."

A dozen questions filled his eyes, but he didn't ask a single one. For some reason, that made her feel even worse. "It was a good enough offer, I suppose. But it doesn't make any sense. I can only think of one reason why Abner would want that land."

"Is that why you turned him down?"

"Partly." Olivia set aside the lamp she'd been filling and wiped her hands on her apron. "You know I don't want to break up the ranch, but if I was going to sell *any* piece of land, I'd get rid of that one."

"How much did he offer?"

"A dollar an acre."

Sam let out a low whistle and sank into a chair at the table. "That much?"

"That much." Olivia joined him at the table and rested her chin in one hand. "Selling that land would make it possible to keep the rest, but I don't want to sell any of it. And why would someone like Abner Grimley want it, anyway?"

"My question exactly."

"It has to be the legend," Olivia speculated. "I wish I could put an end to it, once and for all."

"You and me both." Sam glanced toward the window. He looked less agitated, but a muscle in his neck still twitched to show his aggravation. "Has Kurt found what he's looking for up there?"

Olivia stiffened. "What makes you think he's looking for anything?"

"He's been up there often enough."

"How do you know that?"

"I've followed him."

"You've *what*?" Olivia sat bolt upright. "Why?"

Uncharacteristic anger flashed in Sam's eyes. "Because I'm *worried* about you."

"So you've been sneaking around to watch me and spy on Kurt? How dare you?"

"It's not like that—"

"No? Well, what *is* it, then? And what else have you done?" She couldn't remember when she'd been so angry or felt so violated. She stood abruptly and for a long moment, the sound of her chair teetering on the floor was the only sound in the room. "You've changed since Kurt came," she said. "I don't like what's happening to you. I feel as if I'm always having to explain myself to you— how I act, what I say—"

"I'm your friend, Olivia. I care about what happens to you."

"A *friend* wouldn't do that to me." Her breath came so

hard and fast, her lungs ached. Her heart thudded with anger and something else. A deep, sinking dread settled in the pit of her stomach. This would change things forever between her and Sam. "A friend wouldn't claim to trust me one minute, and then spy on me the next."

"I was keeping an eye on Kurt," Sam shouted. "Not you."

"Did I *ask* you to keep an eye on him?"

"No, but maybe you should have. You're obviously too besotted with him to see what's going on right under your nose."

Her hands trembled almost uncontrollably and she had trouble getting her breath. "Do you really think I'm so stupid that I don't know what Kurt's doing?"

"Are you telling me you *do* know?"

"Yes." The word came out too loud, too harsh. It echoed off the walls for a few seconds while Sam's face went through a series of changes. Guilt warred with her outrage, but outrage won easily.

"Then he's gone up to the mesa with your permission?"

"Yes." The lie nearly stuck in her throat, but she forced it out. Sam *had* to realize that he couldn't keep acting as if she and the Lazy H belonged to him.

Sam's eyes traveled across her face for what felt like forever. She begged him silently not to say anything that would make it worse. His jaw clenched. His fist tightened at his side. And then, without another word, he turned away and let himself out into the afternoon.

The sound of the door closing behind him tore through her like a bullet. She sank into her rocking chair and buried her face in her hands. Her chest ached with unshed tears, but she couldn't cry.

She didn't want to lose Sam, but she had to draw the line. Maybe she'd been wrong to accept his help all this time. Maybe by doing so, she'd inadvertently given him the wrong impression about his position in her life and on the Lazy H.

She loved Sam. He would always have a special place in her heart. But if he didn't understand even the most basic things about her, how could she possibly consider spending the rest of her life with him?

Chapter 13

KURT HAD SPENT the past two weeks waiting for Olivia to return to normal. She'd kept herself virtually locked away inside that tiny little house, emerging only to work in her garden, do her laundry, or carry his meals to the barn. She spoke only to give him instructions or say a quick hello to Sam.

Kurt had tried to forget about finding the Black Mesa ruins. He'd worked hard to put the kiss they'd shared out of his mind. He hadn't been successful on either front. The ruins seemed to call out to him every time he looked up at the mesa.

And when he was successful at forgetting the kiss—which wasn't as often as he'd have liked—the memory would come rushing back at the oddest moments. It didn't matter what he was doing when the memory returned. Even mucking out the stables wouldn't stop his body from reacting as if Olivia were nestled in his arms again.

He was just lucky Sam had decided to follow his advice and make himself scarce. If Sam had been around as often as he'd been a few weeks ago, he'd certainly have noticed how withdrawn Olivia had really become. And he'd have demanded an explanation instead of just hinting around for one.

Sooner or later, Kurt knew he'd have to explain—unless Olivia snapped out of her self-imposed exile first. He hoped she would. He didn't even want to think about how Sam would react if he found out what Kurt had done.

Keeping the kiss secret was putting a strain on his fledgling friendship with Sam. When Sam did show up, he talked about Olivia like a kid with his first crush. The more Sam talked, the less Kurt wanted to hear.

He wasn't the kind of guy who could share a kiss like that with a woman and then pretend that nothing had happened. But if just hearing Sam talk about her bothered him so much, how in the hell could he live anywhere nearby and watch them be married?

He'd heard the term "cruel fate" before, but it had never seemed so appropriate. He was between a rock and a hard place—stuck here in the past, with nowhere else to go and no way to get there.

The day his luck ran out, he saw Sam arrive mid-morning, tether his horse, and start up the stairs toward the house. Hoping to head off trouble, Kurt set aside the saddle he'd been rubbing with oil and left the shade of the barn. Olivia opened the door before Kurt could call out to him, and let Sam inside before he could come up with a reason for interrupting.

He went back to work on the saddle and waited, alternately convinced everything would be all right and afraid he'd ruined everything for Olivia and Sam.

It didn't take long for Sam to come back outside again and make a beeline for the barn. He stopped in front of Kurt, eyes narrowed, face puckered in consternation. "You want to tell me what the hell's going on around here?"

Kurt's hand stilled and a lead weight settled in his stomach. "What do you mean?"

Sam swept a hand toward the house. "I just came from talking to Olivia. Or maybe *talking* is the wrong word."

"Oh?" Kurt began working the rag again . . . slowly, to buy time. Sam looked angry enough to shoot him. But Kurt had created the mess. The least he could do was be a man about it. He set the rag aside and stood to face the consequences. "It's not what you think."

Sam's frown deepened. "All right then, what is it? What *are* you doing up on Black Mesa?"

"*Black Mesa*?" Then Olivia hadn't told him about the kiss. Kurt held back a relieved laugh. "What did Olivia tell you?"

"I'm asking you."

"Right." Kurt thought quickly, trying to decide whether to tell Sam the truth and risk making him angrier, or come up with some other, more believable story. One more glance at Sam's eyes helped him make up his mind. Sam deserved *some* piece of the truth.

"So?" The word snapped out of Sam's mouth, angry, impatient.

Kurt took a deep breath and let it out again. Telling Sam about the time travel shouldn't be any harder than telling Olivia. Sam might look deadly, but *he'd* never actually pulled a gun on him. "Come into the barn with me," he said. "I can explain the whole thing a lot better with a few visual aids."

It took nearly an hour to get the whole story out with all of Sam's interruptions. Sam studied the coins thoroughly, went through Kurt's wallet with a fine-tooth comb, and spent a long time flipping through the pictures of the ruins. By the time they'd finished, Sam's hat had worked its way so far back on his head, it was a wonder it hadn't fallen completely off.

To Kurt's surprise, Sam seemed not only able to believe

him, but almost eager to do so. He handed back the pictures and let out a low whistle. "Does Olivia know?"

"She does. I asked her not to say anything to anyone—including you. Not exactly fair, considering how close the two of you are."

Sam made a face. "Not anymore. I think I've lost her."

That familiar traitorous leap of hope tickled Kurt's belly. He ignored it. He'd slipped once, but he wouldn't slip again. As long as Olivia was confused, she was off-limits. As long as he was in limbo between past and future, he wouldn't take the chance of hurting her.

"You have to remember, she's recently widowed," he told Sam. "That may make her react to things differently than other women. Just be patient with her. Give her some time."

"She doesn't *have* time. Her mortgage is due in a few days. And people in town are starting to talk about the two of you living out here alone together." Sam let out a hefty sigh. "I'm not sure this hard-to-get thing is working like you said it would. Things are worse, not better."

Kurt didn't know why it wasn't working for Sam. The more Olivia avoided him, the more he wanted to be near her.

Sam pulled off his hat and twisted it round in his hands. "Well?"

"Well, what?" Kurt made himself more comfortable. "Are you asking me for more advice?" Bright move. Ask the guy who's never kept a woman happy. Ask the guy who's chomping at the bit for a chance with the woman you want.

Sam crooked an eyebrow at him. "Advice? No. I've had enough of that. But it seems to me that Livvy talks to you a whole lot more than she talks to me. I was thinkin' that maybe you could put in a good word for me. Maybe try to get her to see that marrying me is her only way to save the ranch."

Kurt laughed abruptly. At Sam's narrowed eyes, he sobered quickly. "I would, but I don't think that would do you a whole lot of good right now."

"Why not?"

He nodded toward the house. "You just talked to her. I wouldn't say she's exactly receptive . . . would you?"

Sam rested his hat on his knee and raked his fingers through his hair. "Stubborn woman." He pulled his hand away and fixed Kurt with a look. "What happened between the two of you, anyway?"

Kurt's heart skipped a beat. He turned his attention back to the saddle. "What makes you think anything happened?"

"Something must have." Sam stood slowly. Did he practice looking menacing, or did it just come naturally? "She only changed after you came around."

Kurt indulged in another silent argument over the wisdom of coming clean with Sam, but it only lasted for about three seconds. One to wonder, one to look at Sam towering over him, and one for his brain to scream, *hell no!*

But he'd listened to his instincts for too long, and where had they gotten him? How could he claim Sam as a friend if he didn't respect him enough to be honest? How could he call himself a man if he wouldn't take the heat for his actions?

"It's not her fault," he said slowly. "I've tried like hell not to fall in love with her, but it's pretty damned hard not to."

Sam's expression grew even more ominous. "I see." He paced about ten paces away. "Does she love you?"

"No. I think she's confused about what she feels."

"Do you want her?"

"Even if I did, I'd be a jerk to try. I'm not in the habit of stealing another man's woman. Besides, I can't promise that I'll be here in five minutes, much less tomorrow or next week."

Sam took so long considering that, Kurt's palms began to itch. He kept his eye on the Colt in Sam's holster.

"So," Sam said at last. "What are we going to do?"

Kurt expelled his breath slowly. "Give her time. Do what we can to help, but don't pressure her."

"Her mortgage is due in ten days," Sam reminded him.

"Yeah. But do you really want her to marry you just to keep her ranch? Seems to me, you'd always wonder if she really loved you or not. Believe me, that can make for a miserable life."

Sam turned a glance on him so full of agony, Kurt felt sorry for the big guy.

"When the time is right, I'll put in a good word for you. The best thing *you* can do is to help her find the independence she's looking for. Lighten up a little. Concentrate on finding someone who might be willing to make her a loan or pay her what her horse is worth."

Sam nodded slowly. "Guess maybe you're right at that."

For once, Kurt suspected he might be. Funny. It had taken him a hundred years or so to learn that the way to a woman's heart wasn't so different after all. It just took honesty, truth, integrity, and respect.

And now that he knew, he'd just handed another man the key.

It didn't matter that Sam was the better man. It didn't matter that Olivia would be happier with Sam than she could ever be with Kurt.

Logic did nothing to soften the ache in his heart.

Olivia kept one eye on the road as she hauled a basket full of dirty clothes into the yard. She listened for the sound of Sam's horse as she settled the scrub board into the washtub and took the wrapper from her bar of soap.

She hadn't seen Sam since he'd ridden away, hurt, three days before, and she was nervous about seeing him again. But she wouldn't let herself even think that he might not come.

Sam always came.

And if he didn't?

She shoved the question away and plunged her favorite dress into the water. She worked the bar of soap across its folds and scrubbed, putting her frustration and confusion into her hands.

Avoiding Kurt hadn't been easy. Worse, it didn't help. She was more confused now than she'd ever been. She'd thought staying out of his way, avoiding anything but the briefest of conversations, and making sure they were never together for long might help her put him out of her mind. Instead, she thought about him more with every passing day.

His smile, his laugh, his kindness would flood her mind without invitation. Remembering the feel of his shoulders beneath her fingers weakened her knees without warning. Knowing that he could disappear at any moment ate at her constantly. If not for that, maybe she would have let herself acknowledge the feelings she worked so hard to keep buried.

She carried a dripping dress to the line Harvey had put up for her behind the house, and pegged the heavy cotton to it. As she started back toward the washtub, the sound of an approaching horse caught her attention.

Sam!

Breathing a silent prayer that they wouldn't argue, she hurried to the front yard. But instead of Sam, she found Sloan Durrant giving the ranch and house a once-over.

Olivia wiped her hands on the skirt of her worn house dress and crossed the yard toward him.

Sloan put on a wide, friendly smile when he saw her. "Morning, Olivia. Did I catch you at a bad time?"

"Just doing the wash." She propped her hands on her hips and squinted up at him. He'd positioned himself so that the morning sun hit her full in the face. "What are you doing all the way out here?"

Sloan dismounted and came to stand in front of her, still holding the reins of his horse. His blond hair caught the morning sun and reflected it, but his smile didn't make it all the way to his eyes. "I was out this way on business and thought I'd stop by to see how things are going. Any luck on selling that black yet?"

The shrewdness in his eyes caught her by surprise and made her faintly uneasy. It was almost as if he knew she hadn't had any luck selling Nightmare. Almost as if he didn't want her to be successful. "Not yet," she admitted reluctantly. "But there are still a few days until the mortgage is due."

Sloan laughed easily. "Relax, Olivia. I'm not here to take the ranch from you. Just being neighborly, that's all." He let his gaze travel across the yard again. "I can't help but think about you being out here on your own like this and wish there were something I could do to help."

Olivia hoped she was only imagining the predatory gleam in his eye. But her future was so firmly under his control, she didn't dare show her distaste. If she angered him, he could call in the mortgage payment this minute. And then what would she do?

Forcing a smile that would have made her mother proud, she shook her head and dripped Southern sugar into her voice. "What a kind offer, but I think we'll be all right."

Durrant moved closer. "You'd make things so much easier on everyone if you'd just admit that running this place on your own is too much."

She casually backed away. "We've been over this before, Mr. Durrant—"

"Yes, but I keep hoping that you'll see reason." His

voice had become silky and far too smooth.

Olivia's temper began to simmer, but she did her best not to show it. "Maybe it will interest you to know that I have a full-time ranch hand now."

One of Sloan's eyebrows winged toward his hat. "Is that right? Do you mind if I ask who?"

"It's no one you know."

The eyebrow inched even higher. "A drifter?"

"I wouldn't say that." Olivia worked her fingers into the folds of her skirt.

"Well, what would you say?" Durrant's smile was as slick as his voice. "Much as I like you, Olivia, I'm still a businessman. I have to be realistic."

A chill ran up her spine, but Olivia refused to let him see that he'd had any effect on her. "If you want to be realistic, quit discounting me simply because I'm a woman."

"I'm not discounting you." That predatory gleam reappeared in his eye and this time Olivia realized it wasn't directed at the ranch. "I have endless admiration for your courage and your abilities. But it's not enough just to want to keep the Lazy H afloat." He moved so close she backed against the fence trying to get away.

She had nowhere to go, so she summoned all her courage and looked him straight in the eye. "Your bank's investment is sound." *And you don't have a personal one, you piece of slime.*

"I hope so," he said with a smirk. "But you can't blame me for wanting to keep an eye on it . . . can you?" Just when she thought she might have to destroy all her chances by slapping him, Sloan backed away and the menace faded. "I thought I might ride up onto the mesa and take a look around."

The mesa again. Olivia flicked a glance at it rising up to meet the morning. It looked almost beautiful, but she couldn't forget. She would *never* forget. It must hold powerful secrets to make normally rational men behave like fools. "Why would you want to do that?" she asked innocently. "There's nothing up there."

"If I have to foreclose, that land will be mine. I'm just interested in seeing what's up there, that's all."

She believed that like she believed in fairy godmothers. And if Kurt's ruins *were* up there, she didn't want someone else finding them first. "I'd rather you didn't."

"Really?" Sloan's eyes chilled. "And why is that?"

"It's still my property, Mr. Durrant." For another seven days, anyway.

"Yours and the bank's. Don't forget that." He turned an almost hostile glare on her. "You're hanging on so tightly, I'm beginning to wonder if you know something I don't."

Somehow, Olivia managed a nonchalant smile. "The only thing I know is that Harvey wanted me to keep the ranch—even that worthless piece of mesa land."

Sloan studied her for a minute more. "Yes, but as I told you before, Harvey wasn't the best judge."

"Perhaps not, but he was my husband, and I really must honor his wishes."

Sloan took her arm and led her back across the yard to his horse. She forced herself not to jerk her arm away. "I do hope you'll listen to reason soon, Olivia. Before it's too late. You'd be smart to remember that. I don't need your permission to make an inspection of any piece of this ranch any time I choose."

There was no mistaking the threat in his words, no mistaking the anger and even hatred gleaming in his eyes. Olivia couldn't think of a retort, but she forced herself not to look away until Sloan rode away, leaving her choking on dust.

How was he going to approach Olivia? Kurt asked himself for at least the hundredth time in three days. How could he casually swing the conversation—assuming he could even *start* one—around to Sam? How could he tell her to marry someone else?

He couldn't.

He'd agonized since his conversation with Sam and argued every logical reason, but he still couldn't get around one simple fact: he was falling in love with her. He couldn't send her into another man's arms.

But he had to.

He was in one hell of a place, and he had no one to blame for it but himself. This was one time he couldn't avoid a tough situation. He'd created this mess. He had to fix it, for Olivia's sake. If he loved her, he had to do what was best for her. And *he* was definitely *not* best for her.

He'd finally found the woman he'd consider spending the rest of his life with, and he couldn't tell her. Charlotte would laugh herself sick.

He climbed the steps slowly and paused in front of the door. His heart began to hammer and his hands grew clammy as he knocked. She didn't answer for several agonizing minutes and he was half-convinced she didn't plan to.

And then, suddenly, she was there, so lovely he thought his heart would crack into a million pieces. It was the closest he'd been to her since that kiss. The first time he'd been able to look into those intriguing brown eyes or smell the faint flowery scent of her hair.

Her lips moved and his name danced through the air between them, a half-whisper that nearly made him lose his resolve. "Kurt? Are you all right? Is something wrong?"

"I'm fine," he lied. "I just need to talk with you for a few minutes."

He expected her to at least hesitate, maybe even send him away. But she threw open the door and stepped aside to let him enter. "I'm glad you came. I was going to talk to you when I brought your supper."

Kurt's step faltered. "You were? Why?"

"I need your help."

"*My* help? With what?"

"I want you to show me the ruins."

The abrupt about-face left Kurt almost speechless. "You want me to take you to see the ruins? Why?"

Olivia gripped the back of a chair so hard her knuckles turned white. "I told you in town that Sloan Durrant had offered to buy the ranch. Well, I've had another offer for it, as well."

"From who?"

"A man named Abner Grimley. He says he's doing me a favor, but if you knew Abner, you'd know it isn't true."

Kurt racked his brain, but he couldn't remember the name. But, of course, he'd only really paid attention to those who'd been instrumental in preserving the cliff dwellings. "Does he know about the ruins?"

Olivia's grip on the chair relaxed. "I don't think so. I think he believes the legend, just like Harvey did. But there's more. Sloan Durrant came out here today while you were in the back pasture. He said he was going up onto the mesa to look around." She let go of the chair and ran her hands up her arms. "I've been selfish, Kurt. If the ruins are up there, you deserve to find them."

Kurt wanted to whoop for joy, gather her into his arms, and dance her around the small room. He wanted to smother her in grateful kisses. He settled for a quiet "I'm glad" instead. "If we can find the ruins before anyone else does, we can preserve them—"

"Preserving the ruins may solve your problem, but it won't solve mine. I need cash. Quickly."

Kurt's euphoria vanished. "What are you saying?"

She waved a newspaper in front of him. "Sam brought this from town the other day. I didn't even look at it until after Sloan left. But it says that a museum in Denver paid the Wetherills three thousand dollars for some of their artifacts. *Three thousand*, Kurt. Do you know what I could do with that much money? I could pay off Harvey's mortgage completely and even buy some cattle or horses so I'd have an income."

Kurt dropped into a chair while her words ricocheted around inside his head. "You can't sell them, Olivia."

"Why not? I can't seem to find anyone willing to pay what Harvey's horse is worth. Without money, I can't pay my mortgage. I'm trying to be practical. I need money, and you say I have something worth a fortune on my land."

"But those artifacts belong to the world. They should be preserved here, not shipped off to some museum."

"I can't worry about the world," she said softly. "I'm trying to survive."

The look on her face nearly tore him in two. If he cared anything about her, how could he ask her to let her home be taken away, even for the sake of history? But how could he abandon his ideals, his beliefs, for the sake of one person?

"Will you help me look?"

He hesitated, but only for a heartbeat. His ideals meant nothing if he was going to hurt the woman he loved for their sake. "Of course. We'll saddle up and head out first thing in the morning."

She let out a sigh so soft it brought a lump to his throat. "Thank you. Would you—would you like to stay for supper?"

The invitation stunned and pleased him at the same time. But he couldn't help asking, "Do you think that's wise?"

She stepped away from the table and moved toward the stove. "It's only supper, Kurt, and we're the only two people for miles around. I don't see any reason why we can't share meals and a little conversation."

"No reason at all. I won't even bother trying to pretend that I'll miss sharing my cornbread with Nightmare. He's a terrible mooch."

Olivia laughed softly. "He is, isn't he?" She sobered again and averted her gaze. "You're welcome to come in for meals again . . . as long as there are no misunderstandings. The . . . the other . . . thing . . . can't happen again."

Kurt bit back a laugh at the way she referred to their kiss. Good thing he wasn't easily offended. "I promise to behave myself." Though if she looked up at him like *that* very often it would be pretty damned tough.

A quick blush painted her cheeks and disappeared into her hair. "Yes. Well. As long as we understand that." She clasped her hands in front of her. "And I'd rather not discuss it again after this. I think it would be best to just pretend as if it never happened."

Fat chance of that happening. But she didn't need to know *every* thought that ran through his head. "It's forgotten."

A faint, satisfied smile curved her lips as she turned back toward the stove. "Good. Thank you."

Kurt started toward the door, anxious to earn his keep and to make sure she didn't change her mind. "Looks like you're running low on wood. I'll bring some in while you finish up."

Feeling damned good, he brought in enough to last her for several days. It wasn't until much later as he whistled his way across the yard toward his lonely bed in the barn that he realized he'd completely forgotten the reason he'd gone to talk to her in the first place.

Sunlight streaked across the mesa as Kurt and Olivia set off the next morning, leaving everything in their path burnished with a misty golden hue. The woodsy scents of sage and juniper filled the air.

Last night, Olivia had been convinced she could face Black Mesa again. This morning she wasn't so sure. Her decision to come with Kurt had been rash and impulsive, and she'd seriously considered backing out when he showed up on her porch in the gray half-light of dawn. Only the determination to keep Sloan Durrant from finding the cliff dwellings first kept her in the saddle.

They rode slowly, letting the horses find their own way up the slope. Autumn wasn't far away. Olivia could feel it in the air and smell it on the breeze. And Kurt's high spirits helped keep her from getting maudlin over the rapidly approaching mortgage payment.

He talked as they rode, pointing out things that would be different in the years to come, and his love for the land seemed to radiate from every pore. Olivia loved the land, too, she reminded herself. Just not this part of it.

This part had robbed her of everything—of her husband, her future, and her security. But if Kurt was right about the ruins, maybe it would actually restore some of those things to her. At the very least, she hoped to get back her peace of mind.

Kurt glanced at her frequently, his gaze warm and caring, and the familiar tingles spread through her, chasing away some of the chill of fear as they grew closer to the mesa top. He reined in on the crest of the mesa, frighteningly close to the spot where Harvey had fallen to his death. Shifting in his saddle, Kurt waited for her to draw alongside of him.

Why had he chosen to stop here? Keeping her eyes carefully averted away from the ledge, she drew up beside him.

"By my calculations," he said, "the Medicine Bowl ought to be somewhere below us, and Sandstone Castle half a mile further on."

"Here?" Olivia sucked in a deep breath and glanced around stiffly. The coincidence made her skin clammy.

She had the horrible feeling that if she glanced down into the canyon, she'd see Harvey's broken body lying there.

Lifting her chin, she forced her gaze away from the canyon. "It can't be. I know for a fact there are no ruins here."

"How do you know?"

"This is my property, remember?" Her horse shied away from the ledge and she had to battle for a moment to bring it under control again. Obviously, the animal sensed her rising anxiety. One more reason to put the fear to rest. "This is where Harvey died. Sam has been up and down this piece of the canyon. If there was a hidden village here, he'd have seen it."

Kurt's gaze shot to hers. "Harvey died here? Are you sure?"

"It's not the kind of thing I'm likely to be confused about."

"I suppose not." Kurt ran a hand along the back of his neck. "Are you sure he didn't find the ruins in all the time he spent here?"

"If he had, he would have told me about them." She knew that as surely as she knew her name. Harvey had been so enamored with the legend, he'd talked endlessly about his experiences on the mesa. Of course, she'd grown so tired of listening after a while, she might not have heard *every* word.

Kurt dismounted and looped the reins over a limb. He paced to the lip of the mesa and looked into the crevice far below.

A shiver tore through Olivia. "Please don't get so close to the edge."

Kurt didn't seem to hear her. "I could walk right to the Medicine Bowl if I could just get down there. I could take you to Coyote House and Sandstone Palace in less than an hour."

The thought of Kurt going over that sheer cliff brought on another shudder. "How? You'll fall."

"We'll use ropes. It'll be perfectly safe. We'll tie one end around my waist and let you and Nightmare control the rate of descent."

She couldn't let him follow Harvey over that cliff. She'd never sleep again if anything happened to him. "Can't you get down there another way? A way that's not so dangerous?"

Kurt turned back, poised to argue, but her terror must have been obvious. "There are a dozen ways into the main canyon, but they're all miles away."

"We have all day. We could ride in through Inca Canyon. It's fairly close and not nearly so steep. Harvey used to take horses down there all the time."

Kurt gave that some thought. "How long would it take to get back here?"

"An hour. Maybe two." She prayed silently, willing him to agree.

He hesitated, glanced toward Inca Canyon with a scowl on his face, then smiled up at her. "All right. We'll go in through Inca."

She could have kissed him. She *wanted* to kiss him, and not just because he'd agreed. "And you'll stay with me? You won't leave me alone?" She hated sounding so weak and needy, but she hated these canyons more. She had a resounding fear of riding through the canyons lost and alone.

Kurt's dimples dipped into his cheeks. "Of course. You'll be safe with me. I promise. But are you sure you want to do this? You're white as a sheet. I could get Sam to come with me instead."

She shook her head firmly. "I'm tired of being afraid of this place. How can I ask anyone to take me seriously as a rancher if I can't even ride my own land?"

Kurt laughed softly. "You're really something, Olivia Hamilton. So, are you ready?"

"As ready as I'll ever be."

She spurred Nightmare, determined to get moving before she lost her nerve. After all, what other choice did she have? She could sit around like a scared chicken and wait for someone to take her home away, or she could buck up, look fear in the face, and spit in its eye.

She'd take the second option, thank you, but she couldn't deny that it would be much easier with Kurt by her side than if she'd been alone.

Chapter 14

OLIVIA TOOK OFF in a spurt of gravel and dirt before Kurt could stop her. He remounted quickly, determined not to let her get too far ahead on the treacherous slopes. She sure didn't act like a woman who'd been quaking in her boots only a few minutes before. But Kurt knew how fear could drive a smart person to do stupid things.

He shouted after her to slow down, but either she didn't hear him or she chose to ignore him. Gritting his teeth, he spurred his horse to follow.

Damned woman.

If he'd known bringing her here would make her act like this, he never would have done it. But how could he have known this was where Harvey died?

The coincidence left him uneasy.

Was it coincidence? He didn't even want to voice the thought that lay in his stomach like curdled milk—that Harvey's death may not have been an accident, after all.

Olivia had been through enough lately. Unless or until he had proof to back up his suspicions, he intended to keep his mouth shut around her. It might be nothing.

After a wild chase, Olivia slowed a little and Kurt was able to catch up with her, but the questions stirred through his mind like the dust that swirled in front of him on the hillside. A gnawing uneasiness began as a flutter in his stomach and grew with every mile they put behind them.

Had someone killed Harvey over the treasure of Black Mesa? And if so, who?

Hot and tired, Olivia trailed behind Kurt on foot through the dense growth along the canyon's floor. A mile or so back, he'd stopped suddenly and told her they'd have to go the rest of the way on foot. While she panted and gasped for breath, he seemed to grow stronger by the minute.

Just when she thought she'd have to call out for him to slow down, he turned to check on her and came back on his own. Of course, *he* didn't have six yards of cotton dragging at his heels.

"Am I going too fast?"

"A little. If I ever come back here, I'm wearing trousers."

"Good idea." Kurt handed her his canteen and found a fallen log for them to sit on. "Women wear pants all the time in the future."

"Like the ones in your picture?" Just thinking about how much those clothes had exposed made her blush.

"Sometimes."

"Imagine." She settled on the log beside him. "What else is different in your time?"

"Well, for one thing, a woman wanting to live on her own and run her own ranch wouldn't be a big deal."

Olivia sighed wistfully. "It wouldn't?"

"Not to most people. Most of us have moved past the idea that women need men to take care of them."

It sounded like absolute heaven to Olivia. "Are you one of them?"

He grinned at her, but it looked forced and brittle. "My aunt Dorothy would've boxed my ears if I'd ever *thought* of treating a woman as if she couldn't take care of herself. She never married. Never had any desire to. And nobody would have ever dared say she couldn't take care of herself."

Olivia treasured this rare glimpse into his life. "What about your mother?"

His grin evaporated. "She died when I was ten. My dad had already run out on the family, so Mom's aunt Dorothy took me in and raised me."

"Just you? Didn't you have any brothers or sisters?"

"Just me." Kurt's smile returned, but there was a shadow in his eyes. "What about you? Brothers and sisters?"

"One sister. Melody. I haven't seen her in five years."

"And you miss her?"

"Terribly. She and I used to be so close."

"Used to?"

"She's still in Virginia." She took another sip of water and looked at the canyon wall that seemed so serene from this angle. "We haven't been really close since she had her baby."

"Do you hear from her often?"

"Hardly ever."

"What about your folks?"

"They're still alive. Mother writes occasionally to complain about Melody."

"Then she and her husband live close to them?"

"She's not married," Olivia said quietly. "That was part of the problem. She withdrew from everything, including me." To her surprise, it was easy to tell Kurt about Melody—even the part she usually didn't talk about.

Kurt didn't look even slightly surprised or shocked by

Melody's story. He said only, "If she's so miserable in Virginia, why don't you invite her out here to stay with you?" as if it were the most natural thing in the world.

"I don't think she'd come."

"Have you asked her?"

"No. I just assumed—"

Kurt sent her a playful scowl. "*You*, who's had plenty to say about other people making assumptions for you, *you're* going to do the same thing to your sister? Shame on you."

Olivia's face flamed. "I didn't realize that's what I was doing."

Kurt laughed softly. "Don't feel bad. Most of us don't realize what we're doing until someone else rudely points it out." He held out a hand to help her up. "Shall we? Watch your step. It's steep going from here on."

Olivia spent the next few minutes too breathless to speak. But as soon as they reached another level patch of land, she raised the subject again. That tiny peek into Kurt's world had left her wanting to know more. "Did you really grow up in California?"

"I really did."

"What is it like?"

"Now?" He took a moment to catch his breath. "It's still wide open and beautiful, but in the future it's crowded. There are people everywhere, the air's polluted, and you can hardly see the city for the freeways. That's why I left."

"And came here?"

He nodded briefly. "Why did you leave Virginia?"

She opened her mouth to answer, then caught herself and sent him a quick scowl. "Do you always do that?"

"Do what?"

"Change the subject whenever the conversation is about you."

Kurt shrugged the question away. "We'd better get

moving again. We don't want to come back this way in the dark."

"There! You did it again."

He gave her a slow up-and-down so intense it made the heat creep into her face. "I don't like talking about my past."

"Why not?"

"I don't know. I just don't."

"Is it painful?"

"Parts of it." He looked as if he intended to walk away, then thought better of it. "Yes, parts of it are hard to think about. But I guess everyone has times in their life like that, don't they?"

"I think so. I've told you all about Harvey, and you've never even told me about your wife. Now you know all about Melody, but I still don't know much about you."

He shifted his pack roughly. "You want to know about Holly?"

Olivia nodded.

"I came home from work one afternoon and found her in bed with my best friend."

Olivia could only imagine the heartache she'd have felt in his place. The pain was still evident in his eyes. "But why?"

"Her excuse was that I didn't excite her anymore. That my work with the Anasazi ruins had made me boring. The truth is—" He broke off and turned away. "I don't know what the truth is. Maybe that's why Charlotte accused me of being obsessed with it after all this time. I've never understood what I did wrong."

Olivia touched his arm tentatively and the familiar warm tingles started in her fingertips and spread up her arm. "What *you* did wrong? *She's* the one who violated your marriage vows."

"Because she stopped loving me."

"But why is that *your* mistake? Why does that mean there's something wrong with you?"

He flicked a glance at her, but he didn't speak.

"Obviously, I don't know much about life where you come from," she said, "but I don't understand why you blame yourself for what she did. Any woman would be crazy not to love you." The instant the words slipped out, she wished she could take them back.

Kurt registered them and his eyes darkened. His expression changed and his gaze searched her face as if he expected to find something there. He hadn't even touched her, but everything inside Olivia suddenly seemed alive and on fire. Just being this near him made her tremble. He seemed huge as he stood over her, huge and very much alive, and so close she could feel his breath on her cheek.

He was going to kiss her again. She knew he was. But did she want him to?

In this moment, she'd never wanted anything so much. She wanted to feel his arms around her, his lips on hers. She wanted to hear her name on his sigh.

"What about Sam?"

The question jolted her back to earth in a hurry. "He's my *friend*."

"He's in love with you, and you know it." His glance swept over her quickly, as if he couldn't bear to look at her—or didn't want her to see too much. "If you aren't in love with him, why do you keep him hanging around?"

"I'm also keeping you around," she reminded him. "Does that mean you think I'm in love with you?"

"Of course not."

"Well, then, help me, please. Because I don't understand your logic."

"Sam is in love with you."

And you're not. The implication was perfectly clear. "I don't know why we're discussing this," she said, pushing past him and starting along the trail. "Aren't we supposed to be looking for your ruins?"

She walked quickly, though she had no idea where she was going. She wasn't about to stand around and let him make her feel small and foolish. The fleeting thought that he wasn't to blame darted through her mind. She was the one who'd let dreams get the best of her, who'd let imagination carry her away, and who'd let foolish expectations master her.

She'd only gone a few steps when he grabbed her arm from behind and pulled her around to face him. "Are you in love with Sam?"

She tried in vain to pull away. She didn't want him to see into her eyes, to glimpse the pain and embarrassment she was trying to hide. "What business is it of yours?"

He refused to let her go, taking her chin gently in his other hand and tilting her face until she had no choice but to look at him. Their eyes locked. Her lungs released all the air they held and refused to take in more. Her skin burned where his fingers touched. The look in his eyes started a second fire inside her.

"Maybe it isn't any of my business." His voice came softly, tenderly, like the brush of a lover's fingers against her cheek. "I probably shouldn't even care."

Gentle hope fluttered in Olivia's heart. "But you do?"

"God help me, yes."

The hope turned to a steady beat, a drumming that pulsed through her. "I'm glad."

His gaze moved from her eyes to her mouth. He swallowed convulsively, then lowered his head and touched her lips with an urgency that took her breath away. Her hands and arms went numb as the sensation centered low in her abdomen. Only her heart, thudding like Nightmare on a dead run, seemed to have any power left. His lips were like silk, only better. They were warm and filled with the taste of him.

His breath mingled with hers, his fingers slid into her hair and the leather thong she'd used to tie it back fell away. Warm honey flowed through her veins, and her knees buckled as if she'd been imbibing the aged bourbon her father favored. Even as that thought crossed her mind, Kurt's tongue erased it with the merest flick across her lips.

Someone moaned. Him? Her? Someone sighed. When his hands left her hair, caressed her shoulders, and traveled to her waist, she groaned aloud and tilted back her head. He buried his lips in her neck and the sensation in her abdomen grew more insistent.

She couldn't separate need from want, desire from necessity. She only knew that she didn't want the moment to end.

"Olivia." His lips formed her name against the soft skin of her neck and flame shot through her. She caressed his arms, his shoulders, his face. She couldn't seem to get enough. His hands moved again, this time to her hips and on to her bottom. He pulled her tightly against him, and the groan that escaped his lips sounded like pain . . . or pleasure. Or both.

Olivia melted into him. A traitorous voice inside her head warned her to stop. It whispered of Melody and the misery she'd suffered because of a moment like this. It murmured of shame and embarrassment, of ruination and reputation.

Closing her mind to the warnings, Olivia surrendered to sensation. It had been so long . . . so very long . . . and never like this. Kurt's hands, his chest, his lips, his lean, hard body were all that existed in the world. Her own answering fire seemed to come from somewhere inside herself that she'd never known about before this moment. This was the feeling she couldn't force herself to feel for Sam.

Sam . . .

Incredibly, she heard her voice whisper, "Stop. Please."

His hands slowed, then stopped completely, and his eyes gradually regained focus. "What is it?"

"I . . ." Her voice wavered, cracked. The newfound wanton inside begged her not to say it, but she had to. She couldn't afford to take such a risk with her heart. "I love you, but I can't do this. Not until I tell Sam. It's not fair to him." She got the words out, but it was one of the hardest things she'd ever had to say.

Kurt heard Olivia talking, but it took a few seconds for the words to make their way through the pleasurable haze of passion into his brain.

Stop?

He had to. Never in his wildest dreams would he try to take a woman further than she wanted to go, but it wasn't easy to put the brakes on.

His hands kept moving for a few seconds, as if they had minds of their own, and the rest of him took another pulse or two to realize things had changed direction again. At last, passion began to fade and common sense had a chance to start working again.

"I promised myself I wouldn't do that," he said with a weak laugh. "Guess that shows how reliable I am."

"It wasn't entirely your fault." Olivia slanted a glance at him through the hair he'd loosened. It fluttered in the breeze, teasing him, taunting him, enticing him to indulge himself once more. "I didn't exactly try to stop you."

He liked knowing that she'd enjoyed it as much as he had, but he stuffed his hands into his pockets to keep from reaching for her again. "Did I do something wrong?"

She shook her head quickly. "No." A tiny smile quirked her lips. "It was just too much, too fast. One minute we were talking about your divorce, my sister, and Sam, and the next . . ."

Kurt chuckled, delighted that she wasn't going to start

playing games with his heart. "I can do it all slower if you'd like."

She made a face at him. "That's *not* what I mean. But you're right about Sam. I really should tell him how I feel about you before—" Her cheeks turned a tantalizing pink. "Before. . . ."

Before. Kurt had never heard such a beautiful word. He'd never wanted anything so much in his life.

"And I can't forget that you might not be here for long," she whispered.

Foolishly, knowing he shouldn't, Kurt took her hands in his. "What if I *do* stay?"

Her eyes met his again and the hope he saw in them made him feel like a jerk. "Can you?"

"I hope so. I have nothing to go back for." A little of his common sense returned and he pulled away. "But I can't promise. I don't know what brought me here. I don't know what—if anything—might take me away again. But I can promise to stay with you as long as I can."

"But you can't promise forever."

"No," he admitted. "I can't. Maybe you were right to stop us. You need to save the Lazy H. I need to save the Black Mesa ruins. Neither of us is in a position to make a commitment until we've done that and can see where we are then."

"No, we're not."

"But if I were to be swept out of here tomorrow, I want you to always remember that I love you. Always. Here or there, that won't change." He couldn't believe how easily the words left his lips. Maybe if he'd learned to say them earlier, he'd still be married to Holly. Maybe Charlotte wouldn't have left him.

When he thought of it that way, he was glad he *hadn't* learned to say them before now.

•   •   •

Olivia's eyes filled with tears. He loved her. It should have been one of the most beautiful moments of her life, but a bittersweet pain filled every inch of her. She reached for his hand. "Let's go back."

"Back?" He stared at her as if she'd lost her mind. "Why? Sandstone Palace is just around the next bend."

"Because if we find the ruins, I'll lose you."

"If we don't, you'll lose your home."

"I don't care."

"You don't care." Kurt put an arm around her and rested his chin on top of her head. "Olivia, sweetheart, you might not care right this second, but you will later. All you've been able to talk about since I met you is saving this ranch."

"That was before. Everything's different now."

He pulled away and looked deep into her eyes. "Nothing's different. Even if you and I got married tomorrow, you'd still have to pay your mortgage or lose your home. And *I* certainly don't have any money we could use."

She dashed tears away angrily. "I know. But why does it have to be this way? It's not fair."

He cradled her against his chest again. "No, it's not. If I could make promises, I would. I'd promise you the world and everything in it. The only thing I *can* do is make sure you're safe. If I have to go back, I want to read in the history books that you've had a wonderful life, that you've grown old on the Lazy H, and that you've been happy."

That only made her feel worse. "At least you'd have that. How will I ever know what's happened to you?" She pushed him away. "This whole situation stinks."

"Yes, it does."

She glanced at the sky and realized how late it was getting. She could argue all she wanted, but fate would have its way no matter what she did. "Fine. Let's go find your ruins."

He released her reluctantly and led the way around one last bend. And suddenly, she saw it. Just like in the photograph.

High above her, midway up the cliff wall, the wind had scooped out a cave deep enough and high enough to hold a small village. And someone—some long-ago people—had built one there.

Sandstone walls rose at least three stories high and the hundreds of tiny windows in the multi-leveled walls made her breath catch. A few of the walls had begun to crumble, but the effect was still breathtaking.

Speechless, she looked at Kurt and saw the wonder and triumph in his eyes. A sudden hush fell over the valley and Olivia imagined voices on the delicate breeze. "Are they here?"

"Who?"

"The people who built this village. It almost feels as if they're watching us."

"They might be." Kurt kept his voice low, evidence that he felt it, too. "You'd have liked them, I think. The homes belonged to the women of the tribe because they built them. So the women slept in the upper floors of the houses, and the men slept in the *estufas*, ceremonial rooms below ground."

"I like them already," Olivia said with a soft laugh. "And I thought women who stood on their own was a new idea of the future."

"Nope." Kurt flashed her a smile. "It's just that we keep having to remember it all over again."

She turned her attention back to the ruins. "How do we get up there?"

"Very carefully. There should be some foot- and hand-holds cut into the cliff that the Anasazi used to get up there, but they won't be easy to find. That was one of the ways they protected their villages from their enemies." Kurt led her toward the cliff face and began to search, but

Olivia couldn't stop looking at the village high overhead.

It was at once the most beautiful, inspiring, and magnificent thing she'd ever seen. But their search had been for nothing.

Now that they'd found it, how could she sell a single piece of it?

Olivia rode in front of Kurt on the way back to the Lazy H. The sun had already begun its westward slide as they left the mesa behind, and storm clouds began to cluster as the wind picked up. Silence hung between them like a wet blanket and she knew they were both wondering the same thing.

They'd found the ruins. Now what?

She'd never been afraid of being alone, but neither had she realized how lonely she'd been until Kurt arrived. Sam's visits helped, but it was nice to have another person around all day, nice to know that he was asleep in the barn at night.

They rode into the yard of the Lazy H slowly and headed toward the barn without exchanging a word, as if they each knew exactly what the other would do without having to discuss it.

Kurt dismounted, helped her down, then led the horses into the barn. Instead of heading into the house, she followed him. She couldn't bear the uneasy silence that had ridden along with them all the way home. But at least he hadn't been taken away from her yet.

"So, now we wait," she said as he tethered Nightmare.

"We wait."

She wanted to demand answers but Kurt knew as little as she did, and he looked so miserable that she wouldn't let herself make this any harder on him. But neither could she pretend this was just another evening. They could at least talk about it. They *needed* to talk about it.

She sat on a bale of hay and watched him brush Nightmare, enjoying the play of his hands across the black coat. "What do you think will happen?"

"I have no idea." He smoothed the brush across Nightmare's neck and glanced at her over his shoulder. "If I'm still here in the morning, we could ride into town and try to convince the local law to put the ruins under protection."

If he was still here in the morning. Olivia hated the sound of those words. She couldn't bear to lose him this way.

She must have made a noise because he looked at her, carefully, taking in every detail of her expression. His eyes seemed to hold all the questions and their answers at once.

He set aside the brush and took her into his arms gently. She lifted her mouth, ready for his kiss, wanting it so much she could scarcely breathe, needing it so much she ached everywhere. The barn seemed to dip and sway, to spiral out of control. If he hadn't been holding her so tightly, she would have wrapped her arms around his waist and held on for dear life.

But he didn't kiss her. "We wait, Olivia."

"Then let's wait together. Please . . ." She could hardly get the words out. "Please stay with me tonight."

Kurt's eyes widened and darted over her face. She couldn't tell if she'd shocked or delighted him. "You don't know what you're saying."

"I know exactly what I'm saying. I don't want to wake up in the morning and find that you've disappeared while I was asleep." Not that she *would* sleep.

Kurt pressed a kiss to her forehead, but there was nothing of what she craved in it. "Much as I'd love to take you into that house right now and make love to you, I'm not so much of a weasel that I'll do it tonight."

"Why would that make you a weasel?"

"I've already gone too far. I shouldn't even have

touched you, and I should never have kissed you. I'm interfering in your life too much already. Besides, I thought we agreed not to do anything until the ranch is safe."

"That was before we found the ruins." She tried to keep her chin up, even though the slow heat of embarrassment flushed her face. And the desperation. She'd tried so hard to keep it at bay, but it swelled inside her now. "Now that we've found them, what is there to keep you here?"

"I don't know. I wish I did." Kurt stepped away from her. "You're too vulnerable right now. That decision would haunt you for the rest of your life."

She pulled back, stunned by the firmness in his voice, hurt by the resolve there. "How do you know that?"

"It would, Olivia. If we made love tonight and then I disappeared, where would that leave you? We might have found the ruins, but they're not protected. Your ranch certainly isn't safe and your reputation would be ruined if anyone found out."

She stepped away from him, chilled to the bone. "My *reputation*?"

Kurt went on, relentless. "If you and I were together tonight and I left tomorrow, could you marry Sam? Would you tell him the truth and hurt him? Or would you lie to him and make both of you miserable?"

"This isn't about Sam," she said. "This is about us. At least I thought it was. Even if you disappeared this instant, I still wouldn't be able to marry Sam. I love *you*."

"And I love you. But I can't let you destroy the rest of your life over nothing."

"You can't *let* me?"

Kurt had the decency to look sheepish. "That's not what I meant. But you were right about what you said in the canyon. Even if you and I were to throw caution to the wind, we'd hate ourselves if we didn't tell Sam first."

Olivia frowned at him. "It's pretty hard to argue with

you when you throw my own words back in my face."

Kurt pulled her close again. "If I'm lucky enough to stay here, I don't want anything to come between us. Sam's been your friend for far too long. The guilt would eat you up. I wouldn't have an easy time of it, either."

"Then you've stopped expecting Sam to shoot you?"

He laughed, and she treasured the chance to hear it emanating from deep inside. Here in his arms, she felt safe and secure. She could almost believe that everything would be all right.

"Sam's a good guy," he said. "He didn't even try to shoot me when I told him where I came from."

"You told him?"

"I had to. He was having a little trouble understanding what's going on here." Kurt's hands began to move slowly across her back. "But that's exactly why I have to tell him how things stand before we go any further. I can't do to him what Holly did to me."

Delicious shivers ran in every direction, making it hard for her to concentrate on what he was saying. "We wouldn't have to make love," she whispered. "Just stay beside me so I know you're there."

His hands stilled. "Sweetheart, if you think I could lay down beside you and be a good boy all night, you seriously underestimate your charms." He pushed her away with exquisite tenderness. "Now go. Please. Before I change my mind. And don't argue with me. This is the first time in my life I've put someone else's needs before mine, and the way I'm feeling right now, it just might be the last."

Chapter 15

"YOU'RE QUIET TODAY."

Sam flicked an annoyed glance at Jesse across the irrigation ditch they'd spent the morning digging. "No quieter than usual."

"About a *hundred times* quieter than usual." Jesse tossed a shovelful of dirt onto the ground behind him. "So what's on your mind?"

What wasn't on his mind? Kurt and Olivia were growing closer by the day. Sam could see it in their eyes and hear it in their voices. Even the tension between them the past few days had an intimate quality about it.

"Is it Olivia?"

Sam glared at his brother and speared his shovel into the red dirt at his feet. "No, it's not Olivia."

"Is it me?"

Sam let out a sigh heavy with frustration and leaned on the handle of his shovel. "Partly. It'd help if you'd stop talking and work. I didn't ask you to come with me so I could dig this ditch myself."

Jesse merely smiled and dropped onto the ground to rest. "It's not that I *want* to leave, you know."

"Nobody's breaking your arm, are they?"

"No-o-o." Jesse nudged his glasses up on his nose. "You know my reasons."

"I've heard 'em. Don't understand 'em."

"Don't you?" Jesse folded his arms behind his head to make a pillow. "Be honest, now."

"You want me to be honest?" The sight of him lying there as if nothing had happened during the past few weeks, as if Sam's life wasn't falling apart in front of his eyes, did something to him. He tossed his shovel to one side. "All right, then. I'll *be* honest. If you want to leave, then leave. Nobody's breaking your arm to stay, either. But this is just about the stupidest decision you've ever made."

"Wait just a minute—"

"You asked for honesty," Sam snapped. "Now you're going to get it. The Cinnabar might be mine, but it *should* be yours. You and I both know that. You're the one with the heart to work it, not me."

"You love this land, too."

"Not like you do." Some of the wind left Sam's sails. "Not like you do," he said again. He sat beside Jesse and stared out over the land that was tearing them apart. "The Cinnabar was Pa's dream, not mine. And if you want to know the God's honest truth, it's not worth what it's doing to us." He turned his gaze on Jesse slowly. "If you want the Cinnabar, take it. Take the whole thing, lock, stock, and barrel."

Jesse's gaze flicked across his face rapidly as he tried to take in everything he'd said. "I can't do that."

"Sure you can. If you want to leave, then do it. But if what you've told me about you and Elizabeth wanting to stay here is true, then the Cinnabar is yours. I'll get out of your way."

Jesse sputtered in disbelief. "But what would you do?"

"Something." Sam laughed at the look on his brother's face. "I'll be fine, Jesse. I'll ride out and find someplace new to start over. I've thought some about seeing what it's like up Montana way."

"Montana? Why there?"

Sam shrugged. "Why not?"

Jesse eyed him cautiously. "Have you been drinking?"

"Not a drop."

"Are you sick?"

"Never felt better."

Jesse sat up slowly. He still didn't look convinced. "What about Olivia?"

Sam's smile faded. "I don't think she's going to worry about me being gone—or care much, either."

"How can you say that after everything you've done for her?"

"You asked for the truth. Well, the truth is, I think she's in love with someone else."

"I knew it." Jesse shot to his feet. "I *knew* this was about Olivia."

"Not in the way you think." Sam studied his fingernails for a moment, trying to figure out how to make Jesse understand. "She doesn't want to marry me, Jesse. And I don't think I can stay here and watch her be married to someone else."

Jesse's eyes flashed. "But how can she love someone else? You're the only reason she's still on that ranch of hers. Without you—"

Sam cut him off with a laugh that hid how much Jesse's loyalty meant to him. "Don't be angry with her. A person can't help who they fall in love with. If they could, I would never have fallen in love with her when she still had a husband."

Jesse's mouth fell open and he sat again, slowly. "You've been in love with her that long?"

Sam nodded miserably.

"Does she know that?"

"No, and she's not going to—*is she*?"

Jesse held up both hands and scooted a couple of inches backward. "Not from me."

"Good."

"But I've got to tell you, brother, if you've loved her that long, I think she ought to at least hear it from you."

"No."

"Oh. So you're just going to roll over and play dead while somebody else walks off with the woman you love?"

"And I suppose you have some brilliant suggestion about what I should do?"

"As a matter of fact, yes. I've got a month's wages that say you've never taken her flowers."

Sam glowered at him, but he couldn't lie. "You'd win."

"And how did you propose? Did you make it sound like a business proposition?"

Sam looked away quickly, but not before Jesse saw the color creep into his cheeks. "Tried to make it palatable."

"And is that all you want from her? A merger of the ranches? Or do you love her?"

"Of course I love her. I just didn't think she'd take to a lot of mushy talk, considering Harv's been gone such a short time."

"Well, in my experience, a woman would rather hear mush than a business proposition."

Sam laughed softly. "In your experience? You're just about as green at this as I am."

Jesse plucked a blade of grass and rolled it between his thumb and forefinger. "Just about," he said at last. "But not quite. Elizabeth likes romantic stuff, and I'm pretty sure Olivia's not that much different. Hell, man, at least *try.*"

Sam gave that some thought. He had no idea whether it would make a difference, but maybe Jesse was right. He had to at least try, or he'd always wonder.

•   •   •

Olivia awoke the following morning to the heavenly aroma of coffee and breakfast. Stunned by the realization that she'd slept at all, she scrambled out of bed and tugged on her wrapper. She hurried into the main room to find breakfast and a bouquet of wildflowers in a jar on the table, and the front door standing wide open.

She found Kurt standing on the porch sipping coffee. The sun was just beginning to creep over the eastern horizon and pale clouds of lavender, peach, blue, and pink dotted the sky.

The sight of him standing there sent a shock of relief through her. He held his cup in one hand and looked out over the foothills as if he'd always been here. The scent of his soap mingled with the clear morning air and brought memories rushing back—not vivid memories of Harvey, but of the companionship and the knowledge that someone was there for her. Of lying in bed together and sharing confidences in the night.

And now Kurt was here, but for how long? Could she survive another loss so close on the heels of losing Harvey? Harvey hadn't been perfect, but his death had shredded her heart. If she lost Kurt, she might never recover.

Kurt turned as she stepped through the door and held his finger to his lips. He nodded toward the foothills and she squinted into the dawn, trying to make out what he was watching.

At the base of the hill she saw a doe and her fawn making their way through the piñon and juniper toward the clearing. Their heads were up, ears pricked, senses alert. The doe moved cautiously, picking her way through the brush and checking on her young one frequently.

Harvey would have reached for his rifle and counted himself lucky for finding food for the winter. Kurt only watched without moving and the awe on his face touched her.

Olivia moved closer so she could whisper without scaring them. "They're beautiful, aren't they?"

Kurt nodded. "They sure are. I've always loved watching them. I guess this area must always have been good grazing."

"It's safe," Olivia said, lifting her cup. "Especially since Harvey died. I'm not much of a hunter."

"Neither am I." He smiled over the rim of his cup and sat on the porch rail.

She sat beside him. "I thought all men hunted."

"Not all."

The fawn stopped and sniffed the breeze. The doe's head shot up and every muscle in her body tensed.

"The wind must have shifted," Kurt said close to her ear. "They know we're here."

The sound of his voice and the feel of his breath on her shoulder started the fire in her belly again. She felt wicked and wanton and totally shameless for having such thoughts at sunrise when she should be thinking about the day ahead.

She wondered what Harvey would have done if she'd ever felt like this when they were married, then decided he'd probably have liked it very much indeed. She looked away to hide her sudden blush and pulled her thoughts away from the dangerous cliff she felt herself approaching. It wouldn't do either of them any good to start down that road again.

"I really should get busy," she said.

She stood to escape, but Kurt pulled her back onto the railing beside him. "Just sit for a minute," he said in her ear. "And relax."

"Relax? How can I, considering everything that's going on around here?"

Kurt began kneading her shoulders gently. "What do you have to do today?"

His fingers burned her skin through the thin fabric of

her wrapper and warmth spread from the pressure points through her entire body. It had been far too long since she'd felt anything so sensual.

"Nothing if you keep doing that." She smiled at him over her shoulder. "What do you have in mind?"

"I'd better not say." He grinned and pulled his hands away. "I think we should visit the ruins again—this time with journals so we can record what we find."

She nodded, even though every step they took toward protecting the ruins took her closer to the day when she'd lose him forever. "After breakfast." She kissed his cheek gently. "And speaking of breakfast, thank you. I can't remember the last meal I didn't have to cook myself."

His sudden grin made him look so young, she thought about the lonely young boy he'd been and the life he'd face when he went back to the future. At least she had family, even if she didn't get to see them. But she refused to let herself get maudlin this morning.

She tried to keep spirits light as they ate and cleaned up afterward. "If we're going to go back up there, I want to change. I'm *not* climbing around on those cliffs in a dress, and you're not going up there without me."

She could hear Kurt moving around while she changed into a pair of Harvey's trousers and one of his shirts. While she searched for something to cinch them at the waist so they wouldn't drop off her hips, mysterious sounds drifted through the door. When she finally emerged, she found that Kurt had already packed a lunch for them.

"Two meals in one day? You're going to spoil me."

Kurt picked up the lunch with one hand and took her hand with the other. "At least I can do *something* for you," he muttered as he led her outside.

Olivia forced a laugh. This was hurting him as much as it hurt her, but they couldn't let themselves get mired in misery or they'd destroy what time they had together.

Whether it lasted five minutes or five days, she wanted it to be a beautiful memory for both of them.

Keeping his hands to himself as he watched Olivia climb the cliff face ahead of him was one of the hardest things Kurt had ever done. Only the heavy pack dragging him backwards and the knowledge that letting go even for a second might very well send him plunging to the valley floor kept him in line.

He'd been into these ruins a thousand times. The climb had been easier in his own time, but he couldn't beat the view. This was by far the nicest trip up this cliff he'd ever made.

He bargained with the gods—or whatever had brought him here—as he climbed. If they'd let him stay, he'd do whatever it took to make her safe and happy for the rest of her life. He'd give up everything he'd ever imagined he needed just for the chance to stay with the woman he loved. Money had no power over him. Material things had no appeal. He'd give the world for a life if only they'd let him.

It seemed to take forever to make the climb, hand over hand, searching for the hidden footholds in the rock before Olivia took each step. Dangerous as it was to send her up first, he'd opted to follow so he could catch her if she slipped.

Her courage amazed him. Just two days ago she'd been terrified of these cliffs, yet here she was, climbing them as if she'd never had a moment's hesitation. And knowing that she was doing it for him made him feel as if there was nothing he couldn't do, no foe he couldn't conquer, no problem he couldn't solve.

He'd never been loved so deeply. He'd never loved so completely. He'd never even imagined it was possible to feel like this. No wonder Holly had cheated on him, no wonder Charlotte had walked out if they'd been expecting him to feel this way. He must have seemed like a selfish bastard to both of them.

At long last, Olivia reached the cave and stepped onto the level ground. He handed up his backpack, then climbed up beside her and caught the amazement on her face.

"Oh," she breathed so softly he could barely hear her. "It's incredible." She turned toward him, her eyes glittering with excitement. "It's so *huge*. And beautiful. Looking at it from a distance doesn't do it justice."

"No, it doesn't, does it?" Kurt started toward the first structure, a towering square building with narrow high windows that had probably served as a guard tower. His gaze swept the ground in front of him. Broken pieces of pottery lay everywhere amidst the crumbled bricks, and he wanted to make sure neither of them accidentally stepped on anything culturally important.

"According to the journals kept by the original explorers," he said over his shoulder, "they found blankets and clothing inside the houses, and sandals woven from threads pounded from yucca, pots full of yucca seeds, toys, and even a few skeletons." He reached a hand out to stop Olivia and squatted in front of a round opening in the floor near the cliff's edge. "You'll find these all over," he said, sweeping aside the dust. "They buried pots in the ground to collect rainfall."

Olivia took everything in with wide, eager eyes. "Can you imagine living here?"

"I've tried many times."

She scanned the fronts of the dwellings nearest them and looked back at him with wide, surprised eyes. "There aren't any doors. How did they get inside?"

"The doors are in the roofs. They pulled in their ladders at night for safety. And you'll notice there aren't any windows on the ground floor, either." He stood again and tried to decide exactly where to start. He'd dreamed of this moment for so long, but now that he was here he felt unequal to the task. How could he possibly find time to catalogue everything and still work the ranch?

The thought caught him and made him laugh silently at himself. He was dreaming again. Fantasizing that he'd be allowed to stay here forever. Imagining that life would suddenly become fair.

He looked for a safe place to put down his backpack and froze when he realized what he was seeing. Footprints. Heavy, booted footprints in the soft layer of sand. Prints that hadn't come from the Anasazi and hadn't been here long enough for the wind to blow them away.

"I think we have a problem," he said with a quick glance at Olivia.

"What is it?"

He tried to keep his voice level in spite of his rising anger. "Someone else has been here."

Her smile faded abruptly. "Are you sure?"

"Come here and look at these. See what you think."

She hunkered down beside him. "Sloan Durrant?"

"Probably. And it doesn't look like he was alone, either. There's more than one set of prints here. Two, maybe even three."

"But how did they find this?"

"That's the million dollar question." Kurt ran his sleeve across his forehead and tried to keep his temper in check. "The next one is, what have they taken so far?"

"You think they've taken things?"

"If they've been here more than once, I'd just about bet my life on it."

"How *dare* they?" Olivia stood suddenly, her movements jerky and obviously agitated. "This is still my land. The bank doesn't own it yet. And Sloan Durrant doesn't own it at all."

"He's getting a little ahead of himself."

"He obviously doesn't think I'll be able to pay the

mortgage." She took a jerky step away, realized she might destroy some of the artifacts, and pulled herself up short. "Damn him."

"You took the words right out of my mouth." Kurt stood slowly, pondering their options. "As I see it, we have a couple of choices. We can haul out the artifacts ourselves, and hopefully find a buyer within the next few days, or we can stand guard and catch them. Maybe when Sloan realizes you're on to him, he'll stop."

"For a few days, maybe," Olivia conceded. "But if I can't make the mortgage payment, they'll belong to him and we'll lose any hope of saving them." She looked at the sheer rock face and the plunge to the canyon floor far below. "Besides, it's too dangerous to stand guard here."

"A whole town lived here once," Kurt reminded her. "Including women and children. I think I'll be safe enough."

She started shaking her head with his first word and kept going until he'd finished. "Women and children who were *used* to this kind of life. Not time-traveling men from the future—"

"You're forgetting that this is what I do for a living. I'm in these ruins at least once a month. I know every inch of them, every weak spot, every great place to hide . . ." He smiled to take away some of her fears. "I know them a helluva lot better than Sloan Durrant and his buddies."

She looked slightly less worried, but not much. "I still don't like it. I know it's because of Harvey, but I can't help it. I just know something horrible will happen if you stay out here alone."

With all the strange things that had happened in the past few weeks, Kurt wasn't about to discount a possible premonition. He tried to come up with an option they could both live with. "Tell me about the town marshall. What kind of man is he?"

"Marshall Pulver?" Olivia sent him a grateful smile. "I don't know him all that well, but he's nice enough, I suppose."

"Do you think he'd help keep an eye on the ruins until we can get someone to agree to put them under official protection?"

"How long would that take?"

"Months. Maybe years."

"I wouldn't hold my breath, then. Besides, I only have a few days."

"Then we'd better get busy, hadn't we? Most of the relics are probably buried beneath the rubble. And we'll have to bring in a ladder so we can get inside." He ground his teeth in frustration. "I can't *believe* Sloan Durrant got here first."

Olivia touched his shoulder gently. "Let's talk to the marshall before we disturb too much. He might surprise me."

"I think we should ask Sam to go with us. I have the feeling we'll need him on our side."

Kurt couldn't think of anyone he'd rather have standing beside him in a fight. He just hoped Sam would *be* on their side once they told him everything. He couldn't think of anyone he wanted *less* as an enemy.

Feeling like a damned fool, Sam watched from the top of a hill as Kurt and Olivia rode back into the yard together. Kurt helped Olivia from her horse, then pulled her close and kissed her. Olivia wrapped her arms around his neck and held on, obviously enjoying every minute of it.

Sam clutched the wilting bunch of posies he'd picked, unable to look away. Sure, he'd guessed that Olivia and Kurt had fallen in love. He'd even halfway reconciled himself to the idea. But seeing them together brought a whole new set of feelings to the surface. Feelings he hadn't expected.

He wanted Olivia to be happy. He *loved* her. He *should* hurt like hell.

So why did he feel so . . . free?

God knew, he didn't want to spend the rest of his life alone. And the choices of a wife were mighty slim in Cortez. But for the first time since his father's death, the dream of leaving, of making his own way somewhere new, seemed more like a reality than a dream.

It was the answer to every one of his problems. He could leave the ranch to Jesse and Elizabeth and leave Olivia in Kurt's hands. She looked happier than Sam had ever seen her, even when Harv was alive.

Shaking his head in wonder, he tossed aside the posies and waited out of sight until they took the horses into the barn. Olivia might have made her choice, but Sam figured he'd still have to find a way to let her down easy. He might not know a whole lot about women, but he knew enough not to tell her that maybe he'd never really loved her after all.

Might as well get it over with. Wouldn't accomplish anything by putting it off, except to worry about how she'd take it. He rode into the yard slowly, making enough noise to let anyone for five miles around know he was there.

Kurt came to the barn door first and his eyes widened when he saw Sam standing there. "Sam?" He shot a guilty glance over his shoulder.

Sam waved him forward. "Mind if I talk to you for a minute?" No sense telling Kurt the whole truth, either. Kurt would treasure Olivia all the more if he thought he'd won.

But Kurt sensed something. "How long have you been here?"

"Only a minute." He led Kurt toward Olivia's garden and hoped Olivia wouldn't follow. "I saw you ride back in."

Kurt's eyes shot to his face. Nervous.

Sam bit back a smile. "Relax. I'm not going to shoot you."

"Well, that's a relief." Kurt laughed nervously. "We didn't mean for you to see us like that. We wanted to talk to you and explain everything."

"Yeah?"

"You know how much Olivia cares about you. And you're the best friend I've ever had."

"Best friend, huh?" Sam kept his voice gruff, his expression somber, but the confession touched him. "You have an interesting way of showing it."

Kurt held up a hand in self-defense. "Look, Sam, I know how you must be feeling. I've been there, and it's hell."

The look on his face made Sam feel a little guilty. He waved Kurt's concerns away with one hand. "I'll get over it. The best man won. Congratulations." Kurt tried hard not to look pleased. He failed. "Just take care of her, that's all I ask."

"I'll do my best." Kurt hooked his thumbs in his back pockets. "For as long as I'm here. I still don't know how long I'll be able to stay." He pulled his hands out of his pockets and began to pace. Quick, jerky steps that gave away his agitation. "I shouldn't have let myself fall in love with her, Sam. It's not fair to her."

"I'll tell you what's not fair," Sam told him firmly, "and that's not letting yourself love her. Hell, man, you think you're so much different from anybody else just because you traveled through time to get here? The truth is, none of us knows how long we've got. *I* might not be here tomorrow. I could get thrown by my horse, snake-bit, or take a bullet in the back. But if I'd been lucky enough to win Olivia, I sure as hell wouldn't hide from what *might* happen. You could waste an awful lot of precious time that way."

Kurt stopped pacing and stared at him. "You're right."

"Damn right I am. The woman's in love with you. Don't be a fool."

Kurt grinned slowly. "You're sure you're okay with this?"

"I don't make a habit of lying."

"No. No, I know you don't." Kurt took off his hat and ran his fingers through his hair. "You're a great guy, Sam. I'm proud to call you friend. And after everything you've done to help Olivia out, I'll return the favor whenever I can."

Now came the hard part. Sam let his gaze travel to the bluff of the mesa. "Give the help to my brother if he needs it. I'll be riding out."

Kurt slanted a glance at him. "Riding out? This is something new, isn't it?"

"Not exactly. Running the Cinnabar has never been what I wanted to do, but after Pa died, it just seemed to be in the cards for me. And then when Harvey died . . . Well, I figured that meant I was supposed to stick around and look after Olivia."

"And now?"

"Now I'm thinking of riding up to Montana and starting over. Maybe trying my hand at mining silver. Figure that's a way for a man to test his mettle. No easy life like here on the farm."

"Easy?" Kurt laughed. "I've got news for you, my friend. This is no easy life."

"Maybe not," Sam admitted with a shrug, "but I've never had to test myself. My father built the Cinnabar with his bare hands. He carved it out of this land and proved himself in the process. Everything I have was handed to me on a silver platter. I've spent my life living up to my father's reputation and trying to meet his expectations."

"We all do that in one way or another."

"To some degree, I guess." Sam dragged his gaze back to Kurt's. "But my father *knew* who he was because he proved himself. I'd like the chance to do the same thing, but I'm not going to get it here. Besides, my brother loves the Cinnabar. He really should be the one running it. It's not his fault I was born first."

Kurt glanced behind them toward the barn. "So you plan to leave?"

"Don't know when I'll ever get another opportunity like this one."

"What will you tell Olivia?"

That was one conversation Sam didn't look forward to having. "I'm not sure yet. I don't want her to think it's her fault."

"Well, think fast." Kurt jerked his head almost imperceptibly toward the barn. "She's waiting back there."

Sam adjusted his hat and tried to beat down a flash of nervousness. "I'm counting on you to help her understand she's not to blame. And my brother . . . Don't want him thinking he's done something wrong, either."

"I'll see to it."

Sam stole a glance over his shoulder. Sure enough, Olivia was standing just outside the barn, waiting, and obviously burning with curiosity. "Just one more question. How in the hell did you get her up on the mesa?"

"I didn't," Kurt said with a frown. "Sloan Durrant did."

Sam listened with mounting fury as Kurt told him about Sloan's visit the day before, about finding the ruins, and about the evidence that someone had gotten there before them. "Well, then," he said when Kurt had finished, "the only thing left to do now is take care of this little problem."

"It's not your fight, Sam."

"Maybe not, but I'm not going anywhere until it's taken care of. And if you really want to make me mad, just argue with me."

Kurt grinned and shook his head in wonder. "I'm not stupid. Besides, I can't think of anyone I'd rather have on my side."

Sam laughed. Other than Jesse, he'd never had a friend he'd trust his life with—or his responsibilities. Truth to tell, he'd miss Kurt when he'd gone.

Chapter 16

OLIVIA WRUNG HER hands nervously, wondering what Kurt and Sam were talking about, alternately deciding to join them and deciding to leave them alone. They looked so serious, she decided to give them their privacy. If they'd wanted her there, they would have called her over.

She hated knowing that she was about to hurt Sam. Loathed the thought of causing him even an instant's pain after everything he'd done for her. The thought crossed her mind briefly that Kurt might be telling Sam, but when Sam laughed she decided they couldn't be discussing her, after all.

What felt like hours later, Sam stepped away from Kurt and started across the yard toward her. Her hands grew clammy and her breath caught. When he drew close enough, she studied his face and eyes for a clue to his emotions.

His eyes looked clear and bright and a smile hovered on the corners of his lips. He hooked his thumbs in his waistband and rested his weight on one foot. "Kurt said you might be wanting to talk to me."

"I—" She looked to Kurt, half-wishing he'd come to help her through this difficult conversation, half-glad he was giving them time alone. "I—"

"He told me, if that's what you're worried about."

"He told you?"

"About the two of you."

She took a deep breath for courage and forced herself to say something reasonably intelligent. "I never intended for this to happen. I didn't intend to fall in love with Kurt."

Sam's gaze dropped to the ground at his feet. "Aw, shoot, Livvy. I know that. And I understand it, too. I should've told you I already knew so you wouldn't worry."

"You already knew? How? I didn't know myself until recently."

Sam looked back up at her. "It was plain as the nose on your face, Liv. *You* might not have known, but anyone else with eyes sure could have." He put an arm around her and led her toward the porch.

She followed willingly, surprised by his reaction but not by his kindness. "I'm sorry, Sam. You know how much I care about you."

He waved away her apology and sat on the step beside her. "Don't be sorry. And don't look so sad. If you had to fall in love with someone who wasn't me, I'd say you picked the right guy." He laughed softly, then sobered again. "Look, Livvy. There's something I think you should know."

The look on his face sent a chill up her spine. "What?"

He pushed his hat back and spent a minute studying his fingernails. He looked so uncomfortable, Olivia almost smiled. "Once we get this trouble out at the ruins settled, I'm going to be moving on."

"*What?*" The idea of Sam leaving the Cinnabar was so preposterous, he might as well have said he was planning to fly to the moon. Surely she'd heard him wrong.

A gust of wind lifted the hair away from his forehead and the look on his face made him look like a little boy. Big, tough Sam with his thick moustache and deep bass voice and the gleam of excitement in his eyes. Olivia had never seen him look like this and she wondered how well she really knew him. "Are you serious, Sam? You're leaving?"

"Planning to."

"How long will you be gone?"

He didn't answer immediately, and his silence gave her the answer.

"You're not coming back, are you?"

"Not for a while, anyway."

"But why?" Tears filled her eyes and clogged her throat. She hurt everywhere. "I can't bear to think that I've driven you away from your home."

"Durnit, Livvy. Don't cry."

She glared at him, suddenly angrier with him than she'd ever been. Sadder, too. "How can you say you're leaving for good and then tell me not to cry?"

"Easy. I'm riding out to a brand new life. You should be happy for me."

"*Happy*?" Olivia laughed sharply. But the look on Sam's face made her think again. How could she expect him to stay here after the way she'd hurt him? With effort, she dashed her tears away and forced the best smile she could. "I'll try to be happy for you, if it's what you really want."

"It is."

She sank onto the porch railing and looked at her dear friend's face. Realizing that soon she'd never look into those familiar gray eyes again tore at her heart. "What about the Cinnabar?"

"It's Jesse's. Always should have been, you know that. Truth to tell, Livvy, I never did want it." Sam straightened and sent her a comical look. "Always thought I belonged somewhere new, wild, and untamed . . . being the adventurous sort as I am."

Olivia couldn't stop the laugh that escaped her lips. "You might have shown me a bit of that adventurous side earlier."

"Would it have made a difference?"

"It might have." She glanced toward Kurt who stood near the corral. The surge of love she felt for him gave light to the lie she'd just told. She wouldn't let Sam leave with lies between them. "No, I suppose it wouldn't have." She glanced back at him sadly. "Can you ever forgive me?"

"For not falling in love with me?" Sam snorted a laugh. "There's no predicting love, Livvy. Nor making it follow some set road, neither. Kurt's a good man. And I'm not the kind of man to hold what's in your heart against you. We're too good of friends for that."

"Yes, we are, aren't we?" Olivia reached for his hand. "I guess that means I need to try to understand what you need to do, doesn't it?"

Sam curled his fingers through hers and gave her hand a gentle squeeze—more gentle than she'd ever known him to be. "I'd feel a sight better if you could."

"I hope you find someone who loves you the way you deserve to be loved."

"Me?" Sam made a noise of derision. "I'm heading to the wilds of Montana, Livvy. Not likely to find the kind of ladies up there who'd appeal to me. Saloon girls and fancy ladies, maybe, but not the kind of gals a fella marries." He released her hand slowly. "But that's fine by me. I'm thinking I'll be better off alone anyhow."

"No, Sam. Don't say that. You have too much to offer to spend the rest of your life alone."

"Maybe." He looked uneasy with her comment. "But

for now, alone is exactly what I want. There'll be time enough for a family later."

Olivia tried to keep the moment light. "After you've made your fortune?"

Sam's expression darkened. "I'm not after money, Livvy. You know that."

She thought she did. Now she wasn't so sure. Sam had shocked her thoroughly. "Then why head to Montana? Why not stay closer to home?"

Sam leaned forward and propped his elbows on his knees, his expression suddenly earnest. "Because as long as I'm close to home Jesse will feel as if he's under my shadow. I've lived in Pa's shadow too long to want to put Jesse there. He needs to know that he's on his own." His moustache twitched as he smiled. "And because Montana's new and raw and the silver mines are about as far from ranching the Cinnabar as you can get—less'n maybe I were to head back East."

Olivia laughed, delighted to see his humor peeking through. "Oh, Sam. Much as I love you, I can't see you in Boston or New York—or even the drawing rooms of the South. You belong here in the West."

"Can't see me in fancy pants, eh?"

"You'd be terribly handsome in fancy pants," she said, forcing a smile, "but also terribly uncomfortable, I'm afraid. As I recall, you could hardly wait to get out of your fancy clothes after Harvey's funeral."

Sam chuckled at the memory, then met her gaze sadly. "Aw, Liv. I'm going to miss you. Can't lie about that."

The tears welled in her eyes again. "I'll miss you, too, Sam." She could hardly stand to think about it. "How soon do you plan to leave?" The words hurt to say.

"Not until we've got Sloan Durrant and his boys under control. I won't run out on you until that's settled."

"You don't owe me even that," Olivia assured him.

"We're still friends, Livvy. Always will be, far as I'm concerned."

She hugged him quickly.

He returned the embrace stiffly, then stepped back to put some distance between them again. "You do love him, don't you?"

"Very much." At his arched eyebrow, she amended, "With all my heart."

"Good. Make sure you do. Otherwise, you could've settled for me." He patted her shoulder and moved past her toward the steps again. The moment had passed and he was suddenly the same old Sam. "I'll be back in the morning. Kurt wants me to ride out with him for a while, then we'll sit down and make plans about how to catch us some thieves."

A cold chill rushed up Olivia's spine and that eerie feeling returned. Something horrible was going to happen before this was all over.

The next day dawned gray, with low-hanging clouds that threatened rain. Kurt spent the first hour of it pacing, wondering whether Sam would change his mind about riding out to the ruins with him once he had a chance to think about it.

The sky matched his mood exactly. He couldn't remember ever feeling so helpless before, and the helplessness quickly turned to a stormy anger that kept his feet moving while he waited. He had a chance to save the ruins, and a chance to save Olivia, and he seemed incapable of doing either.

Olivia watched him in near-silence. Most of the women Kurt had known would have badgered him with questions, insisting that he talk about whatever was troubling him. Olivia seemed to accept without being told that he'd talk about it when he was ready.

Only once did she broach the subject during breakfast,

and then only to assure him quietly that Sam would keep his word. And, of course, she was right.

Sam rode in shortly after they'd finished eating, looking just about as ominous as he had the first time Kurt saw him. His duster whipped in the wind and he wore his hat pulled low over his eyes. Within minutes, they were riding out again, each grimly determined to find a solution to their problems.

The ride onto the mesa took longer than usual in the rising wind. Kurt's horse shied several times, as if he knew something Kurt didn't. And when they finally reached the mesa's crest, the howling of the wind made it difficult to speak and be heard.

Kurt rode slowly, leading the way, and signaled for Sam to stop when they were finally directly above Sandstone Castle. "What do you think?" he shouted. "Do you want to come in from the bottom through Inca Canyon or go down from here?"

"Here," Sam shouted back. "It'll save time. Just don't tell Livvy."

Kurt laughed. "Don't worry."

They found a sheltered spot to leave their horses and walked to the edge of the cliff, keeping their heads down against the gale. They found signs that Sloan and his men had climbed down to the ruins from this same spot using ropes, fallen trees, and natural outcroppings in the rock to make their descent easier.

The wind made it slow going at times as it whipped around them, moaned through the trees, and threw grit and sand into their eyes. When they reached the ruins at last, the sky had darkened dangerously, but it was still light enough to see even in the shadows of the cave. And here, they were protected from the worst of the storm.

Kurt watched as Sam took in the sight in front of him. They were both panting from exertion but Sam still managed to let out a whistle. "You mean to tell me these have been here the whole time?"

"Just the last thousand years or so."

"Fancy that." Sam moved a few steps further into the cave. A gust of wind made an eerie whistling sound as it hit the back of the cave and swirled around the deserted ruins. "Harvey always said he knew every inch of his land. Guess he was wrong."

Kurt cut a glance at Sam. "Are you sure he didn't know?"

Sam turned back to him with a scowl. "He would've said something to me. At least, I think he would have." He let his gaze run up the length of the guard tower. "But here they are. No denying that. And I can't for the life of me figure how you found 'em when Harvey never did."

"In Harvey's defense, I did know where to look."

"True enough. But Harvey spent most of his last two years riding these canyons. Stands to reason he might've stumbled across 'em."

Kurt nodded, but it made him sick to think Harvey might have kept such a huge secret from his wife and best friend. "That's what I think, too. And I wonder—" He broke off, reluctant to voice the thought that kept eating at him, but nothing else made sense. "I wonder if he told Sloan Durrant about them. *He* certainly didn't seem to have any trouble finding them."

Sam let out a heavy breath and shielded his eyes against a shower of windswept dirt. "I don't want to think so, but I can't figure anything else." He turned to look at Kurt more closely. "And you say Olivia has seen these?"

"She has."

Sam gave that some thought, scanned the village again, and turned back to Kurt. "So, what are we going to do about it?"

Kurt had spent much of the night asking himself the same question. "First, I'd like to take a quick inventory of what we have here. That way we'll be able to tell if Sloan and his men are just snooping around or actually taking things."

"Sounds reasonable."

"I'd *like* to post an armed guard—one of us up top, the other one in the bottom of the canyon, but Olivia's not too keen on the idea. I told her we'd talk to the marshall and see what he has to say, but I wanted you to see what we're talking about first."

Sam ran a hand along his chin. "Can't hurt to talk to him, I suppose. Tom Pulver's a decent man. Not at all sure he'll do anything about it, though. He doesn't usually get involved in petty disputes like this one."

"It's not exactly petty."

"In his mind it will be. He's going to figure it's not worth his time or effort since the property's going to belong to the bank in a few days anyway. And he's not going to be eager to listen to anything bad about Sloan Durrant. Sloan's made himself a popular man in town."

Kurt's stomach twisted. The situation seemed hopeless, but he refused to give up. "That's why I'd like you to come with us when we talk to him. The marshall doesn't know me. I'm a drifter, coming into town and pointing fingers at folks who just happen to be friends of his. Olivia's a desperate widow who might be willing to do and say anything to save her ranch. But you're a respected member of the community. *You* can accomplish what neither one of us can."

"Maybe." Sam pondered some more, studying the ruins from a distance as he thought and watching his step as he moved slightly closer to make sure he didn't break anything. "You really think these ruins can save the Lazy H for Olivia?"

"Eventually. Not immediately."

Sam scowled thoughtfully. "Then what good will talking to Marshall Pulver do? Olivia can't wait for eventually."

"We've still got a couple of days," Kurt said with more assurance than he felt. "We'll think of something."

Sam's brittle laugh mixed with the wind and echoed off the walls of the cave. "Wish I could be as sure as you are."

"I'm not sure at all," Kurt admitted. "I'm just hoping like hell one of us will have a brilliant idea before Sloan forecloses." He thought again about Olivia's excitement over the newspaper article and said something he'd never thought he'd say. "We could wire that museum in Denver—the one the Wetherills sold some of their artifacts to. If they're interested in buying some of ours, maybe they'd even be willing to wire Olivia some money up front."

"It's worth a try," Sam said. "What does Olivia think?"

"I haven't mentioned it to her yet. I had to talk myself into it first."

Sam grinned slowly. "Guess she *will* be all right with you, at that."

He took off his hat and took one more slow glance around at the broken pottery shards and broken sandstone bricks. Even to Kurt, the task looked insurmountable. He could only imagine what Sam must be thinking.

But Sam found a spot to leave his hat and turned back to him. "All right, then, boss. I'd say we ought to get started. What do you want me to do first?"

Kurt stared at the telegram with growing disbelief. *Not interested?* How could the museum in Denver not be interested? This wasn't right. It wasn't even *close* to being right. He'd been so *certain* Olivia could get money enough to pay the mortgage by selling some of the artifacts.

He looked over his shoulder at Olivia, who stood beside

Sam with hope dancing in her eyes, and at Sam, who looked as if he'd already picked up on Kurt's expression.

"What did they say?" Olivia demanded.

Reluctantly, Kurt handed the telegram to her, kicking himself mentally for building up her hopes. He couldn't bear to watch the light in her eyes die, so he turned back to the wiry, greasy-haired telegraph operator whom Sam had called Texas Jack. "Are you sure you got this right? Maybe you left out a word or two or got an extra one in there where it didn't belong."

Texas Jack scowled at him darkly. "I didn't leave nothing out, mister. And I didn't add nothin' either. I'm not in the habit of getting messages wrong."

"I'm sure you're not," Kurt said quickly. He didn't want to alienate anyone. You never could tell who might be able to help Olivia. "But—" But he sure as hell couldn't explain how he knew this message wasn't accurate. Or why he *believed* it wasn't accurate, anyway.

According to the books he'd read, people had been falling all over themselves to cart away pieces of history. Some had sold them for a hefty profit. Some had added the pieces to private collections. Only a handful of people had been interested in protecting the ruins, and it had taken them until well after the turn of the century to find success. But people had sure been quick to protect their own interests.

In fact, if history hadn't changed completely, the people of nearby Durango would arrest Gustav Nordenskiold, a young scholar from Sweden, in less than a month and charge him with collecting relics illegally, damaging cliff structures in Mesa Verde, and attempting to send a valuable collection out of the country.

How could the museum *not* want the Black Mesa artifacts?

Kurt caught Texas Jack's frown and the slight lift of his shoulders that spoke of aggravation, and decided not to push his luck. Jerking his head toward the door, he stepped out onto the boardwalk.

Sam and Olivia followed close behind. "What now?" Sam asked, crumpling the telegram in his fist and shoving it into his pocket.

Kurt shook his head, thinking quickly but coming up with nothing. "I suppose we could try again to get the museum interested, but I'm afraid we may be fighting a losing battle."

Olivia waited for a man and woman to pass, then said softly, "I think our next logical step is to talk to the marshall."

"Whatever we do," Sam said in a low voice, "we have to move quickly. Now that Texas Jack knows we've contacted the museum, it won't take long for Sloan Durrant to hear what we're up to."

"And when Sloan hears that the museum turned us down, he's going to get braver," Kurt predicted. "We have to figure that he'll be watching every step we take from here on out."

"The marshall will do something," Olivia said, but her eyes gleamed with more hope than certainty. "The artifacts are on my land."

Sam shot a look at Kurt, but neither had the guts to dash her hopes. Besides, Kurt reasoned, they might be wrong about Marshall Pulver. Better to wait and see than to upset Olivia with dour predictions.

They started off together with Kurt on one side of Olivia and Sam on the other. Kurt tried to work up a little faith that things would go the way Olivia wanted them to, but the look on Sam's face made it difficult.

He reminded himself that Sam believed Tom Pulver was a good man, but he couldn't forget that Pulver considered Sloan Durrant a friend. He told himself repeatedly that Sam's opinion would carry some weight, but Sloan's might equal or outweigh Sam's.

He tried desperately to find some flicker of hope to cling to, but he found himself instead trying to come up with a Plan B that didn't involve losing Olivia if she lost the ranch. No matter how hard he tried, he couldn't see any way for her to remain in Colorado. She'd have no source of income, no place to live. And he had nothing to offer her, no way to support her, not even a roof to put over her head.

It didn't take long to reach the town marshall's office, but his mind had been down half a dozen different dead-end roads by the time they got there. Sam led the way inside, Olivia followed, and Kurt brought up the rear.

Marshall Pulver, a paunchy man in his late forties with a thick shock of graying hair and a moustache that rivaled Sam's, looked up when they entered. He smiled at Sam and stood to shake his hand, hesitated briefly before he shook Kurt's, and tipped his hat to Olivia. "Mrs. Hamilton. It's been a while since I've seen you."

She sent him a thin smile and took the chair he offered. Sam took the other, which left Kurt standing near the door. Olivia didn't waste time on social niceties. "I have a problem, Marshall. I need your help."

Marshall Pulver's smile faded. He lowered himself back into his chair and linked his hands on the desk in front of him. "What sort of problem?"

"Someone has been trespassing on my property."

"That's easy enough to fix. Have Sam here build you a fence. That's the best way I know of to keep people out of where you don't want them to go."

Kurt bristled at the marshall's patronizing tone, but he forced himself to let Sam handle it. He'd only make things worse if he opened his mouth.

Olivia flicked a thin smile at the marshall. "It's not that easy. We're talking about my land up on the mesa."

Marshall Pulver leaned back in his chair and regarded her intently. "I'm not sure I understand the problem. Are you upset because someone rode across a stretch of your land?"

"No." Olivia put some starch in her backbone. "I'm upset because someone has been vandalizing some valuable property up there."

"Valuable property?" The marshall looked to Sam as if he couldn't quite believe Olivia.

"Native ruins," Sam said. "Finer than anything they got over at the Wetherills's."

The marshall's eyes widened for a heartbeat. "You seen these ruins, Sam?"

"I have."

"Well. Isn't that something?" Marshall Pulver took a moment to think about that and turned his attention Kurt's way. "What's your part in this?"

"I work for Mrs. Hamilton."

Olivia leaned slightly forward. "Someone has been there, Marshall. Without my permission. They've already broken some valuable relics and probably taken others."

The marshall leaned back in his seat and smoothed his moustache with his thumb and forefinger. "I'm still not sure I understand. You're complaining because someone broke some old Indian pots out at your place?"

"Artifacts, Marshall. Not just old pots. I'd like your help catching whoever is doing it."

Kurt bit back a smile of approval at the way she carefully avoided mentioning names. The marshall would see for himself soon enough.

Marshall Pulver's mouth twisted. "You want me to sit out there in the middle of the canyon to keep people from breaking more of them?"

Sam leaned into the conversation. "We just want help protecting her property."

"I understand that, Sam. But you know better than to ask a thing like that. There's just me and one deputy here. Besides, how do you know they didn't get broken by the wind or something? That's one thing we don't have a shortage of out here . . . wind."

Kurt held back a frustrated sigh. "These pots weren't broken by the wind. There are footprints all over the site."

The marshall's quick scowl warned Kurt to work harder at keeping his mouth shut. "You believe all this, Sam?"

"I've been there. I've seen the footprints. I'm here. That ought to say it."

"If you'd just come out there, you'd see what we're talking about," Olivia bargained. "And I'm sure you'd understand why this is so important."

Marshall Pulver leaned forward and rested his arms on the desk. "Look, Mrs. Hamilton, let me be frank with you. Even if I was a mind to, I couldn't watch every section of land somebody around here wanted to keep folks off of. And I don't see why you're so worried, anyway. You ought to talk to Sloan Durrant and let him worry about it."

"It's not Durrant's property yet," Kurt growled.

Sam shot him a warning look. "He's right, Tom. The bank hasn't foreclosed yet. And this just might be a way for Mrs. Hamilton to save her property, *if* we can keep people from stealing the artifacts out from under her nose."

Marshall Pulver heaved a sigh. "I sympathize, Mrs. Hamilton. But none of what you've told me changes the facts. I don't have the manpower to do what you're asking. If I did it for you, I'd have to do it for everybody." He rocked forward in his chair again. "Tell you what I will do, though. You let Sam and this fella watch the place for you. If they catch somebody actually stealing from you, bring 'em to me and I'll see that they're brought to trial next time the circuit judge rides through. That's the best I can do."

His answer didn't surprise Kurt, but the disappointment

on Olivia's face made him wish they'd been more honest with her about what to expect.

And the realization that he'd gone full circle knotted in his stomach. He'd been guarding the ruins the night he was brought here. He just hoped this wouldn't be what finally took him back.

Chapter 17

OLIVIA LISTENED TO the deep rumble of voices on the other side of the room as she poured coffee and divided last night's apple pie in half. They'd been talking for hours about their visit to town, tossing out alternatives, arguing mildly, but they kept coming back to the same place—Kurt and Sam would have to guard the ruins themselves.

She just couldn't make herself agree. She'd rather give up the Lazy H than be responsible for anything happening to either one of the men sitting at her table. Unfortunately, they had two things in common—bull-thick heads and stubborn pride. No matter how many times she said she'd simply let Sloan Durrant foreclose, Kurt and Sam refused to even consider that as an option.

Now, as she carried the coffee and pie to the table, Sam was at it again. "There's no other option, Livvy. The only way to stop Sloan is to stand guard out there."

She shook her head firmly. "Absolutely not."

"It's the *only way*," Sam argued. "The three of us could sit here speculating for a year, but that wouldn't accomplish anything."

"It's too dangerous."

Kurt scowled up at her. "Not if we're careful. The only other alternative is to let Sloan take the land and you go back to Virginia."

She sat between the two men, breathing deeply to keep her mounting panic at bay. "I don't want to go back to Virginia. I don't want to let Sloan Durrant take anything. But I refuse to let either one of you put yourselves in danger."

"Nobody's going to get hurt," Sam assured her. But he couldn't leave it there. He had to add, "Unless it's Sloan."

Olivia shook her head emphatically. "I don't want *anyone* to get hurt. Not Sloan, not you . . ." She turned a glare in Kurt's direction. "And not you." When it looked as if he might argue with her, she cut him off. "I lost Harvey out of pure stubborn foolishness. I'm *not* going to lose anyone else I care about."

They shared a sheepish glance between them. Sam's eyes darted to hers and away several times. But Kurt met her gaze and held it. "We'll be careful, Olivia. I promise you that."

"No." She stood quickly, unable to stand the look in his eyes. "How careful can you *be* in a situation like that? If Sloan Durrant wants the land and the ruins badly enough to sneak around and lie to get them, what makes you think he'll stop there?"

"I *don't* think he will," Kurt said. "That's exactly why Sam and I need to do something. If we don't, he'll run you out of here. As it is, your options are narrowing by the day."

"I don't care."

"Of course you do." Kurt stood to face her. "We wouldn't be sitting here now if you didn't."

"I don't care *this* much."

Kurt took her shoulders gently. "Look, Olivia, Sloan wants you to be frightened. He's banking on it. That's why he came out here and told you what he was doing. The only mistake we made was in going to town and talking to Marshall Pulver first. Sloan will know by now that we're ready to put up a fight."

"On the other hand," Sam put in, "it might just make him nervous."

Kurt nodded without taking his eyes from hers. "That's what I'm hoping."

Olivia's stomach lurched and her hands grew clammy. "That's what you're *hoping*?" She jerked away from him, so angry she had to clench her fists to keep from striking him. "You're hoping for a confrontation?"

"I'm hoping for a resolution."

His eyes bored into hers. She could see a tiny scar by the side of his lip, the lines that crinkled near his eyes when he laughed, the faint hint of the dimples in his cheek. He'd become so familiar, so dear, and so important, how would she go on if something happened to him?

Sam stood to join them. "We can't do anything without your okay, Olivia. But we need to do something. And it's not just for you. If Sloan Durrant manages to run you out of your ranch, he'll do it again to someone else."

"Why is it *my* responsibility to stop Sloan?" She pulled away from Kurt and put some distance between them. "The people around here have never cared about me. Even after Harvey died, you were the only one who did anything to help. And I know what the women in town think of me for staying on here alone. How can you tell me I owe them anything?"

"You don't." Sam looked as if he wanted to come after her, but he held his ground. "But you do owe it to yourself. I know you, Livvy. If you let Sloan get away with this and he hurts someone else, you'll feel bad about it for the rest of your life."

She wrapped her arms around herself and looked away, wishing he didn't know her so well. He was right, of course. She couldn't just do nothing. She sighed in frustration and resignation. "Supposing I did agree . . . what would you propose to do?"

Kurt bit back a grin as if he knew smiling was the worst thing he could do. "We'll simply stand watch for a few nights until we can figure out what's happening out there."

"At the same time?" She'd feel better knowing neither of them was alone.

Sam nodded. "We'd have to. One of us would take the top of the mesa. The other would stand guard in the valley below the ruins."

"Where would I be?"

"You'd be right here," Kurt said firmly. She opened her mouth to protest, but Kurt cut her off. "No, I'm not saying that just because you're a woman. But my guess is that when Sloan and his boys ride up onto the mesa, they come by here first to make sure you're home and everything's normal. They'll be even more likely to do it now that they know we're not packing up to leave in a few days. And if you're here, you can ride for Marshall Pulver if anything goes wrong."

"How will I know if something does go wrong?" she demanded.

Kurt shot a glance at Sam. "Could you hear gunshots from up on the mesa this far away?"

"Most likely."

"Then that'll be our signal. Three gunshots in rapid succession. Leave Nightmare saddled. But if you do ride out for the marshall, you'll have to be careful. Sloan might leave a man or two watching this place while he and the others are up on the mesa."

Olivia shivered again. The idea of someone watching her without her knowledge made her sick. "And what do I do if Marshall Pulver won't listen to me?"

"You'll have to make him listen," Sam said, then

changed the subject. "Do you still have Harvey's Smith & Wesson?"

She nodded, too numb to speak.

"Kurt's going to need it." And to Kurt, "You know how to use a Smith & Wesson top break?"

"I've seen them," Kurt said, his voice grim, his eyes dark. "It shouldn't be too difficult."

"Spend some time practicing before we ride out," Sam ordered. "I want you able to pop those shells out and reload without fumbling. And make sure you can hit something with it." He stood and crossed the room to brush a light kiss on Olivia's cheek. "I'll be back in a couple of hours. And don't worry. We're not going to kill anybody. At most, we'll just wing 'em to show we mean business—and probably not even that. That's why I want to know Kurt can hit what he aims at."

She managed a tremulous smile. She even managed to act as if she believed him. But the ominous feeling she'd been fighting for the past two days grew decidedly stronger.

As soon as he could see the next morning, Kurt began the climb up the cliff toward the Anasazi village. He'd spent a cramped and chilly night hidden behind a clump of trees in the bottom of the canyon, watching the ruins while Sam kept watch up above. In another few minutes they'd head back to the ranch, but Kurt wanted to check the ruins before they rode out again.

A raven screamed in the clear light of morning and a shower of pebbles from overhead brought his head up sharply. Sam stood silhouetted against the rising sun, his rifle resting on his arm.

"Expecting trouble?" he shouted up to his friend. His voice echoed in the narrow canyon. Every sound seemed magnified by the canyon walls.

"No sense taking chances," Sam shouted back.

"Even Sloan Durrant isn't going to risk being seen out here in broad daylight."

"Maybe not, but it still pays to be careful."

Kurt conceded the point with a nod and returned to his climb. His eyes were gritty from lack of sleep and even his bones longed for rest, but he couldn't ignore the persistent urge to check on the pottery they'd hidden in one of the crumbling *estufas* the last time they were here.

He reached the cave just as sunlight began to crest the mesa and filter through the trees on the opposite side of the canyon. It turned the drab sand-colored walls to a breathtaking gold, and for a few moments Kurt almost believed the city had been built of gold dust instead of sandstone.

He laughed softly to himself and wondered what Harvey would have done if he could have seen the village this way. His laughter faded when he realized that Harvey probably would have destroyed everything in an attempt to get gold out of sand.

Not for the first time, he wondered what Olivia's life had been like with Harvey. He couldn't imagine Olivia, who'd changed her mind about selling the artifacts after just one glance, who'd been sensitive enough to feel the spirits of the ancients with her first footsteps onto the site, married to a man whose only goal seemed to have been exploiting it.

He picked his way carefully across the mound of broken pottery he and Sam had sifted through the day before toward the back of the cave. It took a few minutes to find the opening of the ceremonial room, but he eventually found it and carefully let himself into the darkened room.

He struck a match and took a quick look around the walls blackened with soot more than a thousand years old. But when he saw one of the large waterpots he and Sam had carefully hauled and hidden away lying in a hundred pieces in the center of the room, he froze in place.

How? When? *Why?* The destruction was totally senseless.

He stared at the broken pot while fury took the place of exhaustion, boiling up from deep within him and filling him with the urge to help Sloan Durrant's face meet the same fate as the water jug.

Gritting his teeth in anger, he waved out the first match, struck another, and hunkered down in front of the once-beautiful jug. It had been almost whole the previous afternoon, encircled with an ancient design of triangles and glazed from years of use, scrubbing, and polishing. Now, it was a shattered, ruined mass.

Raw hatred tore through him, knotting his stomach, making the hair on the back of his neck stand on end. *Damn them!* He'd rather see the relics added to someone's private collection than destroyed.

When the second match singed his fingers, he shook it out and let out a string of obscenities. His voice echoed through the *estufa*, bounced around in the cave, and rose through the morning.

A second later, he heard Sam's echoing shout. "Something wrong?"

"Damned right." Kurt scrambled out of the *estufa*, wishing he could take out his anger on something—anything. But the ancient relics around him were too delicate. He didn't dare touch anything in this mood. "Someone must have gotten past us last night."

Sam didn't answer immediately, but a few seconds later another shower of pebbles heralded his arrival at the end of a rope. "How the hell did they get past us? I thought we had everything covered."

"So did I." If he couldn't even protect the ruins when he was sitting right there watching, what good was he?

"What did they do?"

Kurt jerked his head toward the *estufa*. "They found the stuff we hid yesterday and broke that huge water jug."

"Sonofa—" Sam cut himself off and picked his way across the rubble as if he needed to see the carnage for himself. He emerged a few seconds later with a piece of the shattered pottery in his hand. "They couldn't have gotten past us last night. They must have been here while we were in town yesterday. They must have seen us and they knew we wouldn't be back for a while."

Kurt barely resisted the urge to slam his fist into the side of the guard tower. He'd save the fist for when he could look Sloan Durrant in the eye and plant it where it belonged. "Either they think the treasure of the legend is inside the pottery or they're trying to make a point."

"Useless point if you ask me." Sam lowered the shard to the ground again and shook his head. "But they won't come out today. If they come back now, it'll be at night and we'll get 'em."

Kurt tried to find some consolation in that, but the loss of even one irreplaceable artifact made him too angry to see straight. "Let me take the ridge tonight."

Sam glanced up at him with a scowl. "Nope."

"This is my fight, not yours."

"I thought we agreed we were in this together."

"We are, but—"

"Besides," Sam said, cutting him off with a grin, "I'm a better shot."

Kurt glowered at him. "I'll practice."

"Don't be a damned fool." Sam stood to face him. "What would Olivia do if something happened to you?"

The question stopped Kurt cold.

Sensing his advantage, Sam added, "Have a heart, man. Don't make me take bad news home to her tomorrow morning."

Kurt ran a hand over his face and tried to pull himself under control. "Thanks," he said after a long moment.

"For—?"

"For stepping in and helping out."

Sam shrugged casually. "It's only right."

"Yeah, but it's still not your fight. If it gets ugly—"

"We'll deal with it." Sam turned away and made a show of looking at the remaining artifacts, apparently eager to put an end to the conversation. "You want to carry any of these back to Livvy's?"

Kurt had never thought he'd disturb the ruins by carrying artifacts out, but this senseless destruction had quickly changed his mind. "Let's take things that won't break easily, like sandals, pieces of baskets, and the yucca blankets that we can fit into the saddlebags. Tonight, we can bring something to wrap the smaller pieces of pottery in."

Sam nodded and set his hat to one side. "We'll save 'em, Kurt. *And* save Olivia's ranch. I'm not in the habit of losing."

Unfortunately, losing was one of the things Kurt had always done best.

Until now.

Kurt scarcely had a chance to talk with Olivia that day. He and Sam filled her in on the night's work, the morning's discovery, and their plans for the night, then went their separate ways to catch a few hours' sleep before riding out again.

Before Kurt knew it, Sam was back and ready to hit the trail. Olivia stood on the porch to see them off, so beautiful Kurt wanted nothing more than to set her mind at ease. But what promises could he make to her? He wouldn't build up her hopes and then see them dashed.

He couldn't promise anything. Though he'd almost started to believe he might be allowed to stay here instead of returning to his own time, he might still be wrong. In spite of his and Sam's determination to bring Sloan Durrant and his band of merry men to justice, they couldn't guarantee success.

Lost in thought, the ride to the ruins passed quickly. If

Sam sensed something on his mind, he didn't mention it. That was another thing Kurt liked about him. He knew when to talk and when to keep quiet and let a man wallow. Either that, or he was doing some serious wallowing of his own.

They hid the horses out of the way and started toward the edge of the canyon. "Keep an eye peeled," Sam said as they walked. "If I hear anyone coming, I'll step to the edge of the canyon and signal you. There'll be a full moon tonight so you ought to be able to see me."

"Why not just make a bird call or something?"

"Might be easier," Sam said with a wry grin, "but I don't sound like any bird I've ever heard, and I figure a gunshot might give us away."

Kurt laughed softly. "It just might. All right, then. Signal from the top of the canyon. I'll keep my eyes open." He watched Sam amble away, amazed at how much he'd grown to like the guy. He'd be sorry to see Sam go.

What if the unthinkable happened? What if Kurt was allowed to stay until after Sam left and then was sucked back to the future? What would happen to Olivia then? He couldn't think about it now or he'd lose his concentration.

He let himself down into the canyon carefully, sparing a quick glance at the ruins as he passed. Though he couldn't be sure, he didn't think anyone had been there during the day.

Save her.

The whisper nearly made him lose his grip on the rope. He managed to hang on, but he fell against the canyon wall hard enough to knock the wind out of him. He scrambled for a foothold and hung there until he could breathe again.

Save her.

He was trying to save her, damnit! What more could he do? He barely refrained from shouting at the insistent whisper, knowing that if he did he might give them away.

Shaking off the willies, he started moving again down the rope toward the canyon floor. But he could feel something in the air around him, a disturbance, a vaguely unsettled feeling—as if something was about to happen.

Kurt had been pacing for some time when a shout drew his attention. He spun around, took cover behind a rock, and searched the mesa for Sam. Adrenalin sent his heart slamming into the wall of his chest and put all his senses on sharp alert.

Sam might simply have shouted when he spotted someone, but Kurt couldn't imagine Sam losing his cool enough to do that. Maybe he'd slipped on the sharp incline or been hurt in some other way. Maybe he'd been ambushed.

Kurt inched forward carefully, keeping his eye on the rim of the canyon, willing Sam to show himself. An instant later, a silhouette appeared on the canyon rim and Kurt let out a sigh of relief. But when a second figure appeared his short-lived relief vanished.

Two men. And Kurt had the sick feeling that neither one of them was Sam. He forced himself to remain calm and prayed silently that Sam hadn't been hurt or killed. Olivia would never forgive him. He'd never forgive himself.

He shrank back into the shadows and watched for several minutes, itching to check on Sam but knowing that he had to be careful. First, he had to know what he was up against. Two against one were odds he could handle, but he wasn't stupid enough to go charging into battle against half a dozen men or more without a real good plan.

He waited until he was reasonably certain that there were only two intruders, then began to work his way toward the base of the hill inch by frustrating inch. He moved cautiously, testing each step before trusting his weight on the loose dirt. Every sound he made seemed magnified by the silence surrounding him.

The soft murmur of voices drifted down from high overhead, but Kurt couldn't make out what they said. He'd be taking a risk if he used the rope to get back onto the mesa, but he couldn't walk out to Inca Canyon before morning and he didn't dare leave Sam on his own that long.

Scarcely daring to breathe, he began his climb. He moved slowly, hand over hand, chafing under the delay. By the time he'd made it halfway up the hill he'd run a dozen different strategies through his mind, from taking the men by surprise and thwarting their escape to leaping into a clearing, guns blazing, like something out of a second-rate Western movie. It would depend upon Sam's condition when he got up there.

He didn't want to think Sam might be dead, but he also wouldn't underestimate his adversaries. With every nerve screaming alert, Kurt kept climbing until he reached the mesa top.

But there he ran into another problem. No vegetation grew within thirty feet of the cliff's edge. He'd have to be damned careful to make it up over the top without getting caught.

He hung there, listening for voices, until he thought his arms might fall out of his sockets, then heaved himself up onto the mesa. Scrambling to his feet, he pulled Harvey's revolver from the holster on his hip and found cover behind the trees.

To his immense relief, nobody shot at him. Nobody even shouted a warning. In fact, except for normal night sounds, the mesa top was eerily silent. Sweat pooled beneath his arms and trickled down his back and into his eyes, but he stayed down just long enough to catch his breath before taking stock of his surroundings.

The voices had faded, and it took several minutes of watching carefully to realize that the men had gone. Only a shadowed lump against the base of a tree remained.

Sweating bullets, Kurt crept toward it and cursed himself silently for letting Sam get involved until a light moan cut the silence and relief so strong it almost made Kurt sick swamped him.

"Sam?" He spoke softly, still not sure whether anyone was watching.

Another moan, this one stronger, and this time the lump moved. "Hell."

"Sam?" Kurt hurried toward him, still cautious but more anxious to make sure he was all right. "What happened?"

The lump took shape and touched the back of its head gingerly. "Sonofabitch hit me."

"Did you see who it was?"

"No." Sam tilted back his head and looked up at the stars. "But I smelled him."

Kurt laughed, then caught himself and grew silent once more. "Are they still around?"

"Take a whiff," Sam groused. "Can you smell steer manure, whiskey, and that cheap aftershave from the barber shop?"

"No."

"Then they're gone." Sam swore and ran a hand along the back of his neck. "Did they get anything?"

"I don't think so. I think finding you here must have frightened them off."

"Yeah. They acted real scared." Sam found his hat in the dirt and pushed to his feet slowly, but he had to use a boulder to steady himself.

"Who were they?"

"One of 'em's Quincy Albright. He's the only person I know who smells that foul."

"Maybe we should talk to the marshall again."

"Not yet." Sam straightened slowly and gingerly put on his hat.

"Why not? We have proof now that someone's been out here. And you've been hurt. Surely—"

"Because this makes it personal," Sam snarled. "I think I know who Durrant's got working for him, and I'm damned sure you and I can take 'em." He started toward the horses as if nothing had ever happened. "No sense hanging around. They won't be back tonight. Best thing we can do is make sure Livvy's all right and decide what to do next."

Kurt followed quickly, sickened by the realization that his obsession with the ruins had put Sam and Olivia in jeopardy. Important as he still believed the ruins were, they *weren't* worth the life and safety of even one person.

Until an hour ago, they might have been able to put an end to all this simply by letting go. But if someone was willing to hurt Sam over a few ancient artifacts, they wouldn't stop now. They'd set the ball in motion. Now they had to finish the game—whether they wanted to or not.

Chapter 18

B Y THE DIM light of the oil lamp, Olivia leaned back on her heels and looked at the freshly scrubbed floor. For the second night in a row, she'd found herself unable to sit still while she waited.

She'd tried reading more from Kurt's book, but every word made his image form in her mind, so sharp and clear she couldn't concentrate. Scrubbing floors and polishing furniture didn't require much concentration and it helped relieve her helpless frustration a little.

The long hours alone had given her time to think. She'd spent hours thinking about Harvey, remembering their life together with a clarity she'd denied herself for a long time. They'd been happy at first, she would never deny that. But she wondered if they would have been happy if she'd argued with his decision to come West as she had with his decision to abandon the ranch to search for the treasure.

They hadn't been happy for the last two years of their marriage. No matter how much she wished it, she couldn't make it so. Harvey had known how much she missed

Melody. He'd known how lonely she was on the ranch by herself while he spent days in the canyons, yet he'd never once made the simple suggestion that had come so easily to Kurt.

She carried her scrub bucket to the door and tossed the dirty water out into the yard. As she reached for the door to close it again, the sound of approaching horses caught her ears. Dropping the bucket, she raced into the house and pulled Harvey's rifle from above the mantle.

Cautiously, she moved toward the window and nudged the curtain back a fraction of an inch. She couldn't identify the riders at first and her heart jumped into her throat and bounced around there while she waited.

They rode straight toward the house and her fingers grew damp on the rifle barrel. Would she be able to protect herself and her property, or would she drop the rifle? Lifting it to her shoulder, she waited, scarcely breathing, as the riders drew closer.

Finally, the clouds parted and she recognized Sam and Kurt. Trembling with relief, she lowered the rifle to the floor and hurried to the door. They'd set out less than two hours ago to stand watch all night. Why were they back?

She raced onto the porch just as Sam and Kurt started up the stairs. "What happened? Why are you back?" Sam's face looked different somehow and he walked unsteadily. She looked to Kurt for reassurance and answers. "*What happened?*"

"We had company again tonight," Kurt said as he stepped onto the porch. "Let's just say they weren't exactly happy to find Sam waiting for them."

Olivia's dinner curdled in her stomach. Instinctively, she reached up to cup Sam's face. "They hurt you?"

"Not fatally."

"Who was it? Did you see?"

Sam shook his head carefully, wincing slightly with the movement. "They got the drop on me, so I didn't see a blasted thing. But I'm pretty sure I caught a whiff of Quincy Albright."

"Quincy Albright?" Olivia took Sam's arm and guided him into the house. She'd heard the name before, but she couldn't put a face with it. "Are you sure?"

"He's the only person I know of who smells like that."

"But . . ." Olivia settled Sam in a chair and turned to fill a bowl with water at the pump. "So what is this Quincy Albright doing with Sloan Durrant?"

"Some people will do almost anything for money. Sloan might want to keep his hands clean, but he knows Quincy doesn't mind getting his dirty." Sam touched the back of his head gingerly, drawing Olivia's attention to the matted blood there.

Holding back a cry of dismay, she forced herself to stay calm. "How badly did they hurt you? And don't try to lie to me. I want the truth."

"Not bad, Livvy. It's just a bump on the head."

"A bump with a lot of blood."

"We're just lucky Sam's got such a hard head," Kurt joked.

His smile tore at her already jangled nerves. "It's not funny," she shouted at him, fighting the tears that stung her eyes. She *wouldn't* cry.

Kurt's smile vanished. "I know it's not funny, Olivia. But he's not hurt badly."

She parted Sam's hair and checked the wound for herself. "It's not deep, thank God. But it shouldn't be here at all."

Kurt carried two sets of saddlebags into the house while she rinsed a clean rag in the water and began to clean the blood away. "I don't like this," she told both men when Kurt shut the door behind him. "I don't like it at all."

"None of us do," Kurt assured her. He lowered the

saddlebags carefully to the floor. "But we're in it up to our necks now."

"Our necks and Sam's head. What's next?" Fury Olivia didn't completely understand began to beat on steady wings through her and the look on both their faces made a strange dread begin to curl just beneath her anger. She'd seen that look before, and she knew what it meant.

"We can't back down now." Sam pulled her hand away from his head.

Olivia snatched her hand away from his. "Why not? They know we're on to them. Maybe they'll stop."

Sam shook his head slowly. "They aren't going to back down. All we did was talk to the marshall yesterday and send one little telegram." He touched the back of his head with his free hand. "They had to know we'd be there tonight, and this isn't exactly the kind of greeting you normally get from someone who wants to be your friend."

"I realize that," she snapped. "That's why I don't want you going out there again." She whirled to face Kurt, who'd started pouring coffee into three cups. "I don't want either of you going out there. I won't let you two put yourselves at risk, even if it does mean that I lose the ranch."

"For what it's worth," Kurt said, his face frighteningly solemn, "I agree with you. But I'm afraid it may have already gone beyond that."

"What do you mean?"

Kurt handed Olivia a cup of coffee and placed one on the table in front of Sam. Sitting, he motioned for her to join them and waited to go on until she'd forced her agitated body into a chair. "I've wondered about something for a while now, but I'd talked myself into believing I was way off base . . . until now. The attack on Sam has convinced me that maybe I was right after all." He pushed his cup out of the way and touched the back of her hand.

"I have to ask this, Olivia. Is there any possibility that Harvey's death wasn't an accident?"

The suggestion touched Olivia's heart like a red-hot brand and sent searing pain through her. She shook her head quickly, unable—or maybe just unwilling—to even credit the idea. "Of course not. He fell."

She turned to Sam for support, but the look on his face only made the pain worse.

"I think he stumbled across Sloan doing something out there at the site," Kurt said. "Sam and I both think it's almost impossible that Harvey rode those canyons as much as he did and never even saw the ruins."

"He would have told me," she insisted, but a sick feeling in her stomach told her she might be wrong.

"Doesn't it seem like too much of a coincidence that he was killed in the same spot where Sam was attacked tonight? The same spot where I landed when I was brought here?"

"No." Olivia stood suddenly, sending coffee sloshing over the rim of her cup. "Harvey *wasn't* murdered."

Kurt stood to face her. "We have to face facts, Olivia—"

"No!" She backed away, nearly knocking over a chair behind her. "I don't believe it. I *won't* believe it." In spite of her protests, futility and resignation curled through her. Tears filled her eyes and a huge lump blocked her throat, tearing a sob from her. She covered her mouth with both hands and took a fumbling step backward.

Kurt was there immediately, pulling her into his arms and cradling her against his chest. She should hate him for this. She wanted to hate him. But the feel of his arms and chest, the scent of him, seemed to comfort her instead.

Harvey had been her husband, yet it wasn't the thought of him being murdered that frightened her most. It was the thought of Kurt meeting a similar fate that made her numb with fear.

• • •

Later, after she'd made certain Sam really was all right and spent a useless fifteen minutes trying to convince him to stay the night, Olivia stood beside Kurt in the yard and watched Sam ride off toward the Cinnabar.

Silently, Kurt reached for her hand and laced his fingers through hers. "About what I said earlier—"

An overwhelming feeling of comfort pulsed through her. Who would have ever thought that such a simple gesture could convey so much? "It's all right," she said softly. "You might be right."

"I don't want to be right." Kurt pulled her close and slid an arm around her waist.

"I don't want you to be, either." She worked up a weak smile and nestled a little closer to him. "But even more, I don't want something to happen to you while you're out there."

His face grew solemn. "I never should have asked Sam to go out there with me. It's my fault he's banged up now."

Olivia smiled and flicked a glance in the direction Sam had taken. "Sam has his own mind. You couldn't have forced him into anything, and you couldn't have stopped him. But I don't want to talk about the past anymore tonight. Or about the ruins, or Sloan Durrant, or even about Harvey."

"What do you want to talk about?"

Olivia snuggled slightly closer, relishing the heat of his body, the scent of his skin. "Absolutely nothing. I just want to enjoy this moment."

He closed his eyes and breathed in the scent of her hair in a gesture so touching fresh tears pricked her eyes. As if they'd stood this way a thousand times, he wrapped his arms around her and rested his cheek on the top of her head. "Sounds perfect."

She could feel his voice rumbling in his chest, the deep

tones against her cheek as it rose and fell. She took comfort in the rhythm of his breathing, unbelievably familiar even after such a short time. She wondered what it would feel like to lie next to him, to sleep with his arms around her and wake to his smile. Would she ever know?

She let out a wistful sigh almost before she realized what she was doing.

Kurt pulled back and looked down at her. "Something wrong?"

"No."

"Then why the sigh?"

"I was just wondering what the future is going to bring. The *immediate* future. I keep telling myself to be content with what is, but I can't help but wonder how long you'll be here and what I'll do when you leave."

"That's a depressing subject." Kurt's lips brushed her hair as he talked. His hands began to move in slow circles on her back. "Let's forget about the future, too—just for tonight."

"And do what?"

In answer, he bent toward her and covered her lips with his. So much about him was becoming familiar, but the heat he generated with his kiss still took her by surprise. Before she could even catch her breath, he'd ended the kiss and smiled down at her. "Just a suggestion."

"And a mighty fine one at that." She stood on her toes and returned the favor, savoring the feel and the taste of him.

His arms tightened around her convulsively and a low groan sounded in his throat. When the kiss ended, he held her there. "I wasn't supposed to fall in love with you," he whispered.

She wrapped her arms more tightly around him. "Are you sure about that?"

He laughed softly. "I'm not sure about anything anymore—except that I'm hopelessly in love."

"That seems only fair. I feel as if I've always been in love with you."

"Even when you thought I was crazy?"

She grinned impishly. "I never said I was smart."

He dipped his head again and kissed her thoroughly. When neither of them could breathe, he pulled back and cradled her against his chest again. "If I could promise to stay forever, I would."

"I don't want to think about the empty hole you've left in the future," she whispered. "Or about how powerless I am to keep you here. I want to forget all that and pretend like you'll be here forever—if only for one night."

His eyes darkened and the sudden flare of intensity on his face twisted her heart. His hands moved slowly along her back and up her sides until the tips of his thumbs brushed her breasts. She caught a ragged breath and let out a sigh of pleasure.

One more kiss drew them together. His hands moved with a gentleness that surprised her in a man his size. With a nimbleness that pleased her, his fingers released the top buttons on her dress and skimmed the tops of her breasts. For the space of a heartbeat it almost seemed as if their souls became one.

But it wasn't enough. She wanted more. Much more. Words seemed inadequate. Hands and lips weren't capable of expressing everything in her heart. If Kurt disappeared tomorrow, a few kisses and caresses wouldn't be enough to carry her through the rest of her life without him.

Standing on tiptoe, she pressed her lips to his ear and whispered a suggestion so daring, so brazen, it almost made her blush. But it seemed, at that moment, exactly right. "Love me."

His hands stilled and he pulled back to study her. "What did you say?" His voice was thick with desire, husky with longing, and the sound of it sent the most delicious shivers through her trembling body.

"Love me," she said again. "All of me."

His hands shook as he moved them down to her waist again. "I can't promise that I'll stay—"

"I'm not asking for promises." She ran her hands along his chest and pressed her lips to the skin of his neck. "I need you, tonight."

She couldn't understand the garbled sound that escaped his throat but its meaning was crystal clear. Without another word, he lifted her gently and carried her toward the house.

Inside, he moved quickly toward the tiny bedroom and kicked open the door with one foot.

Breathing raggedly, he lowered her to the bed and stood over her for a moment, his eyes bright. "No matter what happens after tonight, you'll always have my heart."

"And you'll have mine," she promised. "Always." The last word caught on the lump growing in her throat, but she swallowed and tried to force it away. She didn't want sadness to ruin the moment.

Gently, Kurt sat on the edge of the bed and bent to kiss her once more. His lips soothed her at the same time his tentative touch ignited a fire deep within her. With agonizing slowness, he worked open the remaining buttons on her dress and let his eyes take their fill.

"You're so beautiful," he whispered so softly she could barely hear him. "I have no right to do this."

"You have no right *not* to do this," she said in an effort to lead him away from the sadness spilling from his eyes. "Unless, of course, you don't want to."

He laughed hoarsely and gathered her to him. "That, my love, is one thing you don't have to worry about."

While he held her, she fumbled with the buttons of his shirt, finally freeing him from the faded cotton. When the shirt lay on the floor, the last memory of Harvey faded with it.

She pulled Kurt toward her, relishing the feel of his body stretched out on the bed beside hers, reveling in the heated skin of his chest against her breasts. Never had anything felt so right. It seemed as if she'd been waiting her entire life for this moment. As if she'd been created for this. For Kurt.

Still moving slowly, almost reverently, he gathered her skirts and pulled off her dress. He took a moment to remove the rest of his things, then lay down and drew her close again. With nothing left as a barrier between them, the agonizing slowness went up in smoke as the fire between them ignited.

Kurt's fingers and lips carried her into a place where she'd never been before and never wanted to leave. A place too high to catch her breath or think. There was no past. There was no future. There was only sensation after sensation, wave upon wave of pleasure. There was only Kurt and fire. Kurt and satin.

Kurt.

She must have cried out his name because she could hear it echoing off the rough pine walls. She must have whimpered it because she could feel it in her throat. The need for him filled her, drew her higher and higher until she couldn't open her eyes. And yet she could see him and the matching need mirrored in his eyes, the answering shout hovering on the edges of his lips.

The rhythm he set made her feel as if she were floating one moment, then being drowned in waves of warm honey the next. Instinctively, she knew he was holding back, waiting for her before he took his own pleasure, but she couldn't seem to tell him that she couldn't bear any more.

Lights burst in front of her eyes one moment. Soft blue clouds enveloped her the next. At long last, Kurt was

unable to hold back any longer and gave her the ultimate
release, the most supreme pleasure she'd ever experienced. And when he collapsed against her, panting
roughly, spent emotionally and physically, he caught his
breath and pulled her to him once more for one last, lingering kiss.

His lovemaking was unlike anything she'd ever experienced. By comparison, Harvey had been rough and
clumsy, shy and quick. But this . . . This was art in its
purest form, love in its truest sense, passion at its most
absolute power.

Olivia waited for him to fall asleep as Harvey always
had, but Kurt stayed awake with her, holding her, running
his hands along her back, cupping her bottom, speaking
love and whispering promises both knew he'd never be
able to keep. But Olivia didn't care what tomorrow would
bring.

For tonight, she wanted to believe.

Kurt lay on his side, his arm draped across Olivia, watching her sleep. Outside, the sun had just begun to lighten
the sky, brushing the underside of the clouds with a soft
orange. He didn't think he'd ever seen a more perfect
morning.

Olivia's hair curled softly on the pillow. The soft, eb-
ony coils drew his fingers toward them. He lifted one and
let it drape across his lip, smiling at the softness, breathing
in the scent. For some reason, her hair fascinated him.

Be honest, he chided himself. The entire woman fascinated him. The way her lashes fanned on her cheeks.
The steady rhythm of her breathing, the softness of her
skin . . .

God, she was beautiful. Awake. Asleep. Standing in
front of the stove, drawing water from the well, even
mucking out the stables, she took his breath away.

And she loved him.

That fact filled him with wonder. *She loved him.*

He trailed a finger across her cheek, softly so as not to wake her. Never in his life had he imagined that he could be so lucky. God willing, he'd spend the rest of his life making her happy.

And what would he do if God wasn't willing?

He couldn't imagine a fate so cruel, so heartless. She'd filled every empty spot in his soul to overflowing. She made him everything he was and then some. She made him feel taller, smarter, and braver than he knew himself to be. Surely if fate had a heart at all, he'd be allowed to stay.

But the library shelves were filled with stories about ill-fated lovers. Movie theaters and video stores overflowed with them.

He'd do anything for a chance to stay here. Anything. And he prayed silently to whatever power might be in charge to grant him that chance.

He must have made a sound because Olivia's eyes flew open suddenly and she sat bolt upright, clutching the sheet to those gorgeous breasts. "Kurt?"

She looked so frightened, he resisted the urge to let his hands loose again. He didn't trust them and he didn't want to scare her off now. He lay back and linked his hands behind his head. "Good morning."

Laughing easily, Olivia lay back down beside him. All modesty and shyness faded and she was suddenly, incredibly the woman she'd been last night. A soft leg inched its way across his. An arm snaked over his belly, leaving his skin tingling as it passed over him. A silken set of lips found a spot just below his chin that he could have sworn turned his insides to molten steel.

"If you don't stop that," he warned, "we won't be leaving this bed."

She sobered instantly and glanced toward the window. "Tempting as that is, I can't stay in bed any longer." She tucked a lock of hair behind one ear and leaned her head against his chest.

"Why not?" Kurt kissed her nose and lay back against the pillows, drawing Olivia back with him. "What could you possibly have to do that's more important than this?"

"You explain to the horses why they haven't been fed," she laughed as she tried once more to pull away.

"Nightmare and I are buddies," Kurt reminded her. "And he mooched enough from me, I think he owes me this morning." He fingered a curl that fell onto his shoulder and tried to recapture his contentment of a moment before, but reality was returning steadily with the rising sun.

He did his best not to let Olivia see his changing mood. He liked seeing her peaceful. He liked knowing he'd helped put that smile on her face. She was beyond beautiful when she smiled like that, and beyond sensuous when she turned those smoldering mahogany eyes on him.

Olivia sat up quickly and held her fingers to her lips. "Someone's coming." She flew out of the bed and began searching for her clothes. "Get up. Get dressed. If it's Sam, I don't want him to catch us this way. He's been too wonderful to hurt him that way."

Kurt waited for a second, indulging one more moment and feasting his eyes on the soft, white skin of her back and the curve of her hips as she searched frantically through the jumble of clothes on the floor.

She looked at him over her shoulder and gave him a playful shove. "Will you get up and get dressed?"

Laughing, Kurt did as he was told. He might want to shout his love from the rooftops, but he had no desire to hurt Sam, either. He slipped into the dusty Levi's and old work shirt that had grown as comfortable and familiar as any of the T-shirts and jeans waiting for him at home.

"Remind me to have a word with Sam, would you? He's got about the worst timing of anyone I know." He grabbed her around the waist as she fastened the last of her buttons and pulled her around for a kiss. "I was just about to suggest that we take up where we left off last night."

Olivia kissed him full on the lips and stepped away. "You mean this morning, don't you? I could swear we've only been asleep a few minutes." She brushed her hair quickly and smoothed her skirt over her stomach, then wrenched open the door and hurried out into the main room.

Kurt hobbled after her, still trying to pull on his shoes. "Wait a second . . ." A step creaked. "Shouldn't I—?" Kurt lost his balance, caught himself on the table, and realized his shirttail was still hanging out. He'd been about to ask if he shouldn't be doing something that might explain why he was inside so early in the morning when the footsteps reached the porch. Come to think of it, why had Sam come back so early?

"Wait," Kurt whispered, stuffing one side of his shirttail into his waistband. "Maybe it's not—"

But Olivia threw open the door before he could finish and a tall blond man wearing an immaculate ivory-colored suit and carrying an ivory-tipped cane took in the scene with one long, slow glance.

And Kurt knew without being told that he was looking into Sloan Durrant's ugly face.

"Excuse me," Sloan said with a knowing smile. "I had no idea I'd be . . . interrupting."

Olivia did her best to look dignified. Kurt did his best not to rush the bastard and give him a taste of what he'd given Sam the night before.

"You're not interrupting anything," Olivia said. "What can I do for you?"

Sloan tore his gaze away from Kurt slowly. "Unfortunately, your mortgage is due in just a few days and— correct me if I'm wrong—it doesn't appear that you'll be able to make the payment. I thought perhaps, since I was out this way, I should swing by and take a quick inventory."

"You can take inventory if and when you foreclose," Kurt snarled. "Not a moment sooner."

"And you are . . . ?"

"Kurt Richards."

"Mrs. Hamilton's . . . ranch hand?"

Kurt wanted to take every suggestive nuance and ram it down the man's throat. "Mrs. Hamilton's fiancé."

"Fiancé?" Sloan turned his gaze to Olivia again. "Well, well. Isn't that wonderful. I had no idea you'd be getting married again so soon after Harvey's unfortunate passing." His gaze slithered back to Kurt. "Sloan Durrant at your service," he said, extending a hand.

Kurt ignored it. "I know who you are."

"Indeed?" Sloan slithered a glance at the inside of the house as if he actually thought Olivia might invite him inside. "May I?"

Kurt slipped a hand around her waist, hoping that his presence would bolster her own incredible courage.

But Olivia's back was already rigid and her shoulders stiff, and she watched Sloan with a wariness that reminded Kurt of a tigress protecting her cubs. "I believe you heard what my fiancé said."

"Indeed. But I did hope you would be smart enough to realize how . . . foolish it would be to deny me access. My bank does hold the mortgage on this property."

"Yes," Olivia said stiffly, "but *you* do not. And— correct *me* if *I'm* wrong—you don't own the bank. Now, I'll thank you to leave my property before I have to contact Marshall Pulver. If the bank directors in St. Louis would like to inspect the property, they're more than welcome to send another representative."

And before Kurt could even blink, she'd slammed the door in Sloan's greedy face.

She didn't move until she heard Sloan remount and ride out. Then she turned to Kurt and tried to smile. "I hope you meant what you said last night, because I believe we're at war."

Chapter 19

THAT NIGHT, KURT paced restlessly in front of a rock outcropping on top of the mesa. After Sloan Durrant's visit that morning, he and Sam had decided to mount a double watch on the mesa crest rather than splitting up as they had for the past two nights.

Durrant was getting braver. No telling what he'd try next. The only thing Kurt felt confident of was that Sloan Durrant wouldn't hesitate to do anything.

The wind whistled through the trees, grating on Kurt's already shattered nerves. Sound seemed to come from everywhere. Night creatures scurried through the brush. Horses nickered softly and uneasily in the half-light of the moon. Wind brushed through the trees. Every sound seemed magnified by the adrenalin pumping through Kurt's veins.

Were those footsteps, or just trees groaning in the wind? A horse shifting position, or someone lurking out there?

He could feel Sam watching him from beneath the brim of his hat, his face shadowed by night, but he couldn't seem to stand still. He couldn't forget the look on Sloan Durrant's face that morning.

Olivia was right—they had declared war. Now it just remained to be seen how Sloan would react. Maybe it was just anticipation of Sloan's next move, but the uneasiness that had been dogging him all day had become almost overwhelming by the time night fell.

Something was going to happen.

"You make a good target, pacing that way." Sam's deep voice mixed with the sounds of the night. "Maybe you'd like to light a lantern to help 'em find us."

Kurt stopped abruptly, realized Sam was right, and took cover close to the ground. Durrant and his men could be anywhere. In front of them. Behind them. On one side or the other. Or they might be nowhere at all. He simply couldn't tell.

"I just wish they'd come," he said, keeping his voice low. "I want to get this over with."

"Oh, they'll come, all right. No doubt about that. Just keep talking so they know where to find us."

Chafing under the reprimand, Kurt clamped his mouth shut and forced himself to wait. He envied Sam's apparent calm. Of course, Kurt had never been in a situation quite like this one before. Sure, he'd carried a rifle. He'd even done a bit of aiming and talking big. But this made his previous experiences seem like child's play.

He inched closer to Sam and lowered his voice even further. "What if they don't come up here? What if they do something to Olivia while we're here?"

"Already thought of that," Sam said. "That's why Jesse and one of our men are standing watch."

Kurt let out a breath, shocked by how weak the relief made him feel. "Why didn't you tell me before?"

"Didn't want to worry you if you didn't think of it yourself." Sam nudged his hat back and sent Kurt a look. "And I don't want Olivia to hear of it, either . . . unless she has to know. I'm not leaving her alone, but I'm not in the mood to be accused of treating her like a woman."

Kurt passed a hand over his face. He was in the middle of a full-scale, old-fashioned, Wild West range war and he was ill-equipped to handle himself. "For what it's worth," he told Sam, "I'd have done the same thing."

Sam nodded and pulled his hat back down again. "Figured."

Silence fell between them and though Kurt's nerves made his skin feel too tight, he forced himself to stay in one place. Time passed slowly. Each minute felt like an hour. Every hour felt like eternity.

Only watching the moon climb steadily in the sky helped Kurt estimate how much time had actually passed. Some time later, the wind died down and the night sounds became less ominous. But the longer they went without seeing Durrant and his men, the more nervous Kurt became.

What if they weren't coming? What if they'd managed to sneak past Jesse and his man? If anything happened to Olivia, Kurt wouldn't rest until every last one of them paid.

He shifted position slightly, inadvertently moving into the moonlight for a moment. Before he could move back, something hot buzzed past his ear, a shot rang out, and the bullet chunked into the rock behind him.

Fear and anger filled his mouth with acid and sharpened his senses. His entire body tingled as if an electric current had passed through it. Hunkering behind a rock, he scanned the horizon and shot a glance in Sam's direction to make sure he hadn't been hit.

Sam had taken cover, his body taut with tension. Kurt couldn't see his expression, but a quiet deadliness radiated across the distance separating them.

How many men did Durrant have out there? How far would they go to get their hands on the ruins? What had once seemed all-important to him now seemed almost trivial. Just a few short weeks ago, he'd been willing to go to any lengths to protect the site. Now, he only wanted to protect Olivia and keep Sam—and himself—alive.

His heart thumped furiously as he scanned the horizon. He couldn't make sense of anything he saw. Shadows all seemed to melt together. Trees and rocks looked infuriatingly the same in the shadowed moonlight.

He could scarcely breathe, but he refused to let himself acknowledge his fear. Later, after they were all safe and this was over, he'd let himself think about it. For now, he needed to keep a level head.

Another shot rang out and the sound bounced back from the canyon behind him. He chanced another glance in Sam's direction, but this time Kurt couldn't see his familiar outline. Before he could decide how best to cross the clearing to check on Sam, a rustling in the trees behind him sent his heart slamming into his throat.

He spun around, leveled his rifle, and got a bead on the spot . . . and waited.

"Some friend you are," Sam said from inside the trees. "If you shoot me, you'll be alone out here."

Weak with relief, Kurt lowered the rifle and waited while Sam stepped into the small clearing. "Get down," he whispered harshly. "They just took a shot at me."

"And then skedaddled." In spite of his news, Sam kept a low profile as he moved into the clearing. "They came on foot this time. Must have left their horses back a ways so we wouldn't hear 'em."

"Great. Glad to see you're all right." Kurt tried to keep his voice level, his tone gruff. He tried to look as if somebody shot at him every day and one more was no big deal. But relief nearly knocked the legs out from under him.

As the immediate sense of danger began to wane, a burning anger replaced it. He could have been killed. Actually dead. Kaput. A goner. This wasn't a game. It wasn't some Wild West movie. It was real.

And, as Sam had said the night before, this made it personal. Kurt wasn't about to sit out here for another night and let Sloan Durrant and his band of thieves call the shots—or take them. It was time to take his fate into his own hands.

Sunlight streamed in through the windows as Olivia lay in the shelter of Kurt's arms. For the first time in days, she felt safe, protected, and secure but in her heart she knew it was all an illusion.

She had a hundred things to do and the sun was already high overhead, but she didn't want to move. As long as she lay like this, as long as she could listen to Kurt's steady breathing as he slept, she could make herself believe they'd be together forever.

He'd come home pale and shaken this morning, and angrier than she'd ever seen him. The look on Sam's face had chilled her to the bone. Though they were all exhausted from staying awake all night, they'd stayed up for another hour talking.

She'd hated listening to them plan their approach to keeping watch that night. She hated knowing that she'd taken the step that had put them in such danger. It had been pure selfishness on her part. Nothing but raw, stubborn pride.

The look on Sloan Durrant's face had raised her hackles and the smirk on his lips had wiped the common sense right out of her head. She felt entirely to blame, and nothing either Kurt or Sam had said made her feel any better.

Just thinking about it made her too agitated to lie still any longer. Carefully, she slipped out from beneath Kurt's arm and pulled on her nightgown and wrapper. In the big room, she stoked the fire in the stove and put on a pot of coffee.

Kurt assured her that it would be over in two days. But how? She still had no money to pay the mortgage, and it seemed to her that they were engaged in a losing battle. A deadly one. Why not just turn over the ranch and the mesa property to Sloan Durrant and be done with it?

"What are you doing up?"

Startled, she let out a cry and whipped around toward the bedroom door. All these nights without sleep were beginning to take their toll. She hadn't even heard Kurt getting out of bed.

He wore nothing but a pair of Levi's slung low on his hips, and the night's growth of beard shadowed his face. Sleep had spiked his hair softly.

Suddenly aware of how disheveled she must look, she tried to smooth the hair out of her face. "I didn't mean to wake you. I just couldn't sleep."

He closed the distance between them and bent to slide his arms around her waist. "You *need* sleep, sweetheart. Come back to bed."

"If I did, you'd only try to distract me." She pulled away gently and turned to face him. "I don't want to do this anymore, Kurt. I want to give the ranch to Sloan and stop all this before someone gets hurt."

Kurt dropped into the chair beside hers. "You want to give up?"

How could he look so disappointed with her? "What happened last night is my fault, but this is just not worth the risks you're taking."

"Tell me what good it would do to give up, Olivia. Explain it to me because I don't understand."

"This would stop. You and Sam would be safe."

"You think so? You think that Sloan Durrant would just back off if we gave him everything?"

"Yes. Why wouldn't he? He'd have what he wanted."

"I don't think so." Kurt's brows knit and his eyes darkened. "I don't think what Sloan wants will ever be satisfied. He's not after money or property. He's not after treasure. He's after power, Olivia. And once a man gets a taste of it, nothing will quench it."

"Then let somebody else stop him."

"Who? Marshall Pulver?" Kurt looked away, agitated. "I'm not giving up. I'm not going to roll over and play dead while Sloan Durrant walks away with my pride."

"Your *pride*? Is that what this is about?" She tried to swallow the fear that rose up inside her. "What is it with you men and your pride? Is it worth so much that you'd give up everything else just to save it?"

"You don't understand—"

Olivia shot to her feet, trembling. "Why do you say that? Do you think *I* don't have pride? Or is that just a male thing?"

"Of course not. I know you have pride, sweetheart. And I do understand how you feel. A few weeks ago, I thought there was nothing more important than those ruins and the artifacts there." Kurt stood to face her and took her gently by the arms. "Now, there's nothing in the world more important to me than being with you. But if I lose this battle, I'm afraid I'll lose you with it."

His words found a place deep within her heart and started to peel away the layers of fear and anger. "What do you mean?"

"I can't explain it, really. Just a shift in the atmosphere around me. A different feeling in the air. It's as if the future's just waiting to take me back."

Olivia sank into her seat again. "So, you feel it too?"

Sadness clouded Kurt's eyes. "Maybe I've brought us to this point. Maybe it was always meant to be. I don't know. I just know that I have to finish what I've started."

"I'm going to lose you, aren't I?" Her throat tightened so painfully she could hardly choke the words out.

"Not if I can help it."

"What if you can't help it?"

"I'll still love you forever."

She hurt so much she could hardly breathe.

Kurt wrapped his arms around her and held her close. "All my life, I've made decisions based on what I wanted, not necessarily on what was right. I've hurt people I was supposed to love and I've kept everything bottled inside."

She tried to remember the man he'd been when he first appeared on her doorstep. She tried to remember the woman she'd been. Both had changed so much over the past four weeks, she could hardly remember.

"You've helped me get past that, Olivia. For the first time in my life, it doesn't hurt to tell someone how I feel. For the first time in my life, I care more about someone else than I do about myself. I'd die for you. I'd give my life for Sam." He tilted her chin and looked deep into her eyes. "I like who I am for the first time, sweetheart. And I have you to thank."

She choked back a sob. "I like who you are, too. I like who we are together."

He grinned, trying to look lecherous, trying to make her laugh and ease the tension. "I do too, believe me."

She slapped at his chest but there was no conviction in it. "I don't just mean that way."

"Maybe not, but it's a great way. You can't deny that."

She knew he wanted to lighten the moment. She could see the need in his eyes to forget the threat that yawned in front of them. But she couldn't make herself joke with him this morning. The future was looming, threatening to end her happiness once again. And she had no idea how to stop it.

That night, Olivia couldn't make herself do anything. Even scrubbing the floor required too much concentration. Agitation filled every pore in her body. Nervousness skittered across her skin. She couldn't put her conversation with Kurt out of her mind, nor could she forget the expressions on Kurt's and Sam's faces as they rode out.

They had something up their sleeves. She was absolutely certain of it. And being left behind night after night was driving her out of her skin. She paced to the window and looked up at the mesa. Without warning, the feeling that she'd done this before washed over her.

Well, of course she'd done this before. Tonight. Last night. The night before. A thousand times.

But the feeling persisted, growing stronger with every passing minute. She lowered the curtain again and turned back toward the table . . . and then it hit her.

She'd had this same feeling the night Harvey died. She'd felt that strange premonition of disaster, that oddly unsettled feeling that wouldn't go away. She'd ignored it that time, writing it off to her irritation with Harvey and the letter she'd received from her mother that day—her first in months—that had been full of complaints about Melody, admonitions to Olivia not to forget who she was and how she'd been taught to behave, and not much else.

There'd been no news about her father, no word of friends or other family members, nothing friendly or loving at all. And Olivia had allowed that letter and the ache it brought to her heart to dull her senses.

But there'd been no letter today, and fear kept her senses razor-sharp. Something was horribly wrong.

Without taking time to think through the wisdom of her actions, she raced into the bedroom and changed into the trousers and shirt she'd worn last time she and Kurt visited the ruins. With shaking hands, she filled her pockets with ammunition and carried Harvey's rifle with her to the barn.

It seemed to take forever to saddle Nightmare. He pranced nervously, nickering and tossing his head as if he, too, sensed something in the air. Her heart slowed with dread. Her fingers refused to work properly as she struggled with the bit, harness, and saddle.

Finally, much later, she rode out into the darkness. Her agitation grew with every passing minute. She imagined eyes watching her, even turned in the saddle a couple of times to check behind her, but she refused to second-guess her decision.

Kurt and Sam were in danger. She had no idea what she could do, but if she could get there in time she could at least warn them.

Nightmare's hooves thundered over the ground, drawing her closer and closer. Her heart rode high in her throat as she covered the distance. Halfway there, a strong wind began to blow from the mouth of the canyon, bending the trees in its path.

Ducking her head and shielding her eyes with one arm, she kept going, urging Nightmare forward and scanning the horizon when she could for some sign of Kurt or Sam, or of Sloan Durrant and his men.

She didn't want to run into them. She'd be no match for them alone. Her only chance was to reach Kurt and Sam and stand against them together.

As she drew closer to the canyon, the howling of the wind began to take on an eerie, mournful sound. Clouds covered the moon and forced her to rein Nightmare in for safety. A heavy storm cloud dropped over the canyon, obscuring it from view.

Nearly numb with worry, she urged Nightmare to go as quickly as she dared. The wind drowned out any other sound. The clouds blocked most of the light. Shivering in apprehension, she tried once more to find Kurt and Sam on the horizon. Instead, she saw three riders slightly ahead and to her left.

She had no trouble recognizing Sloan Durrant. He sat his horse like a king, as if the world and everything in it should, by rights, belong to him. Abner Grimley and

Quincy Albright were most certainly the other two.

Bile rose in her throat and hatred threatened to distract her. But she forced herself to concentrate. She could be angry later. She could indulge *all* of her emotions later. Just now, she had to keep her wits about her.

Sloan and his men were a good hundred yards ahead of Olivia. She was a good shot, but she'd never be able to defeat all of them alone. Torn between concern for Nightmare and worry about the men who were about to be caught in an ambush, she spurred the horse faster and kept her eyes peeled for obstacles that might hurt him.

By the time she'd gone another hundred yards, she realized she was risking the poor horse's life—and her own. And for nothing. The riders had increased the distance between them. She'd never get to Kurt and Sam first.

The attack came out of nowhere—three gunmen, maybe four. Gunfire erupted all around them without warning. Sam threw himself to the ground and took cover behind a stand of trees. Sweat broke out on his brow and ran into his eyes. He dashed it away and tried to get a bead on one of the gunmen, but he couldn't see a thing.

Shadows blanketed everything. Wind howled. Dust and grit flew. Noise, confusion, and dirt seemed to be everywhere.

The gunfire stilled and he took a heartbeat to look for Kurt. To his relief, he didn't see him lying on the ground. He took that as a good sign that Kurt had taken cover as well.

He waited, forcing himself to breathe slowly and find the control that had always served him so well in the past. He wasn't about to waste ammunition until he could see someone or something moving.

Kurt must have decided the same thing because the sudden silence was almost eerie. He just hoped it didn't mean that Kurt was down.

He watched, painfully aware of the sound of his own heartbeat and cursing the wind for masking the noises their attackers must surely be making. Hopefully, he and Kurt would have the same advantage. It seemed to be the only thing going their way.

Without warning, a shadow broke free from the others and started running toward the edge of the cliff. Sam watched for a moment, keeping his rifle trained on it as he tried to decide if it was Kurt or someone else.

It ran. Stopped. Ducked. Spun around and waved in his direction.

It must be Kurt, but what the hell was he doing?

A shot rang out, barely audible over the wailing wind. A volley of shots joined it and the shadowy figure began to run again.

Damn fool! He was going to get himself killed running around like that. How in the hell was Sam supposed to protect him? He bit back an angry shout, knowing that he was their only chance to survive and he wasn't ready to let Sloan and his men know where he was hiding.

A sound to his left pulled him around quickly just in time to see Abner Grimley creeping out of the bushes, his rifle trained on Kurt. Without taking even a second to think, Sam took aim and fired. Abner dropped, but his buddies answered with half a dozen shots in Sam's direction.

One down.

Sam threw himself to the ground again and crawled on his elbows through the trees to take up a new position. He battled to keep Kurt in his sights through the swirling dust. Why didn't he turn around and come back?

Was he running away?

No, Kurt wasn't the type to turn tail. Nor did he look like a man on the run. He looked like a man with a mission. He wasn't running *from* something, but what was he running *to*?

Sam scanned the landscape trying to figure out what it was. And when he saw her standing on the edge of the cliff, bathed in moonlight like an invitation for Sloan and his men, he sucked in a breath and felt everything inside him grow cold.

Olivia.

What in the hell was she doing? How had she gotten here? Where were Jesse and the other man who were supposed to be watching her?

Sam spat out an oath along with a mouthful of grit. Kurt had seen her before Sloan and the others, thank God. He had only a few feet to go. But what Sam saw next made his blood freeze.

Directly in front of Kurt, the wind picked up speed. The dust blew harder there, and he knew it must be impossible for Kurt to see the strange-looking hole that yawned in front of him.

If Sam hadn't known better, he'd have sworn something happened to his eyes. The hole looked for all the world like a wrinkle in the landscape. It shifted shape, waiting, drawing Kurt closer.

Kurt couldn't see it. He was too close. But from this distance Sam could see it clearly. Kurt was about to head into it. Another few yards and he'd be there.

With a certainty he couldn't have explained, Sam knew it was the doorway through time that had brought Kurt here. And with an equal certainty, he knew it would take Kurt back again if he got too close. Away from Cortez. Away from the Lazy H. Away from Olivia.

Swearing under his breath, he darted out of his hiding place and ran, absolutely certain that Sloan and his men would shoot him before he reached his target. He let out a bellow for courage and plowed into the storm. His shout must have carried through the din because Kurt stopped, crouched, and spun back toward him.

He kept the shout going, roaring to keep his courage

up and hoping it would distract Kurt long enough to let him accomplish his own mission. If not, it would make him a damned pretty target.

The wind picked up speed, swirling, blinding him, sucking him closer and closer. He caught a glimpse of Olivia watching him and experienced one brief pang of regret. He heard his name, more a whisper than a shout, but he didn't let it distract him.

One down. With Olivia here, the odds were even. They could survive this.

Gunshots echoed all around him, but miraculously, none of them found their mark. Still roaring—for courage now—he passed Kurt and purposely headed into the crease in time. A second later, the hole seemed to grab him and he knew he couldn't turn back.

The force of the wind sucked his breath away. A strange roaring sounded in his ears. Dust and lights nearly blinded him. One second his chest felt as if it might explode, the next as if a terrible weight might crush it.

And then, suddenly, Sam's entire body went limp, everything grew almost supernaturally quiet, and the lights in front of his eyes disappeared. The only thing he was aware of was the helpless feeling of falling into utter blackness.

Kurt stared at the spot in front of him as it sucked Sam inside and closed in around him. His knees buckled when he realized that he'd almost run straight into it. His stomach lurched when he realized that Sam had sacrificed himself so that Kurt could stay here.

As suddenly as it began, the wind stopped. Sam's sacrifice had satisfied the hungry future. The empty hole Kurt left had been filled. He owed Sam his life, his happiness, his entire future. He just hoped Sam would find his own life there.

A gunshot brought him back to the moment and forced

him to put Sam out of his mind. He searched the cliff for Olivia, but she'd disappeared. Kurt prayed frantically that she hadn't been swept into the future with Sam. Wouldn't that be the ultimate irony? Kurt stuck here . . . alone. Sam and Olivia together in the future.

Another shot forced him to put everything but survival out of his mind. He ducked instinctively—too late, of course. If he heard the shot, it had already hit its mark, but instinct was too strong to ignore.

He looked around frantically for Olivia but resisted the urge to call out to her. If she was still out there, he didn't want to draw attention to her. He struggled to orient himself again, to figure out where she'd been the last time he saw her.

She'd been just ahead on the other side of that blinding dust storm. Straight ahead.

Still shaken from watching Sam disappear, he stayed as close to cover as he could and worked his way toward the lip of the mesa. Without Sam, he felt out of his element, but he couldn't let Olivia down—even if she wasn't here any longer. If she *was* in the future, he wanted the history books to show that he'd succeeded.

He moved cautiously, looking around frequently for some sign of the gunmen. With the dust finally settled, he could at least make out the silhouettes of the trees and rocks, even if he couldn't always tell one from the other.

A twig snapped nearby. Kurt froze and listened carefully to the rustling of the undergrowth. Someone was on his left, not more than ten feet away.

He didn't move, didn't even breathe, while he struggled to make out a shadowy figure creeping almost parallel to him, as carefully, cautiously, silently as Kurt had been trying to move.

He waited, watching to make sure it wasn't Olivia, but when the clouds parted a few seconds later, the moon shone down on the grizzled, bearded face of a man. The

scent that reached him across the distance told Kurt he'd
found Quincy Albright.

Damnation, but Sam was right. The stench was unbelievable.

He had to move quickly before the man slipped into
the shadows again. Before the moon ducked behind the
clouds and Kurt lost him. Taking a chance, he made sure
he had good cover, then cocked his rifle and shouted,
"*Freeze!*"

Quincy spun around, the glint of metal from his gun
clear in the dim moonlight.

"I said *freeze!*" Kurt shouted again. Then, for good
measure, "Don't move, you son of a bitch, or I'll shoot
you where you stand."

Quincy dropped his gun and thrust his hands high
above his head.

Kurt crept closer, keeping his rifle trained on the man's
shoulder, hoping he wouldn't have to kill him. "Put your
hands on the top of your head. Lace your fingers together."

Five feet. Four. Close enough to make out the man's
features. "Kick your gun over here to me," Kurt ordered.

The man hesitated briefly, then nudged his gun with the
toe of his boot. But the cocky grin on his face as he did
so made Kurt's blood boil. "Go ahead, you son of a bitch.
Smile. But your ass is grass, buddy."

Too late, he heard someone behind him. He tried to
whip around, but the cold metal of a second gun pressed
into his back.

"Drop your rifle," a familiar voice said just behind his
ear. "I believe *your* ass is the one in trouble."

Kurt hesitated for only a second, but the ominous click
of Sloan Durrant cocking the hammer on his pistol convinced him to do as he was told. Olivia might be gone
into the future. But there was still a chance that she was
here in the past. If there was even a chance for them to
still be together, he wouldn't risk getting shot.

Chapter 20

OLIVIA WATCHED IN horror as Sloan Durrant cocked his revolver against Kurt's back. Unbelievably, Sam was gone. Kurt was being held at gunpoint. Their only chance to get out of this alive lay heavily on her shoulders.

She was still too far away to hit the broad side of a barn, but she had to do something. She couldn't wait for Sloan to hurt Kurt or even kill him.

She had one thing working in her favor—the element of surprise. Quincy and Sloan must not have seen her. They were too cocky, too relaxed. If she could get closer without being heard, maybe she could take them by surprise.

Their voices carried in the clear night air. Sloan's low and menacing, Quincy's slightly higher. Quincy bent to retrieve the gun he'd kicked to Kurt's feet and brought it up into Kurt's face.

Olivia's stomach clenched, but she stayed low to the ground and inched forward.

"Where's Sam?" Quincy demanded. "Where'd he go?"

"Dead. One of you got him."

Quincy stepped around to face Kurt. "Sam Evans dead? Where's his body?"

Kurt jerked his head toward the edge of the cliff. "Down there."

"And the pots you took?" Sloan demanded. "Where are they?"

"In a safe place."

Olivia took advantage of the conversation to creep closer. Only a few more feet and she'd be able to help him.

Quincy leaned closer to Kurt. "What do you know about the treasure of Black Mesa?"

Kurt lifted one shoulder in a careless shrug. "Only that it's a figment of your imagination."

To Olivia's horror, Quincy backhanded Kurt across the face. The blow echoed across the distance separating them and made bile rise in her throat. "Don't be smart," Quincy warned. "Where is it?"

Kurt wiped blood from his lip with the fingers of one hand. "There *is* no treasure."

Another blow resounded and fury boiled up inside her. All her anger over Harvey's death came rushing to the surface and mingled with emotions she couldn't even name from watching Sam throw himself into the future.

Her fingers itched to shoot Quincy where he stood and put Sloan Durrant out of his greed-filled misery, but she forced herself to hold back. She could only shoot one at a time, and if she tried, the other would kill Kurt before she could reload.

She had to be able to get them both or Kurt would die.

A cloud scuttled across the moon, and she took the chance to move across the small clearing that stood between her and Kurt. She bit her lip to keep from making any noise as she crept closer.

Sloan Durrant's carefully measured voice cut through the distance. "If you don't believe there's a treasure, why are you putting up such a fight?"

"I have a moral objection to watching someone steal from widows."

Kurt sounded strangely calm. Olivia could scarcely breathe.

"Well, now," Sloan drawled. "I *am* impressed. What a paragon of virtue we have here in front of us, Quincy. He thinks we're scum for trying to take something from the poor widow woman, but he doesn't have the slightest objection to letting her feed and clothe him . . . *and* provide him with a soft, comfortable bed."

His leering voice left no doubt as to his meaning. Seething, Olivia's finger curled on the trigger of her rifle. But before she had a chance to decide whether to squeeze it or not, Kurt lowered his shoulder and hit Sloan in the chest. Lightning quick, he brought up his arm beneath Sloan's gun hand just as Sloan fired, and the shot went high and wide.

Horrified, Olivia watched as both men hit the ground and Quincy tried to take aim at Kurt. She couldn't hit Sloan without risking Kurt's life, but she could take Quincy out of the picture.

Without giving herself a chance to be frightened, she stepped into the clearing and aimed straight at Quincy's foul heart.

Kurt was vaguely aware of another person moving into the clearing, but he was a little too busy to see who it was. Without his gun, Sloan had lost a great deal of his power, but he still wasn't backing down.

The man's hands flew, landing blows to Kurt's stomach, chest, face, and back, and Kurt had his hands full just trying to overpower him. Kurt still didn't understand why the treasure of Black Mesa should consume him as it did, but he didn't have time to ask questions, either.

He managed to stay on top of Sloan for a few seconds, but Sloan fought like a man possessed. He bucked harshly and threw Kurt to one side, then landed a vicious blow to his solar plexus. Gasping for air, Kurt hit him with a left jab and a right uppercut. Sloan staggered backward and Kurt lunged, hoping to finish the job.

Sloan ducked the blow and landed one of his own to Kurt's back. Pain exploded inside him, but he wouldn't let Sloan get the best of him. As Sloan dove for his pistol, Kurt launched himself and knocked Sloan to the ground inches away from the gun.

Sloan brought his knee up sharply. The blow fell blessedly short of its mark, but pain shot through Kurt's leg. He fought to pin Sloan to the ground, but Sloan twisted away and edged a few inches closer to his gun.

Bellowing with fury, Kurt kicked Sloan's hand just before it closed around the pistol. Sloan brought his elbow straight up into Kurt's jaw. Razor-sharp pain exploded in his mouth and neck. The taste of blood filled his mouth.

Sloan lunged once more and this time his hand closed around the pistol. He brought the gun around, straight into Kurt's face. A hammer cocked and Kurt waited for the shot that would end his life.

Instead, the barrel of a rifle nudged Sloan's forehead and a distinctly female voice cut through the panting of both men. "Blink and I'll shoot you."

Kurt looked up through the haze of pain into Olivia's beloved face. Fury blazed from her eyes. Hatred tightened her mouth into a thin line. But she'd never looked so beautiful as she did in that moment. And he'd never loved her quite as much.

Fighting the pain that seemed to be everywhere, Kurt lurched to his feet and relieved Sloan of his gun. He glanced behind him and found Quincy lashed to the trunk of a piñon.

She barely spared Kurt a glance. Sloan started to turn

toward her, no doubt thinking he could overpower her or out-think her. But she didn't give an inch. "Give me an excuse, Sloan. Any excuse. I'd welcome the chance to blow your head off."

Sam awoke with a start to the strangest sound he'd ever heard. A roar, almost like the sound of a locomotive, followed by a *whoosh* and a gust of hot air blowing across his face. He sat up quickly, but the pain in his head forced him back to the ground with an *oomph*.

He inched open one eye and tried to make it focus. Where was he? The last thing he remembered . . . His eye opened a bit wider. No, that had to be a dream. He'd fallen asleep out in the pasture somewhere. He'd—

The sound of another approaching locomotive caught his ear. He forced himself to his knees and focused slowly on a strange ribbon of black in front of him. It stretched away as far as he could see in either direction and disappeared over gently rolling hills.

Definitely a road, dark gray with two yellow lines running along the center. Sam bent to touch it. Rock. Sleek, gray rock. The strangest thing he'd ever seen.

His head pounded and the sound seemed to grow closer, but he still couldn't see anything. All at once, a . . . a . . . what *was* that? It passed too quickly for him to get a good look at it, but it hadn't looked much bigger than a buggy. Not even as large as the buckboard they used on the Cinnabar. But saints alive, could it move!

By damn, he'd done it. He'd leaped into the future. Never let anyone say Sam Evans didn't do things up in a big way. He'd already decided to leave Cortez, but he *had* planned to pack a bag and say a few good-byes before he left.

Stunned, he shook his head and looked around slowly. Jagged snow-covered mountains cut into the sky on one side of the valley. A series of rolling hills covered in dried grass stretched away in the other direction. Everywhere he looked, he saw trees, grass, and sky.

Okay, he'd come to the future. It had seemed like a good idea last night. And anyway, there wasn't a whole lot he could do about it now.

The next question—*where* was he?

He glanced around quickly and found his rifle. He'd have to be careful with it. He only had a few rounds of ammunition left and the good Lord only knew whether he'd find game in these hills and how long he'd have to wander before he found civilization.

Resting the rifle on his shoulder, he chose a direction and set off. Unless things had changed in the past hundred years or so, roads led to towns, and towns meant food and shelter.

Guilt over the way he'd sabotaged Kurt's efforts in Cortez tickled him but he pushed it away. Things had worked out for the best. Kurt and Olivia had found each other. And Sam was about to face the test he'd always craved.

He could hear another of those strange wagons approaching, so he stepped off the road and waited. It only took a second for him to catch his first glimpse of reflected sunlight. It disappeared behind a hill and emerged again a second later. Another dip, another hill put it on a level with him.

It streaked toward him and he steeled himself, expecting the sound, the rush of hot air. But this wagon didn't rush past. It slowed, passed in a blur of white, and came to a stop just a few feet from him.

It was the strangest looking thing Sam had ever seen. Low and sleek with a collection of strange red, blue, and white bubbles on top. The bubbles began to turn, throwing beams of colored light across the landscape, and a door on the wagon opened.

A man—a kid, really—wearing a shirt and trousers the

color of tanned deer hide stepped out onto the road. He wore a holster on his hip that held not only a revolver but a whole slew of other contraptions Sam didn't recognize.

"Good morning, sir." He looked Sam up and down slowly. "Lost?"

More lost than you can imagine, son. "Not exactly."

"Where are you headed?"

"Town."

"Town, huh? Where's your car? Did you break down somewhere?"

"I'm on foot."

"Hitchhiking?" The man gave him another slow appraising glance. "Would you mind letting me see your rifle for a minute?"

Sam tensed. "There some reason why I should?"

The man held out an impatient hand. "The rifle, please."

Sam caught the glint of sunlight off a metal badge on the kid's chest. "You a lawman?"

"Sheriff's Deputy Donald Dumont."

Sam couldn't think of a good reason to refuse, and he didn't want to start off his new life in trouble with the law, so he handed over his rifle a tad regretfully.

The deputy spent a minute looking it over, then glanced back up at Sam. "What is this, an antique?"

"You might say that."

"Is it loaded?"

"You bet it is."

"Is that right?" The deputy tucked Sam's rifle under his arm as if he had no intention of returning it. "Have you got plans in town?"

"Just looking for a place to stay."

"Looking for a place to stay with a loaded rifle?" The deputy motioned Sam toward his wagon. "You want to step over to the car, sir? Put your hands on the trunk, bend over at the waist, and spread your legs."

"You mind telling me why I should?"

"Because I told you to." Unbelievably, the little pip-squeak drew his revolver and leveled it at Sam. "Now, move."

Sam had to admit, that revolver made a whole lot of difference in his decision. Figuring the "car" must be the wagon with the red and blue lights spinning on its top, he started toward it, but he didn't see a steamer trunk anywhere. "Put my hands where?"

The deputy gave Sam a shove toward the car's tail-end, kicked his foot gently between Sam's to spread his feet further apart, and started patting Sam's leg. Now, that might not have been too bad, but the little squirt made a big mistake when he started moving his hand up Sam's leg.

Sam jerked up quickly and spun around, put an arm in the deputy's throat and gave him a shove backward. The deputy sprawled backward and lost his grip on his revolver. Sam kicked it out of the man's hand and stood over him, hoping to make his point perfectly clear. "Oh, no you don't, little fella. You just keep them hands to yourself."

But that was Sam's big mistake. The deputy's foot shot straight up, catching Sam in the very area he'd been trying to protect. Pain tore through him, doubled him over, and knocked him to the ground.

In a flash, the deputy had retrieved his gun and had it aimed straight at Sam's head. "Get up."

Sam couldn't even speak, much less follow instructions.

"I said, *get up*." As the haze of pain slowly began to clear, Sam could see the deputy's hand shaking, the red-faced fury. "Assaulting an officer is going to earn you a nice, long stay in jail."

"Assaulting an officer?" Sam choked out, still curled like a baby on the ground. "Seems to me, you're the one who was trying to get fresh."

"And don't get smart." The little guy's hand trembled

so badly, the revolver shook in front of Sam's face. Damn and blast, the little fool was so scared, he might shake the trigger hard enough to actually shoot.

Sam struggled to his feet and put his hands up to show he wasn't going to put up a fight. But that wasn't enough for the little guy. "On your head," he ordered. "Put your hands *on* your head. You, mister, are about to become a guest of Heartbreak Hill, Montana."

A slow smile spread across Sam's face. Montana? Well, doggies! And, as Kurt had told him when their situations were reversed, there were worse things than a few days of free room and board.

But Heartbreak Hill? Well, when he thought about it, he supposed that sounded like the perfect place to start his new life.

His smile spread to a grin. "Well, now, I'd be pleased to, son. Why didn't you tell me that in the first place."

Marshall Pulver turned the lock of Sloan Durrant's cell and turned back toward Kurt and Olivia. "I suppose I owe you folks an apology. Never had it figured to be this big of a problem."

Kurt linked his hand with Olivia's, too grateful that they were both alive to sweat the small stuff. "To tell you the truth, I never had it figured to be quite this big, either. How much did Abner tell you?"

Marshall Pulver grinned slowly. "Abner's a family man, you know. Got five sons and a wife who thinks her life ought to be a sight cushier than it is. Sloan had him convinced this was an easy way to make her happy, but Abner doesn't have the guts for a scheme like the one Sloan really had in mind." He sat behind his desk and sent Olivia a weak smile. "Abner insists that your husband's death was an accident, Mrs. Hamilton. A fight that went too far. But the truth is, I don't think your husband would've fallen over that cliff on his own. Murder or accident, Sloan and his boys are responsible in some way for what happened to Harv."

Olivia's hand trembled in Kurt's, but she managed a brave smile. "I'm just glad to see justice done, Marshall."

The marshall ran a hand over his hair. "Near as I can figure from listening to Abner and Quincy babble, Sloan never believed in the legend of the treasure. Harvey had showed him some of them pots, hoping to get a loan from the bank. Sloan knew what they were worth, and he could see the dollar signs dancing in front of his eyes."

"So that's what he was always after?" Kurt let out a bitter laugh. "I knew he was too smart to be going to all that trouble over a legend."

"Trouble was, Harvey died, which upped the stakes. Sloan didn't want to get caught. He knew it would ruin him. Long as Olivia was willing to ignore the mesa and the ruins, he had a free hand. But once Mr. Richards here showed up, Sloan smelled trouble and decided the only way to protect the fortune he was counting on was to frighten you off."

"He very nearly succeeded," Olivia said weakly. "I came so close to just letting him have it all."

Marshall Pulver's expression sobered a bit more. "It's a damned shame about Sam. I suppose I'll have to ride out and tell Jesse."

Olivia looked at Kurt. Her eyes shimmered with unshed tears and he knew it would be a long time before the mere mention of Sam didn't bring them on. He got a little misty thinking about it, himself.

"May we do it, Marshall? There are some things I know Sam would want us to tell him."

"Sure you want to? It isn't going to be easy."

"Very sure."

Marshall Pulver nodded uncertainly. "Then I guess that's about all there is for tonight. Why don't you folks go on home and get some rest."

Olivia's eyes shadowed. "I'm still not out of the woods. The mortgage is still due, and I still don't have any money."

Marshall Pulver chuckled. "Well, now, it's an interesting thing about that. With Sloan in jail, the bank doesn't have a representative—leastwise, no representative I'd listen to if they told me to evict you from your property." He put his feet up on his desk and crossed one over the other. "I suppose I'll have to wire the bank in St. Louis. And they'll eventually send someone out here to take Sloan's place. But meanwhile, I just don't see how any foreclosures can take place."

Kurt grinned at the marshall. "That's too bad."

"Yeah. Real unfortunate." The marshall smoothed his moustache with his thumb and finger. "Have you ever thought about taking folks up to see those ruins of yours? I hear tell the Wetherills are makin' so much money they've just about given up ranching."

Olivia shook her head. "We won't let people walk all over them. We want to make sure they're preserved for future generations."

Kurt tightened his grip on her hand. "We wouldn't have to let people walk all over them, Olivia. Do you remember how you felt when you saw Sandstone Castle for the first time? You weren't close enough to do any damage then."

"You mean, take them in through Inca Canyon and let them just *look*?"

"That's exactly what I mean."

"Would anyone pay money to do that?"

The marshall pulled a five-dollar gold piece from his pocket and tossed it onto the desk between them. "Count me as your first paying customer, Mrs. Hamilton. I'll make sure the word gets around. I can just about guarantee you'll have more business than the two of you can handle."

Epilogue

CORTEZ, COLORADO
1890

OLIVIA CLUTCHED KURT'S hand nervously and watched the road. The stage from Durango would be arriving any minute and she was so excited, she could scarcely breathe. Imagine, just a year ago she'd been so broke she'd nearly lost the ranch and everything she owned. Now, she had everything she wanted.

She still missed Sam desperately at times, but she had to believe that he'd found happiness in his new life. Kurt slipped his free arm around her waist and pulled her close. "Are you okay, sweetheart?"

"Yes, of course. I'm just so *anxious*."

He scowled at the baby in his other arm. He was such a gentle, loving father, Olivia's heart nearly burst each time she looked at them together. The two men in her life. Kurt and Sam.

Kurt bent to kiss little Sam's soft cheek. "Did you hear that, son? Your mother's anxious. I can't imagine why."

She swatted at him playfully. "Don't tease me."

"I'm not teasing. I think I'm almost as excited as you are."

"What is it? What have you ordered for me?"

His eyes darkened and he scowled. "I'm not going to tell you! What kind of birthday present would that be?"

"Just a hint?"

"Not even that. It's enough that you know it's being delivered on the stage." He looked down at baby Sam again with a scowl. "If I'd known she was going to act this way, I wouldn't even have told her that much."

Sam cooed happily and reached up to give his father's moustache a tug.

The sight of them together made Olivia so happy, she didn't care who might be watching. She stood on tiptoe and pressed a kiss full on Kurt's lips. "You've already given me everything a woman could dream of—a home, a child, and more love than a body has a right to. I don't need anything else."

"But you want it, don't you?"

"I won't turn it down," she said with a grin. "I wouldn't want to hurt your feelings."

"Always thinking of others," Kurt said with a chuckle. "That's your mother."

Before either of them could say anything else, Olivia caught the sound of the stage approaching and everything else flew out of her head. She tried not to look too excited, but Kurt had been so mysterious, she couldn't help but bob onto her toes as she watched the stage roll into town and finally creak to a stop in a cloud of dust.

"Is it breakable? Just tell me that much."

"As a matter of fact, it's very fragile."

"China. You've sent back East for fine china, haven't you?"

Kurt slipped an arm around her waist and led her closer.

"That's all I'm going to tell you, sweetheart. You're going to have to wait to see."

She watched as the driver and shotgun rider began to unload luggage. Several men from town ran out to help as the door to the stage opened.

Olivia was dimly aware of passengers alighting, but she was more focused on the luggage. It wasn't until she realized Kurt's eyes were scanning the faces of the four passengers who'd already climbed out that she shifted her attention—just in time to see a woman dressed in a blue serge traveling suit being helped to the ground by the driver.

She glanced around uncertainly, saw Kurt and Olivia standing a little distance from the stage, and started toward them. She walked slowly, hesitantly, kneading her hands together in front of her. Even then it took a moment or two for the realization to hit.

"*Melody*?" What little decorum Olivia had left after six years in the West vanished in a flurry of tears and a rush of excitement. "*Melody*? Is that you?"

She hadn't even gotten the last few words out when Melody picked up her skirts and raced across the distance that still separated them. "Olivia! I can't believe I'm here. It's really you, isn't it?"

They were in each other's arms, laughing, crying, hugging, both talking at once, pulling away to look at each other and then collapsing in each other's arms again. Never, never, never had Olivia dreamed she'd see this day.

Kurt watched from a distance, waiting for his turn to meet his new sister-in-law, and filled with a deep and abiding love for his wife. He grinned down at his son, who'd somehow managed to come into the world with a pair of steel gray eyes he couldn't possibly have inherited from either of his parents.

"I think she likes our surprise, son."

Sam cooed in answer.

Not for the first time during the past year, Kurt tried to send a message through time to the finest man he'd ever known. It might not work, but it was fun trying.

I hope you're happy, my friend. As happy as I am.

He looked back at Olivia and Melody. They'd finally stopped crying and were headed toward him arm-in-arm.

He had everything a man could want. Friends like Jesse and Elizabeth, whose greatest delight these days was in planning ways to leave messages Sam would find in the future; a wife so dear, so brave, and so loving he still couldn't believe his good fortune; a son who held his heart and soul in his tiny hands; and now a sister.

If he didn't know better, he'd swear he could hear the contented sigh of the ancient ones, and a faint whisper.

It is done.

TIME PASSAGES

❏ CRYSTAL MEMORIES   *Ginny Aiken*   0-515-12159-2
❏ ECHOES OF TOMORROW   *Jenny Lykins*   0-515-12079-0
❏ LOST YESTERDAY   *Jenny Lykins*   0-515-12013-8
❏ MY LADY IN TIME   *Angie Ray*   0-515-12227-0
❏ NICK OF TIME   *Casey Claybourne*   0-515-12189-4
❏ REMEMBER LOVE   *Susan Plunkett*   0-515-11980-6
❏ SILVER TOMORROWS   *Susan Plunkett*   0-515-12047-2
❏ THIS TIME TOGETHER   *Susan Leslie Liepitz*
                                            0-515-11981-4
❏ WAITING FOR YESTERDAY   *Jenny Lykins*
                                            0-515-12129-0
❏ HEAVEN'S TIME   *Susan Plunkett*   0-515-12287-4
❏ THE LAST HIGHLANDER   *Claire Cross*   0-515-12337-4
❏ A TIME FOR US   *Christine Holden*   0-515-12375-7

All books $5.99

Prices slightly higher in Canada

Payable by Visa, MC or AMEX only ($10.00 min.), No cash, checks or COD. Shipping & handling:
US/Can. $2.75 for one book, $1.00 for each add'l book; Int'l $5.00 for one book, $1.00 for each
add'l. Call (800) 788-6262 or (201) 933-9292, fax (201) 896-8569 or mail your orders to:

Penguin Putnam Inc.   Bill my: ❏ Visa ❏ MasterCard ❏ Amex _____(expires)
P.O. Box 12289, Dept. B   Card# _____
Newark, NJ 07101-5289   Signature _____
Please allow 4-6 weeks for delivery.
Foreign and Canadian delivery 6-8 weeks.
Bill to:
Name _____
Address _____City _____
State/ZIP _____Daytime Phone # _____
Ship to:
Name _____Book Total $ _____
Address _____Applicable Sales Tax $ _____
City _____Postage & Handling $ _____
State/ZIP _____Total Amount Due $ _____
This offer subject to change without notice.   Ad # 680 (3/00)

FRIENDS ROMANCE

Can a man come between friends?

❏ A TASTE OF HONEY
by DeWanna Pace   0-515-12387-0

❏ WHERE THE HEART IS
by Sheridon Smythe   0-515-12412-5

❏ LONG WAY HOME
by Wendy Corsi Staub   0-515-12440-0

All books $5.99

Prices slightly higher in Canada

Payable by Visa, MC or AMEX only ($10.00 min.), No cash, checks or COD. Shipping & handling:
US/Can. $2.75 for one book, $1.00 for each add'l book; Int'l $5.00 for one book, $1.00 for each
add'l. Call (800) 788-6262 or (201) 933-9292, fax (201) 896-8569 or mail your orders to:

Penguin Putnam Inc.   Bill my: ❏ Visa ❏ MasterCard ❏ Amex _____ (expires)
P.O. Box 12289, Dept. B   Card# _____
Newark, NJ 07101-5289   Signature _____
Please allow 4-6 weeks for delivery.
Foreign and Canadian delivery 6-8 weeks.
Bill to:
Name _____
Address _____City_____
State/ZIP _____Daytime Phone # _____
Ship to:
Name _____Book Total $ _____
Address _____Applicable Sales Tax $ _____
City _____Postage & Handling $ _____
State/ZIP _____Total Amount Due $ _____
This offer subject to change without notice.   Ad # 815 (3/00)

A Quilting Romance

True love, like a beautiful handmade quilt, pieces
together the many patterns and colors of two hearts...

☐ **Patterns of Love**

by Christine Holden   0-515-12481-8/$5.99

☐ **Pieces of Yesterday**

by Carol Card Otten   0-515-12524-5/$5.99

☐ **The Coming home Quilt**

by Joanna Hampton   0-515-12552-0/$5.99

☐ **Mended hearts**

by Linda Shertzer   0-515-12611-X/$5.99

Prices slightly higher in Canada

Payable by Visa, MC or AMEX only ($10.00 min.), No cash, checks or COD. Shipping & handling:
US/Can. $2.75 for one book, $1.00 for each add'l book; Int'l $5.00 for one book, $1.00 for each
add'l. Call (800) 788-6262 or (201) 933-9292, fax (201) 896-8569 or mail your orders to:

Penguin Putnam Inc.
P.O. Box 12289, Dept. B
Newark, NJ 07101-5289
Please allow 4-6 weeks for delivery.
Foreign and Canadian delivery 6-8 weeks.

Bill my: ☐ Visa ☐ MasterCard ☐ Amex _____ (expires)

Card# _____

Signature _____

Bill to:

Name _____

Address _____ City _____

State/ZIP _____ Daytime Phone # _____

Ship to:

Name _____ Book Total $ _____

Address _____ Applicable Sales Tax $ _____

City _____ Postage & Handling $ _____

State/ZIP _____ Total Amount Due $ _____

This offer subject to change without notice.   Ad # 823 (3/00)

Like a man and a maid in ⟨✦⟩ **S0-BDQ-977**
they helped each other dress, with Will touching,
kissing, laughing with Elodie as she donned her
simple maid's gown. He knew once they reached
Paris she would try to slip away from him, but
he felt too light and euphoric to worry about it.
Happiness was fizzing in his chest like a freshly
opened bottle of champagne.

He'd had many an adventure...but never one like this. Never
with a woman who was a companion as uncomplaining as a
man, as resourceful as any of the riding officers with whom
he'd crept through the Spanish and Portuguese wilderness,
working with partisans and disrupting the French.

Their liaison was too fragile to last, but for now he'd be
like his Elodie and suck every iota of joy from an already
glorious day that promised, once he'd taken care of
provisions for the morrow and found her a room with a
bed, to become even more wonderful.

He twined his fingers in hers as they went back to their
horses. "How glad I am to be out of those monk's robes!
I've been dying to touch you as we travel."

"Good thing," she agreed. "Since you're grinning like a
farmer who's just outbargained a traveling tinker, I doubt
anyone could look at us now and not know we are lovers."

He stopped to give her a kiss. "Do you mind?"

"No. I'm grateful for each moment we have together, Will.
One never knows how many that may be."

* * *

The Rake to Redeem Her
Harlequin® Historical #1133—April 2013

Ransleigh Rogues

**Where these notorious rakes go,
scandal *always* follows…**

Max, Will, Alastair and Dominic Ransleigh—cousins,
friends…and the most wickedly attractive men in Regency
London. Between war, betrayal and scandal, love
has never featured in the Ransleighs' destinies—until now!

Don't miss this enthralling quartet from Julia Justiss.

It started with Max's story in

**THE RAKE TO RUIN HER
March 2013**

**Now follow Will's story in
THE RAKE TO REDEEM HER
April 2013**

**Look for Alastair's and Dominic's adventures
Coming 2014**

The Rake to Redeem Her

JULIA JUSTISS

HARLEQUIN® HISTORICAL

If you purchased this book without a cover you should be aware
that this book is stolen property. It was reported as "unsold and
destroyed" to the publisher, and neither the author nor the
publisher has received any payment for this "stripped book."

Recycling programs
for this product may
not exist in your area.

ISBN-13: 978-0-373-29733-7

THE RAKE TO REDEEM HER

Copyright © 2013 by Janet Justiss

All rights reserved. Except for use in any review, the reproduction or
utilization of this work in whole or in part in any form by any electronic,
mechanical or other means, now known or hereafter invented, including
xerography, photocopying and recording, or in any information storage
or retrieval system, is forbidden without the written permission of the
publisher, Harlequin Enterprises Limited, 225 Duncan Mill Road,
Don Mills, Ontario M3B 3K9, Canada.

This is a work of fiction. Names, characters, places and incidents are
either the product of the author's imagination or are used fictitiously,
and any resemblance to actual persons, living or dead, business
establishments, events or locales is entirely coincidental.

This edition published by arrangement with Harlequin Books S.A.

For questions and comments about the quality of this book,
please contact us at CustomerService@Harlequin.com.

® and TM are trademarks of Harlequin Enterprises Limited or its
corporate affiliates. Trademarks indicated with ® are registered in the
United States Patent and Trademark Office, the Canadian Trade Marks
Office and in other countries.

Printed in U.S.A.

Also available from
Harlequin® Books

Also available from
Harlequin HQN

Did you know that these novels are also
available as ebooks? Visit www.Harlequin.com.

Author Note

Sometimes a minor character grabs your imagination and won't let go, intriguing you so much that you know you will have to uncover the rest of her story. Such was the case with the mysterious Madame Lefevre, the woman who lured Max Ransleigh into friendship at the Congress of Vienna in order to set up an assassination attempt on Lord Wellington in the first book of the Ransleigh Rogues miniseries, *The Rake to Ruin Her.*

Where had she come from? What drove her to participate in the plot? What happened to her afterward? As I explored the answers to those questions I discovered a unique and intriguing woman—a French émigrée whose family was destroyed by the revolution, a survivor dragged along by the turbulent historical forces that catapulted France in one generation from monarchy to republic to empire and back. Taught by remorseless circumstance to depend only on herself, Elodie trusts no one and expects nothing.

Who could I pair with such a resourceful and determined heroine? Though I'd originally intended a different story for him, only one man could match her: Will Ransleigh, Max's illegitimate cousin. Cast into the London slums on the death of his mother, a clergyman's daughter seduced and abandoned by Max's uncle, Will survived by his wits on the streets for six years before Max's father plucked him from Seven Dials and sent him to his country estate, instructing Max and his cousins to make a proper Ransleigh out of this gutter rat.

I hope you enjoy Will and Elodie's story.

I love to hear from readers! Find me at my website, www.juliajustiss.com, for excerpts, updates and background bits about my books, on Facebook at www.facebook.com/juliajustiss and on Twitter @juliajustiss.

Chapter One

Barton Abbey—late spring, 1816

'I wager *I* could find her.' Smouldering with anger against the woman who had destroyed his cousin Max's diplomatic career, Will Ransleigh accepted a glass of brandy from his host.

'Welcome back to England,' Alastair Ransleigh said, saluting Will with his own glass before motioning him to an armchair. 'Far be it from me to bet against "Wagering Will", who never met a game of chance he couldn't win. But why do you think *you* could find her, when Max, with all his official contacts, could not?'

'I never had much use for *officials*,' Will observed with a grimace. 'Would have transported me for stealing a loaf of bread to feed myself and my starving mates.'

'You've cleaned up so well, I sometimes forget you were once gallows-bait,' Alastair said with a grin. 'But to be fair, where would one expect to look? Madame Lefevre was cousin and hostess to Thierry St Arnaud, one of Prince Talleyrand's top aides in the French delegation at the Congress of Vienna. The family's quite old and well known, even if they did turn out to be Bonapartists.'

'That may be. But it's those in the serving class who really know what goes on: maids, valets, cooks, grooms, hotel employees, servants at the Hoffburg, keepers of public houses. I'll use them to track Madame Lefevre.'

'When I visited Max at his wife's farm, he insisted he was content there.' Alastair laughed. 'He even claimed training horses is rather like diplomacy: one must coax rather than coerce. Except that horses don't lie and their memories are short, so they don't hold your mistakes against you.'

'Just like Max to make light of it. But all of us—you, me, Dom—knew from our youth that Max was destined to be one of England's foremost politicians—Prime Minister, even! Would he choose training horses over a brilliant government career, if he *truly* had a choice? I don't believe it.'

'I was suspicious, too, at first,' Alastair admitted. 'Max, who never showed any interest in a woman who wasn't both beautiful and accomplished, happily wedding a little nobody who prefers rusticating in Kent to London society? But I ended up liking Caro. She rides better than I do—an admission I make most unwillingly—and breeds top-notch horseflesh on that farm in Kent. She's quite impressive—which is saying something, given my generally low opinion of womankind.' He paused, a bleakness passing over his face.

He's still not over her, Will thought, once again consigning to eternal hellfire the woman who'd broken her engagement and Alastair's heart.

His fury reviving against the latest female to harm one of his Ransleigh Rogue cousins, he continued, 'The very idea is ridiculous—Max, involved in a plot to assassinate Wellington? I'd have thought his valour at Waterloo put a stop to that nonsense.'

Alastair sighed. 'The hard truth is that the attempt in Vienna embarrassed both the French, who were negotiating as allies at the time, and our own forces, who didn't winkle out the conspiracy. Now that Bonaparte's put away at St Helena for good, neither side wanted to rake up old scandals.'

'Couldn't his father do anything? He's practically run the Lords for years.'

'The Earl of Swynford preferred not to champion his son and risk further damaging his political standing, already weakened by Max's "lapse in judgement",' Alastair said drily.

'So he abandoned him. Bastard!' Will added a colourful curse from his days on the London streets. 'Just like my dear uncle never to let his family's needs get in the way of his political aspirations. Makes me glad I was born on the wrong side of the blanket.'

Alastair shook his head, his expression bitter. 'Whoever set up the Vienna scheme was clever, I'll give them that. There'd be no approach more likely to elicit Max's response than to dangle before him some helpless woman in need of assistance.'

'He always had a soft spot for the poor and down-trodden,' Will agreed. 'His treatment of me being a prime example. We need to get Madame Lefevre back to England! Let *her* explain how she invented some sad tale to delay Max's rendezvous with Wellington, leaving the commander waiting alone, vulnerable to attack. Surely that would clear Max of blame, since no man who calls himself a gentleman would have refused a lady begging for his help. He found no trace of St Arnaud, either, while in Vienna?'

'It appears he emigrated to the Americas. It's uncertain whether Madame Lefevre accompanied him. If you do mean to search, it won't be easy. It's been more than a year since the attempt.'

Will shrugged. 'An attack on the man who led all of Europe against Napoleon? People will remember that.'

Alastair opened his mouth as if to speak, then hesitated.

'What?' Will asked.

'Don't jump all over me for asking, but can you afford such a mission? The blunt you'll get from selling out will last a while, but rather than haring off to the Continent, don't you need to look for some occupation? Unless…did the earl come through and—?'

Will waved Alastair to silence. 'No, the earl did not. You didn't really expect our uncle to settle an allowance on me, did you?'

'Well, he did promise, after you managed to scrape together the funds to buy your own commission, that if you made good in the army, he'd see you were settled afterward in a style befitting a Ransleigh.'

Will laughed. 'I imagine he expected me to either be killed or cashiered out. And, no, I've no intention of going to him, cap in hand, to remind him of his pledge, so save your breath.'

'Then what will you do?'

'There are some possibilities. Before I pursue them, though, I'll see Max reinstated to his former position. I've got sufficient blunt for the journey with enough extra to gild the right hands, if necessary.'

'I'll come with you. "Ransleigh Rogues for ever", after all.'

'No, you won't. Wait, hear me out,' he said, fore-stalling Alastair's protest. 'If I needed a sabre-wielding Hussar to ride beside me into a fight, there's no man I'd rather have. But for this journey…'

Looking his cousin up and down, he grinned. 'In your voice, your manner, even your walk, there's no hiding that you're Alastair Ransleigh of Barton Abbey, nephew of an earl, wealthy owner of vast property. I'll need to travel as a man nobody notices and the alley rats would sniff you out in an instant.'

'You're the nephew of an earl yourself,' Alastair pointed out.

'Perhaps, but thanks to my dear father abandoning my mother, unwed and increasing, in the back streets of London, I had the benefit of six years' education in survival. I know how thieves, Captain Sharps and cut-throats operate.'

'But these will be Austrian thieves, Captain Sharps and cutthroats. And you don't speak German.'

Will shrugged. 'Thievery is thievery and you'd be surprised at my many talents. The army had more uses for me after Waterloo than simply letting me hang about the hospital, watching over Dom's recovery.'

'He's healed now, hasn't he?' Alastair asked, diverted by Will's mention of the fourth cousin in their Ransleigh Rogues' gallery. 'Has he…recovered?'

Will recalled the desolate look in Dom's one remaining eye. 'Dandy Dominick', he'd been called, the handsomest man in the regiment. Besting them all at riding, hunting, shooting—and charming the ladies.

His face scarred, one arm gone, his physical prowess diminished, Dom would have to come to terms with much more than his injuries, Will knew. 'Not yet. Once I got him safely back to England, he told me I'd wetnursed him long enough and kicked me out. So I might as well go to Vienna.'

Alastair frowned. 'I still don't like you going there alone. Max said the authorities in Vienna strongly discouraged him from investigating the matter. You'll get no help from them. It could even be dangerous.'

'Dangerous?' Will rose and made a circuit of the room. 'Do you remember the first summer we were all together at Swynford Court?' he asked abruptly, looking back at Alastair. 'The lawyer who found me in Seven Dials had just turned me over to the earl, who, assured I was truly his brother's child, dumped me in the country. Telling you, Max and Dom to make something of me, or else. I was…rather unlikeable.'

Alastair laughed. 'An understatement! Surly, filthy, cursing everyone you encountered in barely comprehensible cant!'

'After two weeks, you and Dom were ready to drown me in the lake. But Max wouldn't give up. One night he caught me alone in the stables. I tried every dirty trick I knew, but he still beat the stuffing out of me. Then, cool as you please, he told me my behaviour had to change. That I was his cousin and a Ransleigh, and he was counting on me to learn to act like one. I didn't make it easy, but he kept goading, coaxing, working on me, like water dripping on stone, until he finally convinced me there could be advantages to becoming more than the leader of thieves in a rookery. Max knew that if I didn't change, when the earl returned at the end of the summer, blood kin or not, he would toss me back into the streets.'

Will stared past Alastair out the library window, seeing not the verdant pastures of Barton Abbey, but the narrow, noisome alleys of Seven Dials. 'If he had, I'd probably be dead now. So I owe Max. For my life. For giving me the closest, most loyal friends and cousins any man could wish for. I swear on whatever honour I possess that I won't take up my own life again until I see his name cleared. Until he has the choice, if he truly wishes, to become the great political leader we all know he should be.'

After studying him for a moment, Alastair nodded. 'Very well. If there's anything I can do, you'll let me know, won't you? If Max hadn't led you and Dom after me into the army, I might not have survived, either. For months after Di—' he halted, having almost said the forbidden name. 'Well, I didn't much care whether I lived or died.'

Will wondered if sometimes, Alastair still didn't much care.

'I might need some help on the official front when it comes time to get the wench into England.'

'She may balk at returning. After all, if she proves herself a spy, the gallows await.'

'I can be...persuasive.'

Alastair chuckled. 'I don't want to know. When do you propose to leave?'

'Tomorrow.'

'But you have just got back! Mama expects you to stay at least a week and Max will want to see you.'

Will shook his head. 'Your mama's being kind and Max would only try to dissuade me. Better I don't see him until...after. If he asks, tell him the army still has business for me on the Continent. Besides, you were right; it's been more than a year. No sense waiting for memories to fade any more than they already have.'

'Do keep me posted. It might take some time to ride to your rescue.'

'Tonight, all I'll need rescue from is too much brandy. Unlikely, as you're being entirely too stingy with it.'

Laughing, Alastair retrieved the bottle and refilled their glasses. 'Ransleigh Rogues for ever!'

'Ransleigh Rogues,' Will replied, clinking his glass with Alastair's.

Chapter Two

Vienna, Austria—six weeks later

Elodie Lefevre shifted her chair into the beam of afternoon sunlight spilling through the window. Taking up her needlework again, she breathed in the soft scent of the late-blooming daffodils she'd planted last autumn in the tiny courtyard garden below. Nodding violas added their sweet fragrance as well.

She paused a moment, letting the calm and beauty seep into her soul, soothing the restless anxiety that lurked always just below the surface. By this evening, she would have this consignment of embroidery finished. Clara would come by with dinner, bringing a new load of embroidery and payment for completing the last.

Against all the odds, she had survived. Despite the constant imperative gnawing within her to get back to Paris, she must remain patient and continue working, hoarding her slowly increasing store of coins. Perhaps late this year, she would finally have enough saved to return…and search for Philippe.

A wave of longing gripped her as her mind caressed his beloved image—the black curls falling over his brow, the dark, ever-curious, intelligent eyes, the driving energy that propelled him. Was he still in Paris? How had he changed in the nearly eighteen months since she'd left?

Would he recognise her? She glanced at herself in the mirror opposite. She was thinner, of course, after her long recovery, but except for her crooked fingers, most of the injuries didn't show. Her blue eyes were shadowed, perhaps, and long hours indoors had dulled the gold highlights the sun had once burnished in her soft brown hair, but otherwise, she thought she looked much the same.

Suddenly, something—a faint stir of the air, a flicker of light—seized her attention. Instantly alert, moving only her eyes, she discovered the source: a barely perceptible movement in the uppermost corner of the mirror, which reflected both her image and the adjacent window that also overlooked the courtyard.

Scarcely breathing, she shifted her head a tiny bit to the right. Yes, someone was there—a man, perched soundlessly on the narrow balcony beside the window, watching her, all but the top of his tawny head and his eyes hidden behind the wall and the vines crawling up it. Had she not chanced to look into the mirror at that precise instant, she would never have seen him move into position.

From the elevation of his head, he must be tall, and agile, to have scaled the wall so soundlessly. The minuscule amount of him she could see gave her no hint whether he was thin or powerfully built. Whether he was armed, and if so, with what.

Not that the knowledge would do her much good. All she had to defend herself was her sewing scissors; her small pistol was hidden in her reticule in the wardrobe and her knife, in the drawer of the bedside table.

But as seconds passed and he remained motionless, she let out the breath she'd been holding. The afternoon light was bright; he could clearly see she was alone. If he'd meant to attack her, surely he would have made a move by now.

Who was he, then? Not one of the men who'd been watching the apartment from the corner ever since Clara brought her here. No one had bothered her since the foiled attack; so small and damaged a fish as herself, she thought, was of little interest, especially after Napoleon's exile at St Helena put an end once and for all to dreams of a French empire.

Elodie kept her gaze riveted on the mirror as several more seconds dragged on. Despite her near-certainty the stranger did not mean her any immediate harm, her nerves—and a rising anger—finally prompted her to speak.

'*Monsieur*, if you are not going to shoot me, why not come inside and tell me what you want?'

The watching eyes widened with surprise, then in one fluid motion the stranger swung himself through the window to land lightly before her. With a flourish, he swept her a bow. 'Madame Lefevre, I presume?'

Elodie caught her breath, overwhelmed by the sheer masculine power of the man now straightening to his full height. If he meant to harm her, she was in very bad trouble indeed.

He must be English. No other men moved with such arrogance, as if they owned the earth by right. He loomed over her, tall and whipcord-lean. There was no mistaking the hard strength of the arms and shoulders that had levered him so effortlessly up to the balcony and swung him practically into her lap.

His clothes were unremarkable: loose-fitting coat, trousers and scuffed boots that might have been worn by any tradesman or clerk toiling away in the vast city.

But his face—angular jaw, chiselled cheekbones, slightly crooked nose, sensual mouth and the arresting turquoise blue of his eyes—would capture the attention of any woman who chanced to look at him. Certainly it captured hers, so completely that she momentarily forgot the potential danger he posed.

He smiled at her scrutiny, which might have embarrassed her, had she not been suddenly jolted by a sense of *déjà vu*. 'Do I know you?' she asked, struggling to work out why he seemed so familiar. 'Have we met?'

The smile faded and his eyes went cold. 'No, *madame*. You don't know me, but I believe you knew my kinsman all too well. Max Ransleigh.'

Max. His image flashed into her mind: same height and build, thick, wavy golden hair, crystal-blue eyes.

An air of command tempered by a kindness and courtesy that had warmed her heart then—and made it twist again now with regret as she recalled him.

The afternoon sun touched this man's tawny hair with tints of auburn; rather than clear blue, his eyes were the hue of the Mediterranean off St Tropez. But beyond that, the two men were remarkably similar. 'You are Max's brother?'

'His cousin. Will Ransleigh.'

'He is well, I trust? I was sorry to have done him…a disservice. I hoped, with Napoleon escaping from Elba so soon after the event in Vienna, that his position had not been too adversely affected.'

He raised one eyebrow, his expression sardonic. Her momentary bedazzlement abruptly vanished as her senses returned to full alert. This man did not mean her well.

'I regret to inform you that your tender hopes were not realised. As you, the cousin of a diplomat, surely know, the "event" that embroiled him in the near-assassination of his commander ruined his career. He was recalled in disgrace and only the outbreak of war allowed him a chance to redeem himself on the field of battle.'

'I understand the carnage was terrible at Waterloo.'

'It was. But even his valour there was not enough to restore his career, which was destroyed by his association with you.'

'I am sorry for it.' And she was. But given the stakes, if she had it all to do over again, she would do nothing differently.

'You are *sorry*? How charming!' he replied, his tone as sardonic as his expression.

Her anger flared again. At men, who used women as pawns to their own purposes. At a woman's always-powerless position in their games. What matter if this man did not believe her? She would not give him the satisfaction of protesting.

As she remained silent, he said, 'Then you will be delighted to know I intend to offer you a chance to make amends. Since you don't appear to be prospering here...' he swept a hand around to indicate the small room, with its worn carpet and shabby furnishing '...I see no reason why you shouldn't agree to leave for England immediately.'

'England?' she echoed, surprised. 'Why should I do that?'

'I'm going to escort you back to London, where we will call on the Foreign Office. There you will explain exactly how you entrapped my cousin in this scheme, manoeuvring him into doing no more than any other gentleman would have done. Demonstrating that he was blameless in not anticipating the assassination attempt, and any fault should be assigned to the intelligence services whose job it was to sniff out such things.'

Her mind racing, Elodie weighed the options. Her hopes rose crazily as she recognised that travelling to London, as this man apparently had the means to do, would get her a deal closer to France, and immediately—not next autumn or in another year, which was as soon as she'd dared hope her slowly accumulating resources would allow.

But even with King Louis on France's throne and the two nations officially at peace, as a French citizen she was still vulnerable. If she testified to involvement in an attempt on the life of the great English hero Lord Wellington, saviour of Europe and victor of Waterloo, she could well be imprisoned. Maybe even executed.

Unless she escaped on the way. Ransleigh would likely want to journey by sea, which would make the chances of eluding him before arrival in England very difficult. Unless…

'I will go with you, but only if we stop first in Paris.' Paris, a city she knew like the lines on her palm. Paris, where only a moment's inattention would allow her to slip away into a warren of medieval alleyways so dense and winding, he would never be able to trail her.

Where, after waiting a safe interval, she could hunt for Philippe.

He made a show of looking about the room, which lacked the presence of a footman or even a maid to lend her assistance. 'I don't think you're in much of a position to dictate terms. And I have no interest in visiting Paris.'

'A mistake, Monsieur Ransleigh. It is a beautiful city.'

'So it is, but unimportant to me at present.'

She shrugged. 'To you, perhaps, but not to me. Unless we go first to Paris, I will not go with you.'

His eyes darkened, unmistakable menace in their depths. 'I can compel you.'

She nodded. 'You could drug me, I suppose. Gag, bind and smuggle me aboard a ship in Trieste. But nothing can compel me to deliver to the London authorities the sort of testimony you wish, unless I myself choose to do so.'

Fury flashed in those blue eyes and his jaw clenched. If his cousin's career had truly been ruined by her actions, he had cause to be angry.

Just as she'd had no choice about involving Max in the plot.

'I could simply kill you now,' he murmured, stepping closer. 'Your life for the life you ruined.' He placed his hands around her neck.

She froze, her heartbeat stampeding. Had she survived so much, only for it all to end now? His hands, warm against the chill of her neck, were large and undoubtedly strong. One quick twist and it would be over.

But despite the hostility of his action, as the seconds ticked away with his fingers encircling her neck, some instinct told her that he didn't truly mean to hurt her.

As her fear subsided to a manageable level, she grasped his hands with a calm she was far from feeling. To her great relief, he let her pull them away from her neck, confirming her assessment.

'Paris first, then London. I will wait in the garden for your decision.'

Though her heart pounded so hard that she was dizzy, Elodie made herself rise and walk with unhurried steps from the room. Not for her life would she let him see how vulnerable she felt. Never again would any man make her afraid.

Why should they? She had nothing left to lose.

Out of his sight, she clutched the stair rail to keep from falling as she descended, then stumbled out the back door to the bench at the centre of the garden. She grabbed the edge with trembling fingers and sat down hard, gulping in a shuddering breath of jonquil-scented air.

Eyes narrowed, Will watched Elodie Lefevre cross the room with quiet elegance and disappear down the stairwell.

Devil's teeth! She was nothing like what he'd expected.

He'd come to Vienna prepared to find a seductive siren, who traded upon her beauty to entice while at the same time playing the frightened innocent. Luring in Max, for whom protecting a woman was a duty engraved upon his very soul.

Elodie Lefevre was attractive, certainly, but hers was a quiet beauty. Sombrely dressed and keeping herself in the background, as he'd learned she always did, she'd have attracted little notice among the crowd of fashionable, aristocratic lovelies who'd fluttered like exotic butterflies through the balls and salons of the Congress of Vienna.

She had courage, too. After her first indrawn breath of alarm, she'd not flinched when he clamped his fingers around her throat.

Not that he'd had any intention of actually harming her, of course. But he'd hoped that his display of anger and a threat of violence might make her panic and capitulate before reinforcements could arrive.

If she had any.

He frowned. It had taken a month of thorough, patient tracking to find her, but the closer he got, the more puzzled and curious he became about the woman who'd just coolly descended to the garden. As if strange men vaulted into her rooms and threatened her life every day.

Maybe they did. For, until she'd confirmed her identity, he'd been nearly convinced the woman he'd located couldn't be the Elodie Lefevre he sought.

Why was the cousin of a wealthy diplomat living in shabby rooms in a decaying, unfashionable section of Vienna?

Why did she inhabit those rooms alone—lacking, from the information he'd charmed out of the landlady, even a maid?

Why did it appear she eked out a living doing embroidery work for a fashionable dressmaker whom Madame Lefevre, as hostess to one of the Congress of Vienna's most well-placed diplomats, would have visited as a customer?

But neither could he deny the facts that had led him, piecing together each small bit of testimony gathered from maids, porters, hotel managers, street vendors, seamstresses, merchants and dry-good dealers, from the elegant hotel suite she'd presided over for St Arnaud to these modest rooms off a Vienna back alley.

St Arnaud himself had disappeared the night of the failed assassination. Will didn't understand why someone clever enough to have concocted such a scheme would have been so careless about ensuring his cousin's safety.

And how had she sensed Will's presence on the balcony? He knew for certain he'd made no sound as he carefully scaled the wall from the courtyard to the ledge outside her window. Either she was incredibly prescient, or he'd badly lost his touch, and he didn't think it was the latter.

Her awareness impressed him even more than her courage, sparking an admiration he had no wish to feel.

Any more than he'd wanted the reaction triggered when he'd placed his hands around her neck. The softness of her skin, the faint scent of lavender teasing his nostrils, sent a fierce desire surging through him, as abrupt and immediate as the leap of her pulse under his thumbs.

Finding himself attracted to Elodie Lefevre was a complication he didn't need. What he did need were answers to all the questions he had about her.

Such as why it was so important for her to get to Paris.

A quick examination of her room told him nothing; the hired furniture, sewing supplies and few basic necessities could have been anyone's. She seemed to possess nothing that gave any clue to the character of the woman who'd lived here, as he'd learned, for more than a year, alone but for the daily visits of her former maid.

He'd just have to go question the woman herself. He suspected she would be as vigilant at keeping her secrets as she was at catching out uninvited visitors to her rooms.

To achieve his aims, he needed to master both those secrets—and her. Turning on his heel, he headed for the garden.

Chapter Three

Will found Madame Lefevre picking spent blooms from the border of lavender surrounding a central planting of tall yellow flowers.

Hearing him approach, she looked back over her shoulder. 'Well?'

He waited, but she added nothing to that single word—neither pleading nor explanation nor entreaty. Once again, he was struck by her calm, an odd quality of stillness overlaid with a touch of melancholy.

Men awaiting battle would envy that sangfroid. Or did she not truly realise how vulnerable she was?

'For a woman who's just had her life threatened, you seem remarkably tranquil.'

She shrugged. 'Nothing I say or do will change what you have decided. If it is to kill me, I am not strong or skilled enough to prevent you. Struggling and pleading are so…undignified. And if I am to die, I would rather spend my last moments enjoying the beauty of my garden.'

So she did understand the gravity of her position. Yet the calm remained.

As a man who'd earned much of his blunt by his wits, Will had played cards with masters of the game, men who didn't show by the twitch of an eyelid whether they held a winning or losing hand. Madame Lefevre could hold her own with the best of them. He'd never met a woman so difficult to read.

She was like a puzzle spread out in a jumble of pieces. The more he learned about her, the stronger his desire to fit them all together.

Delaying answering her question so he might examine that puzzle further, he said, 'The garden is lovely. So serene, and those yellow flowers are so fragrant. Did you plant it?'

She lifted a brow, as if wondering why he'd abruptly veered from threatening her to talking about plants. 'The daffodils, you mean.' Her lips barely curved in amusement, she looked at him quizzically. 'You grew up in the city, Monsieur Ransleigh, no?'

'Commonplace, are they?' A reluctant, answering smile tugged at his lips. 'Yes, I'm a city lad. But you, obviously, were country bred.'

'Lovely flowers can be found in either place,' she countered.

'Your English is very good, with only a trace of an accent. Where did you learn it?'

She waved a careless hand. 'These last few years, English has been spoken everywhere.'

She'd grown up in the country, then, he surmised

from her evasions, probably at an estate with a knowl-
edgeable gardener—and an English governess.

'How did you come to be your cousin's hostess in
Vienna?'

'He never married. A diplomat at his level has many
social duties.'

Surprised at getting a direct answer this time,
he pressed, 'He did not need you to perform those
"duties" after Vienna?'

'Men's needs change. So, *monsieur*, do you accept
my bargain or not?'

Aha, he thought, gratified. Though she gave no outward sign of anxiety—trembling fingers, fidgeting
hands, restless movement—the abrupt return to the
topic at hand showed she wasn't as calm as she was
trying to appear.

'Yes,' he replied, deciding upon the moment. At least
seeming to agree to her demand was essential. It would
be a good deal easier to spirit her out of Vienna if she
went willingly.

He was still somewhat surprised she would consent
to accompany him upon any terms. Unless…

'Don't think you can escape me in Paris,' he warned.
'I'll be with you every moment, like crust on bread.'

'Ah, warm French bread! I cannot wait to taste some.'

She licked her lips. The gesture sent a bolt of lust
straight to his loins. Something of his reaction must
have showed in his face, for her eyes widened and she
smiled knowingly.

He might not be able to prevent his body's response,

but he could certainly control his actions, he thought, disgruntled. If anyone was going to play the seduction card in this little game, it would be him—if and when he wished to.

'How did you, cousin to Thierry St Arnaud, come to be here alone?' he asked, steering the discussion back where he wanted it. 'Why did he not take you with him when he fled Vienna?'

'Nothing—and no one—mattered to my cousin but restoring Napoleon to the throne of France. When the attempt failed, his only thought was to escape before the Austrian authorities discovered his connection to the plot, so he might plot anew. Since I was no longer of any use to him, he was done with me.'

It seemed St Arnaud had about as much family loyalty as Will's uncle. But still, self-absorbed as the earl might be, Will knew if anyone bearing Ransleigh blood were in difficulties, the earl would send assistance.

What sort of man would not do that for his own cousin?

Putting aside that question for the moment, Will said, 'Were you equally fervent to see Napoleon restored as emperor?'

'To wash France free of the stain of aristocracy, Napoleon spilled the blood of his own people…and then created an aristocracy of his own. All I know of politics is the guillotine's blade was followed by the emperor's wars. I doubt the fields of Europe will dry in our lifetime.'

'So why did you help St Arnaud?'

'You think he gave me a choice?'

Surprised, he stared at her, assessing. She met his gaze squarely, faint colour stirring in her cheeks at his scrutiny.

A man who would abandon his own cousin probably hadn't been too dainty in coercing her co-operation. Had he hurt her?

Even as the question formed, as if guessing his thoughts, she lowered her gaze and tucked her left hand under her skirt.

An unpleasant suspicion coalescing in his head, Will stepped closer and seized her hand. She resisted, then gasped as he jerked it into the waning sunlight.

Two of the fingers were slightly bent, the knuckles still swollen, as if the bones had been broken and healed badly. 'An example of your cousin's persuasion?' he asked roughly, shocked and disgusted. A man who would attack a woman was beneath contempt.

She pulled her hand back, rubbing the wrist. 'An accident, *monsieur*.'

Will didn't understand why she would protect St Arnaud, if he truly had coerced her participation, then abandoned her. He didn't want to feel the niggle of sympathy stirring within him, had that really been her predicament.

Whatever her reasons, she was still the woman who'd ruined Max's career.

'You'd have me believe you were an innocent pawn, forced by St Arnaud to do his bidding, then discarded when you were no longer of use?'

She smiled sweetly. 'Used, just as you plan to use me, you mean?'

Stung, his anger flared hotter. Plague take her, *he* wasn't her bloody relation, responsible for her safety and well-being. If he used her, it was only what she deserved for entrapping Max.

'Why is it so important for you to go to Paris?' he asked instead.

'It's a family matter. You, who have come all this way and worked so diligently on your cousin's behalf, should appreciate that. Take me to Paris and I will go with you to England. I'll not go otherwise—no matter what…persuasion you employ.'

He stared into her eyes, assessing the strength of her conviction. She'd rightly said he couldn't force or threaten her into testifying. Indeed, even the appearance of coercion would discredit what she said.

He hoped upon the journey to somehow charm or trick her out of going to Paris. But unless he came up with a way to do so, he might end up having to stop there first.

Although one should always have a long-term strategy, all that mattered at the moment was playing the next card. First, he must get her out of Vienna.

'It doesn't appear you have much to pack. I should like to leave in two days' time.'

'How do you mean to spirit me away? Though the watchers have not yet interfered with my movements, I've not attempted to leave the city.'

Having drunk a tankard with the keeper of the public house on the corner, Will had already discovered the house was being watched, but he hadn't expected a woman, diplomat's cousin or no, to have noticed. Once again, surprise and reluctant admiration rippled through him. 'You're aware of the guard, then?'

She gave him an exasperated look, as if he were treating her like an idiot. '*Bien sûr* I'm aware! Although as I said, rightfully judging that I pose no threat, they've done nothing but observe. But since I have recovered enough to—' She halted a moment, then continued, 'There have always been watchers.'

Recovered enough. He wasn't sure he wanted to know from what. Shaking off the thought, he said, 'Do you know who they are?'

'Austrians, I expect. Clara has flirted with some of them, and from their speech they appear to be local lads. Not English. Nor French. Talleyrand has enough agents in keeping, he can learn, I expect, whatever he wishes from the Austrians.'

Will nodded. That judgement confirmed what the publican had told him. Local men, hired out of the army by government officials, would be easier for him to evade than Foreign Office professionals. During the two days he was allotting *madame* to settle her things, he'd observe the guard's routine, then choose the best time and manner in which to make off with her—in case the authorities should object to her departure.

'Are you thinking to have me pay off the landlady and simply stroll out the front door, valise in hand?' *madame* asked, interrupting his thoughts.

'You'd prefer to escape out a window at midnight?' he asked, amused.

'The balcony worked well enough for you,' she retorted. 'It might be wise to anticipate opposition. I should probably go in disguise, so that neither the landlady nor the guards at the corner immediately realise I've departed.'

Though by now he shouldn't be surprised by anything she said, Will found himself raising an eyebrow. 'Leave in disguise? Interesting education the French give their diplomatic hostesses.'

'France has been at war for longer than we both have been alive, *monsieur*,' she shot back. 'People from every level of society have learned tricks to survive.'

It appeared she had, at any rate. If being abandoned by her cousin in a foreign capital were any indication, she had needed to.

'What do you suggest?'

'That we leave in mid-afternoon, when streets busy with vehicles, vendors and pedestrians will distract the guards and make them less vigilant. You could meet my friend, Clara, at a posting inn not far from these rooms. Bring men's clothing that she can conceal beneath the embroidery in her basket. She will escort you up, telling the landlady, if you encounter her, that you are her brother. You will then exit by the balcony while I, wearing the clothing you provide, will walk out with Clara.'

Her suggestion was so outrageous, Will was hard put not to laugh. 'I've no problem exiting by way of the balcony, but do you really think you could pass as a man?'

'I'm tall for a woman. As long as I don't encounter Frau Gruener, who knows me well, it should work. She almost always takes her rest of an afternoon between two and four, by the way. Those watching at the corner, if they notice us at all, will merely see Clara leaving the building, as she went in, with a man. Once we are away from the watchers, I leave it to you—who did so good a job locating me—to manage the rest.'

Intrigued by *madame*'s unexpected talent for subterfuge, he had to admit that the plan had merit. 'It might work. As long as you can walk in men's clothing without it being immediately obvious that you're a woman.'

She smiled grimly. 'You might be surprised at my talents. I'm more concerned about you remaining for more than a few hours in this vicinity without attracting attention. You are…rather distinctive.'

'You don't think *I* can pass unnoticed, if I choose?'

'Your clothing is unremarkable, but you, *monsieur*, are not.' She looked him up and down, her gaze coming to rest on his face. 'Both that golden hair—and your features—are far too striking.'

He couldn't help feeling a purely male satisfaction that she found him so notable. As he held her gaze, smiling faintly, a surge of sensual energy pulsed between them, as powerful as if she'd actually touched him. From the gasp she uttered and her widened eyes, Will knew she'd felt it, too.

Hell and damn. Bad enough that he'd been immediately attracted to her. If he excited her lust as well…

It would complicate things, certainly. On the other

hand, as long as he kept his head, if not his body, focused on his objective, he might be able to use that attraction later. Seducing her to achieve his aims would be much more pleasant for them both than outright coercion.

Filing that possibility away, he forced himself to look away, breaking the connection.

'I'm a dab hand at disguises myself. I'll not accompany your friend as her brother, but as her old uncle, who wears spectacles and has something of a limp. The gout, you know.'

Tilting her head, she studied him. 'Truly, you are Max Ransleigh's cousin?'

He couldn't fault her scepticism; no more than she could Will imagine Max sneaking on to a balcony, breaking into a woman's rooms, threatening her, or disguising himself as an old man.

'I'm from the wrong side of the blanket, so I come by my disreputable ways honestly.'

'Ah, I see. Very well, Clara will meet you at three of the afternoon, two days from now at the Lark and Plough, on Dusseldorfer Strasse. She'll look for a bent old man with spectacles and a cane.' She offered her hand.

'Honour among thieves?' Amused anew, he took her hand to shake it…and a zing of connection flowed immediately through her fingers to his.

Her face colouring, she snatched her hand back. No longer annoyed by the hardening of his loins, Will was beginning to find the possibility of seduction more enticing than regrettable.

'Three o'clock, then.' As she nodded and turned to go back into the house, he said, 'By the way, *madame*, I will be watching. If any tall young man with a feminine air exits your lodgings in the interim, I will notice.'

She lifted her chin. 'Why should I try to elude you? I *want* to return to Paris and you will help me do so. Until then, *monsieur*.'

Before she could walk away, a woman's voice emanating from the second floor called out, '*Madame*, where are you?'

'Get back!' she whispered, pushing him into the shadows beneath the balcony.

'That's Clara, isn't it? The maid who helped you?' Will asked in an undertone as footsteps sounded on the balcony overhead.

'Ah, there you are, in the garden,' came the voice. 'Shall I bring your dinner down there?'

'No, I'll be right up,' *madame* called back.

She pivoted to face Will. 'As soon as you hear me above, go back over the wall the way you came. I will do as you ask; there's no need for you to harass Clara.'

'What makes you think I haven't already...harassed her?'

Her eyes widened with alarm before she steadied herself, no doubt realising that if he *had* accosted the maid, she would have probably arrived frightened and frantic, rather than calmly calling her mistress to supper. Still, even now it might be worth following the maid home and seeing if he could dredge out of her any additional information about her mistress.

As if she could read his thoughts, *madame* said fiercely, 'If any harm comes to Clara, I will *kill* you.'

Amused at her audacity in daring to threaten him—this slender woman who must weigh barely more than a child and possessed neither strength nor any weapon—Will grinned. 'You could try.'

Her gaze hardened. 'You have no idea what I am capable of, *monsieur*.' Showing him her back, she paced into her lodgings, a wisp of lavender scent lingering in her wake.

Chapter Four

Her heart beating hard, feeling as weak as if she'd run a mile through the twisting Vienna streets, Elodie hurried up the stairway to her rooms. Having placed her basket on a table, Clara was looking at the embroidery Elodie had just completed.

'Ah, *madame*, this is the prettiest yet! The colour's lovely, and the bird so vivid, one almost thinks it will fly off the gown.' Looking up at Elodie, the maid nodded approvingly. 'You've got some colour back in your face. A stroll in the fresh air agreed with you. You must do it more often.'

Elodie wasn't about to reveal that it wasn't the garden air that had brought a flush to her cheeks, but an infuriating, dictatorial, dangerous man.

His touch had almost scalded her. It had been many years since she'd sought or experienced such a physical response. The sensation carried her back to the early days of her love for her late husband, when a mere glance from him could set her body afire.

She shook the memory away before sadness could follow in its wake. Given her reaction to him, travelling in Will Ransleigh's company might be more hazardous to her well-being than she'd first thought. But she could worry about that later; now, she had more immediate matters to address.

'I've brought you a good dinner,' the maid said as she bustled about, putting plates and silverware on the table and lighting candles. 'Frau Luvens made meat pie and some of her apple strudel. You will do it justice now, won't you?'

To her surprise, for the first time in a long time, Elodie found the idea of food appealing. The knowledge that at last, at last, she would be able to stop marking time and get back to Paris, was reviving her vanished appetite. 'You won't have to coax me tonight; it sounds delicious. You are joining me, aren't you? You can tell me all the news.'

While Clara rambled on about her day and her work at the grand hotel where she'd taken employment after her mistress had recovered enough to be left on her own, Elodie edged to the window. Though from this angle, she couldn't see all the way under the balcony, her surreptitious inspection of the garden indicated that Monsieur Ransleigh had indeed departed.

By now, Clara had the covers off the dishes and was waving her to the small table. 'Come, eat before the meat pies get cold. Gruber gave me some extra bread from the hotel kitchen. I'm so glad to see your appetite returning! Just in time, as we'll be able to afford meat more often. Madame Lebruge was so complimentary about your work on the last consignment of embroidery, I told her the next lot would be ten schillings more the piece. She didn't even protest! I should have asked for twenty.'

Elodie seated herself and waited while the maid attacked her meat pie. 'I won't be doing another lot. I'm leaving Vienna.'

Clara's hands stilled and she looked up, wiping savoury juice from her chin. 'Leaving? How? I thought you said it would be months before you could save enough to travel.'

'My plans have changed.' Omitting any mention of threats or the edgy undercurrent between herself and the man, Elodie told Clara about Will Ransleigh's visit and offer to escort her to Paris.

She should have known the maid would be suspicious. 'But can you trust this man, *madame*? How do you know he truly is Monsieur Max Ransleigh's cousin?'

'When you see him, you'll understand; the resemblance between the two men is striking.'

'Why would he wish to do you the favour of taking you to Paris?'

'Because I am to do him a favour in return. I promised I would go to England and testify about how I embroiled his cousin in St Arnaud's plot.'

'*Gott im Himmel, madame!* Is that wise? Is it safe?'

Though she was nearly certain Ransleigh was gone, a well-developed instinct for caution impelled her to lean close and drop her voice to a whisper. 'I have no intention of actually going to London. Once we get to Paris, I shall elude him.'

Clara clapped her hands. 'Ah, yes, and I am sure you shall, now that you've finally recovered your strength! But…should I not go with you as far as Paris? I do not like the idea of you travelling alone with this man about whom we know so little.'

'Thank you, dear friend, but you should stay here. Vienna is your home. You've already done more for me than I ever expected, more than I can ever repay.'

The maid waved a hand dismissively. 'How could I do less, when you were so kind to me? Taking on an untried girl as your dresser, you who had to appear with the cream of society before all Vienna! Nor could I have obtained my present position without all I learned serving you.'

'You've returned many times over any favour I did you.'

'In any case, my lady, you shouldn't travel alone.'

'That might be true…if I were travelling as a "lady". But I shall not be, nor is the journey likely to be comfortable. Perhaps not even safe. I don't know if the watchers will be pleased when they discover I've left Vienna and you've already faced enough danger for me. I must go alone.'

'You are certain?' the maid asked, studying her face.

'Yes,' she replied, clasping Clara's hand. Even if she'd planned to travel as a lady of substance, she wouldn't have allowed Clara to accompany her. Escaping swiftly, drawing out of Vienna whatever forces still kept surveillance over her, was the best way to ensure the safety of the woman who had taken her in and nursed her back to health after she'd been brutalised and abandoned.

'So, no more embroidery,' Elodie said. 'But I'm not completely without resources yet.' Rising, she went to the linen press and extracted two bundles neatly wrapped in muslin. Bringing them to Clara, she said, 'The first is a ball gown I never had a chance to wear; it should fetch a good price. The other is the fanciest of my dinner gowns; I've already re-embroidered it and changed the trimming, so Madame Lebruge should be able easily to resell that as well.'

'Shouldn't you have the money, *madame*? Especially if you mean to travel. I could take these to her tomorrow. She's been so pleased with all the other gowns you've done, I'm sure I could press her for a truly handsome sum.'

'Press her as hard as you like, but keep the money for yourself. It's little enough beside my debt to you. I've something else, too.'

Reaching down to flip up the bottom of her sewing apron, Elodie picked the seam open and extracted a pair of ear-rings. Small diamonds twinkled in the light of the candles. 'Take these. Sell them if you like, or keep them…as a remembrance of our friendship.'

'*Madame*, you mustn't! They're too fine! Besides, you might need to sell them yourself, once you get to Paris.'

'I have a few other pieces left.' Elodie smiled. 'One

can't say much good of St Arnaud, but he never begrudged me the funds to dress the part of his hostess. I can't imagine how I would have survived this year without the jewels and finery we were able to sell.'

The maid spat out a German curse on St Arnaud's head. 'If he'd not been in such a rush to leave Vienna and save his own neck, he would probably have taken them.'

Elodie shrugged. 'Well, I am thankful to have had them, whatever the reason. Now, let me tell you how my departure has been arranged.'

Half an hour later, fully apprised of who she was to meet, when and where, Clara hugged her and walked out. An unnerving silence settled in the rooms after her footsteps faded.

Though she supposed there was no need to work on the gowns the maid had left, from force of habit, Elodie took the top one from the basket and fetched her embroidery silks.

Along with the sale of some gems, the gowns she'd worn as St Arnaud's hostess, re-embroidered and sold back to the shop from which she'd originally purchased them, had supported her for six months. At that point Madame Lebruge, pleased with the elegance and inventiveness of her work, sent new gowns from her shop for Elodie to embellish.

Letting her fingers form the familiar stitches calmed her as she reviewed what had transpired in the last few hours. Clara was right to be suspicious; she had no way of knowing for sure that Will Ransleigh would actually take her to Paris, rather than murdering her in some alley.

But if he'd wanted to dispose of her, he could have already done so. Nor could one fail to note the fervour in his eyes when he talked of righting the wrong she'd done his cousin. She believed he meant to take her to London—and that she'd convinced him she'd not go there unless they went to Paris first.

She smiled; he'd immediately suspected she meant to escape him there. Just because he was Max Ransleigh's cousin, and therefore nephew to an earl, it would not do to underestimate his resourcefulness, or think him hopelessly out of his element in the meaner streets of Paris. He'd tracked her down here, most certainly without assistance from any of the authorities. He'd not been shocked or appalled by her idea of escaping in disguise, only concerned that she couldn't carry off the deception. He'd then proposed an even cleverer disguise, suggesting he was as familiar as she was with subterfuge.

Perhaps he worked for the Foreign Office, as Max had, only in a more clandestine role. Or maybe he was just a rogue, as the unpredictability and sense of danger that hung about him seemed to suggest.

He'd been born on the wrong side of the blanket, he'd said. Perhaps, instead of growing up in the ease of an earl's establishment, he'd had to scrabble for a living, moving from place to place, much as she had. That would explain his housebreaker's skill at scaling balconies and invading rooms.

The notion struck her that they might have much in common.

Swiftly she dismissed that ridiculous thought. She sincerely doubted that *he* had ever had his very life depend on the success of the disguise he employed. Nor should she forget that he'd sought her out for a single purpose, one that left no room for any concern about *her* well-being. Still, depending on what happened in Paris, she might consider going to London as she'd promised.

She would give much to right the wrong she'd been forced to do Max Ransleigh. After studying the background of all of the Duke of Wellington's aides, St Arnaud had determined Max's well-documented weakness for and courtesy towards women made him the best prospect among those with immediate access to Wellington to be of use in his plot. He'd ordered her to establish a relationship with Max, gain his sympathy and learn his movements, so he might be used as a decoy when the time was right.

She'd been instructed to offer him her body if necessary, but it hadn't been. Not that she found Max unappealing as a lover, but having learned he'd already taken one of the most elegant courtesans in Vienna as his mistress, she judged him unlikely to be tempted by a tall, brown-haired woman of no outstanding beauty.

His attentions to her had been initially just the courtesies any diplomat would offer his occasional hostess. Until one day, when she'd been sporting a bruised face and shoulder, and he'd figured out that St Arnaud must have abused her.

She'd told him nothing, of course, but from that moment, his attitude had grown fiercely protective. Rather ironic, she thought, that it had been St Arnaud's foul temper and vindictive spirit, rather than her charms, that had drawn Max closer to her.

In fact, she'd be willing to bet, had the moment not occurred for St Arnaud to spring his plot, Max would have tried to work out an honourable way for her to escape her cousin.

But the moment did occur. As little choice as she'd had in the matter, it still pained her to recall it.

The night of the attack had begun with an afternoon like any other at the Congress, until Max had casually mentioned that he might be late arriving to the Austrian ambassador's ball that evening, since he was to confer briefly in private with the Duke before accompanying him to the festivities. It was the work of a moment for Elodie to inveigle from him in which anteroom that meeting was to take place, the work of another that night to intercept Max in the hallway before he went in.

She waylaid him with a plea that he assist her on some trumped-up matter that would call down on her the wrath of her cousin, should she fail to speedily accomplish it. Despite his concern for her welfare, so great was his impatience to meet his commander, who had a well-known intolerance for tardiness, that she was able to delay him only a few minutes.

It was long enough. St Arnaud's assassin found his target alone, unguarded, and only Wellington's own battle-won sixth sense in dodging away an instant before the stranger bursting into the room fired his weapon, had averted tragedy.

To the Duke, anyway. Captured almost immediately, the failed assassin withstood questioning only briefly before revealing St Arnaud's, and therefore her own, connection to the plot. Assuming the worst, St Arnaud had dealt with her and fled. She'd been in no condition afterwards to discover what had happened to Max; she assumed that, disgraced and reprimanded, he'd been sent back to England.

Dear, courteous Max. Perhaps the kindest man she'd ever known, she thought, conjuring up with a sigh the image of his face. Odd, though, that while he was certainly handsome, she hadn't felt for him the same immediate, powerful surge of desire inspired by his cousin Will.

An attraction so strong it had dazzled her into forgetting, for the first few moments, that he'd invaded her rooms. So strong that, though he'd coerced and threatened her, she felt it still.

It had also been evident, even in his ill-fitting breeches, that the lust he inspired in her was mutual. Elodie felt another flush of heat, just thinking of that sleek hardness, pressing against his trouser front.

Such a response, she suddenly realised, might be useful later, when she needed to escape him. A well-pleasured man would be languid, less than vigilant. And pleasuring Will Ransleigh would be no hardship.

Eluding him in Paris, however, would be another challenge entirely.

Chapter Five

Loitering at the corner, hidden from view by the shadow of an overhanging balcony, and cap well down over the golden hair Madame Lefevre had found so distinctive, Will watched the guard posted at the opposite end of the alley. He'd grab some dinner and return to remain here through the night, noting how many kept watch and when they changed. Although he'd agreed with *madame*'s suggestion that she leave in full daylight, it would be wise to know how many men had been employed to observe her—and might be sent in pursuit when they discovered she'd fled.

He shook his head again over her unexpected talent for intrigue.

Before seeking his dinner, he would question *madame*'s friend Clara. He'd not bothered the girl before, having worked out where *madame* had gone to ground without having to accost the maid. Although the person who'd protected *madame* would likely be the most reluctant to give him any information, after an interview that had given rise to more questions than it answered, it was worth the attempt to extract from the girl anything that might shed more light on the mystery that was Madame Lefevre.

A woman who thus far hadn't behaved as he would have expected of an aristocratic Frenchwoman who'd served as hostess to the most important leaders of European society.

Now that he'd confirmed that the woman he'd found was in fact Madame Lefevre, it was time to re-examine his initial assumptions about her.

The speed with which she'd come up with the suggestion that she escape in disguise—masculine disguise, at that—seemed to indicate she'd donned such a costume before. Recalling the grim expression on her face, Will thought it hadn't been in some amateur theatrical performance for amusement of friends.

'France has been at war longer than we've been alive...' Had her family been caught up in the slaughter leading from monarchy to republic to empire and back? It seemed likely.

He wished now he'd paused in London to plumb for more detail about the St Arnaud family. Thierry St Arnaud's employer, Prince Talleyrand, possessed an exceptional skill for survival, having served as Foreign Minister of France during the Republic, Consulate, Empire and now the Restoration. At the Congress of Vienna, the Prince had even managed the unlikely feat of persuading Britain and Austria that France, a country those two allies had fought for more than twenty years, should become their partner against Russia and Prussia.

What remarkable tricks of invention had the St Arnaud clan performed to retain lands and titles through the bloodbath of revolution and empire?

Perhaps, rather than spending her girlhood tucked away at some genteel country estate, *madame*'s aristocratic family, like so many others, had been forced to escape the guillotine's blade. They might even have fled to England; the British crown had supported a large *émigré* community. That would explain her excellent, almost accentless speech.

Or perhaps she was such a mistress of invention because she was one of Talleyrand's agents. His gut churned at that unpleasant possibility.

But though Will wouldn't totally discount the idea, Talleyrand was known to be an exacting master. It wouldn't be like the prince to leave a loose end—like a former agent—flapping alone in the Viennese breeze for over a year; Madame Lefevre would likely have been eliminated or spirited away long since.

Still, it wouldn't be amiss to behave around her as if she had a professional's expertise.

He smiled. That would make the matching of wits all the sweeter. And if the opportunity arose to intertwine bodies as well, that would be the sweetest yet.

But enough of carnal thoughts. He couldn't afford to let lust and curiosity make him forget his goal, or lure him into being less than vigilant. He was certain she intended to try to escape him during their journey, and he'd need to be on his best game to ensure she did not.

As he reached that conclusion, Clara exited *madame*'s lodgings. Keeping into the shadow of the buildings, Will followed her.

To his good fortune, since the onset of evening and the thinning crowds would make it harder to trail her unobserved, the maid headed for the neighbouring market. He shadowed her as she snapped up the last of the day's bread, cheese and apples at bargain prices from vendors eager to close up for the night.

The Viennese were a prosperous lot, he noted as he trailed a few stalls behind her, and remarkably careless with their purses. Had he a mind to, he could have snatched half a dozen as he strolled along.

Unable to resist the temptation to test his skill and thinking it might make a good introduction, Will nipped from behind the maid to snag her coin purse while she lingered by the last stall, bidding farewell to the vendor and rearranging the purchases in her market basket.

He followed her from the market until she reached a mostly deserted stretch of street, where the buildings' overhanging second storeys created a shadowy recess. Picking up his pace, Will strode past her and then turned, herding her towards the wall. With a deep bow, he held out the coin purse.

'Excuse me, miss, I believe you dropped this.'

With a gasp, she shrank back, then halted. 'Why... it is my purse! I was sure I put it back into my reticule!

How can I thank you, Herr…' Belatedly looking up, she got a glimpse of his face. 'You!'

Will bowed again. 'Will Ransleigh, at your service, miss.'

Alarm battled anger in her face. 'I should call the authorities and have you arrested for theft!'

He raised an eyebrow. 'How could you do that, when I've just returned your purse? If officials in Vienna arrest every fellow who follows a pretty girl, the jails would be full to overflowing. I mean you no harm.'

She sniffed. 'I note you don't deny you took it! But seeing as how you could have just as easily knocked me over the head as given it back, I suppose I'll not scream the houses down—for the moment. What do you want?'

'I intend to help your mistress leave the city.'

She looked him up and down, her expression wary. 'I warned her not to trust you. Oh, I don't doubt you'll help her, all right—to do what *you* want her to. Just like that worthless cousin of hers.'

Remembering *madame*'s bent and swollen fingers, Will felt a surge of dislike. If he ever encountered Thierry St Arnaud, he'd force the man to test his strength against a more fitting adversary. 'He intimidated her, didn't he?'

'Bastard.' The maid spat on cobblestones. 'I only saw him strike her twice, but she almost always had bruises. I'll not hurt her more by telling you anything.'

'I appreciate your loyalty. But whatever you can tell me—about her relationship with St Arnaud or my cousin—will help me protect her on the journey. I can do a better job if I'm aware of potential threats before they happen. If I know who's been watching her, and why.'

Her expression clouded, telling Will she worried about her mistress, too. 'Herr Ransleigh, your cousin, was an honourable man,' she said after a moment. 'You promise to keep her safe?'

'I promise.' To his surprise, Will found he meant it.

Clara studied him, obviously still reluctant.

'You want her to stay safe, too, don't you?' he coaxed. 'How about I tell you what I know and you just confirm it?'

After considering another moment, the maid nodded.

'You've been with your mistress more than a year. She engaged you when she first arrived in Vienna—September 1814, wasn't it?'

Clara nodded.

'That last night, before her cousin fled the city, he… hurt her.'

Tears came to the girl's eyes. 'Yes,' she whispered.

'Badly?' Will pressed, keeping a tight rein over his rising temper, almost certain now he knew what she would tell him.

'She was unconscious when I found her. Her ribs broken for sure, and her arm and hand bent and twisted. Didn't come back to herself for more than a day, and for the first month, I wasn't sure she would survive. Bastard!' the maid burst out again. 'Blaming her for the failure of his foolish plan! Or maybe just taking it out on her that it failed. He was that kind.'

'You took her from the hotel to rooms at a boarding house and nursed her. Then, once she'd recovered sufficiently, you moved her to the lodgings here,' Will summed up the trail his search had taken him on.

'By then, she said she was recovered enough to work. I'd sold jewels for her those first few months, until her bad hand healed enough for her to use the fingers. She started doing embroidery then.'

'And there were watchers, each place you stayed with her?'

'I guess there were, though I didn't notice them until she pointed them out after she got better. I was frightened, but what could they want with her? After a few months, I got used to them hanging about.'

'Viennese lads, they were.'

'Yes. I spoke to some of them, trying to see if I could find out anything, but they seemed to know only that a local man hired them. I'm certain someone more important was behind it, but I don't know who.'

Will filed that observation away. 'Why is she so insistent on returning to Paris?'

'Her family's there, I expect. She never spoke about herself, nor was she the sort who thought only of her own comfort. Waiting for her at the dressmakers or at those grand balls, I heard other maids talking about their ladies. *Madame* wasn't like most of them, always difficult and demanding. She was kind. She noticed people and their troubles.'

Her eyes far away, Clara smiled. 'One night, Klaus the footman had a terrible head cold, hardly able to breathe, poor man. *Madame* only passed by him in the hall on her way to a reception, but first thing the next morning, she had me fetch herbs and made him a tisane. Not that she made a great fuss about doing so, playing Lady Bountiful. No, she just turned it over to the butler and told him to make sure Klaus drank it.'

'Did you ever wonder why she'd not brought her own maid to Vienna?'

Clara shrugged. 'Maybe the woman didn't want to travel so far. Maybe she couldn't afford to bring her. I don't think she had any coin of her own. St Arnaud paid my wages, all the bills for jewels, gowns and the household expenses, but he gave her no pin money at all. She didn't have even a few schillings to buy ices when we were out.'

So, as she'd claimed, Will noted, *madame had* been entirely dependent on St Arnaud. 'She never spoke of any other relations?'

'No. But if they were all like St Arnaud, I understand why she wouldn't.' The maid stopped abruptly, wrinkling her brow. 'There was one person she mentioned. Several times, when I'd given her laudanum for the pain after St Arnaud had struck her, she murmured a name as she dozed. Philippe.'

Surprise and something barbed and sharp stung him in the gut. Impatiently he dismissed it. 'Husband… brother…lover?'

'Not her husband—St Arnaud said he'd died in the wars. I did once ask her who "Philippe" was, but she just smiled and made no answer, and I didn't want to press. She sounded…longing. Maybe he's someone she wanted to marry, that her cousin had refused; I can see him sending away anyone he didn't think grand enough for the St Arnauds. Maybe St Arnaud promised if she helped him in Vienna, he would let her marry the man. I know he had some sort of power to force her to do his will.'

For some reason he'd rather not examine, Will didn't like the idea of Madame Lefevre pining for a Parisian lover. Shaking his head to rid himself of the image, he said, '*Madame*'s dependence on St Arnaud for food, clothing, housing and position would have been enough to coerce her co-operation.'

'No, it was more than that,' Clara insisted. 'Not that she didn't appreciate fine silks and pretty gems—who would not? But when she had to, she sold them without any sign of regret. She seemed quite content to live simply, not missing in the least the grand society for whom she used to play hostess. All she spoke about was earning enough coin to return to Paris.'

Not wishing to hear any more speculation about the mysterious "Philippe", Will changed direction. 'She's had no contact with St Arnaud since the night of the attack, then?'

The maid shuddered. 'Better that he believe she died of her injuries. She came close enough.'

'St Arnaud emigrated to the Caribbean afterwards.'

'That, I can't say. I only know he left Vienna that night. If there's any justice in the world, someone somewhere caught him and he's rotting in prison.'

Clara looked up, meeting his gaze squarely. 'If God has any mercy, once she's done what you want, you'll let her go back to Paris. To this Philippe, whoever he is. After all she's suffered, losing her husband, enduring St Arnaud's abuse, she deserves some happiness.'

Will wasn't about to assure the maid he'd send *madame* back—to Paris or her 'Philippe'—until he'd finished with her. And resolved what had already flared between them.

Instead, he pulled out a coin. 'Thank you, Clara. I appreciate—'

'No need for that,' the maid interrupted, waving the money away. 'Use it to keep her safe. You will watch out for her, won't you? I know if someone wished her ill, they could have moved against her any time this last year. But still…I worry. She's such a gentle soul, too innocent for this world, perhaps.'

Will remembered the woman in the garden, quietly picking spent blooms from her flowers while a stranger decided whether or not to wring her neck. She was more *resigned* than gentle or innocent, he thought. As if life had treated her so harshly, she simply accepted evil and injustice, feeling there was little she could do to protect herself from it.

Since his earliest days on the streets, Will had faced down bullies and fought to right wrongs when he found them. Picturing that calm face bent over the blooms and the brutal hand St Arnaud had raised against it, Will felt a surge of protectiveness he didn't want to feel.

No point getting all worked up over her little tragedy;

if she'd ended up abused, she'd played her role with full knowledge of the possible consequences, he reminded himself. Unlike Max, who'd been lured in unawares and betrayed by his own nobility.

And of course the maid thought her a heroine. If she could take in Max, who was nobody's fool, it would have been child's play for her to win over a simple, barely educated girl who depended on her for employment.

Suppressing the last of his sympathy towards Madame Lefevre, he nodded a dismissal to her maid. 'I'll meet you at the inn in two days.'

Clara nodded. 'The old man's disguise—you're sure you can carry it off?'

'Can she carry off hers?'

'She can do whatever she must. She already has. Good-night, sir.' With an answering nod, the girl walked into the gathering night.

Will turned back towards the inn where he planned to procure dinner, mulling over what he'd learned from Clara.

According to the maid, *madame* had been brought, without other money or resources, to Vienna and forced to do St Arnaud's bidding. She cared little about wealth or high position. Her sole ambition was to return to Paris…and 'Philippe'.

She can do whatever she must, the maid had said. Apparently, betraying Max Ransleigh had been one of those things. Eluding Will and cheating Max of the vindication due him might be another.

She was surely counting on trying to escape him, if not on the road, then once they arrived in Paris. He'd need to remain vigilant to make sure she did not.

From the maid's reactions, it seemed even she feared the watchers might not be pleased to have her mistress leave Vienna. Madame Lefevre might well have other enemies in addition to the angry cousin of the man she'd ruined.

Her masculine disguise, which he'd first accepted almost as a jest, now looked like a prudent precaution.

For a moment, he envisioned *madame*'s slender body encased in breeches that outlined her legs, curved over thigh and calf, displayed the turn of an ankle. His mouth watered and his body hardened.

But he couldn't allow lustful thoughts to distract him—yet. His sole focus now must be on getting her safely to Paris. Because until they reached London, he meant to ensure no one *else* harmed her.

Chapter Six

Late in the afternoon two days later, garbed in the clothing of an old gentleman, wearing spectacles so thick she could hardly see and leaning heavily on a cane, Elodie let Clara help her into the taproom of a modest inn on the western outskirts of Vienna. As the innkeeper bustled over to welcome them, Will Ransleigh strode in.

'Uncle Fritz, so glad you could join me! The trip from Linz was not too tiring, I trust?'

In a voice pitched as low as she could make it, Elodie replied, 'Tolerable, my boy.'

'Good. Herr Schultz,' he addressed the innkeeper, 'bring some refreshment to our room, please. Josephine, let's help our uncle up.'

With Clara at one arm and Will Ransleigh at the other, Elodie slowly shuffled up the stairs.

Not until she'd entered the sitting room Ransleigh had hired and heard the door shut behind her did she breathe a sigh of relief. The first step of her escape had proceeded without a hitch. Exultation and a rising excitement sent her spirits soaring.

As she sank into a chair and pulled off the distorting spectacles, she looked up to see Will Ransleigh's expression warm with a smile of genuine approval that gratified her even as her stomach fluttered in response. His expression serious, he was arresting, but with that smile—oh, my! How did any woman resist him?

'Bravo, *madame*. I had grave doubts, but I have to admit, you made a wonderfully credible old man.'

'You made a rather fine old gentleman yourself,' she said, smiling back at him. 'I wouldn't have recognised you if you'd not arrived with Clara. You were a wizard with the blacking as well, going from white-powdered hair to brunette faster than I could don the clothing you provided. Now I see you've transformed yourself yet again.'

Though he'd kept his hair darkened with blacking, he'd changed from the modest working-man's attire he'd worn the day he climbed up her balcony into gentleman's garb, well cut and of quality material, but not so elegant or fashionable as to attract undue notice.

Still, the close-fitting jacket emphasised the breadth of shoulders and the snug pantaloons displayed muscled thighs. If he'd appeared powerfully, dangerously masculine in his drab clerk's disguise, the effect was magnified several times over in dress that better revealed his strength and physique.

His potent masculine allure ambushed Elodie anew, intensifying the flutter in her stomach and igniting a heated tremor below. She found herself wondering how it would feel to run her fingers along those muscled arms and thighs, over the taut abdomen…and lower. While her lips explored his jaw and cheekbones, the line of brow over those vivid turquoise eyes…

Realising she was staring, she hastily turned her gaze away.

Not fast enough that he didn't notice her preoccupation, though. A satisfied gleam in his eye, he said, 'I hope you approve of the latest transformation.'

'You're looking very fine, sir, and don't you know it,' Clara interposed tartly. 'Ah, mistress, didn't you make a marvellous old gent! I believe we could have met Frau Gruener herself on the stairs without her being the wiser.'

'It's just as well we didn't. I'm no Mrs Siddons,' Elodie said, arching to stretch out a back cramped from bending over a cane during their long, dawdling transit.

'What do you know of Mrs Siddons?' Will asked, giving her a suspicious look.

Cursing her slip, Elodie said, 'Only that she was much praised by the English during theatrical entertainments at the Congress, who claimed no Viennese actress could compare. With your expertise in disguises, I begin to believe you've trod the boards yourself. Is that how you found this moustache?' Stripping off the length of fuzzy wool, she rubbed her lip. 'It itched terribly, making me sneeze so hard, I feared it would fall off.'

'My apologies for the deficiencies in your costume,' he replied sardonically. 'I shall try to do better next time.'

'See that you do,' she flashed back, relieved to have detoured him from any further probing about her familiarity with the English stage.

'I don't wonder your back is tired,' Clara said. 'I don't know this quarter of Vienna and you could hardly see behind those spectacles. The transit seemed to take so long, once or twice I feared we might be lost.'

'No danger of that; I shadowed you all the way and would have set you straight if you'd strayed,' Ransleigh said. 'I also wanted to make sure you were not followed.'

Reassured by his thoroughness, Elodie said, 'We weren't, were we?'

'No. It was a good plan you came up with.'

Elodie felt a flush of warmth at his avowal and chastised herself. She wasn't a giddy girl, to be gratified by a handsome man's approval. She needed to remember the purpose for which he'd arranged this escape—that hadn't been done for *her* benefit.

Despite that acknowledgment, some of the warmth remained.

A knock sounded at the door and Elodie turned away, averting her now moustache-less face until the servant bringing in the refreshments had deposited the tray and bowed himself back out.

'Shall we dine?' Ransleigh invited. 'The inn is said to set a good table.'

Elodie shook her head wonderingly. 'Just how do you manage to discover such things?'

He gave her an enigmatic smile. 'I'm a man of many talents.'

'So I am discovering.' She wished she could resist being impressed by his mastery of detail, but fairness wouldn't allow it.

'*Fraulein*, will you join us before you leave?'

At the maid's nod, they seated themselves around the table. Since their previous exchanges had been limited to threats on her life and plans for escaping Vienna, Elodie wondered whether—and about what—Ransleigh would talk during the meal.

Somewhat to her surprise, he kept up a flow of conversation, discussing the sights of Vienna and asking Clara about her experiences with the notables she'd encountered during the Congress.

Will Ransleigh truly was a man of many talents. He seemed as comfortable drawing out a lady's maid as he might be entertaining a titled lady in his uncle the earl's drawing room. If he did, in fact, frequent the earl's drawing room.

He claimed he'd been born on the wrong side of the blanket, but his speech and manners were those of the aristocracy. Where was he in his true element? she wondered. Skulking around the modest neighbourhoods of a great city, chatting up maids and innkeepers, or dancing at balls among the wealthy and powerful?

Or in both?

He was still an enigma. And since she was forced to place her safety in his hands, at least until Paris, that troubled her.

Their meal concluded, Clara rose. 'I'd best be getting home. It will be dark soon and I don't know these streets.'

'I'll escort you,' Ransleigh said.

'I'd not put you to the trouble,' Clara protested.

'Of course he will,' Elodie interrupted, relieved by the offer and determined to have him honour it. 'I'd like him to accompany you all the way home…and make sure there's no unexpected company to welcome you,' she added, voicing the uneasiness that had grown since she'd successfully escaped her lodgings.

'Your mistress is right. Though I don't think her flight has yet been discovered, we should take precautions,' Ransleigh said. 'Once whoever has set a guard realises she has left the city, they'll probably come straight to you.'

Dismay flooded her. All her attention consumed by the magnificent prospect of returning to Paris, Elodie hadn't imagined that possibility. Turning to Ransleigh, she said anxiously, 'Should we take Clara with us, for her own safety?'

'I don't think she needs to leave, though she might well be questioned. If we're lucky, not until we're well away. She can then tell them truthfully that a certain Will Ransleigh urged you to accompany him to London and met you at this inn, but how or with whom you left it and in which direction, she has no idea. After all, if they want anyone, it's you, not her.'

'Are you sure? I'd thought my leaving, drawing after me whatever threat might still remain, would keep her safe. But what if I'm wrong?' Elodie turned to Clara, still torn. 'If anyone harmed you—'

'Don't distress yourself, *madame*,' Ransleigh interrupted. 'I've already engaged a man to watch over the *fraulein* until he's sure she's in no further danger. A solid lad, a former Austrian soldier I knew from the army. He's waiting below to help me escort her home.'

'Thank you, sir.' Clara dipped Ransleigh a curtsy—the first sign of respect she'd accorded him. 'I never expected such a thing, but I can't deny it makes me feel easier.'

Surprised, touched and humbled, Elodie felt like curtsying, too. *She* should have realised it was necessary to guarantee Clara's safety after their departure. Instead, this man she'd viewed as concerned only with achieving his own purposes had had the forethought—and compassion—to arrange it.

In her experience, aristocrats such as St Arnaud viewed servants as objects put on earth to provide for their comfort, like horses or linens or furniture. Her cousin would never have seen Clara as a *person*, or concerned himself with her welfare.

Ransleigh had not only anticipated the possible danger, he'd arranged to protect Clara after their departure, when the maid was of no further use to him.

She couldn't prevent her opinion of his character from rising a notch higher.

Still, she mustn't let herself be lured into trusting in his thoroughness, competence and compassion—qualities that attracted her almost as much as his physical allure. They were still a long way from Paris.

Before Elodie could sort out her tangled thoughts, Clara had wrapped herself in her cloak. Elodie's previous high spirits vanished as she faced parting for ever from the last, best friend she possessed.

'I suppose this is farewell, *madame*,' Clara said, a brave smile on her face. 'I wish you a safe journey— and joy, when you get to Paris at last!'

Unable to summon words, Elodie hugged her. The maid hugged her back fiercely, blinking away tears when at last Elodie released her. 'I'll try to send word after I'm settled.'

'Good. I'd like to know that you were home—and *safe*,' she added, that last with a meaningful look at Ransleigh.

'Shall we go, *fraulein*?' Ransleigh asked.

Smiling, Clara gave her a curtsy. 'Goodbye, *madame*. May the blessed angels watch over you.'

'And you, my dear friend,' Elodie replied.

'After you, *fraulein*,' Ransleigh prompted gently as they both stood there, frozen. 'Your soldier awaits.'

Nodding agreement, Clara stepped towards the door, then halted to look at him searchingly. 'Maybe I was wrong. Maybe *madame* should trust you.'

Much as she told herself that after a lifetime of partings and loss, she should be used to it, Elodie felt a painful squeezing in her chest as she listened to their footsteps echo on the stairs. When the last sound faded, she ran to the window.

Peeping around the curtain, so as to be hidden from the view of anyone who might look up from the street, she watched three figures emerge from the inn: Ransleigh, Clara and a burly man who looked like a prizefighter. As they set off through the darkness, the thought struck her that Ransleigh, moving with the fluid, powerful stride of a predator on the prowl, seemed the more dangerous of the two men.

Elodie's spirits sagged even lower as she watched Clara disappear into the darkness. The maid had been her friend, companion and saviour for more than a year.

Now, she'd be alone with Ransleigh. For better or worse.

She got herself this far, she'd make it the rest of the way, she told herself bracingly. And at the end of this journey…was Philippe.

With that rallying thought, she settled in to wait for Ransleigh's return.

Chapter Seven

The maid conveyed safely to her lodging where, fortunately, there had been no one waiting to intercept her, Will left Heinrich on watch and headed back to the inn. Their room above the entry was dark when he glanced up at the window before entering.

He'd already paid the proprietor, explaining he planned an early departure. In truth, he intended for them to leave Vienna during the blackest part of the night. Since it appeared *madame* was already asleep, he'd slip in quietly, letting her get as much rest as she could before what would be an arduous journey.

Taking care to make no sound that might attract the attention of the innkeeper serving customers in the tap-room beyond, he crossed the entry and silently ascended the stairs. As he eased through the door into their room, the dim outline of something by the far wall had him reaching for his knife, until he realised what he'd sensed more than seen in the darkness was Madame Lefevre.

'I thought you'd be resting,' he said, closing the door quietly behind him.

'I couldn't sleep until I knew our plans. And I wanted to thank you for seeing to Clara's safety. That was generous of you…and unexpected. I'm very grateful.'

'She being an innocent in all this, I'd not want to be responsible for causing her any harm.'

Harm coming to *madame* he had less of a problem with, he thought. But if she were threatened, it would be after conviction for crimes committed, her punishment determined by the rule of law, not by an attack in some back alley.

Crossing to the window, he made sure the curtains were securely drawn. Lighting a taper, he said, 'I think we can chance one candle.'

As it flared to life, he saw Elodie Lefevre, still in old man's attire, seated in the corner next to the window— her back to the wall, beside the quickest exit from the inn. The very spot he would have chosen, were he required to wait alone in this room, unsure of what danger might threaten.

While he wondered whether she'd seated herself there by design or accident, she said, 'What have you planned for tomorrow?'

'Actually, I've planned for tonight. As soon as all is quiet downstairs and in the street, we will slip out by the kitchen door into the mews. I checked last night; no one keeps watch there. We'll be out of the city and along the road to Linz well before daylight.'

Madame nodded. 'The sooner we begin, the sooner we arrive.'

'When he travelled from Paris to Vienna for the Congress, Wellington made it in just ten days…but he only slept four hours a night. Though I don't mean to dawdle, I'm allowing a bit longer.'

'I'm ready to travel as quickly as you wish. Much as I enjoyed limping on my cane, though, I think another change of costume would be wise.'

Will had a strong sense that this wasn't the first time Elodie Lefevre had fled from pursuit. Had the Revolution forced her family out of France? She would have been scarcely more than a babe during the Terror.

Quelling for now the urge to question her further, he said, 'What do you have in mind?'

'If anyone interrogates the innkeeper, they'll be looking for a young gentleman accompanied by an older man. If that trail goes cold, they would probably next seek a man and a woman posing as a married couple or lovers or siblings or cousins. Whatever explanation we used, if I travel as a female with no maid and only a single male companion, we'll attract notice, making it much more likely that innkeepers and stable boys and barmaids at taverns and posting inns will remember us.'

'What makes you think we'll be stopping at taverns or posting inns?' he asked, teasing her to cover his surprise about her knowledge of the realities of travel. Had she spent her whole life eluding pursuers?

Ignoring the remark, she continued, 'We could pose as an older woman and her maid, but it's still unusual for women to travel without a male escort, to say nothing of the difficulty of your being convincing in either role for any length of time. So I think our best alternative would be for you to remain as you are, a young gentleman, and I will travel as your valet. Men travel the posting roads all the time; you'd be just one more of many and no one pays attention to servants.'

Her scheme for leaving her lodgings had been good; this one was even better. Trying to suppress the admiration he didn't wish to feel, Will said, 'You think you could play the role of valet better than I could that of an old woman?'

She nodded. 'Much more easily. As I said, a woman of any age travelling would excite curiosity, while a valet would be virtually invisible. Whether we stay at an inn—or under a tree or in a hedgerow,' she added with a quirk of a smile at him. 'And if we need to make a hasty exit, it will be much easier if I'm not encumbered by skirts.'

Will couldn't imagine any of the aristocratic ladies of his acquaintance—Alastair's mother or sisters, for example—inventing so unorthodox a scheme or proposing it in such a straightforward, unemotional manner. 'Why do I have the feeling you've done this before?'

A faraway look came into her eyes, and for a long moment, while he hung on her answer, she remained silent. 'I've had to come up with…contrivances upon occasion,' she said at last.

Which told him nothing. *Where have you been and*

what have you done? Will wondered. 'You're a most unusual woman, Madame Lefevre.'

She gave him a faint smile, but said only, 'These old man's garments will suffice until we can procure others. I've kept two gowns in my portmanteau, in case I might need them before we arrive at Paris. Have you a route in mind?'

Will stifled a pang of disappointment that she'd not responded to his compliment by telling him more about her life. His curiosity fanned ever hotter by each new revelation, he was by now eager to discover what events had shaped her.

Maybe along the way, he'd figure it out, find a way to fit the puzzle pieces together. Or, even better, maybe along the way he'd lure her into trusting him enough to volunteer the information.

It would only be prudent to arm himself with as much knowledge about her as possible. As long as he kept in mind that anything she revealed might contain more craftiness than truth.

'Have *you* a route in mind? Your suggestions thus far have been excellent.'

She dropped her gaze and, though he couldn't tell for sure in the dim candlelight, he thought she flushed. 'Thank you,' she said gruffly. 'I've only travelled this way once, when I accompanied St Arnaud, so I don't know the road. It would be wise, I think, to keep as much as possible to the larger cities, where one gentleman will hardly be noticed among the host of travellers. Have you the means to hire horses? It would make the journey faster.'

'A gentleman travelling with his valet would more likely travel by coach.'

'Not if the valet were a bruising rider. The further and faster from Vienna we travel, the safer we'll be from pursuit.'

Will wasn't so sure. If Talleyrand were keeping tabs on *madame*, they would be more vulnerable the closer they got to Paris. But he didn't want to voice that fact, adding more anxiety to what must already be a difficult situation, with her poised to assume yet another false identity. Despite the maid's assertion that she could do 'whatever she had to', he didn't want to push her too hard and risk having her fall apart.

'Very well; I'll travel as a young gentleman. "Monsieur LeClair", shall we say? And you will be my valet, "Pierre".'

'"LeClair"?' she repeated, a slow smile lighting her face. 'Very good, considering nothing about this journey is "clear" or straightforward!'

The honest delight on her face, so strikingly different from the expressionless calm with which she usually concealed her feelings, struck Will near his breastbone with the force of a blow. Warmth blossomed in its wake. Damn and blast, he didn't want to start…liking her!

While he wrestled with his reaction, she continued, 'I'm pleased you approve my plan.'

'For the time being, subject to change as I feel necessary,' he cautioned, pulling himself back together.

'I've got horses waiting at an inn on the edge of Vienna. With hard travel, we may reach the outskirts of Linz by late tomorrow.'

'Excellent. You are very thorough, *monsieur*,' she said approvingly. 'Anything else I should know?'

'No, Pierre; we'd better get a few hours' sleep. I'll rouse you when it's time. You use the bed.'

'Oh, no, *monsieur*, that would never do. Your valet should occupy a pallet at the foot of the bed. I've left the wig and cane over there—' she indicated the dining table '—for you to return to your store of trickeries.'

Flinging the blanket she'd held in her lap over her shoulders, she crossed to the bed and settled herself on the floor by the footboard—back to the wall, with a clear view of both the window and the door, he noted. '*Bonsoir*, Monsieur LeClair.'

'*Bonsoir*, Pierre.'

She closed her eyes. Within a few moments, the even sound of her breathing indicated she must have fallen asleep.

Will should sleep, too. He had only a few hours before he needed to be up, all his wits about him, ready to spirit them out of the inn unobserved or to improvise some sleight of hand, should that be necessary for them to escape pursuit. But as he blew out the candle and lay down on the bed, Will found slumber elusive.

Partly, it was his ever-deepening curiosity about Elodie Lefevre. What remarkable experiences had shaped this woman who noticed watchers at her corner, came up with plans for escape and evasion and talked of disguises as casually as another woman might discuss attending the theatre or purchasing a bonnet?

When he compared her reactions to the emotion-driven behaviour of the women he'd known, he was struck again by her calm. After leaving the only friend she knew, about to creep away with a virtual stranger in the middle of the night, she'd displayed no more than a natural sadness at parting from the maid. There'd been no panic, no fretting over whether she was doing the right thing. No worrying over her ability to carry out her part in the deception, no endless questioning over what was to happen next and—praise Heaven!—no tears. She hadn't even called down evil upon his head for forcing her into this.

Instead, she'd made a single terse compliment about his thoroughness.

'You truly are an amazing woman, Elodie Lefevre,' he told her sleeping form. *But I'd be an idiot to trust you.*

She had paid him one other compliment in their short acquaintance—she'd called him 'striking'.

For the last few hours, the urgency of getting her out of her lodgings and the necessity of planning their escape had helped him dam up his strong physical response to her. But in the darkness, safe for the moment and all plans in place, that one memory was enough to send desire flooding over the barriers.

Despite the contrivance of having her travel as his

'valet', with her bundled at his feet, her soft breaths filling the silence and the subtle scent of lavender beguiling his nose, it was impossible for him to think of Elodie Lefevre as anything other than a woman. A woman made even more alluring by her unique, exceptional abilities.

A woman he wanted.

He stifled a groan as, despite his fatigue, his body hardened. His mind might be urging him to review each detail of their upcoming journey, but his body was recalling the softness of her neck under his fingers, the surge of connection between them when she took his hand.

Damn and blast, what had begun as a grim mission to vindicate Max had become a challenge that filled him with unanticipated excitement. He relished the idea of being on the road with her, overcoming whatever dangers arose, discovering bit by bit more pieces to the puzzle that was Elodie. At the same time, he must maintain a delicate balance between his growing fascination and the necessity to stay vigilant, lest she lull him into complacency and play him for a fool.

And then there was lust. With an anticipation so intense it ought to alarm him, he looked forward to sharing a room with her at the posting inns—and all the enticing possibilities for seduction that offered.

But when he recalled the disguises they'd agreed upon, he had to stifle a laugh. She could have contrived no better way to keep his amorous impulses at bay. They could hardly travel unnoticed if he was seen to be openly lusting after his valet!

He'd just have to get her back into maiden's attire as soon as possible.

Chapter Eight

Five days later, in a small inn south of Stuttgart along the road to Paris, Elodie loitered in a dim, smoky corner of the taproom, mug of ale in hand. Will sat at a table in the centre, gaming with a disparate group of fellow travellers.

Wearing gentleman's attire, the only disguise he employed was hair-blacking, there being nothing he could do beyond keeping his face downcast to camouflage those remarkable eyes. He lounged with cravat askew, long legs outstretched in an indolent pose, as he held the cards before him.

To a casual observer, he appeared to be just another young man who'd decided to go adventuring now that Napoleon's wars no longer threatened the Continent. A younger son of good family, probably, well born but not important or wealthy enough to require an entourage. A young man seemingly indifferent to his comfort—and that of his humble valet, since he'd chosen to ride on this journey, rather than spend the additional blunt necessary to hire a carriage.

It was an image he'd calculated with care. But Elodie, now better attuned, knew that despite his lazy stance, Will keenly observed every detail of the men in the room and the inn itself, always assessing possible threats, ready to make a quick exit in case of danger. Much as she herself did.

From the beginning of their odyssey, she'd watched him intently, at first apprehensive, since she'd had to commit her safety into his hands. By now she'd relaxed a bit, appreciating the high level of alertness he maintained—with remarkably little sleep—and the care he took to evaluate their surroundings and the people with whom they came into contact.

For as long as she could remember, *she'd* been the one who had to be vigilant to protect herself and those she loved. How much easier it was for a man, who could interact with innkeepers and barmaids and grooms and tradesmen virtually unnoticed, as a woman could not. She'd even allowed—if only to herself—that his skill at disguise, invention and evasion equalled her own.

She was beginning to believe that Will Ransleigh would get her safely to Paris after all.

Though she must never forget he was expending all that effort for his own purposes.

Over the last few days, they'd worked out a routine, riding hard by day, not choosing an inn for the night until well after dark, by which time she was so weary she almost fell out of the saddle. In the early dawn,

Will would arrange fresh horses and buy food to carry with them for the next day, and they'd take their meals by the roadside.

She smiled into the darkness. Breaking their fast in the open might have been a dreary, rushed affair, but in Ransleigh's company, the meals had assumed almost a picnic atmosphere. She had to admit she was intrigued by him. Though she herself said little, with a bit of prompting, she'd persuaded him to regale her with tales of his many adventures.

He was a marvellous storyteller, his vivid descriptions making her feel she was reliving the episodes with him. He had her laughing at his account of dismal billets and narrow escapes from marauders on the Peninsula, the comic ballet of Brussels packed to the gills with foreigners. Unknowing, he fed her starved soul with details of the Paris he'd explored before Napoleon slipped his leash at Elba and plunged France back into war.

Notably missing among his tales, however, was any mention of his origins. Which was only fair, since she'd divulged absolutely nothing about herself. But she'd grown increasingly curious to know more about the man, as the relationship of captor and—though willing—captive subtly began to alter, until it now verged dangerously close to camaraderie.

Which was perhaps the point of his tall tales. Perhaps he was trying to earn her trust, beguile her into thinking of him as a friend, a companion…a lover?

Tightness coiled in her belly and she blessed again the disguise that required them to stay at arm's length during the day, the arduous long rides that made her fall asleep almost instantly when she could finally rest for the night.

Otherwise, the two of them alone in the secret darkness… She didn't think she could have resisted the temptation to taste those sculpted lips that she watched, fascinated, as he spun his tales, acutely conscious of his sheer masculine power and the fierce pull of attraction between them. Resisted the desire to run her fingers down the muscled thighs she watched day after day control his mount with effortless precision. Denied herself the chance to explore the naked torso of which she caught only teasing glimpses when he pulled off his shirt to wash in the early mornings.

Did he wait to do that until he knew she was awake, deliberately tempting her?

Over the years, she'd used her body when necessary and, more often, had it used without her consent. It had been a very long time since she'd *wanted* a man.

But she wanted Will Ransleigh. In his smoky gaze when no one was watching them, in the lingering caress of fingers on her arm or hand the few times touching her had been necessary, she knew he wanted her, too.

The day of reckoning was coming when that mutual desire would no longer have to be denied. Heaven help her, how she *burned* for it!

But that time wasn't here…yet. They were still too far from Paris. And she was still too far from deciding just how—and when—she would seduce Will Ransleigh.

Tonight, announcing he needed to replenish their

funds with a little gaming, Will had insisted, despite her fatigue, that she remain in the taproom and linger in the shadows. So she would be close at hand, in case they needed to leave the inn in a hurry.

She'd forced herself to stay awake by watching the game, counting cards and points. She'd been annoyed to discover she must admire Will Ransleigh's prowess at cards, too.

With the same precision he analysed rooms and roads, he surveyed his opponents with that deceptively disinterested, downcast gaze. Having watched the game for several hours, Elodie was convinced he'd worked out just how much he could win from each opponent without straining their purses enough to provoke a belligerent response and just how much overall so as not to have his skill excite comment. He bolstered her belief by deliberately losing a hand from time to time and by his occasional crows of triumph when he won, as if winning were a surprise. Whereas, she was certain he could have fleeced all his opponents, had he chosen to.

Clara had told her how he'd lifted her purse at the market.

Would he have the skill to fleece her, when the time came? Smiling faintly, she thought of Will removing the rough, scratchy man's garb, covering her mouth with his, her body with his, parting her legs to bare to his touch and possession that hottest, most needy place…

The cold splash of ale on her knee jerked her back to awareness. Lost in sensual imagining, she'd drifted off and nearly dropped her mug. Alarmed to have come close to creating a commotion that would have attracted unwelcome attention, she looked up to find Will staring at her.

Elodie froze; not wishing to bring her to anyone's notice, Will never looked directly at her when in company.

'Pierre, take yourself up to the room before you shatter the mug—or spill any more of that good ale! I can wash up and remove my own coat tonight.'

A quick nod punctuated the command. Too weary to object, Elodie walked quietly out, hearing as she closed the door Will tell the others, 'Doesn't have the stamina of youth, poor Pierre. Old family retainer, you know.'

A murmur of commiseration followed her up the stairs. Old family retainer indeed, she thought indignantly, recognising the subtle taunt. The day was coming, Monsieur Ransleigh would soon discover, when she would be neither 'old' nor slavishly obedient.

Their room tonight was on the top floor. She paused after climbing to the first-floor landing, which boasted a window overlooking the street. Weary though she was, the star-spangled sky called out for admiration.

Just a few days' journey ahead, Paris beckoned. And somewhere within that teeming city, she urgently hoped, was Philippe.

Longing for him swelled within her, the ache sharper than usual. She'd been away so long, she was as apprehensive as she was excited to arrive at last and discover whether the long months of hope were justified. Whether she could find him and make him hers again.

She immediately banished a soul-chilling fear that

she might fail. Of course she would succeed, she reassured herself. They belonged together. No amount of time or separation could change that.

With a sigh, she trudged up the final set of stairs, the starlight from the window below fading as she ascended. Five steps down into the darkness of the hallway, she was grabbed roughly from behind. The hard chill of a blade pressed against her neck.

'Come with me quietly, madam,' a voice murmured, 'or your next move will be your last.'

Elodie tensed, her heartbeat skyrocketing. After an instant, though, she forced back the panic, emptying herself of everything but the need to calculate the physical advantage of the man detaining her and the meaning of his words.

Though he'd spoken in French, his accent was English; he knew she was not Ransleigh's valet, which meant he must have tracked them from Vienna. Would he kill her, or just threaten her to force her co-operation?

'Don't hurt me, sir!' she said, putting some of the alarm she'd suppressed into a voice pitched as low as she could make it. 'You're mistaken; I'm Monsieur LeClair's valet, Pierre.'

'No, you are Elodie Lefevre, implicated in the plot to assassinate Lord Wellington in Vienna last year,' the voice replied. 'You're going to descend these stairs with me to the back entrance. Now.'

Her mind tumbling over itself, looking for some means to escape, Elodie let the man push her ahead of him to the landing, stumbling as much as she dared to delay their progress. 'You are wrong, *monsieur*!' she whispered urgently. 'Speak to my master, he can straighten this out!'

A short laugh huffed against her ear. 'I mean to speak to him. After I take care of you.'

'Take care of me? What do you—?'

'Silence!' the man hissed in her ear. 'Speak again and I'll shut you up permanently.'

The assailant knew what he was doing; he kept her arms pinned behind her as he shuffled her forwards, and the blade at her throat never wavered. Could she stumble, catch her foot under his boot and use his own weight to knock him down the stairs, ducking out of the way before he cut her throat?

Probably not. Dragging her feet from step to step, muscles tensed and body poised to flee at the first opportunity, Elodie let her captor push her down the stairs and turn her towards the back exit leading to the stables.

Once outside, she would have more room to manoeuvre. Her assailant knew she was a woman; perhaps she could pretend to faint. Just a moment's opportunity and, thankfully free of encumbering skirts, she could take to her heels.

Her assailant unlatched the door and thrust her into the deserted stable yard. Knowing this would probably be her best chance, she'd gathered herself to make a break when, out of the stillness, came the unmistakable metallic click of a pistol being cocked.

Her assailant heard it, too, and halted. From deep within the shadows by the wall, Will said, 'Put down the knife, or I'll blow your head off. At this distance, I can't miss.'

'I can cut her throat before you can fire.'

'Perhaps.' A glimmer of humour coloured his voice. 'But you would still be dead, so what would it matter? *Monsieur*, you will oblige me by giving over the knife and keeping your hands well in front of you. Then you will accompany me and my much-maligned valet up to our room.'

When the man holding her hesitated, Will sighed. 'Do not try me, sirrah. I'm not at all averse to decorating this wall with your brains.'

With a reluctant laugh, the man surrendered his knife. Taking it, Will said, 'Pierre, search his pockets.'

Weak-kneed with relief, Elodie turned to face her attacker. She had no idea how Will had discovered them, but she'd never in her life been so relieved to see anyone.

While Will kept his pistol trained on the man, Elodie hurriedly rifled the man's greatcoat, removing a pistol from each pocket and holding them up. 'That's all.'

'Good. Pierre, you go first and make sure no one else is about. Sound an all clear and we'll follow you.'

A few moments later, Will herded her erstwhile attacker into their top-floor bedchamber. After pushing him into a chair, he quickly bound the man's wrists behind him, then motioned her to light a candle.

As soon as he held it close enough to make out the attacker's features, his expression turned from angry to incredulous. 'George Armitage! What the deuce are you doing here?'

'Trying to keep you from catching a bullet or being fitted for the hangman's necktie,' Armitage replied.

While Elodie tried to figure out what was going on, Will said drily, 'Your concern would overwhelm me… if you hadn't been trying to carve up my valet. If I unbind you, do I have your word as an officer you'll not threaten him again or try to escape?'

'You do,' Armitage said.

'Pierre, pour some wine,' Will directed as he set about removing the ropes.

'No need to maintain the fiction; I know he's no lad,' Armitage said.

'But the rest of the inn doesn't need to know. What are you doing here, skulking about and attacking harmless servants? Last time we talked, you were about to leave Paris with your regiment, bound for London.'

'So I was, and did. Sold out and went back to the estate, but as Papa has no intention of turning over the reins any time soon, it was bloody boring. I took myself off to London and lounged about the club, losing at cards and vying for the favours of various actresses until Locksley—you remember him, lieutenant in the 95th—talked me into joining the Foreign Office. Thought it might provide some of the excitement I'd missed since leaving the army.'

'But how did you end up here?'

'You were seen leaving England, bound for Vienna, barely two weeks after returning from Brussels. Knowing what had happened to your cousin Max, it wasn't difficult to figure out what you meant to do.'

'And the Foreign Office was so displeased by that, they sent a bloodhound after me?'

'Though the officials weren't too concerned when Max tried to track down Madame Lefevre, some who knew you felt you might be better at ferreting her out. I can't believe you weren't aware that no one, neither the English, nor the French, nor the Austrians, *wished* her to be found. So when I discovered they meant to send someone to stop you, I volunteered. Fellow officer and all—didn't want to see you come to harm.'

'I suppose I owe you thanks, then. I must say, though your tracking skills are acceptable, if tonight was an example of how you plan an ambush, your Foreign Office career is likely to come to a quick and violent end.'

Ignoring that jibe, Armitage continued, 'The Foreign Office just wants you back in England, out of this, but there are others with less charitable intentions. Once *madame* scarpered, according to my superiors in Vienna, several agents set out after her.'

Will's amused expression sobered. 'Who?'

'They didn't say. Could be French agents, or maybe the same Bonapartists who embroiled St Arnaud, angry the plot didn't succeed and eager to punish those who failed. I don't suppose I could persuade you to abandon plans of bringing the lady back to England?'

As Will shook his head, George sighed. 'Knowing your aim was to restore Max's reputation, I didn't think so. Now that I've warned you, if you're not prepared to listen to reason, you're on your own.'

'What will you do now? Honour among old soldiers

notwithstanding, I don't imagine your superiors would be pleased to learn we had a pleasant chat and you let me go.'

'No, I'll tell them I tracked you to the inn, but you'd left before I arrived.'

'You think they'll believe that?' Will laughed. 'I repeat my advice about seeking another career.'

Armitage waved a careless hand. 'If they do give me the sack, I'll find something else to do. I can always retire in disgrace on Papa's land and die of boredom. What of you? Not knowing who else may be trailing you or how close they are, you'll leave at once, I expect?'

Will frowned—his expression mirroring Elodie's concern as she followed the conversation, too alarmed by Armitage's news to object to being treated as if she were a piece of the furniture.

As the months after the assassination attempt had passed without incident, her worry that someone besides St Arnaud wished her dead had slowly dissipated. In time, she'd even found the presence of the guards keeping watch over her lodgings comforting. Discovering that she was being followed by some anonymous someone had just shattered that peace of mind.

'As soon as it's light enough to see,' Will was saying.

'Let's drink a bottle, then, to friendship and the regiment. Who knows when we'll meet again?'

Will nodded. 'I considered knocking you out before we left, to give you a more believable excuse for not apprehending me, but you could say instead that I drugged you. Much less painful.'

Armitage grinned. 'Much more civilised.'

Will gestured to Elodie. 'Fetch more wine from the saddlebags, Pierre. Then get some rest.'

Chapter Nine

They had left Armitage, who imbibed the majority of the wine, sleeping off his efforts at conviviality. During their hurried preparations to depart and the hard ride that followed, they had not had—or made—time to discuss the events of the previous night.

Not until after mid-afternoon the next day did Ransleigh signal them to a stop. As he led their mounts into the shade of some tall trees, within sight of the main road, but far enough away that they'd not eat the dust of passing carriages with their bread, Elodie wondered if he would speak of it now.

She shivered, still feeling the sting at her neck where the blade had nicked her.

What would George Armitage have done with her, if Will Ransleigh hadn't come to her rescue? He'd wanted to save his army comrade from Foreign Office scrutiny, possible danger—and from her. She warranted no such protection.

No one, neither the English, nor the French, nor the Austrians, wished her to be found, he'd said.

Unease clenched in her belly. Who was tracking her? Not since the earliest days after the attack in Vienna had she felt so vulnerable.

After extracting bread, cheese and wine from the saddlebags, Will parcelled out portions and they settled to eat, making stools and a table out of a fallen log.

Setting down his wine, Will turned to her, his eyes sparkling as they always did when he was about to spin another tale. But whatever he saw on her face made the gleam fade.

'You're wondering who else is out there and if last night's attack is only the first,' he said abruptly.

She nodded, then felt a tingle of shock that he had read so much in her face. Had she been that unguarded?

Or had he just learned her expressions too well?

Pushing back that alarming thought, she replied simply, 'Yes. And I should thank you for rescuing me. How did you know I was in danger, by the way?'

'I heard the two of you on the stairs as I left the tap-room. Since there was only one logical way for your attacker to smuggle you out and you were very cleverly delaying him, it was easy enough to slip out the front and await you in the stable yard.'

Despite his dismissive words, Elodie knew the successful intervention had required skill and timing. Putting a hand to the scratch at her throat, she said, 'Anyway, thank you. I don't know what he would have done, if you'd not intercepted us.'

Will shrugged. 'Since it was George, probably just tied you up while he tried to talk me into turning you over to the local authorities and heading back to England.'

Elodie had a sudden, terrifying vision of being cast off penniless and friendless, under very real threat of imprisonment. Thank heaven Will Ransleigh was so dedicated to his cousin! 'I'm grateful for your help. But what of those who might be more dangerous?'

'From what George told us, everyone from the Austrians to the British Foreign Office knows we're headed for Paris. After failing to stop us, George will have to report where he discovered us and the identities under which we were travelling.'

'Time for a new disguise, then?' She sighed. 'They'll still be looking for two lone travellers, whatever new appearance we assume. If we could somehow merge with a group, it would be easier to continue unremarked.'

'I'm thinking it might be better to head south and take a less direct route. They'll be watching for us on the major posting roads now.'

'They'll be watching for us to arrive in Paris, too, however long it takes,' she pointed out.

'True, but after another week, when they could reasonably expect us to turn up on our present course, they'll be less vigilant. There must be hundreds of people entering Paris every day. The guards can't scrutinise every one of them…especially if we enter in the early morning, with the rush of farmers bringing goods to market.'

She smiled, trying to envision Will Ransleigh in a farmer's smock, driving a herd of pigs. He'd probably do it expertly and look dashing. 'After we travel south, should we purchase some livestock?'

'Yes, valet Pierre should probably become farmwife Paulette.' From the saddlebag, he extracted a map and consulted it. 'If we turn due south towards Bavaria, skirt around the edges of Switzerland and proceed from Strasbourg towards Nancy, we could head west straight to Paris.'

She shook her head. A map! She tapped the saddlebag. 'Hair-blacking, spectacles, canes, wigs—I almost expect there's a flock of chickens hidden in there, too. Is there anything you do not carry in that bag of deception?'

He grinned. 'I like to be prepared.' The smile fading, he continued, 'We shouldn't underestimate the pursuers. The other parties to the affair seem to want to forget it happened, so the most serious threat might be posed by St Arnaud's confederates. He can't have been working alone; if his partners discovered that, contrary to what St Arnaud assured them, you'd not been silenced, they might want to correct his lapse.'

'Quite possibly,' she agreed. The thought was dismaying, but it was useless to panic. It was hardly the first time her life had been in danger. If they *were* being trailed by forces who wanted to eliminate her, there was nothing she could do but take all reasonable precautions—and keep going.

'Well, today seems the very breath of early summer,

with wildflowers blooming under a gentle sun and the sky blue as the Mediterranean. This bread is fresh and crusty, the cheese piquant, the ham savoury, and the wine delicious. I don't intend to allow whoever might be out there to steal my enjoyment of it. So, tell me another story.'

Instead of obliging, Ransleigh remained silent, studying her. 'You are remarkable, you know,' he said after a moment.

'Remarkable?' she echoed, raising an eyebrow.

'You've been threatened by me, forced to leave your only friend, hauled out of Vienna, attacked at midnight at knifepoint and acknowledged that everyone from the British Foreign Office to Bonapartist agents may be looking to snuff you out. Yet all you ask of life, of me, is a story.'

She shook her head, a little mystified by his intensity. 'All we can ever ask of life is the joy of this moment. There are no promises about the next.'

'The joy of this moment,' he repeated. 'Ah, *yes.*' Before she could imagine what he meant to do, he reached over, tipped back her hat and kissed her.

Elodie couldn't have stopped him if Talleyrand himself were holding a pistol on them. For days, she'd been unable to tear her eyes from the play of those lips as he spun his tales…from imagining how they'd feel and taste pressed against hers.

Their touch was hard, demanding, flavored of the wine he'd drunk. The taste of him intoxicated her, as if she'd drained the whole of the wineskin. She heard small mewing noises of encouragement and was shocked to realise they came from her, while, driven by a hunger long denied, she wrapped her arms around his shoulders and plastered herself against him.

His tongue probed her lips, opening her, and plunged deep. It chased hers in fiery dance, then encircled and suckled, pulling her deeper, unleashing a maelstrom of desire so intense her sole imperative was to have all of him.

She fumbled at the waistband of her trousers, desperate to open herself to the sleek hardness pressed against her, to feel it invade her body as his tongue had conquered her mouth.

Suddenly, in a shock of cold air, he pushed her away. In a tumult of clashing sensations—desperate need, impatience to continue, dismay that he had stopped—she finally heard it: the clatter of jangling harness, a murmur of voices as travellers approached down the road.

At least she had the solace of knowing he felt the same desire and disappointment. As he backed away, he grabbed her chin and, one last time, his mouth captured hers. Then, before refastening the single button she'd managed to unloose in her trouser flap, he slid a hand through the opening and stroked his fingers swiftly across the hot waiting flesh.

Just that glancing touch to the sensitive nub jolted through her like a lightning bolt, the sensation so powerful that, had it lasted a touch longer, she would have reached her release.

When had she last felt that joy? Had she ever felt it so intensely?

Gasping, disoriented, Elodie tried to settle her agitated senses as travellers came into view on the road beyond. Soon, a group of friars with cart and cattle slowly lumbered past.

'Would that I could get away with kissing my soon-to-be-former valet one last time,' Ransleigh murmured against her ear, the warmth of his breath setting her still-acutely sensitive body pulsing again. 'But you wished for a group to travel with and I think the Lord just answered that prayer. Given how we were engaged as they arrived, you can't say the Almighty doesn't have a sense of humour.'

Trying to quell the desire still raging through him, Will concentrated on regulating his breathing as he and Madame Lefevre watched the monks plod past.

As soon as the dust settled, she turned back to him. 'Travelling under the protection of the good friars is tempting, but we'd be rather conspicuous, don't you think? Unless you have robes, hoods, sandals and rope belts hidden in that bag.'

'Not yet, but I will. By the quantity of cattle and the amount of goods in the wagon, this group must have been to the farmers' market at Sonnenburg. Moving as slowly as they are, they probably spent the night at the religious guesthouse we passed at mid-morning. You stay here; I'll ride back and obtain what we need to become "Brother Pierre" and "Brother LeClair".'

'That's outrageous!'

'What, you don't think you can pass as a monk?'

'No! Well, yes, but lying to a priest? A whole group of priests?'

She looked so aghast, he had to laugh. 'Ah, so you do possess some scruples! I, alas, have none. Come now, think of it as…divine intervention sent to protect you. It would be a wonderful disguise, you must admit. We could travel south to wherever they are going, spend a few days at their monastery and then head for Paris. Absolutely no one would think to look for us dressed as monks.'

She nodded reluctantly. 'That's true enough.'

'If it chafes your conscience so badly to dissemble to the holy brothers, you could confess the deception before we leave. Besides, even if we admit we are in disguise, have not religious houses for millennia offered sanctuary to those in danger?'

Since she didn't immediately lodge another protest, Will knew she was weakening. Though he thought it a brilliant plan, her concession was all he needed.

'I suppose so,' she admitted at last. 'But how do you plan to obtain the supplies? The guesthouse isn't a clothing shop.'

'I'm sure the friars have a few robes and vestments they can spare. I'll tell the abbot there was a fire at my monastery that destroyed some of the brothers' robes and, as penance for some misdeed, I pledged to replace them. If I let him charge twice what they are worth, I'm sure I can persuade him to sell me a few.'

Frowning, *madame* wrapped her arms around her head. At Will's raised eyebrow, she said, 'I shield myself from the lightning bolt the *bon Dieu* will surely send to punish your sacrilege.'

Will chuckled. 'Never mind the good Lord, just protect yourself from view by passing travellers. It shouldn't take me more than an hour to reach the guest-house. I'll have us outfitted and on our way to catch up with the friars before nightfall.'

As promised, after a glib explanation and a generous donation, Will returned to *madame*'s hiding place two hours later with the necessary robes, hoods, belts and shoes. After giving her some privacy to change into the latest disguise—and trying very hard to avoid the further sacrilege of imagining her naked—he stowed the rest of their provisions and clothing in the saddlebags.

A few moments later, she returned, face lowered beneath the shadowing hood, hands clasped together in her sleeves in a prayerful attitude, looking the very picture of a humble friar.

'What an excellent Brother Pierre you make!' he marvelled. 'If I didn't know your identity, I would absolutely believe you a man of God.'

She shuddered. 'Please, don't tempt the Lord's wrath again by claiming that! Since Armitage knows our current aliases, we should complete the blasphemy by changing names. Shall I be "Brother Innocent" and you, "Brother Francis"?'

'Of Assisi?' he asked with a grin, following her thoughts.

'Yes. A sinner and voluptuary before he came to the Lord. Perhaps the so-divine aura of the name will stick,' she replied tartly. 'I intend to protect what's left of my immortal soul by swearing a vow of silence. You will have to spin this web of lies by yourself.'

Throwing herself up on to her mount, she rode off. He was still chuckling when he caught up to her. But, true to her declaration, she ignored his attempt to converse. After a few snubs, he left her to her chosen silence.

Watching her, bent humble and prayerful over the saddle, Will had to shake his head. Madame Lefevre adopted the role of holy brother as quickly and unquestioningly as she had transformed herself from a gentlewoman into an old man into a valet. Will wished his subordinates on his army missions had understood their roles and mastered them as quickly and completely.

Not that she was merely a follower. Had she not astutely observed that travelling in a group offered them the best chance to evade their pursuers and reach Paris undetected, he might never have recognised the potential in that passing group of monks.

He had to appreciate the good Lord's sense of irony. How much better a rebuke to the raging desire that had nearly made him take her by the roadside in the full daylight, where anyone might have discovered them, than to send a band of friars?

But, as that same good Lord knew, even in men's

garb, Elodie Lefevre posed enough temptation to break the will of a saint and he was nothing close to that.

All those days telling stories, his gaze continually straying to her soft lips and generous mouth, while eyes blue as the lake at Swynford Court in June focused on him with complete concentration, as if he were the only being in the universe. Wisps of brown hair escaping from under the homespun cap made him itch to slide their silkiness through his fingertips, while his hands ached to cup the softness of those pale, freckled cheeks. Mesmerised by her, he rambled on, recounting by rote stories with which he'd regaled fellow soldiers at camps and billets and dinners from the barren heights of Badajoz to the ballrooms of Brussels, all his will needed to resist the ravaging hunger to taste those lips, invade that soft mouth, pull the essence of her into him, possess her and all her secrets.

It had been worth it, worth everything, to begin the process with that kiss. She tasted of the bread and wine she'd praised, of lavender and woman. He'd hardly begun to penetrate her mystery, to discover the source of that amazing ability to block out all the world's dangers and embrace the joy of a single moment, but he'd learned she was no sensual innocent.

She'd kissed him back with fire and expertise, fanning his passion to an intensity he couldn't remember ever reaching so quickly before. If not for the inextinguishable instinct for survival born of six years living on the streets, he would never have heard the travellers approach—or been able to force himself away from her.

Just then, he spotted the dust cloud in the distance that marked the progress of the monks who'd passed them earlier. Gesturing towards it, he said, 'Time for Act Two to begin.' He checked a smile at the scowl 'Brother Innocent' threw him as he spurred his mount forwards.

Reining in beside the group, Will slid from the saddle and greeted the monks with a nod and the sign of the cross. 'God's peace, good brothers! Where are you bound?'

'His peace to you as well,' replied a monk mounted on a donkey, to whom the others deferred. 'We travel to our abbey at Leonenburg, which we should reach just after nightfall. And you?'

'Returning from Vienna on a mission for our abbot. I'm Brother Francis and this is Brother Innocent—who pledged a vow of silence towards the success of our journey. May we join you?'

'Of course. Anyone doing God's work is welcome.'

As they fell in behind the slow-moving cortège, *madame* gave him a reproachful look from beneath her hood—doubtless again fearing the imminent lightning strike.

But in a sense, they were doing God's work, he reasoned with her silently. Righting the wrong done Max and restoring to the nation the talents of a man who could do great good was a worthy endeavour.

Hauling into danger a woman who he was—grudgingly and much against his will—beginning to think might have been almost as much an innocent victim of the plot as his cousin might not, though, a stab of conscience replied.

Was that the reason, rather than a desire to wash her hands of his blasphemous deception, she'd chosen her name? he wondered.

Maybe the influence of *his* name was affecting his views. Though he'd never been a voluptuary, he'd committed sins enough to stay alive on the streets and to survive years of war.

A little humility and some genuine penance wouldn't come amiss. As they travelled in this herd like docile holy sheep, he appreciated having a divine ally in resisting her allure. As last night's attack chillingly demonstrated, he couldn't afford to let the attraction between them diminish his vigilance.

He didn't even want to think what might have happened, had her assailant been someone other than George. Someone who would have cut her throat without a qualm in the darkness of the hallway while he sat gaming in the taproom.

When he'd slipped from the common room up the stairs, the vision of her seized by an unknown assailant, moonlight glinting off the knife at her throat, had punched all the air from his lungs. Savage rage against her attacker and the urgent imperative to rescue her had refilled them.

George confirmed that the danger her maid feared was very real. The hasty, casual promise he'd given Clara to keep her safe was going to require all his wits and every artifice he'd learned as a young thief and perfected as a soldier. For now, he'd just have to keep a tight rein over his increasingly intense need to possess her.

But once they were safely in Paris… If she thought he'd stand aside and turn her over to some no-surname-Philippe before they settled what raged between them, she knew nothing of the iron resolve of Will Ransleigh.

As predicted, Will and Madame Lefevre had reached the monastery just after dark, were greeted by the abbot and invited to rest from their journey for as long as they liked. Billeted in a common room and eating with the group, he had little opportunity to speak privately with *madame*, stealing just a moment to recommend they remain several days at the monastery, and receiving her nod of agreement in reply.

Madame had mimed her willingness to work in the vegetable garden, while Will joined the monks cutting wood in the forest. Outside the walls of the monastery, he could relax a little; within them, unused to the traditions of a monastic order, he needed all his skill at mimicry to carry off the deception.

Madame, however, must have been raised a good Catholic, or was a better mimic than he, for she followed the order of worship and the prayers as if born to them. Or had she learned them after the fall of the Republic, when Napoleon made his Covenant with the Pope and religion returned to a France which for years had functioned without a church?

After five days with the brethren, who accepted their presence, respected their privacy and asked them no questions, Will approached *madame* to suggest they could move on. Silently she gathered her belongings, Will leaving a handsome gift with the abbot before they left the friendly gates of the abbey and made their way west through the foothills towards Switzerland.

Once they could no longer see the sheltering walls of the abbey in the distance, *madame* pulled down her hood and turned to Will. 'Perhaps we should continue this disguise for the rest of the journey. It's served us well enough thus far.'

Will clapped a hand to his chest theatrically. 'Behold, she speaks! Does this mean you've forgiven me for the deception? Or did you ease your conscience by receiving absolution from the abbot?'

She grinned at him. 'I confessed the truth the very first night. Did you never wonder why the brothers were so discreet?'

'Because they are holy men, above the sin of gossip?'

'They are still human and curious. Besides, that tale of being on a mission wouldn't wash; your ignorance of the ways of holy orders would have shown the moment the abbot questioned you about it, if your performance at Compline the night of our arrival hadn't already made everyone suspicious.'

After a moment's annoyance, Will grinned back. 'And here I thought they'd accepted me as an exemplary monk.'

'They admired how hard you worked, if several had

to keep from smiling at your ignorance of the most basic prayers.'

'You broke that vow of silence to discuss me?'

'No, I overheard them talking about you in the refractory. I confessed to the abbot only that I was female, fleeing in disguise under threat of my life, and that you were helping me to reach my family in France.'

'Had you no other sins to confess?' Will teased.

The playful look faded from her face as she stared at him. He felt her gaze roam his face, his mouth, his body and return to focus on his lips. 'Not yet,' she replied.

Her meaning hit him like a punch to the belly, the always-simmering need he worked hard to contain bursting free in a blast of heat that hardened his body and roared through his veins. For a moment he saw only her, felt only the pulse of desire pulling them together.

His mouth dry, his brain scrambled, he couldn't come up with a witty reply. She broke the connection, turning away from him.

'We're still a long way from Paris.' To underscore the point, she urged her mount to a trot.

He didn't dare trust her, but there was no question about the strength of his desire for her. He urged his horse after her, wishing they could gallop all the way.

Chapter Ten

Following their former pattern of hard-riding days and short nights, for almost two weeks Will had led Madame Lefevre around the foothills of the Alps, finally descending to Nancy. Once past that city, they joined a growing stream of travellers headed north-west through the vineyards and fields of the Lorraine towards Paris.

Although in its anti-clerical zeal the Revolution had destroyed or sold off most of France's great abbeys and monasteries, in their guise as monks, they were still able to claim shelter for the night at the re-established churches along their route. Will continued to negotiate for food and fresh horses, joking, to *madame*'s repeated warning about hellfire, that he was fast becoming a model priest.

Allies and collaborators by necessity, they were now an experienced team, able to communicate silently through looks and gestures. Though they'd not encountered any further need for stealth, they maintained their roles diligently. As he'd learned in Seven

Dials, one never knew when rats might come pouring out of some unseen hole.

They still took their meals in the open, and Will still spun the tales, *madame* listening with every appearance of fascination. But she never volunteered anything about herself.

He no longer wanted to ask. Instead, foolish as it might be, Will wanted her to open to him willingly, without his having to trick or pry the information from her.

Though this woman had betrayed his cousin and brought scandal upon his name, he was having a harder and harder time reminding himself of the fact. Much as he tried to resist it, the slender sprig of camaraderie that had sprouted in Vienna had grown stouter and stronger through the intrigue and dangers of the road, entwining itself around him until it now threatened to bind him to her as powerfully as the sensual attraction that tempted him with every breath.

Each day, he'd slip into his stories some comment or observation that invited her to reciprocate with a similar experience of her own. At first, he'd wanted to tempt her into talking about herself, eager to use his wits to separate fact from deliberate falsehood.

Each day, as she had remained silent, disappointment grew sharper. He'd long since given up the suspicion that she had any intentions of feeding him false information to gain some advantage; her behaviour upon the road had been absolutely upright and above-board, just as he would have expected of a comrade-in-arms. Increasingly, it pained him that after their shared adventures, he knew nothing more about Madame Lefevre's past than he'd learned before they left Vienna.

In many ways, he felt closer to her than to anyone else in his life save his Ransleigh cousins. He could sense he was nearing the essence of her, the soul of her that danced always just beyond his reach. But she continued to withhold herself from him, in body and in spirit.

Was that a ploy, too? To disarm him by holding herself apart?

Tactic or not, he hungered for both. He wanted her to hunger for him, too. To yield her secrets.

Before he seduced her. For in a day or so, they'd be in Paris and the game would begin again in earnest. Some time before they passed through the city gates, he intended to bind her to him with the silken ties of physical possession. Before she could try to run, or set off to search for the mysterious Philippe.

Before he took her back to England.

Despite their growing closeness, he still meant to carry her there. He just wasn't so sure now, he admitted with a sigh, what he meant to do with her once they arrived.

Having spotted a likely resting spot under a stand of trees near a small river, he motioned her to turn her mount off the road. While she watered the horses, Will removed his saddlebag and extracted their simple meal, his thoughts returning to the conundrum of England.

Maybe he could stash *madame* at some quiet place

in the country; he owned several such properties. He'd journey to London alone, feel out some contacts in the Foreign Office. Maybe there was a way to clear Max's name without incriminating Madame Lefevre.

The idea of giving her up to the gallows was growing more and more unacceptable.

By the time she finished with the horses, he had bread, ham, cheese and wine set out on a saddle blanket on the sun-dappled grass under the trees. This time, hoping to lure her into speaking, as they sat to consume their meal, he did not immediately launch into a story.

It seemed she was content to eat in silence. Just as Will was about to judge his experiment a failure, she said, 'So, are you out of tall tales?'

'Have you not grown tired of my exploits?'

'Not at all. But there is something else I'd like to know about. Won't you describe your childhood? You've spun many stories of your roguish life, but nothing of how you became who you are.'

The whirlpool of the past swirled in memory, threatening to suck him down into its maelstrom of fear, hunger, pain and grief. He shook his head to distance it. 'There's nothing either entertaining or edifying about it.'

'It was…difficult?'

'Yes.'

'I'd still like to know. I've never met a man like you. It's ill bred to be so curious, I realise, but I feel driven to discover how you became who you are.'

He saw an opportunity and grabbed for it. 'I'll tell

you about my youth—if you tell me about yours. Over our travels, I've blathered on at length about my misspent life. You've told me nothing.'

After a moment, she nodded. Exultant, he exhaled the breath he'd been holding.

'Very well. But you first. How did you learn all these things you seem to do so instinctively? To move as silently as silence itself. To be so aware of everything, everyone, all the time. The ability to be anyone, mingle with anybody, to converse as an English aristocrat or a Viennese workingman.'

'Silence, so as to move and not be seen. Awareness, in order to snatch purses and not get caught. Pickpockets in England are transported or hung. And to be anyone? Perhaps because I have been almost all those things and had to mimic them to survive until I mastered the roles.'

'How did the nephew of an earl, even an illegitimate one, become a thief, a pickpocket and a working man?'

Will thought of the taunts and hazing at Eton that no amount of bloody-knuckle superiority had stopped. Crude drawings of cuckoos left on his chair, muttered obscenities about his mother issuing from within a gaggle of boys, impossible to identify the speaker. Would this daughter of aristocrats scorn him, too, when she knew the truth?

Somehow, he didn't think so.

'During her come-out in London, my mother, a clergyman's daughter, was bedazzled by my father. The younger son of the Earl of Swynford, he was a rogue, gamester and self-centred bastard of epic proportions.

He lured her to his lodgings, a midnight excursion that ruined her reputation. When she refused to slink away to the country in disgrace, her family disowned her. For a time, they lived together at some dismal place just outside Seven Dials, but after losing a fortune at cards one night, he fled to Brussels. His older brother, now the earl, had already warned him he'd pay no more of his debts, and my father wasn't prepared to adapt himself to a debtor's life in Newgate. He left behind my mother, six months gone with child. Mama managed to eke out a few pennies doing needlework, enough for us to survive.'

Though all he remembered was being hungry. Frightened. Alone. And, later, angry.

'And then?' she prompted softly.

'When I was five years old, the local boss made me a runner and the street lads became my family. For the next six years, I learned the finer points of card sharping, lock-picking, house-breaking, knife-fighting and thievery.'

'Did your father never come back for you?'

'No. I heard he died of a bullet wound, courtesy of a man he'd been trying to cheat at cards in some low dive in Calais. But among his papers, later delivered to the earl, were letters written by my mother, begging him to make provision for their child. The earl set his solicitor to investigate and, once paternity was established, he had me brought to Swynford. Although, over the years, I'm sure he's regretted the decision to turn a second-storey boy into a gentry-mort, my cousins did their best to make me into a proper Ransleigh. Especially Max. Now, your turn.'

He caught her chin, making her face him. 'Who are you, Elodie Lefevre? Because if you're St Arnaud's cousin, I'll eat this tree.'

Before she could deny or dissemble, he rushed on, 'Don't you owe me the truth? I've told you about my ill-begotten youth. I've kept you safe and brought you almost to the gates of Paris. I simply can't believe St Arnaud would have left his own cousin in Vienna. Beaten her, perhaps, but not abandoned her; *someone* in the family would have taken him to account. Who are you, really?'

He held her gaze, implacable, willing her to confess, while his heart pounded, frantic with hope and anticipation.

Finally, she said softly, 'I was born Elodie de Montaigu-Clisson, daughter of Guy de Montaigu-Clisson, Comte de Saint-Georges. Our family home was south of the Loire, near Angers.'

He ran a map of France through his head. 'Isn't that in the Vendée?'

'Yes.'

That fact alone could explain so much. 'Was your family involved in the Royalist rising against the Revolution?'

'My papa joined the Comte de La Rochejaquelein, as did almost all the nobility of the Vendée. I don't know much, I was only a babe when the Republic was declared. But I do remember turmoil. Being snatched

from the house in the middle of the night. Fire licking through the windows. Living in a garret in Nantes.
Mama weeping. More fighting. Then that day…that
awful day by the river.'

She'd lived in Nantes. Suddenly he recalled the event
that had outraged all of Europe. 'You witnessed The
Noyades?'

'The Republican soldiers herded all the townspeople
to the quai beside the river. They marched the priests on
to a small boat, locked them below and scuttled the vessel.' He could almost see the rippling surface reflected
in the bleakness of her eyes. 'They did it again and
again, one boatload of priests and nuns after another.
All those holy ones, drowned. I was five years old.'

A child so young, watching that. He put a hand on
her shoulder, stricken. 'I'm so sorry.'

'It was terrible. But it was also wonderful. There
was no screaming, no pleas, no panic. Just…serenity.
Mama said they went to a secret place in their hearts,
where no evil could touch them.'

Like you do now, he thought. 'And after? If I'm remembering correctly, the Revolutionary government
offered amnesty to all Vendéeans who surrendered and
took the oath of allegiance. Did your father?'

'He died in the final battle. We left the garret in the
middle of the night, our shoes wrapped in rags to muf-
fle the sound, and boarded a ship. I remember wind
shrieking, rain lashing, travellers screaming, thinking
we would all drown like the priests and have to swim
to heaven. Then…calm, green land, Mama weeping on

the shore. We travelled north for many days, around a great city, surrounded by people speaking a language I couldn't understand.'

'You sailed to England, then? A number of *émigrés* went to the north, supported by the Crown.'

She nodded. 'Mama, my elder brother and I settled in a cottage on land owned by Lord Somerville.' She smiled. 'He had a wonderful garden. I used to spend hours there.' The smile faded. 'It was *my* secret place when Mama wept, or food supplies ran low. When the children in the village taunted me for my poor English and tattered clothing, for being a foreigner.'

'If you were living in England, how did you come to the attention of St Arnaud?'

'My brother, Maurice, ten years older than me, despised the Republicans who seized our land, killed my father and turned Mama into a grief-stricken old woman. When Napoleon abolished the Directoire and made himself First Consul, instituted the Code Napoleon and promised a new France where merit and talent would be rewarded, Maurice was ecstatic. He hated living as a penniless, landless exile, dependent on charity. He determined to enter Napoleon's army, perform great feats of valour and win back our lands. So we returned to France. On his first army leave, he brought home a friend, Jean-Luc Lefevre.' Her expression turned tender. 'I loved him the first moment we met.'

Instinctive, covetous anger rose in him. He squelched it. Devil take it, he wouldn't be jealous of a dead man! 'Whom you married. He was lost in the war?'

Pain shadowed her face. 'He fell at Lützen. He died the day after I reached the billet to which they'd taken him.'

'Is that when you learned to walk like a man? To disguise yourself on the journey?' At her sharp look, he said, 'I was a soldier, remember. I know what happens in the aftermath of battle. It's…dangerous for women.'

Eyes far away, she nodded. 'There'd been another battle at Bautzen, just after I buried Jean-Luc and left for home. Skirting the battlefield, seeking shelter for the night, I came upon a ruined barn. Inside were several soldiers, deserters probably, with a woman. They were…ravishing her.'

He'd seen enough of war to know what happened to some men when the blood-lust faded. Dismay filling him at what he feared he'd hear next, Will seized her arm.

Caught up in memory, she didn't seem to notice. 'I heard her crying, pleading with them.' Tears welled up, and absently she wiped them away. 'I heard her, but I did nothing to help. I was so ashamed.'

'Thank heaven you did nothing!' Will cried, relieved. 'What could you have done, except invite the same treatment?'

'Nothing, probably,' she admitted. 'But I vowed never to be so helpless again. I went back to the field— the burial teams hadn't covered all of it yet—and "borrowed" a uniform from a dead soldier. It was already bloody, so all I needed was a bandage around my head. I wanted to be ready.'

'In case you encountered renegade soldiers?' Will nodded his approval. 'Ingenious, to use the uniform as protection.'

'As protection, and also to be able to intervene if I encountered a…similar situation.'

'Intervene?' he echoed, appalled. 'I trust you never attempted to! Such men are beyond reason or shame; trying to stop them would have gotten you beaten, or worse.'

'I never had the opportunity. If I had, though, I planned to tell them there were willing women in the next town, and ask that they leave the one they had to me, since I was wounded and lacking my usual vigour.'

Will stared at her a moment, astounded. But foolhardy as such an action would have been, he could believe Elodie would have attempted it—and shuddered to think what might have happened.

'Why did you travel to Lützen alone, anyway? Did your husband have no family to accompany you?'

She shook her head. 'His family were *aristos*, like mine. All but he were killed or scattered during the Terror.'

'Had he no friends, then?' When she shook her head, he burst out, 'But to travel among rival armies after a battle, a woman alone? I can't believe you took such a risk!'

'To save the life of someone you love is worth any risk. You, who have done so much for Monsieur Max, must know that is the truth.'

She had him there. He knew without question he'd face any danger to protect his cousins.

'Soon after I got back to Paris,' she continued, 'Maurice came to me. His mentor, St Arnaud, needed a favour.'

'A hostess for Vienna.'

'Yes. My brother met St Arnaud through the army; he approved of us because we were *ancien régime*, part of the old nobility, like he and *his* mentor, Prince Talleyrand. Maurice had become Arnaud's protégé, so, when he needed a hostess, Maurice suggested me.'

'Did you know about the plot?'

'Not until after we arrived.'

'And St Arnaud used this "Philippe" to compel you to participate? Who is he—your lover?'

Even to his own ears, the question sounded sharp. Elodie merely smiled and shrugged.

'Something like. But enough for now; I've already told you more than you told me and we're losing the light. Besides, as you've said, we will be in Paris soon, perhaps even tomorrow.'

Her eyes on his, she laid her hand on his leg. Every muscle froze.

'In case our pursuers were able to figure out what happened after Karlsruhe, we should refashion ourselves once more. Enter Paris in the early morning with the crowd heading for Les Halles, just another farm couple with something to sell. I still have a simple gown in my pack. I could change here and we could stay at an inn tonight…as man and wife.'

The breath seized in his lungs. There was no question what she offered, with her gaze burning into his and her fingers tracing circles of fire over his thigh.

And no reason not to accept. If this were a trick to impair his vigilance, he'd just have to risk it.

'I thought you would never ask, my dear Brother Innocent. Let me help you change.'

'Not yet. I intend to wash in the river before putting on a clean gown.' She wagged a teasing finger at him. 'You stay here. No peeking!'

But her laughing eyes and caressing fingers told him she wouldn't mind at all if he watched her bathe.

He couldn't have kept himself from following her if the whole of Napoleon's Old Guard stood between him and the river.

Chapter Eleven

The chill of the early summer water shocked her, sending shivers blooming down her skin, but Elodie welcomed its bracing grip. Ah, to be clean, to wear her
own clothes again!

Perhaps as soon as late tomorrow, she would find
Philippe. As always when she thought of that moment,
she felt stirring anew the mingled joy and anxiety that
sat like a rock in her belly.

First, she'd have to deal with Will Ransleigh.

She couldn't deny a groundswell of regret that their
paths must diverge. He was an amusing companion, a
born storyteller, and more skilled at disguise, evasion
and subterfuge than anyone she'd ever met.

Dissembling their way across Europe, they'd made
good comrades. Despite the danger, this journey from
Vienna had been unique and magical, a gift she would
remember and savour, something never to be experienced again.

She would miss him, more keenly than she'd like,

but there was no question of a future. Now that Paris loomed and parting was inevitable, best to get on with it as quickly as possible.

She just hoped she'd be able to carry out her plans for that parting without a check, unease fluttering in her gut. Acquainted now with Will's high level of vigilance and excellence of observation, she'd need to be exceptionally careful in order to make her escape.

But before she eluded him, there was one final gift she could give—to him and to herself. Today and tonight, she would send him to the moon and the stars on a farewell journey of pleasure he would never forget.

Steeling herself to the cold, she strode into deeper water, quickly washing herself and her hair with a small bar of soap from the saddlebag. Despite warning him away, she knew he'd be watching from the copse of trees bordering the stream.

She'd start with a show to whet his appetite.

Shivering in the chill, she waded back to knee-deep water. With slow, languorous movements, she smoothed back the wet mane of hair, knowing it would flow sleekly over her shoulders. She leaned her head back, letting sunlight play over her breasts, the nipples peaked and rigid from the cold.

She lathered her skin again, then cupped her breasts in her hands and caressed the slippery nipples between her thumb and forefinger.

Sensation sparked in them, hardening them further, while matching sensation throbbed below. Half-closing her eyes, she imagined Will's hands mimicking the action of her thumbs. Would he bring his tongue to them, or use that hot, raspy wetness to stroke her tender, pulsing cleft?

She wanted him to tease her body to madness, as she'd imagined so many nights when she lay alone, chaste as the church floor they bedded down upon, acutely conscious of him sleeping beside her.

Heat crested and flowed outward from the slippery abrasion at her nipples, the hotter moisture at her centre. The fire building within now insulated her from the water's chill, made her breath uneven, her legs tremble, eager to part and receive him. She couldn't remember the last time she'd been so ready for a man, or ever wanting one as badly.

She opened her eyes to a muted splashing, and found Will, already shed of coat, boots and hose, wading out to her. Need blazed in his eyes.

Desire squeezed her breath out, gave it back to her in short, shallow puffs. The sensations at her breasts, between her legs, spiralled tighter, stronger.

'Shall I wash you?' she asked, her throat so dry she could hardly get the words out.

'If you'd be so kind.'

Oh, she wanted to be kind! She tugged at his shirt, impatient for an unimpeded view of the bare chest he'd teased her with so many nights on the road.

The skin was golden, sculpted over broad, muscled shoulders. His flat nipples were peaked, like hers. She couldn't wait to taste them. Couldn't wait a moment longer to see all of him.

Impatiently she tugged open the buttons of his trouser flap, freeing his member, which sprang up before her, proud and erect. Wobbling a bit in the current, he yanked the breeches further down and stepped out of them, tossing them back to the bank.

Her pulse stopped altogether, then stampeded. She could only stand, gaping at this Greek god of a man who'd come to earth to bathe in the stream and steal her heart. Would loving him transform her into some other being, a cow, a tree, as so often happened to unfortunate maidens who tangled with the Olympians? she wondered disjointedly.

Her admiration must have been obvious, for when she forced her gaze from his magnificent physique back up to his face, he was smiling. 'Soap?' he suggested.

She looked for it, then realised she still held it in her hand. After dousing him with water, she applied it to his neck, shoulders and chest. Breath catching in her throat, she massaged the film into a froth, touching, caressing, memorising the hard curve of muscle, the hollows between sinew and bone.

She thought he might break then, seize her and take his pleasure, but to her surprise and delight, he remained completely still, allowing her to touch him as she wished while standing so close she could feel his heat down the whole length of her body.

Lower she scrubbed, over the taut belly, the smooth curve of hip bone, until finally she took him in her hands.

His breath hissed out and he shuddered as she massaged the lather around his glorious hardness. Unable to resist temptation any longer, she leaned in and took one nipple between her teeth.

'Elodie!' he cried with a muffled gasp, then jerked her chin up to kiss her, one strong arm binding her to him. His mouth mastered hers, his tongue probing deep, leaving her senses swimming and giddy.

Still, he did not take her. She knew instinctively that even now, if she pushed him away, he would let her go. Awe and gratitude filled her.

And then, suddenly, she had to feel him there, in that aching, needy place that had been unsatisfied for so long. Her body had been handled and bullied, but not since she was very young, falling in love with the man who'd been so briefly her husband, had she encountered tenderness.

Still revelling in his kiss, she wound her arms around his neck and pulled herself up, so she could wrap her legs around his waist. Bringing his rigid erection to the hot, moist openness only he could fill.

Groaning, he broke the kiss. 'Are you sure?'

'Yes! Please! Now,' she gasped back, then uttered a long, slow moan of ecstasy as he entered her.

Then, he was walking with her, his hands cupping her bottom to hold her in place as he took them deeper and downstream, beneath the tender summer-green branches of a huge tree that overshadowed the bank. Kissing her again, he balanced her in his hands, using the river's current and the water's buoyancy to augment his thrusts.

It was delicious, floating submerged in coolness yet captured at her very core by urgent, demanding heat. The sensations built and built and built as she rode him, her breath gone to sobbing gasps, her nails digging into the muscles of his shoulders, until finally she shattered and spun apart into dazzling shards of pure delight.

She came to herself, clinging weakly to him, her whole body limp, his hardness still buried deep within her throbbing core. *'Ma petite ange,'* he murmured, kissing her again, light, feathery touches on her eyelids, her brows, her forehead. He licked her throat, the shell of her ear, the edges of her lips, until the spiral within began to rotate again and she rocked her hips against his.

Exquisite sensation shot through her when he put his mouth to her breasts, rolling the tender nipples between his teeth. Desire accelerated, building hotter and faster, making her thrust towards him while the flow of the river magnified every movement. In a rolling, rhythmic motion, they slid together, tugged apart, the liquid friction within and without catapulting her to the waterfall's peak, where this time, they tumbled over together.

Some timeless interval later, Will pulled her with him to the bank. Under the embrace of the overhanging tree's branches, he sat, settling her between his legs, his warmth cradling her from the chill of air and water. 'I really had planned for there to be wooing, fine food and wine, a bed,' he said, planting a kiss on her head.

'I know,' she said on a sigh. 'I just couldn't wait any longer.'

'I'm glad you couldn't. I've wanted that for months.'

'You haven't known me for months,' she pointed out.

'True.' He wrapped his arms around her. 'But I've been looking for you all my life,' he added, so softly she wasn't sure whether she'd heard the words or only imagined them.

So had she been looking, the thought struck deep. Hoping for a lover who would give back rather than demand, who would care about her, rather than simply use her. She'd lived on her own, by her wits, pummelling some small space of existence from a bully prizefighter of a world for so long, she had to go back into the mists of long-ago childhood to remember when she'd trusted anyone else to keep her safe. When she had last felt so protected. So…not alone.

The realisation was both thrilling and terrifying. Will Ransleigh, who would drag her to the gallows to save his cousin, had no part in her future, and the notion that she could depend on him after tomorrow was madness.

Yes, she'd been touched by his tenderness in seeing to her pleasure. Moved by his respect for her abilities and energised by the excitement of the sleight-of-hand they'd pulled off during their journey. But the sweetness of it was simply the rich dessert at the end of a meal—delectable, but not the sort of wholesome fare it took to sustain life.

Her life was with Philippe and that was an end to it.

She struggled, trying to use logic to disentangle her emotions from him, but like pulling at a fraying cloth, ragged threads of connection remained. Giving up, she made herself move away from him, squelching her body's protest at the loss of his warmth.

'It's good you had the foresight to find us a resting place that cannot be observed from the road,' she said, trying for some dispassionate comment.

'I know you trust me to keep us safe.'

She wanted to deny it, but had to admit the statement was true. It should frighten her anew to realise she'd fallen into such an instinctive reliance on him... but that reliance remained, tenacious as the river tugging at her ankles.

Which was illogical and dangerous. If she weren't exceedingly careful, this man could stop before it ever began her hunt for Philippe in Paris and she must never forget that.

Pushing her ungovernable emotions aside in disgust, she said, 'If we don't dress soon, we will freeze.'

'I suppose. But I don't want you dressed.' He skimmed his fingers over her breasts, down between her legs. She sighed and lay back against him, feeling his spent member stir.

'Don't tempt me,' he said with a groan. 'Just the touch of you arouses me and we need to be sensible. We must dress now and ride quickly if we want to reach the village before dark.'

'Yes, sensible,' she agreed. Movement was what she needed. Returning to their travels, like rewinding a stopped clock, would set her emotions back on their proper course and reanimate her purpose, both shocked to a halt by the intensity of this interlude. Remind her that, but for one night of pleasure, their paths *must* diverge.

'We should purchase some livestock, too. Chickens, perhaps? The easier to blend in with the other farmers headed to market.'

'Another good idea. You're quite resourceful.'

She couldn't help feeling warmed by his praise. 'I've had to be.'

He helped her rise, his hands at her waist. 'Posing as man and wife for tonight,' he murmured, bending to kiss her, 'is your best idea yet.'

Ah, yes, she still had tonight, their last night, to savour. Her reward for all her forbearance along the road.

Passion, she could give him, though she could pledge him nothing else. Framing his face in her hands, she murmured, 'Perhaps livestock isn't so essential. All we really need is a room with a bed.'

'I hope that's a promise.'

She skimmed her fingers from his shoulders over his torso and down his body before leaning to snag his breeches and toss them up. 'Count on it.'

Chapter Twelve

Like a man and a maid in love for the first time, they helped each other dress, Will touching, kissing, laughing with Elodie as she donned her simple maid's gown and he changed back into a combination of working man and gentleman's attire that might be worn by a prosperous farmer. He knew that once they reached Paris, she would try to slip away from him, but he felt too light and euphoric to worry about it, happiness fizzing in his chest like a freshly opened bottle of champagne.

He'd had many an adventure, but never one like this. Never with a woman who was as uncomplaining a companion as a man, as resourceful as any of the riding officers with whom he'd crept through the Spanish and Portuguese wilderness, working with partisans and disrupting the French.

Coming together at irreconcilable cross-purposes, their liaison was too fragile to last, but for now, he'd be like his Elodie and suck every iota of joy from an already glorious day that promised, once he'd taken care of provisions for the morrow and found her a room with a bed, to become even more wonderful.

He twined his fingers in hers as they went back to their horses. 'How glad I am to be out of those monk's robes! I've been dying to touch you as we travel.'

'Good thing,' she agreed. 'Since you're grinning like a farmer who's just out-bargained a travelling tinker. I doubt anyone could look at us now and not know we are lovers.'

He stopped to give her a kiss. 'Do you mind?'

'No. I'm grateful for each moment we have together...Will. One never knows how many that may be.'

Happiness bubbled up again as she said his name for the first time, lifting his lips into a smile. He loved how she pronounced it, rolling the 'l's so it was drawn out, like a caress.

He loved her simplicity and directness, her matter-of-fact approach to life, not fretting over problems incessantly like a shrew with a grievance, but considering them carefully, making the best plan she could and then putting them out of mind. So she was able to draw solace and find joy...in her garden, beside a river.

This time, she'd brought him joy, too. Tonight, in their bed, he would give that back and more, everything, all that was in him.

Only then would he face the dilemma of taking her back to England.

As they approached the village on the outskirts of Paris, they encountered more fellow travellers. After making a circuit of the town, Will chose an inn frequented by respectably dressed men and women—busy enough to indicate its food and service were of good quality, but not elegant enough to attract the wealthy and well connected.

After turning their horses in to a livery, he obtained dinner and a room at the inn he'd selected. It required all his self-discipline, after climbing the stairs and opening the door to a snug chamber with table, chairs and a bed that beckoned, to leave Elodie alone while he went off to purchase a dozen chickens and the cart to haul them in.

Anxious to complete the arrangements, he didn't even bother haggling with the farm woman whose fine fat pullets caught his eye. Settling quickly on a higher price than he'd ordinarily pride himself on getting, he took over the hens, content to leave her thinking she'd struck a good bargain, but not so good that she'd brag to her neighbours about getting the best of a lackwit stranger.

Even this close to Paris, one couldn't be too careful about avoiding notice.

He settled the purchases behind the inn's stables, to the raised eyebrows of the grooms. Farmers, even prosperous ones, didn't usually store their squawking produce at an inn the night before bringing them to market.

But they'd be gone on the morrow before the grooms on duty had a chance to gossip in the taproom, if indeed any watchers had picked up their trail. Will didn't think so; he'd been vigilant—except for a short time at the river—and he'd seen no evidence of their being followed.

Someone would be looking for them in Paris, however. But he'd worry about getting them safely through the city—and out again, Elodie in tow—tomorrow.

Visions of seduction now filling his head, Will hurried back to the inn. For the first time in days, they'd eat a fine dinner and sip wine by their own fire. They'd talk about their adventures, about her life, about Paris.

Maybe she'd even tell him about the mysterious 'Philippe'. Though initially he'd expected during the journey she would try to lull him with lies, when she finally did open up to him, every instinct told him what she'd related was the truth.

Then he'd knead her shoulders, massage her back, take down the honey-brown hair she'd kept hidden and, for the first time, comb his fingers through the long silken strands. Undress her slowly, bit by bit, kissing the newly revealed flesh, as he'd dreamed of for so many solitary nights. Taste the fullness of her breasts, rake the pebbled nipples against his teeth, gauging her arousal by the staccato song of her breath. Finally, he'd taste the honey of her fulfilment on his tongue before he sheathed himself in her and pleasured her again and again.

His body humming with anticipation, he took the stairs two at a time and knocked at the door to their chamber. 'It's Will,' he said softly before unlocking it.

He entered to find the room in semi-darkness, lit by the flickering fire on the hearth and a single candle on the table. From the shadows of the bed, Elodie held out her hands. 'Come to me, *mon amant.*'

She sat propped against the pillows, the bedclothes at her waist. At the sight of her naked breasts, full and beautiful in the candlelight, his member leapt and all thoughts of dinner vanished.

'Nothing would please me more,' he said, pulling at the knot of his cravat, already impatient for the touch and taste of her.

'No, don't! Come here,' she beckoned. 'Let me undress you. I want to honour you, inch by inch.'

Emotion squeezed his chest while his member hardened to a throbbing intensity. Always a success with the ladies, he had been pleasured by blushing maids, loved by neglected wives, seduced by bored matrons who enjoyed the forbidden thrill of bedding an earl's illegitimate nephew. But no woman had ever vowed to 'honour' him.

'Willingly' was all he could choke from his tight throat.

Swiftly he came to the bed, where she urged him to sit. He kissed her head, finding her hair still damp from a bath, that lavender scent enveloping her again. His mouth watered. 'You smell good enough to eat.'

She smiled. 'We shall both eat our fill tonight.' Tilting down his chin, she leaned up to kiss him, slipping her tongue into his mouth.

Not until his brain registered a sensation of coolness at his chest did he realise she'd unfastened his cravat and opened his shirt. Breaking the kiss, she moved her mouth there, licking and kissing until impeded by the shirt's edges. Murmuring, she urged his arms up and pulled the garment over his head.

'Better.' She trailed nibbling kisses along his collar-bone while her fingers shaped and massaged the muscles of his back and shoulders. She kissed from his neck down his chest, flicking her tongue teasingly just to the edge of his nipples, until they burned for her touch. He arched his back, manoeuvring his torso until her lips reached them, shuddering as she suckled them and raked her teeth across the tips.

Meanwhile, her fingers moved lower, beneath the back waistband of his trousers, to cup and squeeze his buttocks. He uttered a strangled groan, his member surging.

She glanced up at the sound. 'You must be tired. Lie down, *mon chevalier*,' she murmured, guiding him back against the pillows.

As he reclined, she removed his boots, giving him a delightful view of her naked back and bottom as she tugged.

The temptation was too great; he seized her and pulled her up to straddle his lap while with the other hand, he undid his trouser flap. She gasped, then uttered a little growling sound as she guided his swollen shaft into her slick passage and rocked her hips to take him deep.

He wrapped an arm around her back to pull her closer. As he branded her neck with his lips and teeth, he slipped the fingers of his free hand between them to caress her soft wet nub while he moved in her.

Panting, she arched against him, pushing him deeper. He moved his lips to her breast while his hand cupped her mound and his fingers played at the entrance, sliding into her to the rhythm of their thrusts.

Sweat coated his body, his neck corded and his arms grew rigid with the effort to hold himself near the peak without going over. And then she came apart in his arms, crying his name. Her tremors set off his own, a pleasure so intense he saw stars exploding against blackness as he spent himself in her.

For some time after, they lay limply in each other's arms. All his life, he'd been impatient, restless, driven by some intangible something to keep moving, searching for a destination he could never quite identify. For the first time, he felt utterly content, filled with an enormous sense of well-being. A deep sense that he belonged here, in this moment, with her.

His suspicions, along with the last bit of the anger he'd harboured against her, both gradually dwindling since they'd left Vienna, vanished completely.

He must have dozed, for he opened his eyes to find Elodie, still deliciously naked, sitting on the edge of the bed, pouring a glass of wine. 'For you, *mon amant*,' she said, handing it to him. 'To keep up your strength. You will need it. Now, where was I before I was so pleasantly interrupted? Ah, here.'

She tugged at the waistband of his unfastened trousers. Obligingly, he lifted himself, letting her pull them free and toss them to the floor. 'That's better. Naked, just as I want you.'

Her eyes gleaming, her expression sultry as a harem concubine intent on enticing a sultan, she gave him a wicked smile. 'Now I may see and taste…everything.

She extracted the wine glass from his fingers and took a sip. 'I'll need my strength also. To make this a night you will never forget.'

Some subtle sound roused him from a fathom's depth of sleep. Will rose slowly to consciousness, the room steeped in darkness, his whole body thrumming from senses wonderfully satisfied, like a chord still vibrating after the last note of a virtuoso's performance. *A night you will never forget.*

He certainly never would.

After that first lovemaking, she'd eased him back against the pillows and straddled him again, taking him within. And then sat chatting of Paris and London as if she were conversing at some diplomatic dinner, all the while moving slowly, rocking him inside her, her breasts bobbing deliciously close to his lips.

It was arousing, erotic, unlike anything he'd ever experienced. At first, he tried to match her aplomb and respond to the conversation, but after several times losing track of his sentences, he gave up the effort and closed his eyes, savouring the sensations.

Breathing itself became nearly impossible when, chatting still, she reached beneath him to where his plump sacks lay hidden, squeezing and massaging them while she urged his cock deeper. Pleasure burst in him, even more intense than the first time.

They dozed, roused to eat their cold dinner, slept again. He woke to find her head pillowed on his thigh. Noting his sudden alertness, she leaned over to trace his length with the tip of her tongue. As his member surged erect, she captured him in the hot velvet depths of her mouth, driving him to another powerfully intense release.

Just thinking about her made him smile. Maybe he could talk her into staying one more day at the inn. What would one more day matter? They'd already spent almost four weeks on a journey envisioned to take just over two. At odd times on the road, he'd considered trying to stretch it out even more, eking out every last second of joy from an experience as unparalleled as it had been unexpected.

Now, for the first time, he was beginning to envision a bond that might last not just a handful of nights, but weeks, months…into the hazy future.

As he stretched languorously, savouring the prospect, suddenly Will realised he was alone in the bed.

He sat bolt upright, his heart hammering. Not the faintest glimmer of dawn showed yet under the curtained windows. Probably she'd gone to the necessary, he thought, trying to force down the alarm and foreboding welling up in his gut.

She'd given him all of her freely, everything, as honestly as he had given it back to her. Stripped bare, with no defences, holding nothing back, they'd created a union of souls as well as bodies. She wouldn't just... leave him without a word.

His anxious, clumsy fingers struggled with flint and candle on the bedside table, but the additional flare of light just confirmed she wasn't in the chamber.

He jumped out of bed. Although the saddlebags he'd given her in exchange for the bandbox she'd packed in Vienna sat against the wall, they were empty; the gown, shift, chemise, stockings and shoes she'd donned after giving him back the monk's robe were gone.

Emptiness chilled him bone-deep as he admitted the unpalatable truth.

Damn her, she'd reduced him to a pudding-like state of completion, not out of tenderness, but so she could escape.

Escape him—and run off to her Philippe.

Nausea climbed up his throat and for a moment, he thought he'd be sick.

Betrayed. Abandoned. An agonising pain, worse than he'd felt after being shot by Spanish banditos, lanced his chest.

He dammed a rising flood of desolation behind a shield of anger. With iron will, he forced back deep within him an anguish and despair he'd not felt since he'd been a small boy sitting beside his dying mother.

It was ridiculous, he told himself furiously, carrying on like a spinster abandoned by the wastrel who had deceived her out of her virtue. The circumstances were nowhere near the same as the tragedy suffered by that five-year-old. He hadn't lost his only love, he'd merely been tricked by a lying jade.

But she'd not got the better of him yet.

Stupid of him to forget one rogue should know another. He'd forced this journey on her, giving her no real choice. Their adventure had been based on a bargain, each of them getting something they wanted.

She was trying to cheat him out of doing her part.

The sound that had roused him moments ago must have been Elodie, sneaking away. Without the instincts for survival Seven Dials had honed so well, he might never have heard her. It had already been nearing dawn the last time they'd coupled, so she couldn't have got far.

If Elodie Lefevre thought she'd seen the last of him, she was about to discover just how hard it was to dupe Will Ransleigh.

Chapter Thirteen

Her few remaining worldly goods concealed beneath the chickens in one of the baskets she carried on each arm, Elodie hurried in the dim pre-dawn with the press of other farmers heading into Paris. Too impatient to stroll at the crowd's pace, docile as the birds in the dovecote on the pushcart in front of her, she darted around the vehicle, causing the startled doves to flutter. Driven by an irresistible urgency, she only wished their wings beating at the air could fly her into Paris faster.

She had to escape Will, before he woke to find her gone. As skilled as he was at tracking, she must lose herself in the safety of the great rabbit warren of Parisian streets well before he set out after her.

There, as she began her quest, she'd also lose this nagging temptation to go back to him, she reassured herself.

It didn't matter how energised and alive he made her feel. Their time together had been an idyll and, like all idylls, must end. Besides, what they shared was only the bliss of the night, no more permanent or substantial than the lies a man whispered in the ear of a maid he wanted to bed.

A dangerous bliss, though, for it made her wish for things that life had already taught her didn't exist. A world of justice not ruled by cruel and depraved men. A sense of belonging with friends, family...a lover who cherished her. Safety, like she'd felt in Lord Somerville's garden. Illusions that should have vanished long ago with her childhood.

It ought to have been easy to leave him. She knew what he planned for her. She'd allowed herself the reward she'd promised, a spectacular night of passion more fulfilling than any she'd ever experienced.

Up until that very last night, she'd been successful in keeping her emotions, like tiny seeds that might sprout into something deeper than friendship if dropped into the fertile soil of his watchful care, clutched tightly in hand.

Her devotion to Philippe was a mature growth, a sturdy oak planted firmly in the centre of her heart. He was her love, her life, her duty. Returning to him should have shaded out any stray, straggly seedlings of affection germinated by Will Ransleigh.

But it hadn't. Even as she hurried to fulfil the mission that had sustained her for the last year and a half, she ached. A little voice whispered that the wrenching sense of loss hollowing her out inside came from leaving a piece of her soul back in Will Ransleigh's keeping.

Very well, so passion had forged a stronger bond

than she'd anticipated. She'd been privileged for one brief night to possess her magnificent Zeus-come-to-earth. But she could no more cling to him than had the maidens in the myths. She'd not been transformed into a cow or a tree; she mustn't let leaving him turn her into a weakling.

She'd just have to blot out the memory of their partnership on the road, forget the sparkle in his eyes and warmth in his smile as he spun tales for her. Obliterate all trace of the feel of him buried in her, catapulting her into ecstasy with skill and tenderness.

She wouldn't have to worry about *him* pining over *her*. When he woke to find her gone, he'd stomp the life out of any tendrils of affection that might have sprouted in *his* heart.

Time to put Will Ransleigh and the last month out of mind, as she always put away troubles about which she could do nothing. Time to look forwards.

The sun just rising in a clear sky promised a lovely summer day. She should be excited, filled with anticipation and purpose. She suppressed, before it could escape from the anxious knot in her gut, the fear that, despite all her scheming, she would not find Philippe.

Losing him was simply unthinkable.

Her agitation stemmed from fatigue, she decided. Certainly it couldn't be pangs of conscience at deceiving Will, she who wouldn't have survived without honing deception to a high art.

Besides, she *had* given him passion—the only honest gift within her keeping. She had no regrets about that.

As she rounded a bend in the road, the walls of Paris towered in the distance, casting an imposing shadow over the west-bound travellers. She forced her spirits to rise upwards like her gaze.

No more time for fear, regret or repining. The most important game of her life was about to begin. After waiting so long and being so close, she was not about to fail now.

Fury and contempt for his own stupidity fuelled Will's flight from the inn, which he quit within minutes of discovering Elodie's deception. Since they'd be entering the city separately, he'd no need to play the farmer. Let the innkeeper roast the fowl for dinner and chop the gig into firewood, he thought, his anger at fever pitch.

Unencumbered by cart and poultry, he was able to move swiftly.

Just a half-hour later, he spotted Elodie as she entered the city gates—his first bit of luck that day, for, once inside, despite her farm-girl disguise, there was no guarantee she'd actually make for Paris's largest market.

Walking quickly, two baskets of squawking chickens on her arm, she did in fact continue towards Les Halles. Camouflaged by the usual early-morning bustle of working men, vendors, cooks, housemaids, farmers, tradesmen, soldiers and rogues returning from their night's revels, he was able to follow her rather closely.

If he hadn't been in such a tearing rage, he might have enjoyed making a game of seeing how close he could approach without being observed. Though anger made him less cautious than he would have normally been, he was still surprised he was able to get so near, once reaching her very elbow as she crossed a crowded alleyway.

Hovering there had been foolish, as if he were almost daring her to discover him.

Maybe he was. With every nerve and sinew, he wanted to take her, shake her, ask her *why*.

Which was more stupidity. He knew why she'd fled, had been expecting it, even. He accepted that she'd out-played him in the first hand of this game, and in the one tiny objective corner remaining within his incensed mind, he realised it was unusual of him to be so angry about being outmanoeuvred. Normally he would allow himself a moment to admire her skill, learn from the loss and move on.

He would not—*could* not—examine the raw and bleeding emotions just below the surface that contrib-uted to his unprecedented sense of urgency and outrage.

He paused on the edge of the market square, watch-ing as she sold off the chickens and one basket, then moved on to purchase enough oranges to fill the other. He could corner her immediately, but it was probably wiser to wait until he could catch her where there were fewer witnesses who might take her part in the struggle that was sure to follow.

After Elodie left the market area, Will dropped back further, though he was still able to follow much closer than he would have expected, based on how alert and careful she'd been during their escape from Vienna. As consumed as he was by fury, he still wondered why.

Basket of oranges on her arm, she proceeded southwest to the Marais. This area of elegant town houses, so popular during Louis XIV's reign, had been already in decline by the Revolution, and many of the magnificent *hôtels* with their courtyards and gardens looked shabby and neglected. Elodie paused before one of impressive classical grandeur which, unlike its unfortunate fellows, was well tended, its stone walls and windows clean, its iron fences painted, its greenery freshly clipped. After staring at the edifice for a few moments, she turned down the alleyway leading to the garden entrance at the back.

Was this the abode of the mysterious 'Philippe'?

Watching her walk towards the gate, Will pondered his next move. Prudence said to take her before she could disappear within, if that's what she intended.

But if he stopped her now, he might never learn who occupied that house. She had to know he'd be furious if he caught her; if she hadn't revealed the secret of this elegant Marais town house to an accomplice and fellow traveller, there was little chance she'd do so to an angry pursuer.

Curiosity—and, though it pained him to admit it, jealousy—battling logic, Will hesitated. If he waited here, intending to seize her after she came back out, it was possible she might exit by the front door and he would miss her. But in her disguise as a farm girl, it was unlikely she'd be permitted to leave by the grand entrance.

Unless Elodie de Montaigu-Clisson Lefevre had resources he wasn't aware of. During his stay in the city after Waterloo, he'd learned enough about official Paris to know this fine mansion wasn't Prince Talleyrand's home, though it might belong to one of the Prince's spies or associates.

While he dithered, uncharacteristically uncertain, she trotted down the pathway and disappeared through the kitchen entrance and his opportunity to grab her was lost. Exasperated with himself, he retreated down the alleyway bordering the *hôtel* and scrambled up the wall beneath a tree conveniently clothed in thick summer greenery that camouflaged him while allowing him a clear view of the kitchen and garden.

Huddled on the wall against the tree, calmer now, he considered his options. There was no point berating himself for not nabbing her when he'd had the chance. After a night of little sleep, his reflexes and timing were off. It had been a long time since he'd enjoyed a woman so much, longer still since he'd met one who affected him as powerfully as Elodie Lefevre. As the sensual spell she'd created continued to fade, these atypically intense emotions would subside and he'd recover his usual equilibrium.

With that encouraging conclusion, he set himself to evaluating whether to wait where he was, within view of the servants' entry, or move towards the front. Before he could decide, Elodie exited the kitchen.

At the sight of her, his pulses leapt and a stab of pain gashed his chest, giving lie to the premise that his intense emotions were fading. Think, don't react, he told himself as he tried to haul the still-ungovernable feelings under control.

Fortunately, after exiting the back gate, she turned down the tree-bordered alleyway and walked right towards him. This time, he'd grab her at once, before she could elude him again.

Heart rate accelerating, breathing suspended, Will waited until she passed beneath him. He jumped down, landing softly behind her, and seized her arm.

She'd been trained well; rather than yelping or pulling away, she leaned into him, slackening the tension on her wrist while at the same time dropping to her knees, trying to yank her arm downwards out of his grip.

Being better trained, he hung on, saying softly, 'Hand's over, and this time all the tricks are mine.'

At his voice, a tremor ran through her and she stopped struggling. Slowly she rose to her feet and faced him, expressionless.

Will wasn't sure what he'd expected to see on her face: shame? Regret? Grief? But the fact that she could confront him showing no emotion at all while he still writhed and bled inside splintered his frail hold on objectivity with the force of an axe through kindling. Fury erupted anew.

He wanted to crush her in his arms and kiss her senseless, mark her as his, force a response that showed their passion had shaken her to the marrow as it had him.

He wanted to strangle the life from her.

Sucking in a deep breath, he willed himself to calm. He hadn't allowed emotion to affect his actions since he'd been a schoolboy, when Max had taught him channelling anger into coolly calculated response was more effective than raging at his tormentors.

It shook him to discover how deeply she'd rattled him out of practices he'd thought mastered years ago.

But one thing *she* couldn't master. The calm of her countenance might seem to deny he affected her at all, but she couldn't will away the energy that sparked between his hand and her captive arm. An attraction that sizzled and beguiled the longer he held her, making him want to pull her closer as, despite the hurt and anger he refused to acknowledge, his body, remembering only passion between them, urged him to take them once again down the path from desire to fulfilment.

Though he didn't mean to follow that road now, just feeling the force crackling beneath his fingertips was balm to his lacerated emotions. He clutched her tighter, savouring the burn.

'*Bonjour, madame.* I had to hurry to catch up to you. Careless of you to leave me behind.'

'Ineffective, too, I see,' she muttered.

'What of our bargain? Did the heat of the night's activities scorch it from your mind?'

When she winced at that jab, he felt a savage sat-

isfaction. No, she was not as indifferent as she tried
to appear.

'I merely wished to begin early to take care of a family matter, just as I told you I would.'

'Here I am, ready to assist.'

'It's better that I do it alone.'

Will shook his head. 'I'll go with you, or you can
leave Paris with me now. I move when you move, like
lashes on an eyelid, so don't even think of trying to give
me the slip again.'

The last time he'd warned her about escaping, he'd
talked of crust on bread and she'd licked her lips. A
flurry of sensual images from their surrender to passion
last night flashed through his mind. In the light of this
morning's abandonment, each gouged deep, drawing
blood. Cursing silently, Will forced back the memories.

'So, what shall it be?' he asked roughly, giving her
arm a jerk. 'Do we head for Calais or...?'

She opened her lips as if to speak, then, shaking her
head, closed them. A bleak expression flitted briefly
over her face before, with one quick move, she wrenched
her arm from his grip and walked off.

In two quick strides he caught back up, grabbing her
wrist again to halt her. 'Tell me what we're about to do.'

Freeing her wrist again with another vicious jerk,
she said, 'Follow if you must, but try to stop me and,
le bon Dieu me crôit, I swear I'll take my knife to you,
here and now. Observe what I do if you must, but in-
terfere in any way and our bargain is finished. I won't

go a step towards England with you, whatever retribution you threaten.'

She delivered the speech in a terse blast of words, like a rattle of hail against a window, never meeting his eyes. Even working with his normally keen instincts diminished, Will was struck by her ferocity and an odd note in her voice he'd never heard before. Something more than anxiety, it was almost…desperation.

Her urgency also shouted of danger, finally giving him the strength he needed to bury emotions back deep within the pit into which he'd banished all loss and anguish since childhood. They weren't in England yet; his first duty to Max was still to protect her so he could get her there.

She resumed walking at a rapid pace, eyes fixed straight ahead, seemingly oblivious to her surroundings. Falling into place beside her, he asked several more questions, but when she continued to ignore him, abandoned the attempt. Instead, he transferred his efforts into assessing all the people and activities in the streets they were traversing, alert for any threat.

While keeping a weather eye out, he was still able to watch Elodie. Her unusual abstraction allowed him to stare at her with greater intensity than she would have otherwise allowed. He tried to keep warmth from welling back up as he studied her striding form and set face, every nuance of the body beneath those garments now familiar to his fingers and tongue.

When his gaze wandered back to her face, he noted it was abnormally pale, her eyes bright, her expression as tense and rigid as her body. She paced rapidly, almost leaning forwards in her haste.

Whatever 'family matter' she was about to address, it was both urgent and vitally important to her.

From the *hôtel*, they passed through the streets of the Marais towards the Seine, south and west until they reached the Queen's gate at the Place Royale. Though some of the houses inside that beautiful enclosure, like those of the Marais, were shuttered and forlorn, even shabbiness couldn't mar its Renaissance beauty.

Rows of lanes, presided over by trees serene in early summer leaf, were well populated by nursemaids with their charges, finely dressed ladies followed by their maids, men with the self-important air of lawyers conversing and a few couples strolling hand in hand. In the distance, on the lawn, several children frolicked.

'Stay here,' she demanded, startling him as she broke her silence. Where her face had been pale before, now hectic colour bloomed in her cheeks. Her eyes blazed, the tension evident in her body ratcheting tighter. Without checking to see if he heeded her directive, she set off.

Neither curiosity nor prudent surveillance permitted him to obey. Will followed at a cautious distance, alertness heightened in him, too, as he sought to identify which of the wandering figures had seized her attention.

As he inspected the several strolling gentlemen, his gaze caught on one who'd paused, leaning over the maid accompanying him. He was too far away to hear their conversation, but the hand the man rested on the girl's shoulder, the juxtaposition of their bodies, nearly rubbing together even in this public space, hinted at intimacy. Had Elodie returned to find the man she loved romancing another woman?

She stopped so abruptly, he had to catch himself before he got too close, though she now seemed so absorbed, he probably could have run right into her without breaking her concentration. Will was scrutinising all the people in the vicinity of her mesmerised gaze, trying to fix upon its object, when a nursemaid nearby called, 'No, no, bring the ball back here, *mon ange*! I'll throw it to you, Philippe.'

A gasp of indrawn breath made him turn back to Elodie. She stood immobile, her gaze riveted on a dark-haired little boy, the basket clutched so tightly in her hand that the knuckles went white. Hope, joy, anxiety blazed in her face.

Philippe. *Philippe*. Comprehension slammed into Will with the force of a runaway carriage, knocking all the preconceived notions out of his head.

A 'family matter', she'd said. It wasn't a lover she'd been so desperate to search for, but a little boy, he realised, even as he recognised her smile, her eyes, in the face of the child. She'd come back to Paris to find her *son*.

Chapter Fourteen

As she neared the children playing in the grass beside the gravelled *allée* in the Place Royale, Elodie picked up her pace. Her heart pounded and her skin prickled as if the mother's love, trapped within her and denied expression for so long, was trying to escape her body and reach him before her feet could get her there.

Discovering from the cook at the Hôtel de la Rocherie that Philippe was, indeed, still in Paris, playing with his nursemaid only a few streets away, had made her desperate to reach him, see him, clasp him once again in her arms. Frantically she raked her gaze from child to child while her thoughts chased one another as quickly as hounds after a fox.

Would his hair still be ebony-black, his eyes still dark and alive with curiosity? He'd be slimmer now, more like a child than the sturdy toddler she'd left, ready for games and to sit a horse. Would he still love balls, play at soldiers, cajole for sweets?

Then she saw him. Her heart stopped, as did her feet, while everything around her faded to a blur.

He was taller, as she expected, his face more angular, having lost the roundness of babyhood. Pink-cheeked from exertions, his skin glowing with health, his eyes bright, his uninhibited laughter as he chased after his ball with that stubborn lock of hair curling down as always over his forehead, made her heart contract with joy.

As her eyes left his face, she noted that his clothing had been fashioned from quality materials and fit him well. The nursemaid tossing him the ball regarded him with an affectionate eye and a husky footman stood nearby, obviously keeping watch.

One anxiety dissipated. She'd for ever blame herself for not recognising the trap before she walked into it, but at least her instincts about the Comtesse de la Rocherie had been accurate. Philippe was well treated and cared for.

But he was *hers*, she thought with a furious rush of determination. Despite all the odds, she'd survived her ordeal, connived her way back to Paris. She would reclaim her son at last and nothing but death would prevent her.

Another swell of emotion shook her and she almost tossed down the basket to run to him, starved for the feel of him in her arms.

She took a shaky breath, fighting off the urge. He hadn't seen her for eighteen months, an eternity in the life of a young child. She mustn't startle him, but approach quietly, let him notice her, inspect her, rediscover her at his own pace.

Then she would work out how to steal him back.

Hands shaking now on the basket, she strolled down the path, on to the grass near her son.

It took two attempts before she could get the words to come out of her tight throat. 'Would you like an orange, little man?'

He looked over at her, his gaze going from the fruit to her face. Elodie held her breath as he studied her, willing recognition to register in those dark eyes, as lively and energetic as she remembered.

After a moment, he looked away, as if concluding she was of no interest. 'Jean, get me an orange,' he commanded the footman before turning back to the maid. 'Throw the ball again, Marie, harder. I'm a big boy now. See how fast I can run after it?'

Hands raised to catch his ball, he trotted off, all his attention now on the maid. Consternation welling within her, Elodie set down the basket and hurried after him.

'Come back, young gentleman,' she coaxed. 'Let me show you my fine oranges. They'll please you as much as your ball.'

'Not now,' he said with a dismissive wave in her direction, eyes still on the maid.

'No, please, wait,' she cried, catching up to him and seizing an arm.

He tugged away from her, but she held on, desperate for him to look at her again, really *look* at her.

He did indeed look back at her, but instead of recognition, as his gaze travelled from her fingers clutching his shoulder to her face, the puzzlement in his eyes turned to alarm. His chin wobbling, he called out, 'M-Marie!'

He didn't recognise her. Even worse, she'd *frightened* him! Aghast, appalled, she stared at him mutely, while denial and anguish compressed her chest so tightly she couldn't breathe.

The tall footman strode over, menace in his face as he pushed her roughly away from the child. 'What d'ya think yer doing, wench?' he growled, while her son ran from her towards the outstretched arms of his nurse. 'I'll call the gendarme on you.'

Then, somehow, Will Ransleigh was beside her, one hand protectively on her shoulder while he made a placating gesture towards the footman. 'No harm meant, *monsieur.* Just trying to get the gamin a treat, that's all. Gotta make a living, you know.'

'Better she sells her oranges at the market,' the man retorted before walking back to the nursemaid, who handed him the child's ball and hefted the frightened child into her arms. With a wary glance at them, the maid hurried off, the footman trotting beside her.

Philippe, his small hands clutching the maid's arms, didn't look back at all as he buried his head against the nursemaid's shoulder.

Just as he used to nestle into her embrace, Elodie recalled with an agonising stab of loss. Had it been that long? Could the eighteen months of separation have erased from his memory every trace of her three years of tender love and constant care?

She stood, staring after them, heartsick denial rising in her, watching until the small party turned the bend of the *allée* and disappeared out the gate. She couldn't, wouldn't believe it.

Suddenly she felt as if the pressure of all the anguish and anxiety, fear and doubt churning within would make her chest explode. Her feet compelled into motion to try to relieve it, she set off pacing down the pathway, light-headed, nauseated and only dimly aware of Will Ransleigh keeping pace beside her.

How could Philippe have forgotten her? His image was etched into her brain. With her first conscious thought every morning, her last every night, she recalled his face, wondered what he was doing, worried about his welfare.

In the depths of her pain after St Arnaud's savagery, his image burning in her heart had given her the will to struggle out of the soothing darkness of unconsciousness. Determination to return to him kept her from despair and lent her patience and courage during the long slow recovery, through tedious hours of needlework, each completed piece adding one more coin to the total needed to fund her journey back to him.

When she pictured their reunion, she always imagined him fixing on her an intent, assessing gaze that would turn from curious to joyful as he recognised her. Imagined the feel of his slight frame pressed tightly in her arms when he threw himself against her, crying, *'Maman! Maman!'*

Instead, he'd called for Marie. He'd clutched *her* arms, buried his head against *her* shoulder.

But he was only a small boy and she had been missing almost half as many years as they'd had together. It had been unrealistic and probably foolish of her to expect he would remember her after so long.

What under heaven should she do now?

Despite the footman being alerted and the maid alarmed, Elodie knew that with a change of clothing and manner, she could weasel her way close to him again, into the house itself if necessary. She'd always envisioned picking him up, telling him to hush as they played a 'hide-and-seek' game while she stole away with him.

She couldn't do that if he were afraid, crying out, struggling against her to escape.

She couldn't do that to him, even if he didn't struggle. The idea of tearing him from all that was comforting and familiar and carrying him off, alone and terrified, filled her with revulsion.

Yet she couldn't simply give him up.

She walked and walked, circuit after circuit, her thoughts running in circles as unchanging as the perfect geometry of the Place. In continuous motion, but always ending up at the same point.

He was young, he'd recover from the trauma, she argued with herself. He'd adjusted to living with the comtesse; he'd adjust again to living with her...even if he never truly remembered her. He was flesh of her flesh; he belonged with her. No one else alive had as much right to claim him as she did.

But could she live with herself if she put him through such an ordeal? Other than the closest kinship of blood, what could she offer him that might compensate for the terror of being stolen away by a stranger?

As she worked patiently in Vienna, she'd always imagined taking him away to a little village somewhere. Using the funds she'd obtain from selling the last of her jewels to buy a small farm in the countryside, where she could plant a garden, eke out a living selling herbs and doing needlework, watch her son grow to manhood. But now?

She was alone with no friends, no allies and very little money. Somewhere St Arnaud might still lurk, a dangerous enemy who might be the force behind those who'd been trailing them. She'd fallen back into the hands of Will Ransleigh, whose tender care was meant to ensure her delivery to England, where he'd press her into a testimony that might send her all the way to the gallows.

Leaving her son, if she stole him away, an orphan in an alien land.

Was it right to catapult him into poverty, peril and uncertainty? Cut him off from the love, security and comfort of a privileged life in Paris?

If he truly was loved, secure and comfortable.

A sliver of hope surfaced, and she clung to it like a shipwrecked sailor to a floating spar. Perhaps, though his physical needs were being met, he was not well treated by the comtesse. Perhaps his adoptive mother neglected him, left his upbringing to servants. Kind nursemaids and protective footmen were well enough, but wasn't it best for him to live with the mother who doted on him, who would make his comfort and well-being the focus of her existence?

If St Arnaud's sister, the Comtesse de la Roche-rie, was not providing that, wouldn't she be justified in stealing back the son she'd been tricked into leaving, despite the dangers and uncertainty of her present position?

Elodie would never have the funds to provide the luxuries available in the household of a comtesse. But did the comtesse love and treasure Philippe, as she would?

Elodie had to know. She would have to return to the Hôtel de la Rocherie and find out.

And then make her terrible choice.

Watching, as Elodie was, the footman and nurse-maid's rapid exit from the square, Will was startled when she suddenly set off down the gravelled path. Quickly he caught up, about to seize her arm and warn her he'd not let her escape again, when the stark, anguished face and hollow eyes staring into the far distance told him she was not trying to elude him; she was barely aware of where she was or who walked beside her.

Knowing he would likely get nothing from her in her current state, Will settled for keeping pace, while he wondered about the story behind Elodie Lefevre—and her *son*.

He couldn't deny a soaring sense of relief that the mysterious Philippe had turned out to be a child of some five summers, rather than a handsome, strapping young buck. Thinking back, her soft laughter and oblique answer—'something like'—to his question about whether Philippe was her lover should have alerted him to the fact that the 'family matter' might not involve the rival he was imagining. He might have realised it, had a foolish jealousy not decimated his usual ability to weave into discernible patterns the information he gathered.

'Something like' a lover. Ah, yes; he knew just how much a small boy could love his mother.

The son in Paris was obviously what St Arnaud had used to compel her co-operation in Vienna. How had he finagled that? A man who'd beat a woman half to death probably would not have many scruples about kidnapping a child.

Had she thought, once she'd got back to Paris, she would give him the slip and then simply go off and steal the boy out from under the noses of the family with whom he'd been living?

Will smiled. Apparently she'd thought exactly that. With her talent for disguise and subterfuge, she probably had in her ingenious head a hundred different schemes to make off with the boy and settle with him somewhere obscure and safe.

Until Will Ransleigh had turned up to spoil those plans. He understood much better now why she'd run.

He wondered which of those hundred schemes she intended to try next. After he gave her time to recover from the shock of seeing her son again, he'd ask her. There was no reason now for her not to confess the whole story to him.

And then he would see how he could help her.

He startled himself with that conclusion. It was no part of his design to drag a small boy back to England. But he had already conceded, despite his anger over her duping him, that he'd moved far beyond his original intention to barter her in whatever manner necessary to win Max's vindication.

Somehow, he'd find a way to achieve that and still keep Elodie safe. Elodie, and her son.

Because, as much as he had initially resisted it, a deep-seated, compulsive desire had grown in him to protect this friendless, desperate woman without family or resources, who with courage and tenacity had fought with every trick and scheme she could devise to reclaim a life with her son. Too late now to try to root that out.

He was beginning to tire of the pacing when, at last, she halted as abruptly as she'd begun and sank on to a bench, infinite weariness on her face. Quickly he seated himself beside her. He tipped her chin up to face him, relieved when she did not flinch or jerk away from his touch.

'Philippe is your son.'

'Yes.'

'St Arnaud used him to make you involve Max in his Vienna scheme.'

'Yes.'

'Why did he choose someone he had to coerce? Surely he knew other families with Bonapartist sympathies. Why did he not ask one of their ladies to join his plot?'

She sniffed. 'If you were at all acquainted with St Arnaud, you wouldn't need to ask. He thought women useful only for childbearing or pleasure, much too feeble-minded to remain focused upon a course of action for political or intellectual reasons. No, one could only be sure of controlling their behaviour if one threatened something they held dear.'

'How did he get the child into his power?'

'Because I was stupid,' she spat out. 'So dazzled by his promise of a secure life for myself and my son, I fell right into his trap.'

Having been homeless and penniless, he could well understand the appeal security and comfort must have had for a war widow with few friends and almost no family. 'How did it happen?'

'As I told you, my brother, Maurice, suggested to St Arnaud that I serve as his hostess at the Congress of Vienna. I dismissed the possibility, for with all his contacts, why would St Arnaud choose a shabby-genteel widow with little experience of moving in the highest circles?'

'Why indeed,' she continued bitterly. 'What a fool I was! I should have been much more suspicious that he invited a woman with few resources and no other protector but a man already deeply in his debt. Instead,

I was surprised and flattered when he confirmed the offer, insisting that my "natural aristocratic grace" would make up for any inexperience. St Arnaud promised if I performed well, in addition to letting me keep the gowns and jewels he would buy me for the role, he would settle an allowance on us. Later, when my son came of age, he'd use his influence to advance my son's career.'

'Inducements hard for any mother to refuse.'

'Yes. At least, until he informed me that Philippe would not accompany us. Upon learning that, I did refuse his offer; there was no way I would leave my precious son behind in Paris.'

She laughed without humour. 'That insistence, I now suspect, probably sealed St Arnaud's conviction that I was the perfect victim for his scheme. Utterly able to be controlled through my son—an easy loss to explain away to the brother who depended on him for the advancement of his career, if something happened to me. In any event, St Arnaud urged me to reconsider. It would only be for a few months, he said. I would be so busy I would hardly have time to miss the child. His sister, the Comtesse de la Rocherie, had recently lost her young son and would be thrilled to look after Philippe.'

She rose and began pacing again, as if propelled by memories too painful to bear. 'When I remained firm in my refusal, he told me he'd promised the comtesse I would bring Philippe to visit her—could we not at least do that? Surely I couldn't be so cruel as to disappoint a grieving mother! And so…we went.'

'He kidnapped the child on the way?'

She shook her head in the negative. 'We did call on her. The comtesse was good with Philippe; he liked her at once, and when she offered to take him up to the nursery to play, he begged me to let him go.'

A sad smile touched her lips. 'She told him she had a toy pony with blue-glass eyes and a mane and tail of real horsehair. What child could resist that? Philippe had grown restless and St Arnaud urged me to send him up to romp while we finished our tea. And the comtesse…there was no disguising the yearning in her eyes as she offered Philippe her hand. So I let him go.'

'I let him go,' she repeated in a whisper, tears welling up in her eyes. 'The next thing I remember, I was in a travelling coach, groggy, nauseated, my hands bound, too weak even to push myself upright. Not until we reached the outskirts of Vienna did St Arnaud allow me to regain consciousness.'

'Vienna!' Will burst out, incredulous that St Arnaud had managed to kidnap, not a child, but a grown woman, and transport her hundreds of miles. 'That's outrageous! Did no one at any of the inns notice anything?'

'I expect it was easy enough for him to spin some story about my being ill. The actions of a man of wealth and authority are unlikely to be questioned by post boys and innkeepers.'

Realising the truth of that, Will nodded grimly. 'Go on.'

'As soon as I was strong enough to stand, I told him

I was returning at once to Paris. That was the first time he struck me.'

'Bastard,' Will muttered, wishing St Arnaud would appear on the pathway before them—so he could strangle the life from him.

'He told me if I loved my son and wanted to see him again, I would do exactly as he instructed. Not to waste my time trying to escape him, for he had swift messengers at his disposal and employees back in Paris. Children, like his sister's son, were so frail, he said. Playing happily one evening, dead of a fever by morning.'

'He threatened to kill your son if you didn't co-operate?' Will said. 'He truly was evil.'

She nodded. 'He said my life, my child's life, was nothing compared to the importance of restoring France to glory under Napoleon. When I asked what assurance I had of ever seeing Philippe again, regardless of what I did, he said he was a "reasonable man". Reasonable! If I did my part to make sure his plot succeeded, he would provide everything he'd promised: clothes, jewels, a handsome financial settlement. I might even be acclaimed in Paris as a heroine of the Empire for helping him restore Napoleon to the throne. But if I refused to play my role…I was finished, and so was Philippe. So I did what he wanted.'

'What about your brother?' Will asked. 'Did he not try to find you when St Arnaud disappeared after the failure of the plot?'

'I don't know. Napoleon escaped Elba within days of the assassination attempt. Maurice's regiment, like all the French regiments, was called up as soon as the authorities learned Napoleon had landed back in France. He died at Waterloo.'

'I am sorry. Did the comtesse know where St Arnaud went to ground?'

'Perhaps. I don't think she was involved in planning this. We were both just pawns in his game, me in my poverty with a young son to raise, her in her grief and need. When I was reported dead, naturally she would raise Philippe as her own.'

'But you still want him back.'

'Of course I want him back.'

'Very well, I'll help you steal him.'

Her eyes widened, surprise and a desperate hope in their depths. 'You'll help me?'

He shrugged. 'I doubt you'll leave France willingly without him.'

A worried frown creased her brow. 'It won't be easy. He's not a purse you can pick at a Viennese market, but a small boy. He'll feel alone after we grab him. Frightened.'

Remembered anguish twisted in his gut. He knew what it was to be a small child, frightened and alone.

'First, I'll need to get back into the house,' she said. 'Locate the service stairs, find the nursery, manage to see him again.'

'How do you propose to do that? The "orange seller" is unlikely to be welcomed.'

'Probably not,' she admitted.

Thinking rapidly, Will said, 'We'll go as a tinker and

his wife. While I keep the staff occupied in the kitchen, distracting them with my wares and wit, you can slip up to the nursery.'

She gave him a wan smile. 'Have you a cart, pots, pans and fripperies in those wondrous saddlebags of yours?'

'No, but I've the blunt to buy some. Have you another gown, one that will make you look like a respectable tinker's wife?'

'I have one more gown in this basket, yes.'

'Good.' Will held out his hand. 'Partners again? No more disappearing at dawn?'

'Partners.' Meeting his steady gaze, Elodie clasped his hand and shook it.

Threading his fingers in hers, Will exulted at the surge of connection, as potent and powerful as ever. It was all he could do to refrain from hugging her, so absurdly grateful was he for this chance to begin again. Abducting a child from the household of a wealthy comtesse was a mere nothing; to keep her beside him, he would have pledged to abscond with the entire French treasury.

His heart lighter than it had been since the terrible moment he'd awakened to find her gone, Will contented himself with kissing her hand. 'We passed a café just outside the entrance to the Place. You can wait for me there.' He offered her his arm.

She took it and he tucked her hand against his body, savouring the feel of her beside him as they walked together. Comrades again, as they'd been on the road.

A few moments later, they reached the small establishment he'd noted. After he'd escorted her to a table, rather than release his arm, she held on, studying him. 'You're a remarkable man, Will Ransleigh,' she said softly.

It wasn't exactly an apology. But it was close enough. 'So I am,' he agreed with a grin. 'Give me about two hours to obtain the necessary items.'

She nodded. 'I'll be ready.'

A spring in his step, Will headed off to the market, running through his mind a list of items to procure. Having spent much time wandering around in markets in his youth, perfecting his skill as a thief, he knew just the sort of shiny objects that would tempt footmen, housemaids, cooks and grooms, and where to obtain them quickly.

He paced through the crowded streets on a wave of renewed energy and purpose, buoyed by the knowledge that Elodie hadn't, after all, abandoned him for another man. She'd been pulled away by a bond he, more than anyone, could appreciate: that between a mother and her son.

That loyalty would no longer stand between them. In fact, her gratitude for his help in rescuing her child would reinforce their powerful physical attraction.

Bit by bit, like a clever spider creating its web, fate and circumstance were adding strand after strand, linking them together. Mastering this last challenge and then completing the voyage to England would take time…time to examine the many subtle threads of connection. Time to sample passion and see if it tasted of a future.

He hadn't solved yet the problem of how to vindicate Max while protecting Elodie from retribution, but he'd figure out something. All in all, he felt more hopeful than at any time since he'd smuggled her out of Vienna.

Chapter Fifteen

Three hours later, in his latest guise as a travelling tinker, Will Ransleigh was putting on his best show for a staff happy for a bit of diversion during the break between the preparation and serving of dinner. After convincing the housekeeper to allow all the employees—including the nursery maid—to come down to the servants' hall, Will's witty repartee, glittering wares and a magic trick or two kept his audience preoccupied enough for Elodie to slip unnoticed to the service stairs.

Before they began their charade, he'd told her he'd give her half an hour to find the nursery, bundle up her son and get him out of the house. He'd then finalise any purchases and meet her with the cart, its contents conveniently configured to hide a small boy, on a side street a short distance away, ready to make all speed out of the city.

She'd nodded agreement. She just hadn't told him that she might not be bringing her son. Her gut twisting at the very thought, she ran up the service stairs, heart pounding in anxiety and anticipation.

As she hurried up, she recalled with perfect clarity every detail of her visit to this house that infamous day eighteen months ago. *Please, Lord*, she begged silently, *let this day not end as that one did, with me leaving without my son.*

The comtesse had told her the nursery was on the third floor. Exiting into the hallway, she peeked behind several doors before, beyond the next, she found a small boy playing with soldiers.

His eyes fixed on the toys he was meticulously placing in assorted groups, Philippe didn't look up as she stealthily opened the door. Taking advantage of his preoccupation, she studied him, her heart contracting painfully with joy at seeing him, with sorrow for the years together that had been stolen from them.

He was a lithe-limbed, handsome little boy where she had left a toddler just out of babyhood. He had her eyes, her lips, his now pursed in concentration as he positioned the soldiers just so, Jean-Luc's nose and sable hair that always fell over one brow and his long, graceful fingers.

Just then he looked up, his bright blue eyes curious. 'Who are you? Where is Marie?'

'Down in the kitchen. She asked me to come stay with you while she looked at some fripperies my man is selling.'

'"Fripperies"? Is that something to eat? I hope she brings me some!'

She smiled; Philippe obviously still loved his sweets. 'No biscuits or cakes, I'm afraid. Things like hair ribbons or lace to trim a collar, glass beads for a necklace, or a shiny mirror.'

Suddenly his eyes narrowed and he frowned. 'You were selling oranges in the Place today. You're not going to grab me again, are you? I don't like being grabbed.'

The wariness in his eyes lanced her heart. 'I won't do anything you don't like, I promise.' Trying to buttress her fast-fading hopes, she said, 'What nice soldiers you have! And a pony, too.' She gestured towards the infamous glass-eyed toy horse against the wall behind him.

'I'm too big for it now,' Philippe said, seeming reassured by her pledge. '*Maman* says this summer, she'll get me a real pony. I love horses. I shall be a soldier, like my papa.'

If you only knew, Elodie thought. 'Is your *maman* good to you?'

Philippe shrugged. 'She's *Maman*. Whenever she goes away, she brings me a new toy when she comes back. And reads me a story before bed at night.' He giggled. 'She brings me sweets, too, but you mustn't tell! Nurse says they keep me from going to sleep.'

Elodie pictured the comtesse in her elegant Parisian gown, sitting on the narrow nursery bed, reading to *her* son, ruffling his silken hair, kissing him goodnight. Tears stung her eyes. *It should be me*, her wounded heart whispered.

'I won't tell,' she said.

Philippe nodded. 'Good. I don't like storms. When

wind rattles the windows, *Maman* comes and holds me.'
His eyes lit with excitement. 'And in summer, when we
go to the country house, she lets me catch frogs and
worms. And takes me fishing. But she makes Gasconne
put the worms on the hook.'

Each smile, each artless confidence, drove another
nail into the coffin of her hopes. Anguished, frantic, she
said, 'I could take you to the bird market, here in Paris.
They have parrots from Africa, with bright feathers of
green and blue, yellow and red. Wouldn't you like to
see them?' She held a hand out to him.

His smile fading, he scuttled backwards, away from
her outstretched hand. 'Thank you, *madame*, but I'd
rather go with *Maman*.'

She'd frightened him again, she thought, sick inside.
'Can I ask you one more thing? Will you look very
closely and tell me if I remind you of anyone?'

Obviously reluctant, he focused on her briefly. 'You
look like the orange lady from the park. Will you go
now? I want Marie.'

He scuttled back further, seeming to sense the fierce,
barely suppressed instinct screaming at her to seize him
and make a run for it. Keeping a wide-eyed, wary gaze
on her, he clutched two of his soldiers to his chest…as
if hoping they might magically spring to life and defend him from this threatening stranger.

From her. From a desperate need to be together that
was *her* desire, not *his* any longer.

Agonising as it was, she couldn't avoid the truth.
With her own eyes, she could see her son was healthy,

well dressed and well cared for. From his own lips, she'd heard that the comtesse was an attentive, loving mother. One who could afford to give him a pony, who had a country manor probably as elegant as this town house where they could escape the disease and stink of the city in summer.

He was loved. Happy. *Home.*

Her breath a painful rasp in her constricted chest, she stared at him, trying to commit every precious feature to memory.

A patter of approaching footsteps warned her the nursery maid was approaching. Though her mind couldn't comprehend a future beyond this moment, she knew she didn't want to risk being thrown into a Parisian prison.

Even so, only by forcing herself to admit that fear of *her* lurked behind the mistrustful stare of her son, only by repeating silently the plea that had stabbed her through the heart—*will you go now?*—was she able to force her feet into motion.

'Goodbye, Philippe, my darling,' she whispered. With one last glance, she sped from the room.

To Will's surprise, Elodie returned to the kitchen well before the thirty minutes he'd allotted her...and alone. Pale as if she'd seen a ghost, eyes staring sightlessly into the distance, she took a place at the back of the crowd, not meeting his gaze. Wondering what new disaster had befallen her, Will wrapped up his cajolery with a few short words, curbing his impatience as the customers he'd enticed took their time purchasing laces, ribbons and shaving mirrors. At last, he was able to pack up the remaining merchandise and bundle them both back outside.

As soon as they turned on to the small street bordering the Hôtel de la Rocherie, he halted and turned to her. 'What happened? Is the child ill?'

'Oh, no. He's in excellent health.'

'Then why did you not seize him?'

She shook her head. 'I couldn't.'

'Ah, too difficult in full daylight?' he surmised, well understanding her frustration. 'No matter. You know the lay of the house now. We'll come back tonight. It's clouding over, so the sky will be—'

'No,' she interrupted. 'We won't come back.'

Will frowned at her. 'I don't understand.'

Shivering, she wrapped her arms around herself, as if standing in a cold wind, though the summer afternoon was almost sultry. 'He was playing with soldiers. Very well made, their uniforms exact down to every detail. His own clothing, too, is very fine. He summers at a country manor, where there are streams to fish and ponies to ride.' A ragged sigh escaped her lips. 'I can't give him any of that.'

'What does that matter?' Will asked, his gut wrenching as from the depths of his past rose up the anguished memory of losing his own mother. 'You're his mama!'

'I used to be,' she corrected. 'I'm just the "orange lady" from the park now; it is the comtesse that he calls *Maman*. She dotes on him, reads him stories, even takes him fishing. All I could offer is love, and he already has that, along with so many other things I could never provide.'

'Besides…' she turned to face him, her expression pleading, as if she were trying to convince him—and herself '…bad enough that stealing him, tearing him away from everything familiar and comforting, would terrify him. The comtesse married into a powerful family; she would very likely utilise all her contacts to track him down and drag him back, putting him through another round of terror and uncertainty. He's only four and a half years old! I can't do that to him.'

'So you're just…giving up?' Will asked, incredulous.

Elodie seemed to shrink into herself. 'He doesn't need me any more,' she whispered.

Abruptly, she turned and moved away from him down the street. Not trying to escape him, he realised at once. There was nothing in her movements of the purposeful stride that had taken her from the Hôtel de la Rocherie this morning into the Place Royale, or even of the frenzied tramp around the pathways that followed her first rendezvous with her son.

This was the aimless walk, one plodding foot in front of the other, of someone with no goal and no place to go.

When he had obtained the cart and goods necessary for their current reincarnation as tinkers, Will had also provisioned them for a rapid flight to the coast. Avoiding the usual crossing points at Calais or Boulogne, he intended to engage a smuggler's vessel from one of the smaller channel ports to ferry them over to

Kent, where several easy days' travel would get them to Denby Lodge, Max's horse-breeding farm.

They had no need for a cart now—and no reason to linger any longer in Paris. With some additional blunt, he could exchange the vehicle and its wares for horses, and they could head for the coast at once.

An instinctive itch between his shoulder blades kept telling him to put as much distance as possible between them and the danger posed by Paris. Philippe, intelligent child that he was, would doubtless have told his nursemaid about the 'orange lady's' return. It wouldn't take any great leap of imagination for that woman and the footman who'd guarded the child in the park to connect the sudden arrival of a tinker and his wife to the man and woman who'd accosted Philippe in the Place Royale. After viewing the sumptuous, well-tended Hôtel, he didn't need Elodie's warning to realise the comtesse had powerful connections who wouldn't hesitate to set the authorities after anyone who threatened her child, an annoyance Will would rather not deal with.

But Elodie looked so limp and exhausted, her face and body drained of the fire and energy that normally animated them, Will wasn't sure she could stand a gallop to the coast now. Perhaps he should settle for obtaining horses and getting them to an inn north of Paris, and start the journey in earnest tomorrow.

Remaining within easy return distance of the city would probably be prudent in any event. Though at the moment Elodie seemed to have lost all the purpose and determination that had driven her to survive St

Arnaud's brutality, evade pursuers on the road—and elude *him*—in order to find her son, that might change, once she'd had a chance to rest her exhausted body and spirits. No point getting her halfway to England aboard some smuggling vessel and having her decide she must return to Paris and try again.

He knew only too well the agony of thinking you'd lost the one person you loved most in the world. But unlike a mother claimed by death, Elodie's son was very much alive. Though he understood that love made her put her son's best interests over her own desires, everything within him protested the unfairness of forcing her to make such a sacrifice.

He ached to ease her pain by urging that they return to reclaim her son, but at the moment, he had no reasonable answers to the objections she'd raised to simply stealing him away. By dint of skilful gaming and even more skilful investing, he was no longer the penniless orphan who, at Eton, had taunted the boys into gaming with him to earn a few pence to buy meat pies. But the property and modest wealth he'd thus far accumulated was no match for the resources of a comtesse, even if he could persuade Elodie to accept some.

As for influence, his only elevated connection was his uncle. Not only was the earl highly unlikely to embrace any cause supported by his black-sheep illegitimate nephew, he might well forfeit even the loyalty of his Ransleigh Rogue cousins if, after pledging to restore Max's reputation, he appeared instead to champion the woman who'd ruined it.

He wouldn't suggest they do anything, raise her hopes to no purpose, until he could consider the matter more carefully and come up with a better plan.

An inn north of Paris it must be, Will decided.

After a quick exchange of cart and contents for horses, Will had got a listless Elodie mounted. For the rest of the day, they had ridden north at a pace he thought easy enough for her to tolerate. Just before dark, they stopped at a village along the coaching road, where Will located a suitable establishment and engaged a room.

For the whole of their journey there, Elodie had neither looked directly at him nor spoken, seemingly lost in an abyss of despair and fatigue too profound for anything to penetrate.

Gently he led her to the room and helped her to the bed. 'Sleep. I'm going to arrange our horses for tomorrow and get some food. I'll be back with your dinner very soon. Men's clothing, too, perhaps, for this last leg of our journey?'

But even that mild jest produced no response. Sighing, Will stripped her down to her chemise and guided her back against the pillows. She was still staring blankly into space when he closed the door.

Darkness had fallen by the time he returned. As he quietly lit a candle, he noted Elodie dozing in the same position in which he'd left her, head thrown back against the pillows like a broken doll, her face pale and her hands limp beside her.

Will considered setting out food and wine and leaving her in solitude with her grief. The last thing he wanted was to witness her pain and be dragged into remembering the anguish of his own youth. Yet, aching for her, he realised he couldn't leave her so alone and vulnerable, even if it meant fending off memories he had no wish to revisit.

Dragging a chair beside the bed, Will settled himself to watch over her.

Suddenly, she shuddered and cried out. 'Hush, sweeting,' he soothed, gathering her in his arms.

Her every muscle tensing, she jerked away before her eyes opened and her hazy gaze fixed on his face. 'Will,' she murmured. Going limp again in his arms, she slumped back.

He plumped up the pillows and eased her up to a sitting position. 'I've brought food and drink,' he said, going over to fetch the supplies from his saddlebag. 'You must eat. It's after dark and you've had nothing but a little wine since before dawn.'

She didn't reply, but when he put the cup to her lips she sipped. After asking how she felt and what she wanted—and receiving no answers—he lapsed into silently feeding her bits of cheese and bread, which she ate mechanically, without seeming aware of him or the nourishment she was consuming.

When she would take no more, Will finished the wine and bread. As he was returning the remaining meat and cheese to the saddlebags, Elodie wrapped her arms around her torso and began rocking back and forth.

Tears welled up in her eyes and, a few moments later, she was weeping in earnest. Tossing down the saddlebags, Will climbed into the bed, gathered her into his arms and held her as deep, racking sobs shuddered through her body.

He cradled her against his chest as she wept out her grief, wishing there was some way he could ease that terrible burden. Finally the sobs grew shallower, slowed, stopped, then she fell asleep in his arms.

He must have dozed, too, for when he woke some time later, the candle had burned out. Too weary himself to light another, he slid far enough away from Elodie to divest himself of his clothing, then rolled back into the bed's inviting warmth.

Gathering her against him, he found her lips in the darkness and kissed her tenderly. 'Sleep, my darling. We've a long journey tomorrow.'

To his surprise, she reached up, pulled his head down and kissed him back.

This was no gentle caress, but a demanding capture of lips, followed by a sweep of her tongue into his mouth that banished grogginess and instantly turned simmering desire into boiling need.

While her tongue probed and demanded, her hands moved up and down his hardness. Still caressing him with one hand, she urged him on to his back and, breaking the kiss, in one swift motion raised her chemise and straddled him, guiding his swollen member to her soft inviting heat.

'Love me, Will,' her urgent voice pleaded in the darkness.

This was anguish seeking the oblivion of pleasure, he knew. But if pleasuring her would keep the pain at bay, he was happy to assist. Grasping her bottom, he thrust hard, sheathing himself in tight, seductive heat.

He would have stilled then, slowed, made it last, but Elodie was having none of it.

Pulling his thumbs to her nipples, she angled her hips and moved to take him deeper still. With him buried within her, she thrust again and again, riding him faster, harder, deeper, her nails scoring his shoulders, her teeth nipping his skin, until she cried out as her pleasure crested.

An instant later, he reached his own release. Wrapping her in his arms, still joined, Will rolled with her to his side and snuggled her there as together, sated, they fell into the boneless sleep of exhaustion.

Chapter Sixteen

William woke just after dawn the following morning. At the feel of Elodie beside him, her head nestled on his shoulder, a glow of joy and well-being suffused him. The warmth lingered even after his groggy brain, lagging behind his senses, grew alert enough to remember how despondent and grief-stricken she'd been the previous night.

She'd also come alive in his arms, allowing him to sweep her away for a time from the anguish and sorrow. That had to count for something.

As long as her son was alive and well, there was hope. If whoever had been watching Elodie wanted to harm the boy, they could have done so long since, so there was every reason to expect he would continue to be healthy and content, living with the comtesse. Eventually, Will would figure out a way to reclaim him that would place no hardship on the boy. For now, he must get Elodie, who might still be in danger, safely back to England.

She stirred and he kissed her lips, his joy multiplying when she murmured and wrapped her arms around his neck to kiss him back. Desire surged as she fit herself against him and, for a time, the problems awaiting them outside their bedchamber receded as he made love to her, long and sweet and slow.

Eventually, they could avoid them no longer. 'You wanted to leave early for the coast?' Elodie said, sitting up. 'It's long past dawn now. I'd better dress.'

'You're sure you don't want to return to Paris and try again to take your son?'

Her jaw clenched and she closed her eyes briefly, as if reeling from a blow. 'He doesn't even recognise me, Will,' she said softly when she reopened them. 'Even if he did—what was I thinking? I have a few paltry jewels I could sell, enough, perhaps, to buy a small cottage somewhere in the country. But beyond that, I have no money, no family, no resources. Nothing to fall back on, nothing put away to pay for schooling or to assure his future. If Maurice were still alive…but he's not, and there's no one else. Besides, who's to say what will happen after we get to England? How could I drag him into that? No, we should just leave today, as you wished.'

Much as it pained him to see the bleak look back in her eyes, empty platitudes wouldn't comfort her. Until he formulated some intelligent plan that offered real hope, it was better to say nothing.

Apparently taking silence for agreement, she slipped from the bed and picked up her scattered garments. 'So

I travel as a woman this time? Or have you yet another disguise in that bag?'

Trying not to be distracted by the arousing vista of Elodie, naked but for the bundle of clothing she held, he forced himself to concentrate on the imperative of getting them quickly to the Channel and on to England, before Talleyrand or whoever else had been following them discovered their current location. Realising now what her objective in Paris had been, any French agent worth his pay must know her story and would have kept the comtesse's house under surveillance. So their pursuers must know they'd made it back to Paris.

'I'm afraid the bag of tricks is rather empty and the funds are running low. We'll travel as we are for now and, as you suggest, go at once.'

Giving him a wan smile—so pale an imitation of the brilliant ones that had warmed his heart during their journey that his chest ached—she dressed quickly. He did the same, then assembled their bags and walked down to pay the landlord. After retrieving their newly hired horses from the stables, with Elodie waiting listlessly beside him, Will fastened their bags on to the saddles.

At first, he paid little attention to the private coach that was progressing slowly down the street, the roadway already filling with the usual early-morning assortment of farmers, maids, vendors, clerks and townspeople going about their business. Until, its driver apparently distracted by an altercation between two tradesmen whose carts had collided, the vehicle began heading almost directly at them.

Will had been about to shout a warning to the driver, when the coach inexplicably began to pick up speed. Preoccupied with controlling their now shying, stamping mounts, he was trying to shift both sets of reins into one hand and pull Elodie back out of harm's way with the other as the coach swayed by them, dangerously close.

Suddenly, the door opened, a man leaned out and grabbed Elodie by the arms. Before Will could finish transferring the reins, the assailant dragged Elodie into the vehicle. Will caught one last glimpse of her struggling figure before the door slammed shut and the driver sprang the horses, scattering people, poultry and produce in its wake.

An hour later, the bruiser who'd muscled Elodie into the closed carriage and bound and gagged her, dragged her from the coach and up the back stairs of an inn. After shoving her into a room, he closed the door behind her. Her anxious ears were relieved to hear no key turn in the lock before his footsteps retreated.

Since the henchman who'd grabbed her had said nothing the entire journey, she still had no idea who had abducted her or why.

Furiously she worked at the bonds, desperate to escape before anyone else arrived to manhandle her. After a few moments, she succeeded in freeing her hands. She'd just ripped off the gag when, her eyes finally ad-

justing to the dimness of the shuttered room, she realised she was not alone.

Her skin prickled and the sour taste of fear filled her
mouth as she recognised the shadowed figure seated at
the table of what appeared to be a private parlour. 'St
Arnaud!' she gasped.

'Indeed,' he said, giving her a nod. 'You appear to
be as delighted to see me as I was to discover you'd apparently come back from the dead. I must admit, I was
quite distressed when Prince Talleyrand informed me
you'd been sighted in Paris. He advised me to take better care of you this time.'

Fury and loathing coursed through her, swamping
the fear. 'You *took care* of me before. You took my son!'

He shook his head. 'Very maladroit of you to be
manoeuvred into it. A bit of money, some promises of
advancement dangled before you, and it was done. So
distastefully predictable. Ah, well, your foolishness has
made my dear sister very happy.'

Never in her life had Elodie truly wished to harm
someone, but at that moment, she would have bar-
tered her soul for a weapon. She wanted to pummel St
Arnaud, carve the sardonic smile off his face, make him
scream with pain. Not for the beatings he'd inflicted on
her in Vienna, but for the blow to the heart from which
she'd never recover.

'Bastard,' she spat out, her eyes scanning the room
for anything she might use against him.

'Not me, my dear! That epithet belongs to the hovel-
born Englishman who's been attempting to assist you.

And don't bother to agitate yourself searching; I'm not foolish enough to leave lying about anything you might use to defend yourself. Now, how shall we dispose of you this time? Something quick and merciful?'

'You mean to do it yourself? You haven't the stomach.'

His gaze hardened. 'You think not?'

'You let others do the difficult work before. What happened to the poor wretch who pulled the trigger on Lord Wellington?'

St Arnaud lifted an elegant brow. 'He was hanged, I suppose. Only what he deserved for being sloppy and inaccurate. Anyway, he was just a means to an end.'

'Like me.'

'Like you. Although unlike Franz, whom the Austrian authorities took care of long ago, you're much more trouble, turning up again after all this time.'

'Then let me relieve you of her,' said a voice from the doorway.

'Will!' Elodie cried, her fear and anger swamped in a surge of surprise, relief and gladness.

St Arnaud's eyes widened with alarm for an instant before he smoothed his features back to a sardonic calm. 'Ah, the bastard appears.'

'Surely you were expecting me. A horse can easily keep pace with a carriage and, with the driver on the box and only one flunky within, there was no one to prevent my following. It's about time you had to deal with someone more up to your weight. And after I do, we'll go.'

'You think I'll just let her leave with you?' St Arnaud laughed. 'How quaint, that you survived soldiering and a childhood in Seven Dials with such naïve notions intact. I would have thought you'd expect me to go for the kill.'

'She's no threat to you.'

'Is she not? What about the testimony you want her to give in London? Dredging up that old scandal could cause a great deal of unpleasantness, just as I'm re-establishing my career.'

'Re-establishing?' Will echoed. 'There's a king on France's throne now. What of your love for Napoleon?'

St Arnaud shrugged. 'He'll never escape from that speck of rock in the Atlantic. I don't deny I regret that France has been saddled with fat old King Louis, but one must adapt to changing circumstances, as Prince Talleyrand always says. I'm a St Arnaud; I belong at the centre of France's political affairs. Now, *monsieur*, I don't know how you convinced Raoul to let you in, but I've no quarrel with you. Leave now and I'll not call the gendarmes and have you thrown in jail.'

'Magnanimous of you,' Will said, showing his teeth.

'Quite. I doubt your uncle would bestir himself on behalf of the bastard branch of family and French prisons are so unpleasant.'

'At least I earned that title by birth. Being a bastard, though, don't you think I would have taken care of such small details as a few retainers? As you said, I was breeched in Seven Dials. It's not wise to leave loose knives lying about that might get thrown at your back.'

Had he really eliminated St Arnaud's henchmen, or was he bluffing? Elodie wondered, shooting him a glance. He gave her a wink.

After weeks on the road from Vienna, witnessing all his skill and ingenuity, she'd bet on Will against odds much higher than these.

St Arnaud wasn't sure, either. His arrogant confidence wavering a bit, he stepped towards the door.

Will stationed himself in front of it, his gaze challenging. 'Let her leave with me now and I might consider letting you live.' He moved his hand so quickly even Elodie didn't follow it and extracted a knife from his pocket.

Making no attempt now to disguise his alarm, St Arnaud reached into his own pocket, uttering an oath when he found it empty.

'Didn't bring a weapon with you? How careless!' Will taunted. 'But then, against a slip of a woman, I suppose you thought your fists would be sufficient.' His eyes narrowing to slits, his expression so murderous the hair raised on the back of Elodie's neck just watching him, Will stepped towards St Arnaud.

Swallowing hard, St Arnaud retreated behind the table. 'Raoul!' he called. 'Etienne! *Venez immediatement!*'

Will laughed and took a step closer. 'Bellow all you want. Your watchdogs are "taking a nap" and the landlord's gone deaf. I outbid you, you see.'

Looking around wildly, St Arnaud fixed his gaze on Elodie. 'Do you really want to go with him? Hanging's an ugly death. I'm sure we can settle our little misunderstanding after all.'

'She knows better than to trust a miscreant like you. Elodie, step behind me, please.' He gave her a quick, pleading glance, as if he weren't sure she would choose him over St Arnaud.

How could he have any doubt? Swiftly she crossed the room. He gave her arm a reassuring squeeze as she passed him, then tucked her behind him. 'His men are tied up, unconscious,' he murmured in an undertone. 'Our horses are at the back. As soon as I deal with this abomination, we'll go.'

Twirling the knife between his fingers, Will looked back at St Arnaud and sighed. 'This is awkward, isn't it? Whatever am I to do with you now? Should I upset my uncle by committing murder? Ah, well, he's upset with me most of the time anyway.' He stepped purposefully closer to St Arnaud.

As he advanced, St Arnaud put his hands out in front of him. 'I'll pay whatever you want! Talleyrand told me the earl never settled on you the sum he promised. I can have a handsome amount transferred to any bank you like.'

'Can you?' Will halted, as if he were considering the offer. Before St Arnaud, looking relieved, could say another word, Will extracted a pistol from his pocket. 'Perhaps I should make it look like you shot yourself instead? Crazed by worry that the old scandal might compromise your new position? I'm sure Elodie could write quite a convincing suicide note.'

'No, please!' St Arnaud wailed. '*Monsieur*, reconsider! What benefit to you if I die? Let me live and I can—'

'Silence, vermin,' Will spat out. 'I've never met a man more deserving of murder, but I'd not soil my blade. However, I might just work the itchiness out of my fists by beating you into the carpet…like you beat her in Vienna.'

'Will, if you're not going to kill him, don't beat him,' Elodie urged, unsure she didn't prefer murder as an option. 'He might hurt my son. He couldn't best you, but he could handle a little boy.'

'Ah, yes, your son.' Will frowned. 'That does present a dilemma. If I let him live, what assurance do we have that he won't harm the boy after we've gone?'

'Of course I wouldn't harm him!' St Arnaud cried with a show of indignation. 'My sister has claimed him as her own, which makes him nearly a St Arnaud. Prince Talleyrand himself dotes upon the boy.'

'I don't know,' Will said, twirling the blade again. 'It would be simpler to gut you and be done with it.'

Elodie didn't know what to think. Much as she detested St Arnaud, she wasn't sure she could live with her conscience if she allowed Will to murder him. Which she was nearly certain Will would do, coolly, cleanly and efficiently, if she told him to.

She didn't trust St Arnaud one bit, but she'd seen for herself that Philippe was treated as the comtesse's beloved son, and she knew St Arnaud was inordinately proud of family and position. Nor would he be foolish enough to cross a man as powerful as Prince Talley-rand, whom he must have already had to appease after the débâcle in Vienna.

'*Madame*, I swear to you, the boy will come to no harm!' St Arnaud cried, recalling her attention.

Will glanced back at her. 'Elodie?'

While Elodie hesitated, agonised, there was a knock at the door, followed by the entrance of a tall, imperious figure.

He halted inside and surveyed the scene, seeming neither surprised nor perturbed to have come upon a woman clinging to the back of a man who was threatening a second man with a knife. 'Madame Lefevre,' he said, bowing to her. 'And you must be Monsieur Ransleigh.'

Glancing at the knife, he wrinkled his nose in distaste. 'Please, *monsieur*, there is no need for such vulgarities. Allow me to introduce myself. Antoine de Montreuil, Comte de Merlonville, assistant to the Duc de Richelieu, who succeeded Prince Talleyrand last autumn as Prime Minister of France.'

Turning his gaze to St Arnaud, he sighed. 'Thierry, must you ever be rash, acting without thinking? When the Prince learned you had rushed off to…detain this lady, he informed Monsieur le Duc at once, telling him he'd made it quite clear to you that you were to speed her on her way.'

'Speed her on—' St Arnaud echoed. 'He told me to "take care of her"!'

'Precisely. However, though the Prince, ah, advises,

it is the Duc who makes policy now. Only your family name and lineage persuaded Talleyrand to retain you after the Vienna fiasco. Monsieur Ransleigh has sought *madame*'s assistance to deal with a matter that is of personal interest solely to his family, and perhaps the British Foreign Office. His Highness the King does not need to be troubled about it, so I suggest that you cease obstructing their progress immediately…or I must warn you, the Duc is likely to be much less forgiving than the Prince.'

Turning from St Arnaud in clear dismissal, de Merlonville addressed Elodie and Will. '*Monsieur* and *madame*, I am so sorry you were inconvenienced. The Duc would be happy to offer you an escort to the coast, to ensure no other…recalcitrants trouble you.'

After studying the Duc's self-professed assistant warily for a moment, Will shook his head. 'Thank you, but I don't think that will be necessary.'

'What of the child?' Elodie cried, needing to be sure about this.

'Child?' de Merlonville repeated.

'Philippe. Philippe…de la Rocherie.'

'What has the Prince Talleyrand's godson have to do with this?' the official asked.

'Philippe is Prince Talleyrand's godson?' Will interjected.

'Well, not officially. But the comtesse's late husband being a close associate of the Prince for many years, he watches over the widow.'

'I see.' Her relief that the comtesse did, in fact, have

a powerful protector who would ensure her son's safety faded rapidly when she realised the full implications of the association.

In her wildest imagining, she might envision some day acquiring a settled home and enough coin to challenge the comtesse's control over her son. But never in any imagining could she hope to find Philippe a sponsor who had the wealth, power and influence of Prince Talleyrand, who'd been at the highest level of France's political life through three successive governments.

Will seemed to sense her dismay, for, after stowing his knife and pistol, he reached over to take her hand. 'Are you ready to leave?'

There seemed nothing further to do or say. 'I suppose so.'

Looking to de Merlonville, Will gestured towards St Arnaud. 'If we might have a moment?'

'Only if you'll promise me not to carve him up once my back is turned. So distressing to the innkeeper and so damaging to the carpet, all that blood.'

'I give you my word.'

De Merlonville nodded. 'Monsieur Ransleigh, you will convey my kind regards to your uncle, the earl? I had occasion to meet him and some other leaders of Parliament when I visited London for the Duc last fall. And, Thierry, I trust you now understand your position? The post to the Caribbean for which the Prince recommended you has not been confirmed…yet. I'm certain you would not wish to compromise your political future by delaying these good people any further.'

'Of—of course not, my dear Comte.'

'Then I suggest you gather up your effects and make ready to return to Paris, while they continue on their way.'

Nodding quickly, St Arnaud pivoted to collect his coat and a snuffbox and some other items strewn about the table. While his back was turned, the comte murmured to them, 'A lovely island, St Lucia. But an area rife with tropical fevers, not to mention the danger of pirates. Many venture there and so few return.'

He gave them a wink, then bowed himself out of the room.

After he departed, Will turned to St Arnaud. Having retrieved his personal items and shrugged on his greatcoat, he was careful to keep the table between himself and Will, while his still-florid face gave evidence of his fury and chagrin.

'Well, vermin, it appears that you'll get to live after all. Though I don't count *your* assurances about the boy worth a ha'penny, I do respect the Prince…and his plans. Still, I want you to know I'll be watching. You'd better pray that Madame Lefevre's son lives a healthy, happy, prosperous life. If I learn he's suffered so much as a sniffle, I'll track you down and snuff out your miserable life.'

Taking Elodie's arm, Will said, 'I believe there's a packet at the coast awaiting us in Calais.'

Chapter Seventeen

Though Will and Elodie had politely declined de Merlonville's offer of an escort, even in her state of diminished awareness, Elodie sensed a subtle presence trailing them during the long days of riding towards the Channel. It wasn't until after dark of the fourth day, when Will hustled her from the room he'd engaged at a Calais inn down narrow back stairs to a pair of waiting horses and rode off with her into the night that she realised he, too, had noted—and mistrusted—whatever force was following them.

Silently he led her horse along narrow back lanes, with only the stars and the distant lights of Calais to guide them, until they reached a small port some miles further south down the coast. Will finally brought them to a halt before a mean-looking inn which boasted only one smoky lantern by its entrance to announce its calling.

Warning her in a low voice to remain outside, he disappeared into the structure. A few moments later, he returned to lead their horses to a lean-to barn at the rear and then escort her up the back stairs to a low-ceilinged room under the eaves whose tiny window overlooked the road and the harbour beyond.

'Sorry to drag you out of your comfortable accommodations for something I fear will be much inferior,' he said as he waved her to the table by the window. 'Not that I don't appreciate the good wishes of the Prime Minister's own man. But I'd rather return to England on transport of my own choosing—and hopefully without the Duc or the Prince's knowledge.'

'On a smuggling vessel? This certainly looks disreputable enough to be a smuggler's inn. You have the most interesting contacts, Monsieur Ransleigh.'

His eyes lit at the gentle barb in her response. 'Are you feeling better?' he asked, pulling a flask of wine from his saddlebags and pouring them a cup.

Better? she asked herself, accepting the mug. She'd gone from agony to numbness, like a recent amputee after the opium took hold. Other than that, she felt… empty, barren as a seashell-dotted beach after a storm had swept it of its treasures, scouring it down to elemental sand.

'I'm feeling…here, I suppose.'

'That's progress. You've been gone quite a while.'

It occurred to her that Will had been unusually taciturn for the whole of their journey north from Paris, trotting steadily beside her with minimal chat, stopping to share bread, cheese and wine at midday without attempting to regale her with any of his stories, settling them in an inn long after dark with only a brief caress before they both fell into the sleep of exhaustion.

Not surprising. In the paralysed state in which she'd existed since emerging from the first shock of leaving Philippe, she'd probably been oblivious to any conversational attempts he might have made. The awful reality of losing her son again had been like staring into the sun, the terrible brilliance blinding her to everyone and everything else around her.

Aside from the vivid encounter with St Arnaud north of Paris, she scarcely remembered anything about the days between walking out of Philippe's bedchamber at the Hôtel de la Rocherie and arriving at the coast tonight. Trying to piece events together now, she could come up with only snippets of memory.

Will, walking beside her across Paris. Settling her into a bed. Feeding her with his own hands. Cradling her against his warmth while grief smashed her like a china doll into shards of misery. And when the anguish had been past bearing, helping her escape into the oblivion of passion.

No friend, companion or lover could have treated her with more gentleness and compassion. A tiny flicker of warmth—affection, gratitude—lit the bleakness within.

'Thank you, sweet Will,' she murmured.

'For rescuing you from St Arnaud? That was my pleasure, though I would have preferred to have beaten him into pudding, if I was not to be allowed to gut him.'

'Would you have gutted him?'

He paused. 'I don't know. Would you have wanted me to?'

'Yes. No. Oh, *je sais pas*! How can I know, when it would make no difference? Killing him wouldn't get Philippe back.'

'It would have guaranteed Philippe could never fall under his power. Although it does seem both Talleyrand and the Prime Minister have united to send him far away, far enough that your son will be safe—and they will be freed from his scheming. Apparently they've also given us their blessing, or so it seems. What do you make of de Merlonville's appearance?'

Like an old iron wheel gone rusty from disuse, she had to scrape away a clogging coat of apathy to focus her mind on the question.

'Talleyrand has been replaced. I didn't know that.'

'Nor did I, but it seems he retains a good deal of influence.'

Thinking more swiftly now, she ran back through her memory the whole exchange between St Arnaud and de Merlonville in the upstairs parlour. 'De Merlonville said Prince Talleyrand had informed the Duc about St Arnaud snatching me, so he must still have agents trailing us…but apparently the Duc now controls who takes action. St Arnaud is tolerated, but just barely. With his thirst for power, I expect St Arnaud will be very careful not to make any further moves against us—or Philippe—without the Duc's approval.'

'In any event, it appears he will soon be leaving France—permanently, de Merlonville seemed to suggest,' Will said. 'The comte also seemed to want to make clear that the French government had no interest in any testimony you might give.'

She nodded. 'Which seems logical—with the king's throne secure, no one would wish to remind Louis of the unhappy past by bringing to his notice a long-failed Napoleonic plot.'

'That matches what George Armitage told us outside Linz—neither the French nor British governments want to dredge up the old scandal now. Which would leave those de Merlonville called "recalcitrants" as the most likely group looking to harass us.'

'Yes, St Arnaud and any of his remaining associates trying to claw their way back into government would be keen to make sure no embarrassing evidence of their former Bonapartist leanings came to light,' Elodie summed up. '*Eh bien*, de Merlonville was instructed to provide us an escort to prevent them from harrying us.'

'Perhaps. Unless de Merlonville's offer was intended to put us off our guard and we are still in danger from Talleyrand's forces, too. Although, since they could have apprehended us any time during our travel north, that seems unlikely, I prefer to remain wary. Hence, this draughty inn.'

'A precaution of the wisest sort.'

'I hope you continue to think so after you've slept in bedclothes clammy from its dripping eaves.'

She tilted her head at him. 'You have slept under its dripping eaves before, perhaps?'

Will grinned at her. 'Never underestimate the contacts of a former thief, cut-purse and salesman of illegal goods.'

'You were involved in smuggling, too?'

'Smugglers make landfall all along the coast, then use a network of agents to move the goods inland. The boss for whom I worked used to have us distribute lace, silk and brandy that had never had duty paid on it to eager, if clandestine, clients. A profitable business, as long as the revenue agents didn't catch you.'

'You *have* led an adventurous life.'

'No more so than you. *Émigrée* creeping from Nantes in the dead of night, returnee to the "New France", soldier's bride, grieving widow disguised as a wounded soldier passing through the detritus of two armies, Vienna hostess, seamstress in hiding, old man, valet, monk, farm girl, orange seller…' Will ticked them off on his fingers.

She'd been smiling at his list until the last disguise reminded her of Paris and the final resolution of her quest. 'Then back to Elodie again,' she said quietly. 'Without home, without family, without my son.' Her voice breaking on the last word, she slumped back in the chair, despair and weariness suddenly overtaking her.

She felt Will's hand cover her own. 'At least you need no longer worry about St Arnaud's interference.'

'Perhaps not,' she replied with a sigh, looking over at him. 'Praise God, my son is safe. But he is still lost to me.'

'Where there is life, there is hope, so—'

She put her hand to his lips, stopping his words. 'Please, Will, no more schemes!' she cried. 'I can't bear it.'

He must have realised how close she still walked to the precipice of falling apart completely, for when she removed her finger, he let the topic drop. Silently he took her hand again, stroking it, his sympathetic gaze on her face.

'I wish I could help. I know how much you've lost.'

Though her rational mind appreciated his attempt at empathy, the wounded animal in her turned on him.

'You *know*?' she spat back. 'How could you? *Je te jure*, you have no idea what I feel!'

'Swear if you like, but I do. I held my mother's hand and watched her die. I was five years old.'

The expression on Will's face struck her to silence, her anger withering in its wake. No wonder he'd never wanted to talk about his childhood.

Five years old—almost the same age as Philippe! And she had thought stealing her son from his home a trial too great for any child to bear.

Compassion—tinged with shame—filled her.

'I'm so sorry,' she whispered.

'She was the only being in the world who'd ever cared for me or tried to protect me,' he said softly, staring beyond her, seemingly unaware of her presence. The anguish in his eyes said he was reliving the experience. 'Though I was always hungry and ragged, even at that age, I knew she was doing the best she could for me.'

Elodie hesitated, unsure what to say that might bring him back from the emotional abyss into which he'd tumbled. Then he shook his head, as if throwing off the memories, and turned to her with an apologetic smile. 'I told you the tale wasn't edifying.'

'How did you survive?'

'I already knew the street boys, though Mama had tried to keep me from running with them. They found me at the market, going through rubbish piles with another, smaller boy, looking for the bits thrown away by the vendors as too tough or rotten to sell. When two of them tried to take away what the younger lad had gleaned, I fought them off. Their leader, an older boy, stopped us. He probably could have finished me with one fist, but instead, he ordered them to leave me alone. Said he liked my spirit and they could use another fighter. So they took me in, taught me the ways of the street.'

'How to thieve?'

He nodded. 'Thieving, house-breaking, lock-picking, card-sharking, knife-fighting. Sleight-of-hand and how to do a few magic tricks to beguile the gullible while a mate picked their pockets. The real trick was to become skilled enough to win without using a weighted deck or marked cards.'

'It must have been quite a change, when the earl brought you to Swynford Court.'

Will laughed, a rueful smile on his lips. 'By then, I was in line to become a street leader for the boss, and resisted mightily being dragged into the country by the brother of the toff who had abandoned my mother. Nor was I interested in exchanging my mates for three dandified cousins. Alastair and Dom were as unimpressed by me as I was by them. But Max…for Max, it was different. I was a Ransleigh by blood and that was that: whatever it took, he would turn me into one.'

'What did it take?' she asked, curious. 'I don't imagine you would have made the task easy.'

'I did not. After beating some respect into me, he used a bit of everything—coaxing, challenging, empathising, daring, rewarding. By the end of the summer, much to the chagrin of Alastair and Dom, who had bet him the transformation couldn't be done, he'd instilled in me a sufficient modicum of gentlemanly behaviour that the earl agreed not to return me to Seven Dials.'

Elodie thought about the dangers of a child's existence on the streets and shuddered. '*Grace à Dieu* he didn't send you back!'

'I thank God, too. Max saved my life, plain and simple. But passing muster with the earl was just the first step. In many ways, Eton and Oxford were more difficult, not a single test but a limitless series of them. It was Max who taught me there would never be an end to bullies wanting to pummel me, or better-born snobs trying to shame me, and it was smarter to outwit and outmanoeuvre them rather than fight. A born diplomat, even as a boy, he knew I was too proud to take money from him. Though the earl paid my school fees, I had no allowance; it was Max and my cousins who lured the other boys into playing cards or dice with me, or betting on my magic tricks. I'd always win enough for a meat pasty at Eton, or steak and a pint of ale at Oxford.'

'So that's where you perfected your beguiling ped-lar's tricks.'

He cupped her chin in his hands and tilted her face until she met the intensity of his gaze. 'So you understand why I'm so loyal to Max and my cousins? Why the bond between us is as strong as the one between a mother and her son?'

He wanted her to realise why, despite all they had shared, he was still willing to sacrifice her to redeem his cousin. Though she'd thought by now she was incapable of feeling anything, a sharp, anguished pang stabbed in her gut.

'Seeing all you've done since Vienna, I already understood. I respect Monsieur Max, too. He was kind to me, even tried to protect me as best he could from St Arnaud's abuse. Nothing but the imperative to get my son back would have forced me into tricking one of the very few true gentlemen I've ever met. A gentleman who offered to assist me, not to further some scheme of his own, but out of genuine concern.'

As everything else, that story led back to her loss. Recalling it like a knife slash across her heart, she said, 'Ah, *mon Dieu*, it's even worse, knowing I entrapped him and lost my son anyway. At least now I can attempt to make amends by fulfilling our bargain. I will testify to whatever you wish to vindicate your cousin and clear his reputation.'

Will hesitated. 'That might not be such a good idea.'

'Not a good idea?' she echoed, confused. 'Haven't

you just spent the last few weeks dragging me across Europe to do just that?'

'True, but your testimony might have…severe consequences if, instead of viewing this as a personal matter concerning only Max's reputation, the Foreign Office decided to open an official enquiry. The penalty for being judged an accomplice in an attempt to murder the allied commander…' His words trailed off.

Would be a long sojourn in prison, or death, she knew. 'That outcome is always a possibility, although both de Merlonville and Armitage said neither government wants a formal investigation. But if they should, it would be as you told me in Vienna: a life for a life. Not so bad a bargain. Monsieur Max would become a great man, who could do much good. I could do this one thing and then I…I am of no more good to anyone anyway.'

For a long moment he held her gaze. 'You're good for me,' Will whispered.

The tenderness of it made her already-decimated heart ache. 'Sweet Will,' she said, attempting a smile. Their strong mutual attraction didn't change the melancholy facts. The unique, incomparable interlude of their journey from Vienna, wary co-conspirators who'd become mutual admirers, then friends, and then the most passionate of lovers, was almost over.

The silly, battered heart she'd thought was beyond feeling anything contracted in a spasm of grief that she must lose Will, too. She stifled its instinctive demand that she find some way to extend their time together.

But the English coast loomed just beyond a narrow

stretch of restless sea and she'd never been one to deny reality. It was time to see the bargain she'd made to its conclusion.

Gently pushing Will's hands away, she took the last sip from her mug. 'I imagine you've conjured a vessel and some good sailing weather for tomorrow. We should rest now, if we're to be away early in the morning.'

Looking troubled, Will opened his lips as if to speak. Elodie stopped him with a hand to his lips. 'There's no more to say. Rest easy, Will. *C'est presque fini.* Your quest is almost done.'

Putting aside her mug, Elodie swiftly disrobed down to her chemise and climbed into the uneven bed, settling back on the pillows with a sigh. In the hollow emptiness within, lit only by the warmth of tenderness for Will, the decision to testify, come what may, sat well.

She wasn't sure when she'd made it. Some time during the long silent hours of moving north from Paris, probably, as the reality of life without Philippe settled into her shredded heart. She could repay the debt she owed Max Ransleigh, even the balance between. Like a person suddenly blinded, she could see no future beyond sitting before a green baize table in a Foreign Office enquiry room.

'May you have a happy, distinguished life, Philippe, *mon ange*,' she whispered, as a rip tide of exhaustion swept her towards sleep.

Bone-weary, Will climbed in bed beside Elodie. During the last of their discussion, he'd wanted to interrupt her, to disagree, to tell her how unique and beautiful she was. But as he hadn't yet worked out a remedy for her stark assessment of her condition— a woman without home, without family, without her son—she would have seen any such speech as pretty, empty words.

He wanted to tell her she meant too much for him to let her become a sacrifice to Max's redemption. But how could he expect her to believe him, when every step he'd taken since arriving in Vienna had been directed towards doing just that?

Unable to voice or reconcile the conflicting claims of loyalty clashing within him, he fell back to the only language that wouldn't fail. Gently he turned her pliant body towards him.

She murmured when he kissed her, then encircled his head with her arms and pulled him closer. He took the kiss deeper, moving his hands to caress her, filling her when she opened to him, showing her with his mouth and hands and body how much he cherished her.

Afterwards, as she dozed in his arms, exhausted and satisfied, Will lay awake, unable to find sleep. Tormented by a dilemma with no satisfactory answer, his mind spun fruitlessly round and round the final points of their discussion, like a roulette wheel before the croupier settles the ball.

For all his early years and then his time in the army, his survival had depended on making the correct, lightning-quick decision. But from the beginning of his doubts in Vienna through betrayal and reconciliation in Paris, he'd put off deciding what the final move in his game with Elodie would be. With arrival in England imminent, he could put it off no longer. And he was still not sure what to do.

He owed Max his life. But, he might as well admit it, Elodie now held his heart.

A vagabond all his life, he'd never thought of settling down on any of the small properties he'd been acquiring the last few years. Never thought of finding a wife or begetting children.

No more than she had he a home to offer her, and his only family were his cousins. The earl would sever their tenuous connection in a heartbeat, and if he were to betray his vow to Max to side with the woman who had ruined his cousin's life, he wouldn't have them, either.

He wished Max lived in the far reaches of Northumberland, so he would have longer to figure out what to do.

He would still willingly give his life to save Max's. But he was no longer willing to let Elodie give hers. Though he'd been dodging around the fact since the attack on her outside Karlsruhe, after almost losing her again to St Arnaud, he finally could no longer avoid admitting the truth. He'd fallen in love with Elodie Lefevre.

He wasn't sure what he'd expected love to be, but it wasn't the hearts-and-flowers, bring-her-jewels-to-woo-her-into-bed sort of fancy he'd imagined. More a gut-deep bond that made the air fresher, the sun brighter, the taste of wine sweeter because she shared it with him. A deep hunger to possess her, to be one with her, to satisfy her, that seemed to increase rather than diminish the longer they were together. A sense that losing her would suck all the joy, excitement and pleasure from life, leaving him like a mechanical doll, gears and levers taking it through the motions of life, but dead and empty inside.

He simply couldn't lose her.

Admitting this didn't make the way ahead any clearer. Though Elodie desired him, she'd given no indication that she felt for him anything deeper than fondness. But whether she returned his affection or not, he now had no intention of bringing her to the Foreign Office to testify. Despite what Armitage and de Merlonville avowed, it was too risky, when her testimony could too easily detour down a path to prison or the gallows.

Instead of leaving Elodie at one of his properties and going first to London to snoop around the Foreign Office and see if he could discover what evidence would be sufficient to clear Max, perhaps they should proceed straight to Max himself. Max, much better attuned to the intricacies of the Foreign Office, would be in a better position to know if there were a means for Elodie to absolve him without her having to testify in person. By means of a sworn deposition, perhaps, which he could have delivered after he'd gotten her safely out of England.

His heart quickened at that solution, then slowed and he frowned. But if Max thought there was no way to clear his name but for Elodie to appear before a tribunal in London, he might press Will to take her there. And Elodie, in her current state, would agree to go.

Perhaps it would be better to sail around the south coast to Falmouth and catch a ship to the Americas... except he didn't have sufficient funds with him for such a trip; he'd need to visit his bankers in London first.

Maybe he should just go to Max, explain to him privately why he was breaking his solemn vow. Max had never been vindictive; even if Will's betrayal meant Max would lose for ever the life that should have been his, he knew Max wouldn't force him to risk the life of the woman Will now realised he loved.

But at the thought of facing the man to whom he owed more than anyone else on earth and admitting he was reneging on his pledge, his gut churned. The earl would say that Will had no honour to lose. But Max had always believed in him.

So, if he was prepared to betray Max, and it seemed that he was, he might as well make a clean break. Travel through Kent without stopping to see Max, go to London, obtain funds and head at once to Cornwall to take ship. He could write to Max later, when Elodie was safe in America, beyond the reach of French or English law.

His heart torn with anguish at the thought of leaving behind the only family he'd known—and losing the respect of the one man whose good opinion he valued more than any other—Will sprang up and paced the small room. After several circuits, as he gazed down again at Elodie's sleeping form, he knew if he must choose between Max and Elodie—between cousins, friendship, family, honour and Elodie—he would choose her.

They would go straight to London, obtain funds and leave for the Americas.

Then, the thought of betrayal bitter in his mouth, it struck him that leaving England immediately would only compound the dishonour. Max had believed in him, counselled him and championed him since they were boys. He couldn't just disappear without facing him. If he was going to break his pledge and for ever doom his cousin's government aspirations, he owed it to Max to tell him face to face.

He'd not add the white feather of cowardice to his disgrace.

Max might try to change his mind, but Will knew, on the bond they shared, that Max would never try to prevent him from leaving, or put Elodie in danger by sending the authorities after them.

So tomorrow they would sail in the smuggler's cutter to the Kentish coast and make their way to Max's farm. He'd confess his intentions to Max, receive his curses or farewells, then take Elodie to the safety of the Americas.

In her present despairing and listless state, Elodie might not agree to go with him. Well, he'd figure out a way to persuade her. She'd probably end up liking it, with new adventures to share and a whole continent to explore, not a town or river or meadow in it tarnished by anguished memories of the past. Maybe they could

end up at the French-speaking colony at Nouvelle Or-
léans. He could contact his friend Hal Waterman, investigate the possibilities of investing in this new land.

Some of the terrible burden lifted from his chest,
leaving lightness and a peace that testified to the right-
ness of the decision. Though the agony of abandoning
Max still hollowed his gut, Will returned to the bed,
took Elodie in his arms and slept at last.

Chapter Eighteen

On a drizzly grey afternoon three days later, mud-spattered and weary, Will and Elodie pulled up their tired mounts before a set of elaborate wrought-iron gates with the image of a running horse in the centre. 'This must be it—Denby Lodge,' Will said, dismounting to knock on the gatehouse door. 'I have to say, I'll be glad of a bath and a good dinner.'

'I still think we should have engaged a room for me at the inn in the last village,' Elodie said. Now that the moment to confront Max Ransleigh had almost arrived, anxiety was filtering through the fog of lethargy that had cocooned her through their Channel crossing—Will having managed to order up fair seas and a swift passage—and the two days of hard riding since. 'I'm sure Monsieur Max will be happy to offer you hospitality. I'm not so sure he'll be willing to offer it to me.'

'You needn't worry,' Will told her as an elderly man trotted from the brick house to unlock the tall gates. 'Max is a diplomat, remember; he'll receive you with such perfect courtesy, you'll never be able to tell what he's really feeling.'

Turning to the gatekeeper, Will asked, 'Is the Lodge straight on?'

'Aye, sir,' the man replied, bowing. 'Follow the drive past the barns and paddocks. The manor will be to your right once the drive rounds the parkland.'

After handing the gatekeeper a coin and acknowledging his thanks, Will ushered Elodie through the entry gates, then remounted and proceeded with her down the gravelled drive.

'The Denby Stud is quite famous,' Will told her as they trotted past lush, fenced meadows. 'Several army comrades purchased their cavalry horses from Sir Martin and swore by their quality. Swift, strong-boned, long on stamina and well mannered.' He laughed. 'Though I can't imagine what Max finds to keep himself busy here, I am curious to meet his wife, Caroline. My cousin Alastair says she's nothing in his usual style. Max always preferred ladies of stunning beauty and alluring charm. A horse breeder is definitely a departure.'

Surprised by Will's sudden loquaciousness, when they had travelled mostly in silence the last few days, Elodie was about to question him when she realised that, so attuned had he become to her, he must have sensed her uneasiness. His commentary was meant to inform her about the farm and the owner she was about to meet—but also to distract her from worrying about Max.

Once again, his thoughtfulness warmed the bleakness within her. How she wished they might have met years ago, when she was young and heart-whole, when she believed the future bright with possibilities.

She would just have to appreciate each moment of the very few she had left with him.

And if he was kind enough to try to cheer her, she could rouse herself to reply. 'It seems a very handsome property.'

'Yes, the fields and fences are in excellent condition. And look, there on the hill!' He pointed off to the left, where a herd of several dozen horses roamed. 'Mares with their foals. Beauties all!' he pronounced after studying them for a moment. 'It seems Max's wife is maintaining her father's high standards.'

After riding steadily for thirty minutes past pastures and occasional lanes leading to thatched cottages in the distance without encountering barns or paddocks, Elodie said, 'The farm seems very large.'

'Larger than I expected,' Will agreed. 'I'm glad I asked directions of the gatekeeper, else I would fear we'd taken a wrong turn. Ah, finally—I see a barn over that rise.'

After passing an impressive series of barns surrounded by paddocks used for training the colts, Will told her, at last the lane entered a wood and turned to the right. As the trees thinned, they saw a fine stone manor house crowning the top of a small hill, flanked by oaks and shrubbery.

Trepidation dried her mouth, while the fluttering in

her stomach intensified. Would Max Ransleigh receive her—or order her off his property?

Then they were at the entry, a servant trotting out to take their horses, a butler ushering them into the front parlour. Trying to be unobtrusive, Elodie stationed herself behind a wing chair set by the hearth, while Will stood by the mantel, toasting his hands at the welcome warmth of a fire.

With Will poised on the threshold of accomplishing all he'd set out to do, she'd expected he would be excited, impatient to see his cousin again, triumphant to be bringing home the means to redress all Max Ransleigh's wrongs. Oddly enough, he seemed as tense as she was, almost...uncomfortable, Elodie thought.

Before she had time to wonder further about it, the door opened and Max Ransleigh walked in, as handsome and commanding as she remembered. 'Will, you rascal!' he said, striding to the hearth and clasping his cousin in a quick, rough embrace. 'Though I ought to spot you a good round of fisticuffs for returning to England and then leaving again without even the courtesy of coming to meet my bride.'

Just as Elodie thought she'd escaped his notice, Max turned to her. 'And Madame Lefevre,' he said, bowing. 'My cousin Alastair told me Will intended to bring you back to England and I see he has succeeded. Welcome to my home.'

Elodie sank into a deep curtsy, studying Max warily beneath her lashes as she rose. If he was angry, he hid it well; his smile seemed genuine and his greeting sincere. A diplomat, indeed—or far more forgiving then she deserved.

'It is of everything most kind of you to receive me, Monsieur Ransleigh. When you would have every right to spit on me and toss me out of your house.'

He surveyed her with that quick, perceptive gaze she remembered so well. 'To be frank, a year ago, I might have. But everything has changed since then.'

'I deeply regret the disservice I did you. Let me assure you, I'm fully prepared to do whatever it takes to make amends.'

'We'll talk of that later,' Will interposed.

'Yes, later,' Max agreed. 'For now, I'm happy to see you without bruises, *madame*. Will must have been taking good care of you.'

For an instant, she recalled the whole amazing, wonderful journey and how well in truth Will *had* cared for her. Suppressing a sudden urge to weep that their time together was over, she said, 'Ah, yes. Most exceptional care.'

'Good.' Suddenly Max's eyes lit and a smile of joy warmed his face. 'Caro, I didn't know you'd come down! Come, my dear, and meet our guests.'

Elodie turned to see a slender woman enter the parlour, her simple green day dress setting off the auburn tints in the dark hair that crowned her head in a coronet of braids. Eyes the bright green of spring moss glowed when she looked at her husband, who walked over to meet her, wrapping an arm around her shoulders. 'Are you feeling strong enough to be up?'

'I'm fine. When Dulcie told me there were riders approaching, I had to come down. Isolated as we are, Denby Lodge doesn't often receive unexpected guests.' Turning towards the hearth, she said, 'But this gentleman needs no introduction. You must be Will! Alastair told me you and Max favour each other strongly.'

'Guilty as charged,' Will said, giving her a smile and a bow. 'Alastair said you were lovely and talented. An understatement on both accounts; we've just had a most enjoyable ride past your fields and some of the handsomest mares and foals I've seen in a long time.'

'Flatterer! You could find no faster way to my heart than to praise my horses.'

'I warned you he was a rogue, my dear,' Max murmured to his wife.

Will moved to Elodie's side, putting a protective hand on her arm. 'Mrs Ransleigh, may I present Madame Elodie Lefevre.'

'You, too, are very welcome,' Caro said, holding out her hand to Elodie, who, after a moment's hesitation, shook it.

'Caro, why don't you show Madame Lefevre up to a room, while Will and I get reacquainted?'

When Will gave his cousin a look and tightened his grip on her hand, Elodie murmured, her voice pitched for his ears alone, 'Don't worry. I'll not try to run away again.'

'It's not that. I feel…better when you're close.'

Watching their interplay with an appreciative smile, Max said, 'You needn't worry to let her go. Caro will take even better care of her than you do. *Madame*, you look exhausted—why don't you rest before dinner? And if you don't mind my saying so, Will, after a quick chat, you could use a bath.'

'Won't you come with me, *madame*?' Caro said. 'After a hard day's riding, there's nothing so soothing as a long soak in a hot tub. I'll have some tea and biscuits sent up, too, to tide you over until dinner. We'll see you later, gentlemen.'

And so Elodie allowed herself to be shepherded out of the room, down the hall and up the stairs to an airy bedchamber that looked out over the expanse of front lawn to the barns in the far distance.

She found herself instinctively liking Caroline Ransleigh, who offered her hand to shake like a man, dressed simply and whose unassuming, straightforward manner spoke of a self-confidence that had no need to impress.

Upon first seeing Max's wife, she'd been surprised, even though Will had told her his cousin said Caroline Ransleigh was not in Max's 'usual style'. She was certainly different from the beautiful, seductive Juliana Von Stenhoff, who'd been Max's mistress at the Congress of Vienna. That lady would never have deigned to greet guests in so simple a gown—nor would she have passed up an opportunity to try to entice a man as handsome as Will.

With that observation, Elodie liked Caroline Ransleigh even better. Though she doubted her hostess would return the favour, once her husband informed her just who she was harbouring under her roof.

Waving her to a seat on the wing chair near the hearth, Caroline Ransleigh turned to direct the footmen who were bringing in a copper tub, while a kitchen maid started a fire. A moment later, a butler appeared to leave a tea tray on the side table and a freckle-faced maid, carrying Elodie's saddlebags, bowed herself in. 'I'll be happy to wash up your things, ma'am,' she said.

'Excellent idea, Dulcie,' Mrs Ransleigh said. 'Having been travelling so long, you probably don't have any clean garments.' She gave Elodie a quick inspection from head to toe. 'You're a bit slighter than I, but we're of a height. You are very welcome to borrow something of mine while your own things are drying.'

A clean gown, one no doubt newer and in better repair than the well-worn few she still possessed! The idea was almost as welcome as a soak in a tub. 'That is most kind of you, Madame Ransleigh, and you, Dulcie.'

The offer confirmed her suspicion that Max's wife, who appeared to be a straightforward woman with no diplomat's artifices, could not know what role she'd played in Max's life, else she'd be much less accommodating. Feeling guiltily that she ought to acquaint her with the facts before the woman did her any more kindnesses, she was wondering just where to begin as her hostess seated herself and poured them each a steaming cup of tea.

'Here, this will help warm you. Such a raw day for midsummer! After riding in the damp, you must be chilled through.'

Murmuring her thanks, Elodie had just taken a reviving sip when a knock sounded and an older woman came in, carrying a wrapped bundle. 'Dulcie said you was in here, Miss Caro, and that you'd want to tend the young master as soon as he woke.'

'Andrew, my love!' Her face lighting, Mrs. Ransleigh reached out to take the bundle—a closely wrapped, newborn child.

Elodie gasped, her teacup sliding from her nerveless fingers to clatter against the saucer, her gaze transfixed on the baby's face.

In a sweeping vortex of memory, she saw in rapid succession bright dark eyes, a pink bow mouth and waving arms as the newborn Philippe surveyed his world. His drunken-sailor, wobbling steps as he determined, at nine months, to walk upright. The restless toddler fixing his intent, curious gaze on every object that caught his attention, asking 'What is it? What it do? Why?'

And then the boy she'd left, that intense gaze focused on the soldiers he meticulously arranged in battle formation.

As if lying in wait to ambush her after she had thought she was safely over the worst, the pain of his loss attacked her with the blunt impact of a footpad's club. She couldn't draw breath, couldn't move, could do nothing but stare at Mrs Ransleigh's beautiful child, the very image of all she had lost.

'What is it, *madame*?' Over the roaring in her ears, Elodie dimly heard Mrs Ransleigh's voice, saw her turn to look at her with concern. 'Are you ill?'

Elodie struggled to pull herself together. 'No, no, I

am fine, really.' Her fingers shook as she picked up her cup again and took a determined sip.

'You have children, *madame*?'

Elodie nodded. 'I have a son. Had…a son,' she corrected, biting her lip against the urge to weep.

Mrs Ransleigh's face creased in concern and she hugged her infant tighter. 'He died? How horrible!'

'No, he is alive. But…living in Paris. Another lady looked after him for some years, while I was away. She is wealthy, from an important family. He is happy with her and she can give him many advantages, so I…left him with her.'

'But you miss him,' Mrs Ransleigh said softly.

'With every breath.' A few traitorous tears forced their way to the corners of her eyes. Determinedly, Elodie wiped them away. 'Your Andrew is a handsome child. How old is he?'

'Three weeks today. A lusty lad. His proud papa is already planning his first pony.'

With a pang, Elodie thought of the traitorous toy horse with the glass eyes. 'He may need to wait a few more weeks for that.'

The magnetic power of the newborn still held her. 'May I?' she asked, extending a hand. At the mother's nod, Elodie reached over to stroke the infant's soft cheek. Immediately he turned his mouth towards her, rooting. She gave him her fingertip to suckle.

'Always hungry, too, just like his papa,' her hostess said.

After vigorously sucking for a moment, the baby spat out her fingertip, giving her a mildly indignant look.

Mrs Ransleigh laughed. 'I know that look. I'd better go feed him, before he demonstrates just what a fine pair of lungs he has. Ah, here's your hot water,' she said, as the kitchen maid and two house boys brought in steaming urns of water to pour into the tub, followed by the lady's maid with clean clothing and a towel.

'Ring for me when you're ready, ma'am, and I'll help you into the gown,' Dulcie said, depositing the garments within reach of the tub.

'We'll leave you to your bath.' Mrs Ransleigh rose, cradling her son.

Elodie put a hand on her hostess's arm. 'Treasure every moment with him.'

'I intend to.' About to walk away, Mrs Ransleigh hesitated. 'He's my miracle child. Nearly all the women of my family died in childbed and I almost did, too. So I take nothing for granted. Not Andrew. Not Max. Not the farm and the horses that are my life's blood. They are all precious gifts.'

Elodie smiled. 'You are very wise.'

'Actually, I'm very grateful to you.' At Elodie's startled look, she said, 'Yes, I know who you are and what happened in Vienna. But you see, if Max hadn't been in disgrace after the assassination attempt, I would never have met him. I wouldn't have now the sweetest love a woman could ever desire and the joy of bearing his child. And Max truly is content here.'

With a wife who obviously adored him and a healthy

newborn son, Elodie wasn't about to suggest otherwise, but her hostess continued, 'I did try to resist him, you know. I urged him to return to Vienna, to look for you and do everything he could to clear his name and resume his government career. But as he began to work with me, training horses, he discovered he had a real gift for it. He says he's happy with his life here and, of course, I want to believe him.'

It eased her guilt to think that perhaps she hadn't ruined Max's future after all. That their interaction in Vienna had merely sent him down a different path, perhaps an even more rewarding one.

She still intended to do what she could to restore his reputation. For now, he was content training horses, but some day he might long to rejoin the circles of power for which he'd been born and bred. If that happened, she wanted to make sure nothing from their association in Vienna prevented him.

'With a lovely wife and a handsome son, how could he not be content? But I thank you for telling me.'

As if trying to remind his mama of his presence, the newborn squirmed in her arms and gave a preliminary wail.

'My master calls,' Mrs Ransleigh said with a grin. 'Enjoy your bath. We're very informal here, so we dine early. Dulcie will get you anything you need, and then we'll let you rest until dinner.'

With that, shushing the baby with a kiss on the nose, she put him to her shoulder and walked from the room.

Swiftly divesting herself of her grimy clothes, Elodie

climbed into the tub and sank with an ecstatic sigh into the hot scented water. Even in the grimmest of times, one should not fail to savour the wonder of a warm bath.

Tired as she was, the water both soothed and made her drowsy. Perhaps, as his wife suggested, Max was no longer angry at being reduced from a rising star of government to a breeder and trainer of horses. What was it he'd said—'everything has changed'?

For the better, she hoped. But she was too weary and the water too deliciously relaxing to contemplate the matter any more. Doubtless Will and Max were discussing it at this very moment. All she need do was be ready, at last, to fulfil the bargain she'd made with Will.

And then see him walk out of her life.

Chapter Nineteen

William watched Caroline Ransleigh usher Elodie out the parlour door with a panicky feeling in his gut. There'd been no time to reassure her that he didn't suspect she would try to run away. It was just that, after two attacks against her, he didn't feel comfortable about her safety when she was out of his sight.

He turned from the door to see Max studying him and another layer of dread overlay the first. He'd give anything not to have to say to Max what he was about to say. Anything but Elodie's life.

That thought put matters in perspective, so he swallowed hard and looked for a way to begin. The very idea of cutting himself off from his cousins and losing Max's esteem was so painful he'd not been able to bear thinking about or planning what he meant to say, as he normally would have done before broaching a matter of such gravity.

While he stood there, staring at Max and dithering, his cousin shook his head and laughed. 'I should have known if anyone in the world could have turned up Elodie Lefevre—and I gave it more than a go myself—it would be you. A tremendous, and I fear costly, crusade that Alastair said you insisted on funding and carrying out alone. How can I ever convey the depths of my gratitude and appreciation?'

Wonderful—in his very first speech, Max had made him feel even worse. 'I appreciate your kind reception of Elodie; under the same circumstances, I'm not sure I would have been so forbearing.'

'You always were a hothead, faster with your fists than your tongue,' Max observed with a smile.

'You were responsible for teaching me to use my wits instead.'

'I did my poor best.'

'Whatever improvement there is, I owe to your persistence. As for Madame Lefevre, you know the facts of what she did, but you don't know the "why". I think it's important that you do.' *Maybe then you will understand a little better why I'm about to betray you*, he thought.

'Very well, I'm listening. But something tells me the story would be better heard over a glass of port.'

Will didn't object. He'd need all the reinforcement he could get to force himself through the next half-hour. At the end of which, he would likely be saying goodbye to the best friend he'd ever had.

After a gulp of the fortified wine that warmed him to his toes, Will launched into a halting recitation of how he'd found Madame Lefevre and how she'd become involved in her cousin's plot. But as he began to describe

Elodie and her life, the words flowed faster and faster, the stories tumbling out one after another: her childhood trials as an exile, her struggles as a young soldier's wife and then widow, her courageous tenacity in Vienna, when, abandoned by all but her maid after the attack, she found a way to survive, and finally, the return to Paris and the wrenching second loss of her son.

He finished, his glass untouched since his first sip, to see Max watching him again, that inscrutable, assessing gaze on his face.

'A remarkable woman,' Max said.

Will nodded. 'Yes, she is.' *Now for the difficult, agonising part.* 'Max, you know better than I how much I owe you. I promised Alastair I would find Elodie, bring her back to England and make her tell the Foreign Office how she'd involved you in the plot, corroborating your account of the affair. So your reputation might be restored at last, along with the possibility of resuming the government career to which you've aspired as long as I've known you. But…but if she goes to London and the authorities open an official investigation, she could well be imprisoned as an accomplice to an attempt on Lord Wellington's life. Maybe even hung. I can't let her do that.'

Max frowned. 'Are you sure? If her testimony cleared my name, I might indeed be able to revive my government career. There would be no limit to my gratitude! I don't know how you mean to get on, now that you've resigned your army commission. Papa should have made you an allowance when you returned, but…' Max grimaced '…no great surprise that he'd conveniently forget his promise. If I'm in London, Caro will need help here. She'd never give up the stud; breeding horses is in her blood. You could take my place as manager, be the go-between at Newmarket, take a percentage of the sales. She raises excellent horses; it would pay well. You could have a comfortable position for life, accumulate enough to buy property of your own, if you wished. Become a "landed Ransleigh" at last.'

'Thereby finally earning your father's respect?' Will said derisively. 'Though I thank you for the offer, as it happens, I've accumulated sufficient funds on my own. And even if I hadn't, I'd never bargain for Elodie's life.'

Max's frown deepened. 'You obviously care for this woman. Does she return the favour?'

Will swallowed hard. 'I'm not sure. She's fond of me, I know. But…losing her son again has devastated her. I don't think she's capable of feeling anything now.'

'She's "fond" of you,' Max repeated, a bit dismissively. 'You would betray your oath to me for a woman who you're not even sure loves you, or has any appreciation of the consequences of your dishonouring your pledge?'

Trust Max to strip fine rhetoric down to its bare essentials. Unpalatable as it was, that was truth. 'Yes.'

To Will's utter shock, Max gave a crow of laughter. 'So, it's happened at last! Wagering Will's bet was called by a lady with a better hand.'

Sobering quickly, he clapped a hand on Will's shoulder. 'As I said at the outset, I can't begin to express my appreciation and admiration for all you've done, going to Vienna to find *madame* and bringing her back. I'm not sure any man deserves such loyalty. But you needn't risk the life of the woman you've come to love.'

'So, you're…not angry?' Will asked, amazed, too rattled by Max's unexpected response to dare believe it to be true. 'Then why did you try to tempt me with a position here?'

'From the look on your face when you spoke of Madame Lefevre and how protectively you hovered around her, I suspected you loved her. I've never seen you that way with any other woman. But I wanted to discover just how deeply the attachment ran. True, I might not always have felt so forgiving towards her. After Vienna I was angry, dismayed, disbelieving. My world and the future I'd always dreamed of had been destroyed and I didn't think I'd ever be content or fulfilled again. But then I met Caro. Worked with her. Fell in love with her and the farm. I have what I want now, Will. I think, in Elodie Lefevre, you have what you want, too. Am I right?'

'Would I have abandoned my vow for any other reason?'

Max nodded. 'I thought as much. I suppose I recognised the devotion; I feel the same about Caro, as if I'd battle the whole world to keep her safe. Give up the rest of the world, if that were the price of keeping her.'

'Then you do understand. But you know your Caroline loves you. I'm not sure what Elodie feels or wants. I planned to take her away to the Americas, where she'd be safe, but I'm not even sure she'll go with me. When she lost her son after directing all her efforts for nearly two years towards reclaiming him, it was as if she felt her whole life was over.'

'I can appreciate her grief and despair. I thought losing the career I loved the greatest tragedy that could befall me…until Caro had difficulty in childbed and I almost…' his voice broke for a moment '…I almost lost her and my son. I can't imagine how one recovers from such a blow. But as I understand it, Madame Lefevre's son isn't dead, so surely there is some hope of seeing him again?'

'Yes, I'm examining some possibilities, but they'll take time to work out. Grieving as she is, I don't want to propose anything; if the plans went awry, I don't know how she would bear another disappointment.'

'She'll need time to heal. I did, and I lost only the career I thought I wanted, not the persons most dear to me. Teach her there is still beauty and fulfilment in life.' He grinned. 'And that you can provide them.'

'I'm not sure I know where to begin,' Will admitted. I don't even know if she'll agree to stay with me, once she learns we won't be taking her to the Foreign Office. I wouldn't put it past her to disappear in the night, thinking she offers me nothing and I'd be better off starting anew, without her.'

'Is she that elusive?'

Will thought of how she'd loved him to satiation and then slipped away. 'Oh, yes.'

'If you love her that much, surely you're not going to

despair of winning her before you've even begun! I've seen you beguile women from blushing dairymaids to bored *ton* beauties. I can't imagine you're not capable of beguiling a lady you actually love. True, trying to win her is a gamble. But Wagering Will never met a bet he wouldn't take. Comfort her, stand by her and marry her.'

Will sighed. 'I want to, but what do I know about being a husband, creating a family?'

'I thought your cousins taught you a good bit. My father, you remember, wasn't much of a model, either. But then, when you hold your wife's hand while she brings your child into the world, then touch his perfect, tiny hands…' A sense of awe and wonder passed over Max's face. 'I can assure you, the rewards of fighting for a life with the woman you love far outweigh the risks of failing.'

How Will wanted that, too, a life with Elodie, her lovely face finally freed from the shadows of pain and sorrow! He hadn't thought beyond the dread of this interview and the necessity of making all speed to catch a ship to the colonies. Now, buoyed by Max's encouragement, Will started rapidly examining other alternatives.

Winning Elodie's heart, forging a life here…with his cousins nearby. In time, perhaps, giving her another child to cherish, a complement to the one she'd already borne with whom, if the scheme Will was pondering came to fruition, she would forge a new relationship.

'There is another property I've had my eye on, over in Sussex,' he said, running a vision of it through his mind's eye. 'It has a wonderful garden.'

Max raised his eyebrows. 'Another property? Just how many do you own?'

Will grinned. 'Not as many as Alastair or your family, but several. What, you think I just frittered away all my gambling winnings? You remember Hal Waterman, from Eton?'

'That large, inarticulate lad who'd never be lured into playing cards because, he said, the odds were always in the dealer's favour? A sort of mathematical genius, as I recall.'

'Yes. Two misfits, he and I, who later banded together. I happened to meet him in London after Oxford, when I'd had my first really big win at faro. He said if I liked gambling, he could recommend something for which the odds were as risky as gaming, but the potential rewards much greater. Not just in blunt, but in forging the future of the nation. Turns out he's fascinated by finance and technology, and with that limitless fortune of his, has begun exploring the opportunities to invest in new scientific developments. He talked me into putting almost all the blunt I'd won at faro into a canal-construction project he'd put together. With the earnings from that, I bought my first property. I'm also invested in coal mines, mechanical stoves and what Hal claims will be a system that will revolutionise transport, the railroad.'

Max shook his head. 'Does my father know?'

Will laughed. 'Know that his barely civilised, reprobate nephew has become a man of means without his will or intervention? Certainly not! The shock could probably kill him.'

Max chuckled. 'It might at that.'

'However, manufacturing and commerce are close enough to vulgar middle-class shop-keeping that if he does learn of it, I'm sure he'll manage to maintain his disdain.'

'You could have told the Rogues,' Max reproved.

'I would have, had the war and…other projects not intervened.'

'So you're a man of means.' Max shook his head ruefully. 'It's almost as hard for me as for Papa to think you no longer need my help.'

'I'll always need your friendship.'

'That, you'll always have. So, go buy your manor. Would you like us to watch over your Elodie until you return? I must admit, the story you've told piques my curiosity. I liked her when I knew her in Vienna. I'd very much enjoy becoming better acquainted with the remarkable woman who performed so many amazing feats. Not the least of which was capturing my elusive cousin's heart.'

'Would you let her stay here and watch out for her? Although…' Will hesitated, trying to guess how his complex, devious Elodie might react. 'I know it's not fair to keep the knowledge from her, but could we let her go on believing that a visit to the Foreign Office is forthcoming? Not that you need to tell any deliberate mistruths, just be evasive, if she asks directly. I don't think she will. She's committed enough to making recompense for the harm she did you in Vienna that if she thinks I've left Denby Lodge to make preparations for London, she'll not…wander off before I return. It will also give me a chance to think how best to woo her.'

'I may now be a horse breeder, but I'm still a diplomat at heart; I can finesse anything. Especially if it involves the happiness of my dearest friend. So, if you're not going to linger at Denby—and while you're still muddy and smelling of horse—let me give you a quick tour of the stables and stock. My world now.'

'Do you not miss being involved in government?' Will asked, still finding it hard to believe Max could have abandoned so completely the goal that had driven him for as long as Will had known him.

'The idea that I am working for something larger than myself? A bit. But the back-biting and intrigues of those whose mindless ambition far outweighs their concern for the public good? Not at all. I have considered perhaps some day standing for Parliament. Being elected by the men of the district whose respect I've won, whom I respect in turn, giving voice to their concerns in the halls of power, is a more worthy task than what I would now be doing, had Vienna not intervened. Lurking about the Lords, a lackey for my father.'

'Standing for Parliament is an excellent idea.'

'Well, we shall see. For now, I'm just grateful for the blessings of being able to watch my son grow and spend every day—and night—with my wife.'

'So…' Max raised his glass, motioning Will to pick

up his own '…to your safe return. To finding love, and cherishing it. To Ransleigh Rogues.'

Now that he was recovering from the shock of realising he would not lose Max's friendship after all, Will felt a rising euphoria and an eagerness for the future he hadn't known since that moment he'd awakened before Paris, marvelling at the peace he'd found in Elodie's arms.

'To all of that,' he replied. 'And to "Ransleigh Rogues, for ever".'

Chapter Twenty

Two weeks later, on a mild summer afternoon, Elodie sat embroidering her new gown in a beam of sunlight in the front parlour at Denby Lodge. Strange, she thought as she methodically set small, perfect stitches, that she was now marking time awaiting the trip to London as she'd spent the hours before leaving Vienna. But instead of longing and anticipation, she passed her days numb and drifting, the only small joy on her horizon the hope to see Will Ransleigh again before the final resolution.

She did wish Will had taken her with him when he left to consult with the authorities about setting up her interview. After he returned, there would be very little time left to share with him. It would take them a few days at most to travel back to the metropolis before she gave her testimony, that end of the road beyond which she could envision nothing further.

Dull as her spirits still were, she missed him. His acute observations, his teasing eye, his stories…and the surcease from sorrow she found in his arms, when he loved her so sweetly and completely that nothing, not even anguish and loss, could tarnish the bliss. She'd hoped he would come to her some time during the one night he spent at Denby Lodge before leaving for London, but he hadn't.

The day of his departure had dawned all the more dreary for that lack.

Surprised at first that Max Ransleigh had not gone with Will to instigate the proceedings, she'd thought he must want to consult with her about the now-distant events in Vienna, so her account of it, when she at last spoke to the authorities, would reinforce what he'd told them of the affair. But to her bewilderment, he had not sought her out in private to quiz her about her memories, nor had he referred to the matter in any way when in company.

Her host and hostess had insisted she dine with them, and though Max had initiated several discussions of Vienna, their object seemed more to entertain Caro than corroborate what she remembered. He described some of the most notable balls and receptions they'd attended, asking her to share her recollections, or else he traded impressions with her about the colourful array of notables and hangers-on who'd attended the Congress.

Perhaps he didn't wish to distress his wife, who was still recovering from her confinement, by referring to the scandal. Elodie's initial favourable impression of Caroline Ransleigh had quickly deepened to a friendship she would sorely miss when the time came to leave for London. Not since Clara in Vienna had Elodie had a female friend with whom she could converse freely, and growing up an exile with no sisters, she hadn't ever had a confidante from her same level in society.

Though Caro insisted she might borrow any garments she liked, not used to being idle, Elodie had asked Max to sell one of the small pieces of jewellery she'd carried with her, so she might purchase material to make herself some garments. Accompanying Caro to the village, she'd bought several dress lengths, and was now completing the second of two stylish gowns.

In addition to the sewing keeping her occupied, she thought that, if she wished the officials at the enquiry to find it credible that she had been the hostess of a high-ranking French diplomat at the most glittering assemblage of aristocrats and government leaders ever gathered in Europe, she couldn't appear in one of her tattered old gowns, looking like a rag picker.

If prison were the outcome, she might be able to sell the new garments to obtain the coal and candles that would make her existence less miserable. And, if the worst happened, at least she'd have something attractive to be buried in.

At that moment, her hostess entered the parlour with her characteristic, brisk step. 'Elodie, what exquisite work!' she exclaimed, coming over to inspect her embroidery. 'I can easily believe an exclusive Vienna modiste clamoured for you to embellish her gowns.'

'Hardly "clamoured",' Elodie replied. 'But she did pay me promptly and rather well for a seamstress.'

'I'm so hopeless, I can't sew a stitch! I ought to commission you to make some gowns for me. I've never cared two figs what I wore, as long as it was modest and serviceable, but now that I'm regaining my figure...' A blush heated her cheeks. 'I'd like to have something new to intrigue my husband and remind me I'm more than just a mama.'

'Something that shows to advantage that fine mama's bosom,' Elodie teased, smiling when Caro's blush deepened. 'I would be happy to make you something, if I have time enough before I leave.'

A shadow crossed Caro's face. 'I do wish you didn't have to go. But I don't mean to speak of that, for it will only make me melancholy, and heavens, it seems lately the merest nothing has me wanting to burst into tears! Me, who has never in her life been missish,' she finished with disgust.

'It goes with becoming a mama,' Elodie said.

'The nursery maid is just finishing Andrew's bath. Shall I bring him down?'

'Please do! I've been working on a gown for him, too.'

'You're sure? Sometimes I worry that seeing him must make it...more difficult for you.'

'I should miss Philippe every day, even if I never saw another child. But a baby should be a joy. Not for the world would I want yours to diminish, because of my loss! It lifts my spirits to see you with him and know that such happiness still exists in the world. Besides, who could resist such a handsome charmer as your son?'

Caro beamed. 'He is handsome, isn't he? And demanding. Which is good. If I didn't have him to occupy me, I don't know how I would bear the inactivity. I know the doctor said I must not ride for another two weeks, but I'm feeling perfectly fine and cannot wait to get back to my horses!'

'Go get your son and we'll let him entertain us,' Elodie said.

Smiling, she went back to her stitching. She'd not just reassured her new friend to ease her anxiety; she did enjoy seeing the child. Holding and playing with the infant, recalling as it did memories of happier times with Philippe, always lifted her spirits and eased the dull anxiety that sat like a boulder in her gut, an ever-present worry over a future she didn't want to envision.

What if they only interviewed and then released her? Though she tried to keep herself from contemplating anything beyond that meeting in London, occasionally speculation about a different, better resolution crept into her thoughts.

What was she to do with herself if she did not end up in prison or on the gallows? Though she knew her new friend would invite her to stay indefinitely at Denby Lodge, she didn't wish to be a burden. Perhaps she could get lodgings in London and find employment as a seamstress. Rich women would always need new gowns.

There was no question of returning to Paris. The Ransleigh name might command the attention—and protection—of the Prime Minister and the respect of Prince Talleyrand, but Elodie Lefevre, her brother dead and his rising career with him, was no longer of any importance. Besides, sojourning in the same city that contained her son, but unable to be with him, would be a torment beyond enduring.

So, London it must be. Unless…unless Will wanted her. They had been excellent comrades on the road and passionate lovers. Perhaps he would keep her as his mistress for a while, until he tired of her. Such a handsome, charismatic man would make any woman who set eyes on him try to entice him; it wouldn't take Will Ransleigh long to find another lover to share his bed.

As the door opened, she looked up, expecting to see Caro and her babe. Instead, the object of her imaginings walked in.

'Will, you're back!' she cried, jumping up. Within the dull empty expanse of her chest, her moribund heart gave a small leap of gladness.

She couldn't seem to take her eyes from his face as he approached her, smiling faintly, his sheer physical allure striking her as forcefully as it had that first day.

'Sewing again, I see,' he said. 'Just like when I found you in Vienna.'

Was he thinking of their first meeting, too? 'Although this time, you enter, quite boringly, by the door, rather than thrillingly through a window.'

'I see I am failing in my duty as a rogue. I shall have to redeem myself.'

It seemed the most natural thing in the world to walk into the arms he held out to her, to lift her face for his kiss.

He took her mouth gently, but she met him ardently.

With a stifled groan, he clutched her tighter, deepening the kiss. She moulded herself to him, her body fitting his like a puzzle piece sliding into place.

After a moment, he broke the kiss, his turquoise eyes dark. 'Does that mean you've missed me?'

'I have. I feel…' At home? At peace? As content as it was possible for her to be? 'Safe when you're near,' she finished.

His expression grew serious. 'And I mean to keep you that way.'

'Must we leave at once for London? I…I had promised Caro to make her a new gown.'

'She has treated you well?'

'Very well. We so very quickly became friends, I shall miss her when we leave for London.'

'We're not going to London.'

'Not going?' Elodie echoed, puzzled. 'Is the Foreign Office allowing me to give a deposition here, rather than testifying in person?'

'No deposition. No testimony at all. I don't want to risk it.'

She shook her head, more confused than ever. 'But what of Monsieur Max? How is his name to be cleared, if I do not testify? What of his career?'

'Max is quite happy with the career—and the family—he has at Denby Lodge. And if, in future, he has a longing to return to government, he means to go on his own merits, elected to Parliament by the men of this district, not relying on the prestige of his family or the patronage of some high official.'

'This is truth? You are sure?'

'Absolutely sure.'

She would not have to testify. After girding herself for that trial for so long, she could scarcely comprehend she would not be facing the looming spectre of prison or the noose. Dizzy and disoriented with relief, she stumbled to the sofa. 'What is to become of me, then?'

Will seated himself beside her, took her hands and tilted her chin up to face him, his gaze intent. Taking a deep breath, he said, 'I want to take care of you, Elodie. I love you. I want you with me.'

'My sweet Will,' she whispered, freeing a hand to stroke his cheek. 'I want you, too. For as long as you'll have me, I am yours.'

'I want you in my life always, Elodie. I want to marry you.'

'Marry me?' Never in her wildest imaginings had the possibility of marriage occurred to her. 'But that is not at all sensible!' she exclaimed, her practical French mind recoiling from a union of two persons of such dissimilar resources. 'I bring you nothing, no dowry, no family, no influence. You don't have to marry me, Will. I will stay with you as long as you wish.'

'But you can't be sure of that with a mistress. One night, she shows you the moon and the stars, gives you bliss beyond imagining. And the next morning, poof, she is gone, without a word of farewell.'

Feeling a pang of guilt, Elodie looked at him reprovingly. 'That was under very different circumstances, as you well know.'

'What I know is that all my life, I've been missing something, here.' He tapped his chest. 'But in your arms that night outside Paris, I found what I didn't even know I'd been searching for. I felt…complete. I don't want to ever lose that again.'

He stared at her intently, as if waiting for her to reply in kind. She felt a strong bond, something deeper than just the physical, but within her broken and battered heart all was confusion. Better to say nothing than to profess a love she wasn't sure she felt, or wound him by admitting how uncertain she was.

Instead, she shook her head. 'You can have that. It is not necessary, this marriage.'

He drew back a bit, and she knew she'd hurt him, much as she'd wanted to avoid it. 'I know I'm only the illegitimate son of a rogue, while you are the daughter of French aristocracy—'

'Oh, no!' she interrupted him. 'How can you believe I think myself above you? I am the daughter of French aristocrats, yes, but one who has no home, no title, no influential family, no wealth. It is you who are above me, a man linked to a rich and prominent family that still wields great power.'

That seemed to reassure him, for the pain in his eyes receded and he kissed her hands. 'I want to marry you, Elodie de Montaigu-Clisson, whether you can ever love me or not. But don't give me a final answer now. So much has changed since Vienna. You've lost the hope that sustained you for so long and must grieve for that. You need time to reflect, to heal and find consolation, before you can move forwards. I want you to take that time. Will you come with me, let me take care of you? I pledge to keep you safe, so safe that one day you'll stop looking over your shoulder, worried about being followed or threatened. Come with no obligation but friendship. And when you feel ready to begin your life again…if I must, I'll let you go. No force, no bargains.'

Elodie felt tears prick her eyes. She couldn't let him commit the idiocy of tying himself legally to a woman who brought him nothing in worldly advantage, but she would stay with him as long as he'd have her.

'No force, no bargains,' she agreed. 'I go with you willingly and will stay as long as you want me.'

'That would be for ever, then,' Will said and bent to kiss her.

Chapter Twenty-One

On a sunny morning a month later, Elodie strolled through the vast garden at Salmford House. Taking a seat on one of the conveniently located benches with a view of the rose parterre, where the potent, drifting scent of the Autumn Damask 'Quatre Saisons' never failed to soothe her, she smiled.

Her enjoyment of it this morning was just as intense as it had been the afternoon Will first brought her to the property he'd purchased near Firle on the South Downs of Sussex, a lovely land of rolling hills and meadows. After touring her through the snug stone manor and introducing her to the staff, he'd led her out the French doors from the library into the first section of walled garden.

Her reactions of surprise and delight had been repeated many times over as he strolled her through each garden 'room', from the topiary terrace adjoining the library with its precisely clipped boxwood and yew, to the white garden of iris, daisies, sweet alyssum, campanula and snapdragons, the multi-hued perennial border backed by red-leaved berberis, to the artfully arranged herb-and-vegetable knot garden adjoining the kitchen and finally to the central rose parterre, where the 'Old Blush' and damask roses were still blooming after the albas and gallicas had ended their early summer show.

As he'd coaxed her reluctantly to return to the house for an early dinner, saying he, for one, was famished, she'd thrown her arms around him and kissed him soundly. 'What a magnificent garden!' she exclaimed.

'When I was considering where to bring you, I remembered the agent showing me this property. Is it as lovely as the garden of Lord Somerville?'

'Oh, yes, and larger, too! Did you truly choose this house for me?'

'You have had enough of sadness in your life, Elodie. I want you to be happy.' He tapped her nose. 'Clara made me promise.'

'Oh, thank you, my sweet Will! Only one thing under heaven could make me happier.'

But when she took his arm going back to the house and murmured in his ear that she could show him just how grateful she was, pressing herself against him suggestively, he eased her away from him and primly repeated what he'd told her on the drive to Salmford House; that here, they would be friends only, not lovers.

She hadn't believed him, of course, for the idea of refraining from enjoying the powerful passion they shared made no more sense to her than an English aristocrat from a prominent family marrying a penniless exile.

She was not at all happy to discover he'd not been teasing. 'Why, Will? I give myself freely, for your pleasure and mine. Why do you not want such a gift?'

'Oh, I want you—with every breath. But when I make love to you again, I want it to be with you as my wife.'

She sighed in exasperation. 'Is it not the woman who is supposed to withhold her favours until the man succumbs to marriage?'

'Usually, yes. But you see, I'm enamoured of a very stubborn, peculiar female—the French are often stubborn and peculiar, I find—and persuading her to marry me calls for desperate measures. Passion can be very persuasive, so why should I not dangle before her one of my most potent weapons in securing her consent?' He sighed, too. 'Though, in truth, this remedy is so desperate, it may kill me. But were we not true friends and companions on the road, without being lovers?'

'Yes, but only at first, when our disguises prevented it. And we are not on the road now, but in a *hôtel* of the most fine, with, I am sure, beds of quite amazing comfort.'

'You are distressed. I can always tell; your speech becomes more French.'

'Of course I am distressed. This…this show of chastity is ridiculous!'

'Well, as long as there's a chance this "ridiculousness" might help convince you to become my wife, I am content to wait.'

'It may convince me you are an *imbécile*. And I am

not content to wait!' she declared, stamping her foot, frustrated and furious with him, the surge of emotion seizing her the strongest she'd experienced since the loss of Philippe had paralysed all feeling.

'Calm down, *chérie*!' he soothed. 'You need diversion.'

'Yes, and I know just what sort,' she flashed back.

'So do I. A hand of cards after we've dined should do the trick.'

She'd whacked his arm and stomped away, leaving him to follow her to the dining parlour, chuckling. But she couldn't stay angry, as he coaxed her with fine ham, an assortment of fresh vegetables from the garden, aged cheese, rich wine, followed by strawberries and cream, which he fed her with his own hands, rubbing the ripe berries against her lips and then kissing the flavour from them, until she was certain he was going to relent.

Instead of leading her to a bedchamber—by then she would have been quite content with a sofa or even a soft carpet—he handed her into the parlour and produced a deck of cards.

At first, angry with him again, she'd refused to play. But he'd teased and dared, finally winning her grudging agreement by accusing her of avoiding a hand because she was afraid she'd lose.

Within a few minutes, tantalising her with his skill, he'd drawn her into the game. She'd watched him play enough to know he was not trying to let her win, but challenging her to exercise all her skill, which made her redouble her concentration. Interspersed with the hands, he set her to laughing with outrageous observations about the people and events they'd encountered on their travels. When the clock struck midnight and he gathered up the cards, she was surprised to find the hour so late.

It was the most carefree evening she'd spent in years. And she hadn't thought once of her loss.

The yearning returned as he walked her to a bed-chamber. She clung to him, trying to entice him to remain with her.

'Marry me,' he'd whispered against her hair as he held her close. 'Marry me, *mon ange*, and be mine for ever.'

When she'd tremulously replied that she couldn't, he'd sighed and gently set her away from him. And then bid her goodnight.

That same frustrating routine had recurred each night of their stay here.

Though he'd laughed at her anger, teased her, given her deep, thrilling kisses as if he meant to relent, he had not. To her extreme irritation and regret, they continued to live as chastely as brother and sister.

She'd thought about slipping into his chamber and into his bed, pleasuring him with her hands and mouth, when, groggy with sleep and tempted by arousal, he would surely yield to her. For the first few nights, she talked herself out of it, worried about embarrassing herself if she were wrong and he refused her still, even in his bed.

By the time they'd been at the manor for a week,

she'd grown too desperate to worry about embarrassment. In the early hours of the morning, unable to sleep, she'd crept through the silent house to his chamber—and found the door locked against her.

The following morning, grumpy from sleeplessness and frustration, she'd sulkily enquired if he thought she were dangerous, that he must lock himself away from her. He'd replied that he was not so much of a fool as to subject himself to a temptation he knew he'd never be able to resist, a reply which mollified her somewhat, though it did nothing to relieve the frustration.

But for that one—and very major—fault, Will had been a perfect companion. He had encouraged her to take him on walks through her beloved garden, telling him the names of all the plants—and later making her laugh by deliberately bungling them. Noticing how she loved to linger in the rose parterre, breathing in the potent scent of the autumn damasks, he had bouquets of the spicy blooms put in every room.

As she gradually began to emerge from the cocoon of grief into which she'd spun herself, it was impossible not to notice his cherishing care of her. Some might have found it suffocating, but Elodie, who had experienced precious little cherishing in her tumultuous life, drank up the attention and concern.

Sitting here now, she recalled all the ways he'd seen to her comfort. Foods she mentioned liking would appear regularly on the table. When she thanked him for a new gown in blue or azure or gold, several more of similar style and hue appeared in her wardrobe.

He even found her, heaven knows where, a little French girl to be her lady's maid. Chatting with the homesick lass in their native French tongue helped ease the sadness within her at the loss of her home and language.

Whatever activity he engaged with her in, whether cards or riding or billiards, he roused her from her recurrent bouts of melancholy by teasing her or cheating her back to attention—or indignation. Sometimes, in the evenings, he read to her, surprising her with the wide-ranging breadth of his knowledge and interests. He talked about his friend, Hal Waterman, and the fascinating new technologies they were investing in that would, he told her, eventually change the way people heated their homes, cooked their food and travelled.

Methodically, slow day by slow day, he was drawing her out of the greyness of grief and death back into the light of his life. Letting her bask in the brilliant warmth of his love.

She hadn't earned such devotion, probably didn't deserve it, but he gave it freely anyway. Wanting, in return, only her happiness.

For the first time in a long time, anticipation stirred in her. What was wrong with her, moping about as if her life were over? Yes, she'd lost her child, a tragedy whose pain would never fully leave her. But along the way, she'd found a matchless lover, who was trying by every means he could devise to woo her and win her love in return.

Almost every day, he repeated his request that she

marry him and share his life. And then, praise heaven, his bed!

Will being normally an intense, restless man, she was astounded that he had managed to content himself staying placidly here, doing nothing more exciting than riding in the countryside and playing cards with her. Surely he was ready to go off exploring new places, investigating new projects. He'd said he longed for her to come with him and share the excitement, companions on the road again.

A sense of wonder and enthusiasm filled her. Salmford House's gardens and Will's tender care had worked their magic. She was, she decided in that moment, now ready to put her losses behind her and start living again—with Will.

Suddenly, she couldn't wait to see him.

Picking up her skirts, she rushed back into the manor, hurrying from room to room until she found him in the library.

He looked up as she entered, his handsome face lighting in a smile, and her healing heart leapt. How could she not flourish in the brightness of that smile? In such tenderness, as she leaned down for his kiss and he caressed her cheek with one gentle finger?

She'd been a fool, not for the first time. It was time to be foolish no longer.

'Are you ready for luncheon, *chérie*?' she said. 'I'm famished.'

Smiling up at Elodie, Will twisted in his hands the letter he'd received in the morning's post. The position he'd discussed with his friend Hal Waterman had been arranged; in the letter was his authorisation to go to Paris and enter discussions with the French Ministry of the Interior about the possibilities of developing railway lines in France.

Hal had pledged considerable financial backing to make the venture happen and tapped his network of influential contacts to persuade the British government to approve Will for the task and to give the endeavour their support. The challenge of persuading the French government to permit the work was exhilarating and Will would need to leave almost immediately.

He wanted Elodie to go with him—as his wife. They'd grown so much closer over the last month. Several times, the tender light in her eyes as she gazed at him had sent his hopes winging to dizzying heights, sure that he'd won her at last and she was about to confess her love.

But thus far, that hadn't happened. And now, if he was to put into motion the scheme he'd been devising ever since they left Paris, he would have to tell her of his plans and propose again, even if he wasn't sure of her love.

He wanted her to marry him because she'd realised she loved him and could not imagine spending the rest of her life without him, not because doing so would allow her to be reunited with her son. Even if she did come to love him later, he would never be able to trust that she loved him for himself, not out of gratitude for his ingenuity in bringing her son back into her life.

But he knew, if he must, he would marry her on those terms. Loving her as he did, he couldn't withhold from her the one thing she wanted most in the world because he hadn't had the good fortune to secure her love in return.

Dropping the letter, he rose to take her arm. She danced around him as she took it, mischief sparkling in her eyes.

His heart turned over to see it, as it always did when she looked happy. He knew a reserve of sadness would always remain with her, but it delighted him to see her look so carefree. It was deeply satisfying to know he'd played a vital part in banishing the shadows from her eyes.

From the naughty glances she was giving him, she was probably plotting to seduce him again. Maybe this time, he'd let her. Heaven knows, resisting her was about to drive him mad.

There wasn't enough cold water in the lake beyond their meadow to cool his ardour for his bewitching Elodie, and he'd been swimming at least twice daily. He'd lasted nearly a month without her managing to break his resolve, far longer than he'd thought he could.

'I'm glad to see you have an appetite, sprite. For so long, you have only toyed with your food.'

'Oh, I have quite an appetite today.' Turning suddenly to push him against the bookshelves, she said, 'Shall I show you how much?'

Anticipation roared through his veins. If tempting her to agree to marriage by withholding passion hadn't worked by now, knowing the proposal he was about to make would contain a temptation she wouldn't be able to resist, why not give up the futile fight and let her have her way with him?

He kissed her hungrily, opening willingly when she slipped her busy tongue inside his mouth. He groaned, pulling her against his hardness.

With a little mewing sound, she reached down to stroke him, and this time he didn't catch her wrists to prevent her. What crack-brained notion had made him deny himself this? he wondered, revelling in her touch.

He returned the favour, caressing her breasts through the fine muslin of her gown and light summer stays, until her breath came in gasps as short as his own.

Picking her up, Will kicked the door closed. It had been too long; desperate for the taste of her, he couldn't possibly wait the few minutes it would take him to carry her up to his bedchamber. The desk would have to do.

In a few quick strides, he reached it and set her on the solid mahogany surface, kissing her ravenously as he slid her skirts up and peeled her stockings down, smoothing the soft skin as he bared it. After working the muslin up to her waist, he parted her legs and knelt before her.

His thumbs teasing the curls at her hot, wet centre, he kissed the tender skin of her inner thighs, tracking up the velvet softness until his tongue met his fingers and he applied the rasp of it to the swollen bud within.

Gasping, she writhed under him, until a very few minutes later reaching her peak. His fingers still caressing her, he took her cries of ecstasy on his lips, then carried her, limp and pliant, to the sofa and cradled her on his lap.

'Oh, my sweet Will, how I've missed you!'

'And I you, *ma douce*.'

'My love, I've been such a fool and you've been so patient with me! I am of a slowness quite remarkable, but finally, finally, I understand. Can you forgive me for being so stupid, clinging to my grief like a child with a broken toy, too stubborn to let it go? But I shall be stupid no longer.'

His heart leapt. Could she mean what he hoped she did? Trying to restrain the hope and excitement bubbling up within him, he said, 'What are you trying to tell me, *chérie*?'

'That no one has ever cared for or loved me like you. Why I have been so fortunate to have received this gift of wonder, I do not know, but my heart rejoices and I love you with everything in me. I want to belong to you for always, be your companion on your adventures and in your bed. I want to be your wife, and though I still believe it is most nonsensical of you to throw yourself away on so undeserving a woman, I shall accept quickly now, before you recover and change your mind. So, will you marry me, prince of my heart? *Parce que je t'aime*, Will. *Avec tout mon coeur*.'

He'd dreamed of hearing her say those words for so long, he could scarcely believe she really had. 'Truly, *mon ange*? You love me with all your heart?'

'Well, with my body, too, as soon as you'll let me.

And from this position…' she wiggled on his lap, rubbing her soft bottom against his hardness '…I am thinking you are ready for me to do so immediately.'

He knew he was probably grinning like the imbecile she'd once called him, but he didn't care. 'Not just yet, in spite of my need. Perhaps tonight, though, if you'll excuse me so I can collect the special licence I brought back from London with me and go to the village to find the rector. If he's available, he can come back and marry us at once. That is, unless you'd like a new gown, or want to plan a ceremony with Max and Caro—'

She stopped his words with a fingertip. 'They can give us a party later. By all means, find the vicar and bring him back at once. I want to be your wife by tonight.'

'I'll kidnap him, if necessary. We've much to discuss tomorrow, but tonight I want to be in your arms.'

Chapter Twenty-Two

The next morning, Will awoke in his bedchamber at Salmford House tired, well loved and with a euphoric sense of well-being that glowed all the brighter when he opened his eyes to see his wife's silky head pillowed on his shoulder.

His wife. He grinned, loving the sound of the words. Fortunately, since he would rather not have had charges brought against him for kidnapping on the eve of his departure for an official mission to France, the vicar had thought his request to wed them immediately romantic rather than foolhardy. Gathering his prayer book, he'd hastened to accompany Will back to Salmford House, where the staff, along with the blushing French maid, witnessed the marriage and the signing of the parish register.

He wanted to wake up like this, with Elodie in his arms, for the rest of his days, Will thought, bending to give her a kiss.

Her eyes fluttering open, she smiled sleepily at him. 'Can it be daylight already?'

'It's halfway through the morning, slug-a-bed.'

'Well, when one has spent hours attending with much concentration to long-delayed and important work, one becomes exhausted.'

He chuckled. 'I think I fell in love with you the moment "Uncle Fritz" limped on his cane into that inn, the night we left Vienna.'

She traced a finger from his shoulders to his chest. 'I lusted after you from the moment you launched yourself from the balcony into my room. But I never appreciated in full measure how wonderful you are until after…after Paris. I thought my life over, that I would never experience joy again. Until with patience, care and tenderness, you taught me I was wrong. You say your cousin Max saved your life; you have given mine back.'

It was a good opening and he took it. 'I'd like to do more. Are you ready to go travelling?'

She shifted up on the pillows to face him, looking so delectably mussed and seductive that only the gravity of what he must discuss with her kept him from pulling her back into his arms and making love to her all over again.

'You have a trip arranged?' she asked while he curbed his amorous appetites. 'To investigate one of those investments you've been telling me about?'

'Yes. This one will be to Paris.'

The excitement faded from her eyes. 'No, Will, please. Anywhere but Paris. I don't think I could bear it.'

'Nor do I, Elodie. It isn't right that your son was snatched from under your nose and you were prevented from reclaiming him. No, hear me out,' he said, forestalling the protest he could see she was about to make. 'Remember, you are no longer Elodie Lefevre, a woman with no home and no family. Elodie Ransleigh is wife to a man of considerable wealth, whose relations, I have it on respected authority, are rich, prominent and wield a good deal of power.'

Though she still looked troubled, he could tell she was cautiously weighing his words. 'What do you intend to do?'

'I've been given an official mission, sanctioned by the British Foreign Office and arranged and financed by my friend Hal Waterman, to approach the French government about the possibilities of constructing a railroad. So not only will you return to Paris as the wife of a wealthy, well-connected man, but one who will be entertained at the highest levels of government.'

'And that will benefit me…how?'

'While in Paris discharging the mission, we will call on the Comtesse de la Rocherie and propose a bargain. It is true, as you said before, that Philippe doesn't remember you and considers the comtesse to be his *maman*. So we won't demand that she give him up— yet. For the moment, we will insist only that you are allowed to become reacquainted with him. I expect this business regarding the railroad will take some time; if it should terminate more quickly than expected, I have other interests that can keep me in France.'

She pushed herself to sit upright against the pillows, joy and hope, anguish and doubt warring in her face. 'Are you sure, *mon amant*? You really think it is possible?'

'I do. Once Philippe knows you better and is comfortable in your company, he can come stay with us. When you think he's old enough to understand, you can tell him that you, not the comtesse, are in fact his mother. And then he will be yours once more.'

'Oh, that would be heaven! But what if the comtesse refuses? To be so close and be denied again…'

'She won't refuse. Elodie, I've been planning this for a long time. I didn't want to say anything until every piece was in place. It will work, I absolutely guarantee it. Have I ever lied to you?'

'No. Oh, Will, if you can truly reunite me with my son, I will be grateful to you for ever!'

He smiled at her tenderly. 'You can show me how much, right now. And then we'll get packing for Paris.'

After a flurry of shopping in London to equip Elodie for her role as Madame Ransleigh, wife to the economic envoy blessed by the Court of St James to engage in discussions with the Interior Ministry of His Majesty, King Louis XVIII, Will and Elodie sailed for France. Though Elodie remained calm—as she had been in every crisis they'd faced together, whether fleeing Vienna in the middle of the night disguised as a valet or while being held, a knife to her throat, by a British foreign agent—

Will knew that beneath the surface, she was torn between anticipation and anxiety.

Knowing every hour of delay before they visited the Hôtel de la Rocherie would be an agony of suspense for her, Will made only the essential calls to present his credentials to the British Ambassador and King Louis's chief advisors before returning to fetch Elodie from the luxurious hotel in which he'd installed her.

He found her pacing the room, from the gilded mantel to the door to the large windows with their view of the Place de la Republique, like a wild bird frantic to escape a jewelled cage.

As soon as she saw him, she rushed to her dressing table, jammed the stylish bonnet on her head and began dragging on her gloves. So nervous was she, she had difficulty pulling the tight kidskin over her trembling fingers.

He walked over to assist her.

'Quite an improvement over our accommodations the last time we were in Paris,' Will said, nodding towards the view of the Tuilerie Gardens in the distance as he coaxed the soft leather on to her hands. 'Though if it would make you less fretful, I could try obtaining some chickens.'

She tried to smile, but her lips were trembling, too. 'Will, I'm so frightened.'

He took her in his arms, wishing he could make this anxious process easier for her. 'You needn't be, my love! Don't you believe I know how important this is to you? I would never have suggested we attempt it if I were not absolutely convinced we shall succeed.' *Even if Will the Rogue has to make a return engagement to guarantee it*, he added silently to himself.

The concierge knocked to inform them their carriage was ready, and he ushered Elodie outside for the short drive to the Marais.

When they arrived at the Hôtel de la Rocherie, Will sent in his card, telling the lackey who greeted them that though he was a person previously unknown to the comtesse, he was in Paris on important government business and must discuss with her a matter of utmost urgency. After showing them into a drawing room elegantly appointed with striped wallpaper and Louis XVI furniture, the man withdrew.

Too nervous to sit, Elodie walked about, trailing her hand over the back of the sofa, down the edges of the satin window hangings. 'Oh, Will,' she whispered, 'This is where *madame* received us when St Arnaud and I called on her with Philippe. The last place I saw my son, before they stole him from me.'

'It's fitting, then,' Will said bracingly, 'that, in this same room, he will be restored to you.'

A few minutes later, an elaborately gowned woman Will assumed to be the comtesse entered the room. As he bowed over her hand, she said, 'Monsieur Ransleigh? I cannot imagine what business you might have with—'

'And Madame Ransleigh, too,' Will interrupted, nodding towards Elodie, who stood frozen by the mantel.

As the comtesse's gaze followed the direction of

his nod, the polite smile faded and her face went pale. 'Elodie Lefevre?' she gasped, stumbling towards the Louis XVI fauteuil and grasping the arm so tightly, Will thought she might have fallen without its support. 'My brother told me you were dead!'

'Sorry to disappoint,' Elodie replied with some asperity, 'but as you can see, I am still quite alive, *moi*. St Arnaud claimed I'd died, did he? How was I supposed to have met my demise?'

'He—he said you'd been injured during the…the attempt on the Duke's life. He did everything he could for you, but you died in his arms later that night. And then he fled.'

'He got the last part right,' Will said drily. 'Shall we sit, *madame*? This must have been quite a shock. You will need time to recover, before we place our proposal before you.'

'Yes, let me order refreshment. I, for one, could use a glass of wine.'

Even while giving orders to the lackey who responded to her summons, the comtesse kept staring at Elodie, as if unable to believe she had truly survived Vienna. After they'd been served, she drank deeply of her wine, then looked back to Elodie again and asked, 'Are you going to try to take my son?'

'Philippe is not your son,' Will reminded her.

'Perhaps not always, but he is now! For nearly two years he has known no other mother. You have only to ask him, he will tell you I am his *maman*.'

'I know,' Elodie said. 'I do appreciate the tender care you have taken of him.'

'You know?' the comtesse repeated with a puzzled frown. Then her eyes widened and she gasped, 'Was it you who accosted him in the park, two months ago? The servants said someone with an oddly intent manner had approached him. That they came back again to this house the very next day. I was so alarmed, I considered informing the gendarmes, but Prince Talleyrand advised against it.' Her questioning tone turned accusatory. 'You frightened him! How could you, if you care for him?'

'I'd hoped that if he studied me long enough, he would remember me. Can you imagine how it felt to see him again and realise he did not even recognise me?' she burst out. 'When I had thought of nothing but his welfare, every day, since he was taken from me?'

'Taken from you? My brother said you'd agreed to go to Vienna without him.'

'That report was as accurate as the one about my death!' Elodie retorted. 'I regret to disillusion you about your brother, but the only reason I left this *hôtel* without my son was because St Arnaud drugged my tea and abducted me. Once he had me in Vienna, he used the threat of harming Philippe to force me to participate in his plot. Did you truly not know?'

The comtesse dropped her eyes, not meeting Elodie's gaze. 'I am…aware of my brother's strong convictions, and the sometimes ruthless means he uses to carry them out. I knew there was something…suspect about your leaving Philippe so abruptly. But the child enchanted me from the first moment. When St Arnaud told me that he was setting out for Vienna immediately and that you had returned home to finish your preparations without seeing Philippe again, so you wouldn't have to distress him by telling him goodbye, I was too thrilled at being able to keep him to want to question the arrangement.'

'Was he…distressed when I did not come back for him?' Elodie asked.

The comtesse nodded. 'Of course. But I had a nursery full of toys to distract him and he loved listening to me read stories. When he would ask for you, I would tell him you were doing an important task, but you would be back soon. He cried at nights, mostly, so I slept in the nursery with him for the first month. And gradually he stopped asking.'

A sheen of tears glazed Elodie's eyes. 'Thank you for being so kind to him.'

The comtesse shrugged. '*Eh bien*, I love him, too. But what do you mean to do now? It was many weeks after you disappeared before he was happy and comfortable. Surely you won't upset him again, by wrenching him from my care?'

'It was to safeguard his happiness and well-being, and for that reason alone, that I did not take him with me when I had the opportunity two months ago. But as much as I appreciate your care of him, he is *my* son and I want him back.'

The comtesse was shaking her head. 'But you cannot

mean to take him *now*, surely! Give him some time! He is too young to understand all of this. You would only confuse and upset him.'

'We don't intend to take him away from you immediately,' Will inserted. 'Right now, he thinks of this as home and of you as his *maman*. What we propose is that my wife be reunited with him, spend time with him, let him become comfortable with her again. Once he is enough at ease with her to agree to it, we will take him to stay with us.'

Tears gathered in the comtesse's eyes. 'And then I will never see him again? Ah, *madame*, if you only knew what it is like to lose your son for ever, you would not be so cruel.'

'Believe me, I know!' Elodie retorted. 'Mine has been lost to me for nearly two years.'

'He wouldn't be far away,' Will said. 'I was sent to Paris on an economic mission to the French government. If negotiations succeed and we proceed to implement the plans, I could remain in Paris for many months. You would be able to see Philippe daily, if you liked.'

'I would like him to remain here,' the comtesse replied wistfully. 'My own son is dead; never in this life will I hold him again. But your son, *madame*, is alive. Though in taking him back you cut out my heart, I…I will not prevent you. Only, I beg you, don't drag him away until he is ready to go willingly.'

'I would take him no other way.' Elodie walked over and put a hand on the comtesse's arm. 'Thank you. I know how difficult it must be for you to agree to let him go. But as my husband said, we will be in Paris for an extended time. It will be weeks yet, probably, before he is willing to leave you, months after that before we would return to England.'

The comtesse shook her head sadly. 'There are not enough months in eternity to reconcile me to losing him.'

'You shall never lose him,' Elodie reassured her. 'Not completely. How could you, when you will always hold a special place in his heart? I promise I will never attempt to erase your image there.'

'Even though I let him forget you?' the comtesse replied. 'But surely you see that was different. I thought you were dead! Why should I remind him of a woman who would never return to him?'

'As long as you both make his welfare your first concern, I don't see why we can't all come to a sensible agreement,' Will said.

'Can I see him now?' Elodie asked.

Knowing her so well, Will could hear the longing in her voice. Knowing, too, that negotiating the terms of Philippe's custody would cause her anxiety—and wanting to make sure, in case the comtesse possessed any of her brother's perfidy, that the woman understood exactly what Will was prepared to do to enforce the agreement—Will said, 'Yes, comtesse, would you please have Philippe sent down now? Elodie, my love, you're too distracted and anxious to think clearly. Why don't you go out—' he gestured towards the French doors

leading out to a small, formal garden that stretched between the *hôtel*'s two wings '—and take a stroll while
we wait for the boy? The comtesse and I can discuss
the particulars.'

Gratitude and relief in her eyes, Elodie said, 'Thank
you. I would like that.'

Will kissed her hand. 'Into the garden with you,
then.'

After the doors shut behind his wife, Will turned
back to the comtesse. 'I'm pleased that you are choosing to be reasonable, *madame*.'

She sighed. 'I don't wish to be. I should like to pack
Philippe up and run away with him to a place where you
would never find us. But...I do know what it is to lose
a son. I'm not sure I could live with myself, if I were to
deliberately cause another such pain.'

'I applaud your sentiments. My wife, too, wants only
what is best for her son, else I would have snatched the
boy for her when we first found him. But I should also
warn you, in case your longing to have sole control over
the boy should ever triumph over your more noble feelings, that having grown up on the streets of London, I
myself possess no tender sensibilities whatsoever. There
is nowhere you could run where I would not eventually find you. I'd steal the boy back without a qualm,
and he'd be halfway to a Channel port before you even
knew he was missing. Once safely with his mother in
England, protected by the influence of my family, you
truly would never see him again.'

The comtesse gasped. 'You would do that, *monsieur*? But that is monstrous!'

'Perhaps, but there's not need to do anything "monstrous" as long as you are sensible. Considering that Philippe isn't truly your son, the arrangement we propose is quite favourable for you.'

'Favourable or poor, you do not leave me much choice, do you?'

'That was my intention,' Will replied. 'Some day, when he's older, Philippe must be told the truth, preferably before he works it out on his own. Come now, *madame*, let us put away our swords. We need not be opponents. Both you and my wife love Philippe. How could he not benefit from having two mothers to love him? The arrangement will work, I promise you.'

The comtesse sighed. 'It had better. Your wife has you, *monsieur*. Philippe is all I have left.'

'Then you will do everything necessary to make sure you keep him in your life. So we're agreed?'

At the comtesse's reluctant nod, Will said, 'Excellent. The boy should be down soon; I'll go fetch my wife.'

Will went quickly into the garden to find Elodie, who, pale and nervous, was pacing around and around the intricate knot garden.

As always, her distress made his chest ache. 'Have courage, sweeting!' he soothed. 'Philippe will be with you soon and you'll never lose him again.'

'Oh, Will, I know you promised me this would work, but are you sure? The comtesse is not just acquiescing to get us to leave, with no intention of honouring the agreement?'

Wrapping an arm around Elodie, he tilted up her chin and gave her a reassuring kiss. 'Do you really think I would let that happen?'

She gave him a wobbly smile. 'No. If I've learned nothing else since Vienna, I know I can trust you to make happen whatever you promise you will.'

'Then stop worrying, *mon ange*. All you desire will soon be yours.'

Taking her hand, he led her back into the salon.

Hardly daring to believe that she was truly going to have her son back again, Elodie fixed her gaze on the hallway door, hungry for her first glimpse of Philippe. When, a few minutes later, he skipped in, a joy of unimaginable sweetness filled her.

'Are we going visiting, *Maman*?' he asked, trotting over to the comtesse. 'Will there be cakes?'

That lady bent to give him a hug, as if to subtly underscore to Elodie that he still belonged to her. Magnanimous in her happiness, Elodie didn't even resent the gesture.

With the impatience of a little boy, Philippe wiggled free. 'Will we leave now, *Maman*?'

'No, Philippe. This kind lady is a…family connection. She's visiting Paris and wanted to become acquainted with you.'

Philippe looked up at Elodie curiously. Recognition flickering in his eyes, he said, 'I know you. You sold

Jean an orange in the park, and you came to the nursery and looked at my soldiers.'

'That's right,' Elodie said with a pang, wishing he could have remembered her as well after Vienna. 'What a clever boy you are!'

'This gown is prettier. Why were you selling oranges?'

'I dressed up to play a game of pretend. You pretend, too, don't you, when you play with your soldiers?'

He nodded. 'I am a great general and win many battles. I have a tall black horse and a long, curved sword and I am brave and fierce, like my papa.'

Elodie's eyes misted. 'I am sure you will be just like your papa. He would be so proud of you.'

'You said you would take me to see the parrots at the market. You said the birds had red and green and blue feathers. Can we go now? *Maman*, will you come, too?'

The comtesse wrinkled her nose in distaste. 'I do not wish to visit the bird market, Philippe.'

'Please, *Maman*? I do so want to go!'

'He seems to have a memory like a poacher's trap now. How unfortunate he didn't develop the skill earlier,' Will murmured, echoing Elodie's thoughts.

'Please, *Maman*, let me go now!' Philippe repeated, focusing with a child's single-mindedness only on the part of the conversation which interested him.

'I suppose, if you take Jean and Marie and don't stay long, you may go,' the comtesse said.

'Do let us go, then,' Elodie said. Longing welling

up in her for the touch of him, she held out her hand to the boy.

To her delight, Philippe put his small hand in hers. After closing her eyes briefly to savour the contact, she opened them to see Will smiling at her, love and gladness in his eyes. She mouthed a silent 'thank you'.

'What is your name? Can we not hurry? I know I shall like the red parrots best. Can I bring one home?'

Elodie laughed, revelling in the sorely missed sound of her son's voice. 'You may call me "*Maman* Elodie". Yes, we will hurry. As for the red parrot, you must ask your *Maman* about that.'

'Can I have a red parrot, *Maman*?'

'Not today, Philippe. Perhaps the next time.'

As they nodded a goodbye to the comtesse, who watched them walk away, her expression sad but resigned, Philippe said, '*Maman* Elodie, would *you* like a red parrot?'

Elodie looked up at Will, and he groaned. 'Somehow, I fear by the end of this excursion, I'm going to own a bird.'

Several hours later, having inspected all the colourful flock and narrowly avoided the purchase of the red parrot, they had returned a now-sleepy Philippe and his attendants to the Hôtel de la Rocherie. During the outing, Will had let Elodie take charge, following her indulgently as she wandered through the market hand in hand with Philippe, answering his volley of questions, even purchasing some sweets for him from a market vendor.

In the carriage on the way back to their lodgings, Elodie threw herself into his arms, so euphoric and brimming over with emotion, she wasn't sure whether to laugh or weep.

Hugging her tight, he said, 'Was it all that you wished for, sweeting?'

'Oh, my love, it was wonderful! The blessed angels must have been smiling on me the day you climbed up my balcony in Vienna! I still can scarcely believe you convinced the comtesse to agree to our arrangement—and, no, don't tell me how you managed it. I will sleep better not knowing.'

'My dear, your suspicions wound me,' Will replied, grinning. 'Sheer charm and persuasion, that was all.'

'The charm of a rogue!'

'A rogue whom you've bewitched completely.'

'It is I who am bewitched.' She looked at him wonderingly. 'You arranged all of this for me, didn't you? The mission, the railroads. You could have negotiated investments for your friend anywhere. But you chose Paris.'

He shrugged. 'Paris held the key to your happiness.'

Awed at the magnitude of such selfless love, humbled to be its object, she said, 'I can almost forgive St Arnaud for embroiling me in his scheme, for otherwise, I should never have met you. I thought it already a gift that you brought me from despair back to life. And now, you have given me back my soul. How can I ever repay you for such treasures?'

'Hmm, let's see,' Will said, drawing her on to his

lap. 'You could give *me* a son, I suppose. You, Max, Caro, even the comtesse seem to think having one is so wonderful, it would be rather selfish to keep it all to yourself.'

She smiled, it occurring to her that the only thing as marvellous as having Philippe back in her life would be bearing another son—Will's son.

'Sharing that blessing with you, sweet Will, my husband, my life, would be my greatest pleasure.' Framing his face in her hands, she leaned up to give him a kiss full of passion and promise.

* * * * *

COMING NEXT MONTH from Harlequin® Historical
AVAILABLE APRIL 23, 2013

HER HESITANT HEART
Carla Kelly
Tired and hungry after two days of traveling, Susanna Hopkins is just about at the end of her tether when her train finally arrives in Cheyenne. She's bound for a new life in a Western garrison town. Then she discovers she doesn't even have enough money to pay for the stagecoach! Luckily for her, the compassionate Major Joseph Randolph is heading in the same direction.
(Western)

THE GREATEST OF SINS
The Sinner and the Saint
Christine Merrill
Having spent years believing a lie about his birth, Dr Samuel Hastings has been condemned to a personal hell of his desire's making—his sinful thoughts of the one woman he can *never* touch would damn his soul for eternity. Lady Evelyn Thorne is engaged to the very suitable Duke of St Aldric when a shocking truth is revealed—and now Sam will play every bit of the devil to seduce the woman he thought would always be denied him!
(Regency)

TARNISHED AMONGST THE TON
Louise Allen
Brought up in vibrant Calcutta, Ashe Herriard is disdainful of polite London society, but something about Miss Phyllida Hurst intrigues him. There's a mystery surrounding her. A promise of secrets and a hint of scandal—more than enough to entice him!
(Regency)

THE BEAUTY WITHIN
Marguerite Kaye
Disillusioned artist Giovanni di Matteo is setting the *ton* abuzz with his expertly executed portraits. Once his art was inspired; now it's only technique. Until he meets Cressie... Challenging, intelligent and yet insecure, Cressie is the one whose face and body he dreams of capturing on canvas. In the enclosed, intimate world of his studio, Giovanni rediscovers his passion as he awakens hers.
(Regency)

You can find more information on upcoming Harlequin® titles, free excerpts and more at www.Harlequin.com.

REQUEST YOUR FREE BOOKS!

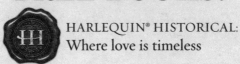

HARLEQUIN® HISTORICAL:
Where love is timeless

2 FREE NOVELS PLUS 2 FREE GIFTS!

YES! Please send me 2 FREE Harlequin® Historical novels and my 2 FREE gifts (gifts are worth about $10). After receiving them, if I don't wish to receive any more books, I can return the shipping statement marked "cancel." If I don't cancel, I will receive 6 brand-new novels every month and be billed just $5.19 per book in the U.S. or $5.74 per book in Canada. That's a savings of at least 17% off the cover price! It's quite a bargain! Shipping and handling is just 50¢ per book in the U.S. and 75¢ per book in Canada.* I understand that accepting the 2 free books and gifts places me under no obligation to buy anything. I can always return a shipment and cancel at any time. Even if I never buy another book, the two free books and gifts are mine to keep forever.

246/349 HDN FVQK

Name	(PLEASE PRINT)

Address		Apt. #

City	State/Prov.	Zip/Postal Code

Signature (if under 18, a parent or guardian must sign)

Mail to the **Harlequin® Reader Service:**
IN U.S.A.: P.O. Box 1867, Buffalo, NY 14240-1867
IN CANADA: P.O. Box 609, Fort Erie, Ontario L2A 5X3

Want to try two free books from another line?
Call 1-800-873-8635 or visit www.ReaderService.com.

* Terms and prices subject to change without notice. Prices do not include applicable taxes. Sales tax applicable in N.Y. Canadian residents will be charged applicable taxes. Offer not valid in Quebec. This offer is limited to one order per household. Not valid for current subscribers to Harlequin Historical books. All orders subject to credit approval. Credit or debit balances in a customer's account(s) may be offset by any other outstanding balance owed by or to the customer. Please allow 4 to 6 weeks for delivery. Offer available while quantities last.

Your Privacy—The Harlequin® Reader Service is committed to protecting your privacy. Our Privacy Policy is available online at www.ReaderService.com or upon request from the Harlequin Reader Service.

We make a portion of our mailing list available to reputable third parties that offer products we believe may interest you. If you prefer that we not exchange your name with third parties, or if you wish to clarify or modify your communication preferences, please visit us at www.ReaderService.com/consumerchoice or write to us at Harlequin Reader Service Preference Service, P.O. Box 9062, Buffalo, NY 14269. Include your complete name and address.

HH13

*Christine Merrill wraps a sensual haze of
desire around you with her brilliant new novel
THE GREATEST OF SINS,
available May 2013.*

"This is what I want," he whispered, his breath in her ear even hotter than his kiss. "And it has nothing to do with a romantic declaration, or a marriage. I want to have you, right now, here in the garden, naked like Eve. I want to use you for my pleasure, without a thought to what is right or good. I want what I want, and I do not care if it destroys us both. That is why I left six years ago. And that is why I must leave now."

And then he pushed her away, out of his lap and onto the bench. She could feel the cold night air against her exposed breasts, and the constriction of the bodice pulled low under them.

"Compose yourself. And then go back into the house and find your betrothed." His voice was cold and passionless. "Marry St. Aldric, Evie. He will care for you. I cannot." He stood then and walked away.

She tugged the bodice back into place and laid a hand against her cheek, waiting for the blush to subside. If she sat here awhile longer, she would be as cold as he was, but not as emotionless. She was angry.

Sam Hastings was all she had ever wanted. She had followed him here like a fool, only to be refused again. He had brought her to the brink of fulfillment. And then left.

Did he not realize that she might have taken some pleasure in the act that he found so base and unworthy? Her body still seethed with desire. It was as if she was waiting for some gift that only Sam could give her. He had shown it to her, held it close and then snatched it away at the last minute.

It would not happen again. Tonight, she would make her choice once and for all. She would go to another man, and she would never turn back.

Don't miss this sensational new
Regency duet from Christine Merrill
THE SINNER AND THE SAINT
Brothers separated at birth, brought together by scandal.

From the birth of a secret to the death of a lie, two brothers have been torn apart. While the duke behaves like a saint, the doctor believes himself a sinner. And only a scandal can bring them back together.
THE GREATEST OF SINS
May 2013

Look for the second in the duet,
Coming soon

Copyright © 2013 by Christine Merrill

HHEXP0413

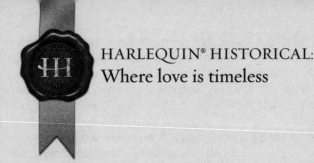

HARLEQUIN® HISTORICAL:
Where love is timeless

THE SECRET LIFE OF MISS PHYLLIDA HURST

Having survived the scandal of her birth with courage
and determination, the beautiful Phyllida has reached a
precarious balance within the *ton*. And in just one moment
Ashe Herriard, Viscount Clere, blows her world and her
carefully made plans to pieces.

Brought up in vibrant Calcutta, Ashe is disdainful of polite
London society, but something about Phyllida intrigues him.
There's a mystery surrounding her. A promise of secrets and a
hint of scandal—more than enough to entice him!

Look for

Tarnished Amongst The Ton

by Louise Allen in May 2013.

Available wherever books are sold.

www.Harlequin.com

HH29737